CHAMELEON

Copyright © 2011
Lance K. Steele

ISBN-13 9780982703144
ISBN-10 0982703147

DISCLAIMERS

This book is fictional; any resemblance to any real persons, places or things is coincidental and unintended.

Where I'm picking on cops, the medico-pharmaceutical establishment or other institutions, *that too, is bullshit*. Everybody knows that all cops are good, all doctors care and all lawyers are honest.

Like I said; it's ALL FICTION.

Well, except for the parts about the Blackeagle Hotel and Ed Kemper... I actually met him during his *alleged killing spree*. While attending college in Aptos I went to pick up my girlfriend, who worked at a convenience store just a stone's throw from the surf. Her shift was up at 11:00 pm. He stood at the counter flirting with her. She introduced me to the huge guy. We shook hands; mine just disappeared into his huge mitt. He was quite polite and very likeable.

Later she told me he'd been hanging out for a few nights, asking her for a date. Since we weren't a firm couple yet, I said; *'Be careful; you don't know this guy.'*

Two days later, authorities found his latest alleged victim in several pieces strewn up and down the coast. I probably saved my girlfriend from becoming that corpse. But ever since meeting him, something *still gives me the willies*... I mean, how much do you *really know* about anybody?

I hope my book gives you the willies, too.

ONE...

LIFE ACCORDING TO

HOWARD

Howard Carver grew up in rural Wisconsin, a preacher's son. He had chores by age six, and by ten, a job at a neighboring farm. His parents applied the belt at any hint of laziness or resistance. By twelve he had his major life lessons; shut up, work hard, keep your nose to the grindstone. It was a good plan.

Then the Great Depression hit; plenty of hard working people lost their farms. Naturally, church tithing dried up, so the Carvers felt the depression just like everybody else. By 17, he formed his lifelong tenet; you had to be strong... d*amned strong.*

He joined the army, fixing radios and teaching soldiers how to communicate effectively on the airways. That got him into the fiercest fighting in the South Pacific. He went to a radio outpost; the tiny atoll was a strategic spot. Naturally, the Jap forces wanted it too.

Arriving to service the radio, Howard and the radio operator dug in to fight off Japanese soldiers stalking the position. The first dozen Japs died before they got a chance to shoot back; two grenades and stereo Garand volleys saw to that. Bullets whizzed and ricocheted. international shouts mixed with groans of the dying; mostly, Japanese, Australian from the wounded operator and the rest of it, roaring and swearing in a mixture of English and Holland Dutch, Carver's lingos of lineage. The last three Japs stormed him; everyone was out of ammo. He fought 'em off with bayonet, rifle butt and Red-blooded American cussedness. When it was over, 36 Japs lay dead or dying. The Aussie bled out just as the last warrior ate Howard's bayonet. The radio outpost kept saving lives 'til the war's end. Later they got medals for it. At war's end he married and moved to California, got a job with the P.D., thanks to his hero status.

Applying his intense work ethic, Howard showed his true strength, long before the position was known as 'Profiler.' Life went according to Carver, until the boy was born. Howard's initial pride slowly began to erode. It wasn't something tangible, really. The boy just lacked vigor. He would never be mistaken for an athlete. He wouldn't fight other kids, which pissed the old man off. He even gave the kid a hearty name, but it didn't help. Clearly, Vinny would never cut the mustard. He was a pussy. But at least he wasn't a fag; the old man would have drowned him. *THAT* he wouldn't stand for, *"In any son of MINE."* Fortunately, puberty saved his ass; The boy went girl-crazy.

Howard sublimated his disappointment. His work took up most of his time. He became the best crook catcher in the nation. He took pride in his fame. It wasn't like having a Heisman-winning son, but it was something.

Carver steadily outgrew the confines of the local precinct. Other orgs would solicit his input. Usually it was the FBI asking. A few times, Scotland Yard. He liked the Scots; they could really put away the booze.

TWO...

VINCENT

It's too bad Howard never took time to know his boy. Whatever Vinny lacked in machismo, he made up for it with intellect. By the sixth grade he knew German and Italian and had a solid grasp of physics. His IQ tested between 140 and 160, depending on which type of test. Some were too lame to merit his full attention.

He had an insatiable mind. Naturally, he hated school, a most boring and painfully slow institution, geared down to spoon-feed the dullest dolts in a community. So when he wasn't in school he could feed his brain at the proper speed. He was as likely to be found pouring over an architecture book as a Playboy centerfold.

At first Vinny thought everyone felt it, but when he tried out for Little League, it dawned on him; the emptiness was his alone. Other boys had dads, big brothers or step dads showing them how to hit, catch and steal a base. Well, he had his mother in the bleachers but that was almost worse than having nobody. It wasn't really a surprise when he failed to make a team.

He graduated high school two years early. He should have felt pride but he just felt hollow. His father never showed up for graduation. He was chasing some bad guy in Atlanta or Bumfuck Ohio. He was always off somewhere, with something more important than Vincent.

With each passing year, he tried to get on a team, any team, to make his dad take notice. The hollow feeling grew. He kept building his brain, until it felt like his head would burst. His mom ran off with a Cuban relief pitcher half her age. Once in a while she'd send a postcard. But mostly he lived alone in the big house with his dad's Top Cop plaques and awards, alone in the shadow of a great man who just happened to be a shitty father.

He gave college some thought, but feared it might be like high school; regimented and slow enough for the dumbest asshole in class. That seemed more like prison than 'higher ed'. On a whim, he went incognito, to apply for his first job. That would be his first real-world lesson. He landed a job in a rest home, so his summer turned out to be a study of senescent degeneration, a neglected field. At first he didn't mind changing shitty sheets and washing incontinent old crotches. The boy had never been around old people. They had loose hide draped over brittle bones. Many were younger than his father, yet couldn't chew pea soup. Vinny's insatiable curiosity kept him going for two months. But the job had drawbacks, not the least of which was the additional twisting of his previously torqued psyche. He was too busy categorizing new stimuli to notice. However, he soon grew bored. People got old, shit their beds, then died. There wasn't any magic in it after all.

To allay the boredom he started studying medical books at the nurse's station. Night shift was quiet, except for answering a few bells and a loose bowel movement or two. Aside from that, he was in med-school heaven. Pharmaceuticals intrigued him. Oddly, the Physician's Desk Reference was rarely consulted, but Vincent sure studied it; especially four dozen drugs that held the most interest.

Next he read Merck's, amazed to learn that eighty percent of common diseases were self-limiting. His old man thought doctors were gods who maintained a tireless vigil between patients and certain death. And now the raw data contradicted the Great Santini. Hell, for 80 percent of all the things that go wrong, doctors weren't even needed. They were far from the heroic vanguards that his father worshiped. He read next about poisons. He wondered why they had such a book; the bedridden patients weren't likely to go out and eat poison mushrooms or antifreeze; too bad, because some of them could benefit from a lethal dose.

After that he dove into Guyton's Physiology. His brain fed voraciously on Prime Rib. He even re-read several chapters for pleasure, much as one re-runs a favorite movie. He really liked the sections on blood loss, liver function and potassium transport. He absorbed a basic med school curriculum during those night shifts. A dim notion began to form. He didn't know what it was yet, but the first subtle stirrings of the mental embryo quickened his heart. He liked the feeling.

Then he met Connie, a comely brunette nurse. One night as he finished a patient's bed, she pressed against him. Connie wasn't much for foreplay; *"I need to show you something."* They went into a linen closet; they showed each other plenty. For the first time in his life he didn't give a shit about what his old man said or did. Later she gave him a Valium. With his mental chemistry altered, the mental embryo grew faster. Something had to give.

In time he grew quite attached to several of the patients. There was an old man, Clarence Minkle; according to the photos around his room, he'd lived quite a life. One pic showed him in a Pitts with a huge trophy, around the time when that was the biplane to beat at an airshow. The background looked like Stead.

Another photo showed him in khaki, holding an English double rifle. He was young, heavily muscled and tanned. At his feet lay a huge Cape Buff, bracketed by PH and trackers, their skin bittersweet chocolate. All other eyes looked at the camera, but Clarence solemnly gazed at the heavily bossed bull on the ground.

There were shots with kids, wife and parents. Vinny wondered where Clarence's support people went. One photo really nagged; a youthful Clarence held a longbow and a quail. Judging from his quiver of Flu-Flu's, he shot it out of the air. Such a shot justified displaying the photo. The man next to Clarence had to be his father. There was no mistaking the genetics, despite three decades of solar wear and tear. *That's* what bothered Vincent. He wondered what it felt like to have a dad that took him hunting, fishing and to ball games. He hated Howard; why couldn't he be more like Clarence's dad? How differently life might have been, with a father like that.

The next night he showed up early. Normally he wouldn't bother Rachel Crackett, R.N. Her work ethic inspired him, and he was basically un-inspirable. She was completely about the job. Her uniforms were spotless and starched. She always wore her hair high and tight. Every day was a carbon copy for Crackett. She brought her best to work, no matter what happened in her personal life. Vincent wondered if she even *had* a personal life. All he could see was a wiry sixty-something, ironing her uniform, counting the minutes 'til she could go to work. As he walked up to her, a Buddhist precept flashed in front of his mind. He'd read it... six years ago, while listening to Willie's "On the Road Again" in the spring, on the back porch. The calligraphy scrolled, like a stock market ticker.

"To be a master, simply do what masters do."

That was it; Crackett did a masterful job. As long as nobody messed with her, she got it right, every damned day. A man had to admire that kind of discipline. He walked up as she charted some patient's latest bowel movement;
"Miss Crackett, may I ask you a question?"
"I believe you just did."
"I was wondering about Clarence; why doesn't his family ever visit him?"

Crackett almost dropped her chart. Her blue eyes bored hotly through him, then they softened to ordinary contempt as she processed the query, then she understood; this new boy probably didn't know about the wreck. Except for that little whore Connie he was probably screwing, the kid never interacted *with anyone.* He was a good worker, but very quiet. She lowered her voice; "Oh, you don't know about it, do you? Sit down."

"Yes ma'am; thank you."

"Fifteen years ago, Mr. Minkle and his family were coming back from an Idaho elk hunt. A drunk ran a rural stop sign and crashed into them at high speed, ripping their vehicle in half..."

"OH, I'm sorry!"

"Be quiet or I won't tell you."

"Yes ma'am. Sorry."

Crackett dispatched information like she meted out medications. That's how she maintained her Zen-like state; "Clarence was driving. His daughter Elizabeth sat in front. She was killed instantly."

Her voice cracked, then she regained composure, determined to finish in one take; "The rear half burst into flames. Beatrice, his wife of 22 years and his 19 year-old son Ethan were in it. Ethan was decapitated; Beatrice didn't have it so lucky. She was pinned down. Gasoline poured everywhere. Clarence... ahem... *Mr. Minkle...* was trapped in the front half. He regained consciousness just in time to hear his wife screaming. He could only scream with her, while she burned to death." Crackett paused to let the vision register; "He couldn't do anything. His cord was severed at T12, paralyzing his legs."

She tried to think of a way to soften the data, but there was no sugar-coating such a story. "In one insane act, that damned drunk took away all Clarence had, and all he was ever going to have. The drunk survived with minor injuries... *Any questions?"* Her eyes shot fire.

"No, ma'am."

He went to daily rounds. They called it a 'progress report', but there never was any progress; Ted Banks, 112, had a bowel movement, 800 cc, semisolid and absent of blood. Merry Monroe, 122, took an extra pain shot at 4:30. Harry Harris drank 300 cc of OJ. She droned on, but she lost Vincent at Harry's 'Battle of the Juices.'

Poor old Harry had Parkinson's. He was in a constant state of spasm, with practically no swallow reflex; he choked and gagged on every drink. Harry's life was a constant state of bodily contraction, known as hypertonus clonus... medi-babble for 'hellish cramps & writhing-pain.' But Clonus sounds better to those not suffering the malady.

Harry was stuck in bed, hollering one word over. Due to his pharyngeal spasms, the word came out garbled and slow, like old dry toothpaste squeezed from a clogged tube, on chunk at a time; *"H..O..RR... B... LE.... H..O..RR..IB... LE...."*

If Harry was conscious, he was hollering *'horrible'*. This spawned his inevitable nickname, but saying it was grounds for termination. "Horrible Harry" was the icon for everything bad about a lifetime of treatment for an incurable illness, wrapped up in a writhing, dying package.

Harry fought in World War One. While others panicked and ran, Harry shit his pants and stood his ground, fighting like a fucking lion. Krauts finally overtook his position and found him straddling eight dead Germans. He was stabbed through the left guts and weak from blood loss, still swinging his bayonet from side to side. His courage kept them from killing him. Later he escaped, moved through the French underground, made it back to the army just as the war ended.

Harry married; started a plumbing business, but the damage to his pancreas and spleen took its toll. Medicine was too primitive back then to help him. Doctors gave him every experimental drug. Predictably, some were worse than the conditions they tried to cure. Still, Harry was a fighter. He raised a family, sold his business and took his wife on a world tour that excluded Europe. Then the Parkinson's hit and everything went to shit. It really was HORRIBLE after that. Harry lay in the same bed, looking at the same off-white cinder-block walls, moaning 'Horrible' non-stop, for 36 hours at a stretch. Then his body would commit treason, forcing sleep until an orderly would come, brandishing the dreaded paperboard carton. Harry's eyes would bulge in fear, pleading with the assailant to *NOT* give him the juice. But no matter how he pleaded, the idiots kept choking him. They were just following orders, like the fuckin' Nazis.

Suddenly the change of inflection in the nurse's voice broke up Vincent's thoughts. Rounds were over. She smiled and folded her chart closed; "So that's about it. See you tomorrow." The new shift plodded off to their posts while the departing RN grabbed her car keys.

Working nights, he didn't have to pass out meal trays or coax unwilling wilted old people to eat. He would cruise the halls and answer the rarely pushed button. He could read, flirt with the nurses or slip into the linen closet with Connie and hump like shore-leave sailors. The only drawback there were the incontinent clean-ups.

Some clients had hale minds but infirm sphincters. They would apologize for crapping their beds, but the Alzheimer's patients had it lucky; they might be embarrassed, but it only lasted a second. Now for old salts like Harry or Clarence, the degradation lasted much longer. It's better for heroes to die on the battlefield.

13

Horrible Harry never shit his bed. He would lay on his left side facing the open door, alert for intruders trying to choke him to death; all he saw were huge cartons of grape, cranberry and orange juice. Then sometimes he saw just a big, white glove walk in. He hated the glove most of all. Two decades in the joint taught him a thing or two about vigilance. He knew every sound in the hellhole. He knew the sound of the death moan, whenever another of the old guard expired; he envied his peers their death.

Over the years he managed to lose all speech, save for a few choice words. Not only couldn't he kill himself, but he lacked the ability to ask someone else to do it. Horrible Harry was horribly fucked. He studied the young man; he always had the look of someone going somewhere, but tonight the kid looked uncertain. Harry was relieved to see no juice carton in his hands, and no gloves, so he wasn't there to drown or rape his ass.
"Hi, Harry… how you doin?"
He softly uttered his mantra. "HO…RR…I…BLE."
"Oh, yeah? I'm sorry."
Harry's special pillow was in place to prevent wounds to his inner knees from Adductor spasms. The staff would insert a firm, thin pillow. This required three people; one to rip each knee apart, one to jam the pillow in. Then they let go the knees, which sprang shut like a bear trap. Harry would wear a hole through the pillow every three weeks. Fortunately an Alzheimer patient loved to make pillows during her lucid phases.

Harry wondered why he wasn't humping that brunette in the linen room adjoining Harry's room. He liked to hear their noises through the wall; damned good sounds for an old fart to hear. Too bad he couldn't ask why the kid came to him. But decades of institutionalized torture teaches extreme patience; sooner or later he'd know. It didn't matter when, either. It might even be good to ponder the kid's motives; might help take his mind off the searing pain wracking his brain twenty-four seven, 365 HORRIBLE days a year.

14

The kid drew up a chair and sat at eye-level;

"Harry, *do you WANT* to die?"

Harry almost had an orgasm. He chanted 'horrible' as long as possible, but nobody got the clue. Well, maybe they got it, but lacked the compassion to end his life. Instead, they tortured him with juice every four hours, knowing damned well it caused him pain and suffering. They stuck tubes down his throat whenever he tried to hunger-strike his way out. And now finally, this young kid had it right. Hell yes, he wanted to die, but Harry couldn't say the words; they just bounced around in his head, like bees in a hive whose exit was plastered shut. He tried staring into the young man's eyes. Emboldened by Harry's uncustomary silence, he asked him; *"Is that your way of saying you want to die?"*

Harry struggled to say yes, but he heard his mouth say one of the few other words he could say;

"THANK... YOU."

Damn, he hoped the kid could take a clue.

"Is that yes, Harry? *Thank you' means... yes?"*

*"THANK... YOU... **THANK... YOU!**"*

The old man's eyes sparkled with tears. Something welled up in Vincent. He cried, for the first time since he was a kid. He got a napkin and daubed Harry's tears away. He reached to pat his head, but Harry hated being touched. Instead, he whispered to the tortured old war horse; *"Ok, Harry, I'll see... what I can do."* He left the room while 'THANK YOU's echoed down the hallway. Harry felt ecstasy for the first time since he escaped the Nazis. He fell asleep and dreamed a good dream, for a change...

"Je suis Americaine... j'ai chocolat."

The best words the fuckin' army ever taught him. She answered fast, as any good French hooker would;

"Je m'appelle Dominique; alons y"

Before he could say toot sweet, they were humping like mad. Not only was it his first hooker, it was his first ever. He tipped her so much that she insisted on seeing

15

him again. And again. Wartime love has no equal for intensity. They danced in lush vineyards. The musty smell of rain, mushrooms and spring earth hit him like a wet blanket. He led, she followed, breasts jiggling. Horrible Harry had legs, lungs, and a big swinging dick. God, it felt good. He put his arm around her. Dom cooed in his ear;

"Je vous aime beauc…"

Just then the lights went on, shattering his dream. A mammoth orange juice carton walked in. Harry started pleading; "Horr ib… LE… *Noooo!!!!"* His scrawny arms tried to parry the carton while he also wondered about the dream. And that kid, too; *"Was his promise to kill me just a dream too?"* But Harry didn't have time to ponder it. The batle of the juices resumed, round twelve thousand. Fuckin' horrible, indeed.

THREE...

KILLING HARRY

The idea began to take form; just as some were born to climb Everest or cure cancer, he felt bound to kill Harry. It wasn't really murder, any more than a vet snuffing a sick cat. Clearly semantics and nothing more. But Harry was no sick cat. He was an honest to god war hero. He sure as hell didn't deserve to live out his life under the constant, agonizing hellfire. Someone should have respected him enough to kill him already. Only a heartless asshole would let a cat suffer like Harry did. Men like him purchased our freedom with blood, severed limbs and sizzling-shrapnel deaths. They ran unflinchingly toward machine guns, bayonets and Panzers, so others could live a life of liberty without ever tasting the hell of battle.

But nobody got the death sentence for killing a cat, so Vincent had to plan it carefully. In fact, that's about the only thing he and his dad ever talked about; a few precious minutes here and there, trying to convey to his son how great Howard Carver was, hoping it would rub off; cojones by osmosis, if you will. Trying to get closer to his dad, he feigned attention, then learned how Howard found the bad guys. Not too hard for a kid with perfect recall and plenty of time. So he hacked into Howard's files and began reading the profiling database. Soon he could distinguish a spree killer from a serial as easily as a dog lover tells a Labrador from a Poodle.

17

Killing a willing, incapacitated nonagenarian ought to be easy; getting away with it? Not so much. He dove into it with Zen-like ethic. For a week, he didn't even mess with horny little Connie; now, *that's* a work ethic. If his dad were to know about it, he'd shit his bed, wherever that was.

Vincent couldn't see anyone getting too excited about a bed-ridden old man's long overdue demise. Certainly the staff wouldn't care. They loathed his incessant chanting. Late at night Harry's hollow voice reverberated in the hallways and resonated into every patient's room; Alfred Hitchcock, Vincent Price and Edgar Allen Poe rolled into one ghoulish mantra; *'horrible, HORRIBBBLLE...'* He was the Grim Reaper that refused to shut the fuck up, the town crier for Deathville, shouting that it's almost midnight and *all is DEFINITELY NOT WELL.* Nobody gets out alive.

It reminded Vinny
of a Buddhist precepthe'd read once;

'SUFFERING IS UNIVERSAL AND <u>INEVITABLE</u>'

He wondered if anyone might miss Harry's chant, once it was gone; like a tooth aches after it's pulled. The registered nurses *clearly* would be glad he checked out. Every three days, an RN had to reach up into Harry's bony old rectum and dig out the clay. It had to be done, if Harry was to remain alive. And somehow, quantity of life was the only god medicine worshiped. So they mined Harry's ass clay twice an ass-raping week. It was the only time he said words other than 'horrible.'

BACK in the day, a real man would never take it up the ass. So when the glove entered his room, Harry's eyes always widened like a slaughterhouse sheep. He'd scream out a garbled *"NO... NO!!!"* And then a magical transformation occurred. Black magic maybe, but magic nonetheless. Harry's Nazi-killing willpower surfaced, overpowering his clonus. His hands would crawl away from center chest like the hands of a clock, but they fuckin' moved, until the right arm got back to repel the coming assault. It's always his right hand. They would put him on his left, pointing his belly at the open door, presumably to save passersby from witnessing the grisly scene. It sure as hell wasn't to give Harry any dignity or they'd close the door or place a blanket over him. Instead, his withered white belly faced the hallway while sanitized vultures with gloves dug at his ass.

Near the halfway point, Harry's willpower collapses; the right hand defaults back to center-chest. He whimpers while the nurse clinches her jaw and keeps digging marble-hard shit, so Harry can live some more of this wonderful life. If he could speak, he'd say; *"Good bye, bon jour, je suis outtahere. I hope your shit-digging fingers fall off every one of you heartless bitches!"*

Vincent refocused; he was going to kill a hero that no longer mattered. There wouldn't be an autopsy. Or perhaps there were different levels of autopsy. He searched the Net to find out. Sadly, the mortuary business was a secretive one. Aside from superficial platitudes and coffin prices, he found very few post mortem logistics online. Some things are best seen firsthand, so he took the next step to find out.

FOUR...

THE MORGUE

Nobody answered the ad for three weeks. He used his newest false identity. It would work longer than he would. Vincent Carver became Lou Morgan. The job paid well to compensate for the grisly factor. There was only one problem; they wanted him to start that night, on graveyard. Only in the trade, they didn't call it that.

He took the job on the spot, calling in sick at the rest home. His task was in-taking each dead person. The doctors called them decedents or bodies. The gophers called them stiffs. Louis' job was to take stiffs from the ambulance, tag, bag and roll 'em to a drawer. Finally he entered the data into the computer. People got fussy about knowing where their departed were, as if it mattered.

He saw a woman with the biggest implants and trimmest snatch he'd ever seen. She had a bullet hole through her liver, a rare on-the-job hazard for a mobster's hooker. He touched her monumental tits, purely out of awe. They were stiff, cold and uncaring... dried leather fun bags.

He saw doctors' screw-ups. One guy had two abdominal wounds; the first was neatly sutured and partly healed. The other, hurried and un-sutured. The stiff was 25, chiseled muscles, six pack abs and a tan line to his pubes. A pretty boy ski bum with a bad appendectomy outcome. Three days post-op, complications demanded an x-ray;

21

some scrubbed idiot failed the post-op tool count. Part of Ski-bum's Ileum wrapped around the scissors' open blades and burst. The second incision would have been the right thing to do, if only they'd done it three days sooner. He wondered about it, long enough to draw ire;

"Hey, kid... roll him to the cooler; we're backin' up!"

"Oh, yes sir- - sorry!"

He vowed not to draw any more attention. The hard body went into drawer 26, next to the liver-shot mob hooker. He would've liked that. Louis startled at the voice;

"Hey, KID... if you wanna play, you gotta pay. Come here! Hand me that bone saw!" Dr. Mike Jones had taken a liking to Louis.

"Yes sir... right away!" He jumped at the chance to learn more. The docs were glad for a free set of willing hands. They let him make Y incisions, draw blood, weigh organs and open skulls, the grunt work of the trade. Encouraged by his voracious curiosity, Dr. Mike made the other gophers take up Carver's slack. He had himself an assistant.

Louis worked the morgue for two months; he'd seen everything he needed. He had their passwords, coding system and he even hacked a back door into the morgue's two most-used independent pathology labs.

He had seen it all. Or so he thought. One Saturday night around two in the morning, one of the gophers whispered to Doc Jones, who personally escorted this particular stiff right to the autopsy table, removing a manila packet from the stiff's blood-soaked jacket. Meanwhile, the dark blue unmarked Mercedes hearse drove off. Then he saw Jones close the drawer on the stiff; no autopsy, no paperwork. Jones caught him looking. The kid nonchalantly proceeded with his work. As he left for the night, the doc caught his shoulder, then slipped him some cash;

"Here... you didn't see *anything,* right?"

Surprised, he took the bills; "Thanks. See what?"

At home he counted it; 500 bucks glowed in his hands. He hacked into the morgue's system. Sure enough, the late night arrival never got logged in. The next night, Dr. Jones took him into the lunch room for some insurance work; "You been talking?"

"Nope. I can keep a secret."

"Good. I knew I could trust you. Sometimes I do a favor for a... friend. I get paid well; *NOW, so do you,* cool?"

"Yep. So, am I in danger?"

"We both are... I mean, we're talking *MOB,* right? Don't worry; just go with the flow. What's not to love?"

Louis shook his hand; "*I'm IN!*"

After that, Jones made him privy to the under workings... When things got busy, they gave the homeless and the elderly a cosmetic Y and scalp slit, but no autopsy. They used a canned narrative, your basic form letter for the dead. There was money in body trafficking. Jones' turf was the temporal bone, sold to audiology researchers and med schools. The removal isn't visible once the skin flap is sewn back. He had an account with a research lab; paid off two student loans with them so far.

The double-burying and cadaver selling was the turf of the senior staff. The kid was amazed at how many med schools bought John Does. He was also surprised to see the underside of the death business, with the mob, medicine and the law rolling around in bed together. But he was no hypocrite, so he got over it fast. After all, it wasn't so long ago when he started planning to kill Harry.

Now that he knew that Harry wouldn't get an autopsy, he was ready to kill him. One weekend Vincent Carver went to Arizona under false identity to acquire the insulin; more than enough to kill a healthy young man. Harry was neither young nor healthy, but he wanted to err on the side of overkill. Then he went to a farm supply store for a large veterinary syringe.

What he wasn't ready for was Harry's body rolling into the morgue. The chart said Harry died of a heart attack, but charts often lied just to cover someone's butt. His body was still on his left side, with the pillow stuck

23

between his knees. His sinewy muscles shrank, giving the curled corpse an even scrawnier, bonier look. The doc checked the chart; "No kin. *Perfunctory*, Chad."

Dr. Chadwick Haversham M.D., was formerly a plastic surgeon from Surrey. Bernie loved screwing anesthetized breast implant patients. He got a lot of sleepy pussy, thanks to bribing his greedy staff. But one day, his staff got greedier and Bernie got indignant, refusing to pay the escalating bribes. He actually expected his staff to keep quiet while he got rich *AND* got his rocks off. For a doctor, he was pretty stupid. He left England under mysterious pretenses, barely managing to snag the American morgue job before his UK credentials imploded.

But if Bernie was quick with his dick, he was quicker with a scalpel. Harry's Y cut took all of one minute. Louis was glad Harry was spared the grisly process. He only wished he would have killed Harry months ago; would have saved him a bunch of juice-choking and clay-rapes. For a moment, he actually wondered about Harry's actual cause of death; it just *had to be* choking. Louis put in his notice; the morgue had lost its usefulness.

FIVE...

KILLING CLARENCE

Since Harry finally managed to die on his own, Vincent Carver hung in an incomplete cycle; he basically HAD to kill, and pretty damned soon. If anyone else needed killing, it was Clarence Minkle. Perhaps he was in the back of Vincent's mind all along, while Harry was just the perfect prototype. But deeper psychic issues plan such things. These mental ghouls live in the basement, where the ego dares not venture, so I can't say for sure.

Killing Clarence wouldn't be the same; where Harry lived in constant suffering and was a pain in the ass, Clarence just lay there quietly. He was a model patient. Or so it seemed. Clarence was a real Type A. His photos showed just a fraction of his accomplishments, but to show them all would require a gallery. He held patents in aviation tools. One was an improved version of the pop rivet tool, allowing for low-drag flush rivets. With the royalties, Clarence was free to service his passion, sharing outdoor experiences with his family. For a man with plenty of money, he had surprisingly few vices. This was good, because a shady business partner ended up finessing Clarence out of his royalties.

Any other man would have been caught off balance, but not Clarence. At a time when telephones still had cranks, Clarence was already building a company to make phones with buttons. When those hit the market, who cared about pop rivets? Still, those were milestones in the distant past, shrinking billboards in life's rear view mirror.

When the drunk killed his family, Clarence's world collapsed. The sharks circled. His business partners declared him non-compis mentis. The bastards took every asset. But compared to losing his family, the business loss was nothing. A man without family can have too much time.

Along with a broken spine, Clarence had a busted soul, and there is no fixing that. He tried to shut out the images. Sometimes it worked, but they always came back; a sideways view of the rear half of their Suburban burning and smoking like the hinges of Hades; his soul mate's horrific screams for him, then for God. Then the flames burned her lungs into silence. After that came only the crackling, sizzling sounds as Bea's and Ethan's bodies turned to chitlins, popping in the burning liquid vinyl and hydrocarbon puddle on the blistering pavement. The smell was always there, too. God has a sick sense of humor. The wind could have blown in any direction. Clarence could never forget the smell. Or the horrific loss. His pain meter was pegged too long. There's no coming back from that.

He had moved mountains, but couldn't move his limbs. He'd heard all the false hopes and superficial platitudes from candy stripers and idealistic nurses. What did they know of pain and loss? How can cheerful words and bouncy steps truss such a soul chasm? Clarence prayed for death. With each passing year, he shut down more of his mental systems, as if he could shrink himself to death. That's what made him perk up when he heard the young man's voice;

"Clarence, should I kill you?"

He tried to come out of his fog to say yes, but had been reliving the flesh-charred memories for too long. The next time he heard the question, it sounded better. "Blink twice if you want to die. I'll help you." Clarence tried to get an eyelid to drop. He sure couldn't see the point of 20 more years of *this* bullshit. The right lid blinked, then again, faster.

"OK, but confirm it. Blink again." He blinked six times in a row. Hell yes, he wanted it. Carver nodded; "I thought so; it won't be long, I promise."

Carver went home and reviewed his short checklist. Clarence's associates didn't care about him, now that they'd ravaged his assets. Clarence had no kin. He had no hope of recovering. It seemed his only hope was to die, and for that he'd need help.

Three nights later he walked into Clarence's room an hour after his shift started, the usual time he'd settle down to read his medical books or get Connie in the linen closet. There was a strange light in the old man's eyes. Vincent closed the door, the nonverbal sign for an incontinence cleanup. Vincent sat down next to him; "I'm ready... If you're ready, blink."

The blink came fast. Since Clarence was numb from the waist down. He still had a huge dick, for all the good it did him. At the morgue Vincent learned that the penis was never cut. Vaginas, sure, but nobody messed with a stiff's dick; one of medicine's unwritten double standards, no doubt. Probing the urethral slit with the needle, Vincent ran the needle alongside the catheter wall for an inch or so. Then he bent Clarence's penis sideways and shoved the needle deep into the Corpus Cavernosum, the muscle responsible for swelling a noodle into an erection. Clarence never twitched while the killer pumped 35cc's into the swelling shaft, giving Clarence a boner the size of Houston.

There was no bleeding or insulin dripping, so Vincent replaced the covers. He crouched to eye level; "Mr. Minkle, I'm sorry nobody helped you pass, before this. You'll be with your family again. God bless you." Clarence tried to say thanks, but it had been too long since he spoke. He blinked twice. Vincent resumed rounds. He felt incredibly warm.

The penis was a balloon with a tiny leak, shrinking as insulin extruded into his pudendal veins. He felt a headache. His heart fluttered, so he took it as a good sign. His mouth got dry. Then he took charge, as he'd always done. He prayed;

"Lord, forgive me, but thank you for this orderly's brave act; hold no grudge against him. He did what any decent man would. Now take me so I may bathe in your light. Amen."

He wished that he could walk, just long enough to kiss his killer's ass. He felt giddy. Then his head started to hurt. His heart quit. He heard a chart drop onto the tile, somewhere near the nurses' station. Then he saw his family; happy, healthy, hugging. Amen. Damn right. At morning rounds there was news; Clarence Minkle expired during the night shift. They were going to miss him. His bed would be filled by Mildred Gord, 78, Huntington's Chorea; she was a real pain in the ass. On the drive home, Vincent felt the rush like a prolonged orgasm. When he hacked the morgue, he saw the canned narrative they used for society's dregs. For such a good man, it wasn't right. His obituary two days later was likewise canned;

"Clarence Alfred Minkle, 89, natural causes. No Memorial. Donations to St. Francis' Academy for Excellence."

His whole life summed up in two chickenshit lines in the Observer, which would be perused only by others waiting to die. And by Vincent; it was sort of like returning to the crime scene.

Clarence would go the way of all poor flesh; cremated, his ashes unceremoniously tossed in the Dumpster. The state would foot the bill. Three hundred bucks won't buy what it used to; barely paid for the propane to cook a stiff.

Vincent flashed back to Minkle's photographs; it would've been better if Clarence would have crashed in that acrobatic biplane. Compared to lingering in a rest home, a flaming crash in Nevada's sagebrush was an act of godly compassion. At least he would have left a hale family to immortalize him, remembering his life and times. That's how it was supposed to work.

Then it hit him like a beer truck; he had made a big mistake. Something about those photographs always bugged Vincent. They were always free of dust and smudges. Clarence had no family, and staff was forbidden to touch clients' personal effects, so WHO the hell thought enough of Clarence to keep them in such perfect order? It had to be Crackett... He remembered how she looked when she told him about the crash. Maybe they had been lovers once. Or maybe she saw the champion in Clarence. Clarence had soared with eagles; reason enough to love the guy, especially for a nurse in polyester, too busy giving pills to live a life of her own. It had to be Crackett.

He got his answer two days later. She took him in the pill room and shut the door; "Bernard, here's two weeks' severance pay. I'm letting you go, with a good reference. You needn't work tonight; I filled your position." A thousand ice picks jabbed his guts; Vincent already felt handcuffs biting his wrists. He couldn't say a word. Then she really blew his young mind. She hugged him and whispered in his ear; "Thank you for helping Clarence... and me."

She exited the pill room and never looked back at him. He slipped out the side door, scared and astonished. He tried to sort it out. Crackett *never hugged.*

29

The boy didn't have much experience in human nature. He raided the old man's liquor cabinet, slammed two shots and poured a third. Settling into the overstuffed leather couch, he began dissecting his conundrum. He broke down her statement into smaller bites; *"thank you"* meant grateful, *"helping"* meant she saw his act as beneficial. "Clarence", not *'Mr Minkle'* meant she really did love him. But the last words really got him; *"... and me."* To utter those two words must have come at great cost. She was sworn to preserve life, no matter the consequences. Maybe she had been tempted... Hell, she *HAD* to, but her oath got in the way. In her typically clipped rhetoric, she summed up her conflict; *'and me'*. For that, she was grateful enough to look the other way... What a woman.

Bernard Simpson dodged one hell of a bullet with his first kill. Carver was always fascinated with disguises; it was part of the twisted dynamic between him and his famous father. Everyone at the home knew him as Bernie the bedpan guy. Nobody knew where he lived, except his fuck partner, Connie. Bernie's paychecks went to a mail service. Nobody at the mail service knew Vincent by sight, but they sure knew Bernie Simpson. The only link to his real identity was Connie, already matriculated into a snob college in Maine. It would take a sharp cop to make that connection. Since Crackett indicated he was free to go, the cops wouldn't be sniffing. The rest of the bourbon numbed him, but doubt still nagged. He spoke aloud to himself; *"What if her conscience gets to her 'n she rats me out?"* He considered killing her, but Clarence was probably already cremated; only the report remained. Vincent knew the morgue dudes would cover their asses if a warrant were served. The whiteout would fly. Besides, Crackett already had two days to turn him in, but hadn't. Finally he decided to forget about it, to write off his paranoia as mere placental afterbirth of a recently spawned killer. His instinct said move on, and a killer has to trust his gut. He wished Clarence bon voyage. The man deserved no less.

Vincent opened the paper to look for a job.

SIX...

THE PREACHER

Reverend Augustus Hightower surprised Bobby Thompson by greeting him personally. He practically drooled at the tall, handsome lad; "AH, Mr. *Thompson*? Nice to meet you, praise Gawd... Please, uh... sit down."

"Thank you, sir."

Hightower was unlike his TV image. He had crags and boils all over his neck and face. He wasn't wearing his trademark angelic mane. Six long hairs swirled all over his shining globe, like dried spaghetti. It was the worst comb-over on earth. Thompson tried not to stare at the pearlescent scalp, like skull bones under plastic wrap. He forced himself not to look, as one vows not to stare at someone's glass eye. The preacher hadn't built an empire by lollygagging;

"Son, I'll hire you as my personal assistant."

"Sir, I mean... Reverend, that's great!" He wouldn't have been so eager if he knew what 'assistant' meant.

"Well, Mister Thom... may I call you Bobby, Robert or... *how shall I call you, son?*"

"Oh, my friends call me Bobby."

"Well, I suppose Bobby is fine, *just between us*, but when we're in public, I shall use your given Christian name, Robert. And you shall call me Reverend. When we are alone, call me Jim, please."

"Of course... *Jim.*"

His real Christian name was Jim Jones. No relation to the murderer of nine hundred-plus followers in Guyana. *THIS* Jones lacked the spiritual intensity to be a mass murderer. Although he did have the background for it. He grew up in Bath, Missouri; hit the road at 16. Got in a bar fight on the outskirts of Albuquerque. At issue was a plump, horny short-skirted Mexican girl. Her lover caught them in a compromising position in the ladies' room. Jones had his dick all the way in, both hands jammed into her ass. The deeper he stuck his hands, the more she shoved her pelvis at him. This posed a serious tactical drawback; he had no free appendages to parry the switchblade, which pierced his liver, right kidney and adrenal gland. Before his cock went limp, Jones passed out from hemodynamic shock right there on the shitter floor.

The Mexican grabbed his woman and split. There was only one way to deal with the slutty bitch; take her home, throw her naked ass on the kitchen table. He called her filthy whore names; she loved every hot-blooded stroke; they'd just learned how to spice up their sex life.

If it hadn't been for the barkeep's need to piss while the mens' room was locked, Jones would've died. The bartender opted for the ladies' room, finding Jones in a pool of thick burgundy liver blood, writhing slow saurian squirms of the reptilian survival brain. They saved his life by giving him half the blood in the hospital. He lost most of his liver to infection, got sicker than hell, then recovered. From then on his skin suffered huge eruptions and boils; a classic sign of impaired elimination.

Most employers shy away from lesions, so Jones drifted, stole and fenced things to make a living. He made it to L.A. where life was easier. There were plenty of free handouts, loose morals and looser women... in the City of Angels. Such irony. Jones' skin issues weren't a problem while working the 900 phone-sex lines, or as they called it, 'telemarketing.' He discovered his latent oratory skills. He was a natural at bullshitting people, he had the prerequisites, being familiar with all vices, he was seamless when talking to perverts.

33

With a background like that he was destined to become a great preacher. It only took the right set of circumstances for the rose to bloom. To everything there is a season. One morning, he woke up in a no-tell motel with a skanky redhead snoring like a chainsaw. On the nightstand were empty whiskey bottles and a few condom wrappers. He tried to dodge the hangover pain by focusing on the TV, still on from the night before. A televangelist waved his arms and preached like hell. A collection plate floated through the congregation. Jim Jones' vision began to clear. He took a medicinal slug of whiskey. May Gawd bless the hair of the dawg.

Before the skank woke up, Jones saw his calling; he'd be a preacher on TV. It *HAD* to pay better than phone sex. He poured another shot and opened the nightstand drawer for the Bible, placed by do-gooders. Within two months he had the spiritual buzzwords down pat. For the princely fee of ten bucks, he got a preachers' degree from some Caribbean diploma mill. The he gained access to public TV to spread the WORD according to "Reverend Augustus J. Hightower".

It was amazingly easy to dupe the audience. They begged for instruction and hope. He'd bullshit people and they'd beg for more. Compared to phone sex or picking pockets, this preacher stuff was a piece of cake. Women threw themselves at him, hoping to be saved. He saved the shit out of some of them. It was a sexual predator's perfect lair. He grew his sideburns to biblical lengths, then died blue-silver, to match the toupee over his horrific bald spot. He called it 'Moses silver'. One dentist in his flock donated the caps. A dermatologist lanced boils and re-worked his pepperoni-face. "Reverend Hightower's HIGHER POWER HOUR" was soon posed for syndication. His main fear was that someone would out him as a fake, but the more success he had, the less they questioned his authenticity. The TV producers had high ratings for a Sunday spot that was typically a loser. His sponsors didn't care either; they sold more crap.

Jones' show netted half a million per show, puting almost 200K in his pocket. The rest went to overhead, salaries, and *"taxes"* to the greedy palms. Every hustler knew the rule... When you fleece a flock that large, you can't keep all the wool.

There were other payoffs, too. Most of his flock bore the molesting and fucking quite well, but there was the occasional complaint about how he counseled a girl or occasionally, a young boy. Fortunately, Jones had excellent hush lawyers. A few grand would shut the victim up. If that didn't work, they would threaten to vilify the victim. Most closets hold skeletons, if you know where to look.

With fame comes power, the greatest aphrodisiac. This led him to hire Bobby. Not knowing much about the world, Bobby's job initially came as a shock. The Rev had so much pussy lined up, he couldn't save it all. Bobby's job was to screen them. Every Monday he made appointments for the Rev's special counseling. Personal assistant was the wrong term. He was a risk management specialist for fucking... for the fucking reverend.

Jim Jones liked firm young women who hadn't born child. But he really liked 'em young... say, right after those first little hairs sprouted, but these were hard to acquire in the Golden State. Next priority were firm young boys, the more idealistic the better. His luck improved when taking his dog and pony show on the road; those Bible Belt revivals really paid off.

But even a pervert like Hightower had *SOME* standards, so Robert had to screen them, to see it they had scars or blemishes. It wasn't easy, considering the presumed nature of the interview; some of them actually wanted help with matters spiritual, not sexual.

Bobby learned to unlock this information quickly; spew a biblical phrase and look for tells. A raised eyebrow, enlarging iris, whatever. Laying down one's life for another; women ate that shit up. And for the young tender boys...

35

Hit 'em where they live; why not a passage about jacking off? Their irises opened like night blooming Jasmine. At first he worried about how to get strange women to disrobe, but it was actually easy. He told them that in order to get to the Reverend they had to don a special gown. He studied their reactions. A sex flush, pointy nipples, maybe a sinful glance. Some would strip right in front of him, strut a little, then don the gown; obviously proud of their bodies, new implants, whatever. The excuse to flaunt, a form of sexual foreplay by proxy. As for the gorgeous femmes with blemishes, he couldn't turn them away. They got their counseling straight and hard from Robert. And, for those who were reluctant to disrobe in front of the lad, he'd leave the room while hidden cameras scanned for scars, warts or any likely to turn off the Rev.

So for the first months, he had a river of discrete women practically raping him for a shot at the Reverend's salvation. That was the fun part.

However, some of them tried return to Hightower for additional sessions, but the Rev didn't want relationships. He wanted carnal encounters with strangers. The riskiest part was turning away those who knew his dark secret. Hell hath no fury like a woman scorned by her preacher. Robert was the first firewall. He just sucked it up and took his best shot; if he failed, there were always the hush lawyers.

Thompson was barely 19, with a river of women, drugs and cash flowing, but he hated pimping. Reverend Jones sensed it and nipped it in the bud. He decided to add to his job description, to stimulate the boy's hungry mind. He would bring the kid into the act.

SEVEN...

THE POWER HOUR

The show was being audited for syndication. The Rev wanted it perfect, right down to the biblical numerology His choir of 49 professional singers wore satin blue gowns. They were seven rows of seven. They sang the same set every week, but he rehearsed them to be sure they weren't wired or drunk. He had twelve 'disciples' working the crowd, to make it appear that Hightower had spiritual connections. This needed the most rehearsal. The runners worked in concert with Bernie the computer freak, who took the raw ingredients and blended them; his cameras spied on them in the parking lot, restrooms and the Tablets Cafe.

Bernie was good at hacking stuff. When he was 13 he hacked the Pentagon payroll. He was actually surprised when the Secret Service beat down the door, locked & cocked. They cuffed him, took his computers, zip drives, phones, cd burners... *everything*. To Bernie, hacking the Pentagon was just a joke, a bit of a challenge on a rainy day. But when they cuffed his parents, and secured their assets he gleaned the salient details; apparently our nation's security had something to do with people getting paid. The feds made it clear; Bernie touches another keyboard, parents go to San Quentin. All assets go to the task force auction mallet. His parents gave Bernie a big time-out. He was so sorry; never do it again. It took him less than a month to be online, using a new hacked identity and a hot laptop. Feds were so stupid... They'd never catch his young ass again.

Bernie's antics caught Hightower's attention on the evening news, so he drove to Cloverdale; cash and contracts emerged. Rev promised to take care of the problem child. Bernie's parents were relieved beyond words; their son had a good Christian future... and no more feds would batter down their doors and confiscate their Land Rovers.

It was his fantasy job. He actually *got paid* to drink energy drinks and play with the latest technology. He would spy on adults and feed data to the runners. Hidden mikes monitored buzzwords, feeding them to a smaller version of the Homeland Security search engine that spies on citizens. Bernie's computer listened for the seven deadlies in English, Spanish, Italian and Mandarin. If parishioners were foolish enough to say it, Bernie caught it. He caught Christians sniffing coke, whacking off and screwing in bathroom stalls. It was a fun job for a punk.

At rehearsal he checked cameras, mikes and the burning bush, Hightower's basic flaming wishing well. The trashcan resembled a biblical bush. Deep in the flame-less center core, projectors pointed upward, ready to display images upon the wall of flames. Ten frames per second was about right; subliminal marketing for the aching psyche; a crown of thorns or an old rugged cross. Other images resembled a baby, old man, whatever. Bernie had a million of 'em ready at the press of his keyboard.

The time finally came for the sermon. The theater filled with yearning flock. Spillovers crammed the aisles. TV crew and runners threaded their way through the throngs. Tailgaters sweated in the titanic parking lot, watching big screens or cell phones for a glimpse of their beloved Reverend. The lights dimmed. Digital organ music cued up; the choir rattled the rafters and got everyone spiritualized. Spotlights blasted Hightower's flowing mane and his diamond-rimmed frames. Luminescent bullets ricocheted off into the darkness.

He began with a solemn voice; "Praise Gawd for this wonderful assemblage of fine people. Please say that, right now, *will you?*" A few dozen murmured in unison.

"Praise God".

"I mean... *PRAISE GAWD!*"

Half the house chimed in. On the third try it became one roof-lifting voice; *"PRAISE GOD!"*

He barely let the hum die; "You know, on the way here this morning I saw some young people, uh, smoking marijuana. Gawd opened my heart, SO I spoke with them. Remember, Jesus spoke with sinners and concubines. It's time we do what Jesus did."

When it came to harlots, he knew his shit; "If a man can't uplift his brother or sister, then he's not on his way to glory. Well my friends, I want to be *bound for glory!* "

The place went nuts. Just then, Rev got his cue for commercial. The cameras shut off. Digital filler music cued to keep the crowd heated up. Meanwhile, the runners and Bernie prepared for the next segment. His producer whispered into his private mike; "CUT the Pot talk! we'll *lose California!"*

But he had plans; "Don't worry, *I won't lose 'em!"* The cameras lit up again; "And so I sat down with those kids and I asked them a simple question. I said; **'When you die, WHERE ARE YOU GONNA GO?'**

Dozens cheered him; "Hallelujah!"

He shook his head sadly; "They had the wrong answers. One said; *'I'll come back as a German Shepherd.'* Another said; *'I'm gonna live forever.'* And the last man asked me; *'Who cares, dude? I'm gonna LIVE fast, die young and be a good lookin' corpse.* That's all there is, Dad."

The crowd waited, but not for long; "If that's how they feel, *who could blame them?* why not take drugs and steal, lie, kill and covet? "

Then he hit them right between the eyes with fist-pounding-the-pulpit, rock-solid conviction; "I'LL TELL YOU WHY! The *bible doesn't mention german shepherds!"*

More Amens. Christians loved it when he took shots at reincarnation.

"And to the *"I'm going to live forever"* man, I have news; **Nobody** gets out alive... And for the die-young, good-looking corpse dude... Here's your news flash. You'll be dead for a long time!"

He was a hell of a preacher, for a scam artist pedophile sex-monger. He had them spellbound; "Death is forever, Dude... Stars will nova, oceans will freeze, the universe shall collapse... and you'll be *STILL BE DEAD! Man,* that's about as dead as you can get!"

Nervous laughter from the pews; death talk always does that. He was quick to uplift them;

"That's a long time to be *without Jesus!"*

The crowd cheered; "You can be dead forever... OR you can *live with Jesus FOREVER.* As for me and my house, *we choose JESUS, dude!"*

It was time for damage control; "Now don't get me wrong. Some people smoke a little Marijuana and they're still on the righteous path. Others manage a sip of whiskey or wine and they're still with Gawd. Remember, Jesus himself took wine..."

He took his big chance; "And maybe, if Jesus were here today, he might even smoke a little Pot with those dudes this morning. But that's not what I'm talking about. He looked into the camera; "I'm talking about society's obsession with drugs, to escape reality. You see, when drugs wear off you are right back in *REALITY!*

There is a grim reality to face; Some of us ARE gonna die, maybe on the way home today." Nervous 'amens' pierced the pregnant pause; "So I ask again. *WHEN YOU DIE, WHERE YOU GONNA GO?"*

He held up his bible so that its gild reflected the spotlight's intense rays. "We can choose eternal bliss with Gawd. We can live forever in glory, while an infinite number of universes rise and collapse, until the very END of time. OR die without Gawd, dude... it's *YOUR CHOICE!"*

40

He laid the bible down, lowering his head for effect. Meanwhile, runners passed out pens and special paper to the audience. Bernie put the burning bush igniters into pre-heat. The TV crew broke for commercial while the choir pumped them all up with Hallelujah music. In two minutes flat, the flock was primed to donate. As the cameras lit up, Hightower rocked them again;

"Our lives are all about choices. We can choose to walk the strict path, do good things and ask God to save a us seat in heaven. I want you to write down something you wish to change about yourself. You might say; 'Lord, I'm through with drugs'... or 'help me quit adultery, gambling, whatever; sign it and bring it to the Burning Bush, the Flame of the Future... and *throw it in!*" The lights dimmed, showing only the Rev and the Burning Bush. Malibu lights lined the walkways to prevent tithers tripping in the aisles. Jones shifted into overdrive; "Bring your sins, toss 'em in... Give up drugs, give God a hug. Throw in your sinning, start your winning. Come, brothers and sisters, start your new life. Praise Gawd, Hallelujah!"

They knew the drill; toss their sins into the drive-by confessional. Seven aisles converged near the Burning Bush. Seven at a time, they knelt, prayed and tossed their contracts into the flame, then returned to their seats. Bernie cued yellow flames, indicating the papers burned. Actually, the fireproof paper sank to the bottom. Later the hustlers would scan them for extortion leverage.

The next phase would be Q & A, with a little faith-healing to boot, so they could toss the dope now and get healed in the next segment. Meanwhile, Bernie's facial recognition software worked the lines; when he found a match, he'd cue the hologram; a related image would momentarily flash in the flames. It was damned near subliminal, but just enough to push the old love button. They ate that shit up. Robert watched the show with abject fascination. They'd follow Hightower anywhere. It was easy to see how the pervert got what he wanted; just by tapping into their 'urge to purge'.

41

This week, there were only three sheep with dark juicy secrets; they had to be first in line. Behind them stood the shills, ready to throw away their crutches. Of course the real cripples had to wait behind the shills. They would never get to the microphones. Hightower exited stage left and changed into his blue suit; donations were higher with blue. He swapped the eyeglasses for colored contacts giving a semi-fluorescent spiritual haze. As the last of the bush people settled back into their seats he returned. The music came up. Already, lambs were lining up for healing, behind the shills.

Hightower loved to bait them to frenzy and then change gears; a psychic cock tease, much more fun than phone sex. A runner keyed the mike and spoke reverently; "Reverend Hightower; Brian needs SPECIAL help. Would you please pray for him?"

"Special" meant alimony and child support issues, but it wasn't special at all. In California, one in four men were deadbeat dads. Hightower gave the cameras time to focus on him, then peered into the close-up lens, so a million flocksters saw those hazy lenses; "I surely will pray, but the Lord has already made it known to me... Brian, your problems are financial. Gawd wants you to get a better job. That's the easy part. The *HARD part* is doing the right thing with the extra money."

He waited for the amens hallelujahs to fade; "Give unto Caesar that which is Caesar's... and give to HER that which belongs to your ex-wife... And give your soul to Gawd... **THAT** will set you free!"

The next runner prefaced her mark; "Reverend, Carla has a problem. It's growing bigger all the time. Can you help her?" Bigger was Code for 'she's knocked up and the jerk skipped town. Jones nodded sagely; "My dear Carla, the Lord says you are better off alone, than to have that sinner anywhere near you and your baby! PRAISE GOD for *your freedom,* sister!"

Carla went slack-jawed. She was only four months along… Nobody knew, except her best friend whom she told five minutes ago in the bathroom. She slumped into the runner's arms. Hightower surely seemed to be linked to Gawd Almighty.

By the time the shills got to the mikes, the crowd was drooling. Some cried. Many prayed. Some spoke in tongues. Hightower performed three miracles with his best three shills. They went to commercial just before the real cripples had their say. Then the offering plates went out. The collection wasn't really needed, but the tradition was. Most churchgoers expected a collection, just as one expects cops to wear blue or bellboys to linger for tips.

Next the Rev plugged next week's service, then exited stage right while the choir closed the show with old time gospel songs. They had 'em salivating for next Sunday.

Robert quickly followed Jones off stage. A bit too quickly, maybe. He opened the Rev's door unannounced. Jones was swallowing a pill and tried to hide it; "Oh, sorry, Jim… I mean, Reverend, I…"

"Oh, Robert, this is just nitro. When I get excited, the old ticker sets to thumpin'… What's on your mind?" But Robert forgot what he'd come in to say, so he begged off and went home.

It was two weeks later when Robert decided to kill the Reverend. Maybe it never would have happened, but who could say? The rush of killing Clarence was gone. And for a while, there was a chance Vincent Carver's life might have turned out normally. But whatever chance he had, the Reverend stole it. One might also blame drugs for Vincent's decision. First he took drugs with Connie, and now with the Rev's posse. But to blame pharmaceuticals is bad logic; many people take drugs without becoming serial killers… But whatever the reason, it was moot. Truth is, nobody knows what events spawn a serial killer.

One evening, Bernie called him on his cell phone; "Bobby! Get your ass over here to the Rectory, *FAST!*" He sprinted while his mind raced. Bernie sat in the doorway, holding a boy of twelve, with classic signs of shock, according to the medical books in the rest home; pallor, sweating, weak pulse, catatonia. The kid wore the special consultation gown. Blood stained the rear of it, proving what Jones really meant by '*suffer the children*'.

Few decisions have been made with such swiftness and clarity. Were it not for witnesses, he would have killed Hightower right then. It took three calls to reach the hush lawyers; seemed like a lifetime before two young doctor-types swiftly padded into the building, more like gangsters than doctors. Their body language indicated two things; they didn't like cleaning up this shit, but they were really good at it. Within two minutes they treated for shock, complete with gurney, blankets & battlefield I.V. They drove the kid away; no siren, noise or paperwork. He wondered how often they pulled that little trick for the Rev.

Killing a famous preacher would take more planning than snuffing a decrepit rest home patient. He couldn't sleep a wink. The more he wrestled with it, the bigger the urge grew. The next week's counseling session took forever to arrive. Had it taken longer, Bobby would have gone stark raving mad.

Instead of the unwed mother scheduled to be saved, he switched a young hooker of prior acquaintance. She hated cops and loved cash. Robert prepped her on what he wanted; catholic schoolgirl, plaid skirt, knee high socks, no panties, and please shave the pussy, try to look thirteen. When she got there, he was amazed to see how well she pulled it off. He tried to ignore the boner; "Wow, you're good! Here's your cash, Cinnamon."

She looked around; "So, where are we gonna…"

"Oh, no; it's not for me, it's for my uh, my boss."

He pointed to the Rectory, across the grass quad; "C'mon, I'll walk you over."

"Whatever you say, honey." He gave instructions, as if good hookers needed any; "My boss wants it long, hard and quiet. He's fairly famous, so mum's the word." "Sure thing, sweets." Underlings were always nervous. Hell, half the hookers in town talked about Hightower; his promotional skills didn't stop at preaching.

Robert had pre-planned it all. He had the Reverend on a high fat, low-potassium diet. This was easy, since the Rev never ate health foods. The next ingredient was a freebie, but Robert couldn't have planned it any better; Hightower had a stressful three-hour meeting with those bloodsucking TV syndication lawyers. Finally, Bobby served his last meal; two double martinis, 30-ounce New York steak, French bread soaked in butter, mashed potatoes, Southern style pork-chunk gravy. Two bottles of Redwood Valley Zinfandel. After dinner he had his usual glass of sour mash and Cuban cigar. If there's one flaw in the heart patient's psyche, it's the sweet bliss of denial; eat whatever the hell you want, smoke like a chimney and drink like there's no tomorrow. Then with the dying breath, actually have the nerve to ask Gawd why your ticker's quitting, when the bigger question is… *Why didn't it quit years earlier?* Hightower's denial went all the way to the penthouse. He thought of nitro pills as after dinner mints… No big deal, really; don't worry that the ischemic cardiac muscle is so heavily burdened that merely eating food causes pain. Denial, sweet denial…

Robert's most important act was an earlier visit to the Rev's private bathroom. Finding the nitro and switching the fast-dissolving look-alike candies was the easy part. Getting the color right was a bit trickier, but with food coloring and trial and error, he got it… although he doubted Jones would be in any condition to study the pills when the time came. The rest of the plot fell neatly into place; Hightower's night aide had to leave early, for some brunette reason. And thanks to one of Bernie's stolen spy cams feeding Robert's laptop, he sat back and watched the death-play unfold. Cue the hooker.

45

First there was audio foreplay; soft porn chat; '*My, you're a virgin schoolgirl… now I'm horny*'… that sort of shit. Soon she had her skirt draped over the reverend's lap. She taunted, not really engaging but flirting with it. After the heavy meal, it might take some taunting to get his twisted old noodle hard, but deep inside, Jones was already dying; he just didn't know it yet. Normally, he had no problem getting a world-class boner; one look at white thighs and green plaid would swell him right up. But the body has a survival priority system. Hightower's blood was busy trying to digest steak, potatoes, gravy and butter. The liver needed more blood too, to detoxify Cuban nicotine and sixty-something ounces of wine and whiskey. It was a lot to ask… no, it was TOO MUCH. He could have survived another 20 years, by pacing himself. But Jones never lived a life of pace; that was for fools like the sheep he duped.

His first brush with death in Albuquerque's hospital branded the message into his psyche; life's short; play hard, fuck harder. At first he hated that Mexican motherfucker who stabbed him, but later he was thankful. The lesson drove Jones to unimaginable achievements. Ironic, to think that both of his brushes with death occurred while fucking… Perhaps there is justification for celibacy in the ministry after all.

The vascular prioritizing system hit a conflict-of-interest snag. First, blood should go to the vital organs; brain, heart, lungs… then everything else, according to life's priorities. One of which is the primal life expression, reproduction… Or life beyond one's own life. Salmon know all about this. They breed, then die.

This bitch deserved his best effort, so he tried like hell to make it happen. While the hooker's tits rubbed his thighs and her schoolgirl lips smeared lipgloss onto his flaccid shaft, synaptic pathways opened in his primal pleasure centers. He felt the building erection with a great sense of relief. The last thing he wanted was impotence in the presence of such a great piece of ass.

46

He rolled her over and rammed her writhing, shaved schoolgirl pussy. Pleasure at first, then crushing chest pain stopped him, setting fire to his jaw. The anterior coronary artery plugged; the heart sent out distress signals like the Titanic sent off flares, too late to do anything but herald the impending tragedy. His jaw clenched, cracking two molars; his face and left arm burned like Hell's Door.

Meanwhile Robert watched the video feed of the hooker's fantastic body. Then he saw the Rev clutch his chest, roll off the hooker and stagger for the bathroom. Before you could say *"Police; open up"* she was gone. She knew how cops handled 'Death in the Saddle' cases. Robert sprinted for the Rectory. He found Jones sitting on the edge of the bed, slumping forward. His pain was so great that he couldn't remove the childproof cap. Robert couldn't find a pulse; just tiny butterflies, quivering V-tach chaos. It was over, unless someone brought a crash cart.

Bobby hissed quietly; "Lay back; let me help!" Jones was no longer in denial. Expecting CPR, he eagerly lay back and put his arms down. Robert straddled him, a knee on each forearm, then held Jones' chest down, determined to finish whatever the steak, booze and hooker started. Actually, he would have died soon anyway, but Carver wanted the sensation again; "This is for that kid you RAPED last week; you're dying, so where are *you* gonna go, motherfucker?"

The hypocrisy wasn't lost on Jim Jones. With his last breath he weakly groaned; *"OH, GAWD."* The back half of his heart gave up the struggle. Bobby got off Hightower, grabbed the spy cam and the hooker's forgotten socks. The place looked clean. Then he remembered the fake pills. He ate the candies and replaced the real ones, placing the vial in the southpaw's left hand. With one final look around he closed the door on the dying scammer. The Reverend had raped his last child.

News of the famous preachers' demise traveled like wildfire. Robert answered routine questions, but the cops seemed glad to have Hightower off the planet. If trouble came, it wouldn't start with the cops but the media. But they didn't give a crap about the aide de camp. They had bigger fish to fry. Carver put Bobby's costume in a Dumpster. He bought hair dye matching his original color; he was tired of being blond, with the bleaching and bullshit. He was glad to have it over, and happier still with his second kill. He felt... *fantastic*.

The vultures circled. Lawyers and media squabbled for position, as the sex scandals surfaced. By ten o'clock news on the second day, the Rev's estate lay bloating in the sun, like a dead whale on a crowded beach.

Predictably, Hightower's sex-capades only held the public's fickle attention a few days. The only ones still interested were those pressing class action suits for deep-pocket dollars. Vincent watched the news nightly, but apparently he managed to get away with the kill. The good feeling lasted almost as long as Minkle's kill. But when it faded, he felt worse. He'd have to kill again, and that felt OK.

The stiff lay in the morgue longer than most. He had religious and legal documents requesting 'no autopsy'. Nonetheless, with the huge financial empire and so many civil suits pending, the Honorable Judge Tony Pescatore was the best judge money could buy. He signed the order for autopsy. After all of the legal saber rattling, the post mortem didn't show anything unusual; no petechial hemorrhages, broken Hyoid or other evidence of homicide. Lab work showed elevated SGOT and SGPT, alcohol, coke, nicotine, diazepam, and high cholesterol. All of it, proof that the scam artist died from natural causes, if a lifetime of dietary abuse can be called natural. Everything pointed to a life in the fast lane and its inevitable myocardial infarct. This left the lawyers gleefully free to press their lawsuits. By then, there were plenty buzzards circling Hightower's decaying estate.

EIGHT...

THE PROFILER

He was old, but still had charisma. Kay Baker liked the rugged crags in his face and neck; mute testimony to years of hard work and exposure. It wasn't a booth tan, but real-world sunshine that did it. Deeply grizzled, Howard Carver still looked pretty damned good.

Armed with FBI training and a monster brain, Kay didn't take long to get bored with rank and file fed-cop work; most crooks got caught because some cop stumbled upon him; a dangling seat belt, a busted taillight or Hollywood stop. These crooks were the imbeciles parked in a McDonald's at three in the morning, slapping their wives around, while stolen goods still smoked in the back seat; cop magnets, pure and simple. The bastards were too easy. Kay needed more challenging work.

Cold cases appealed but she preferred to think of them as 'failed cases' because in her opinion they were unsolved due to bungled investigations. Many a bad guy roamed free, thanks to a missed clue during an interview; a dismissed inflection here, an ignored body language there. Most men missed so much, especially nonverbal clues. Surely if *she* had performed those interrogations there wouldn't be *ANY* cold cases. To be young and smart is to conquer the world.

This brought her to Howard Carver; he caught the bad guys nobody else could. He blended basic investigation technique, real-world street smarts and intuition. Some guys think outside the box, others inside. But catching the *really bad guys* went beyond boxes; Carver thought outside the universe.

Kay liked him the first time she saw him; Levi's, cowboy boots and a sweat-stained polo shirt with a racquetball tournament logo, various sponsors silk-screened on the back. On the front left; "Finalist, Falling Leaf Classic". He had that look in his eye, which made him look even better to the crook-hound bitch. He was one tenacious son of a bitch. Howard was on the fresh scent of a serial rapist, which meant no sleeping, resting or bullshit. The bloodhound pushed, the stag ran on, just out of sight, its scent lingering heavily. Every hunter knows the feeling; signs of the tiring beast, hooves splaying, strides shortening. Soon the chase will switch to sight trailing. Then it will be finished.

Kay wondered how he found time for a tournament. It wasn't until she'd worked with him for a while that she found out how oddly he managed his time. He was cut from a different cloth, as likely to work six weeks straight or go Tarpon fishing and swill beer with the skipper. Carver answered to damned near nobody; a special trick, for anyone in law enforcement. If someone wanted to contact Carver, they had to know a friend. True, he had an answering service but he rarely checked in while working.

And, when he was off fishing or otherwise horsing around, he never took calls. He had a simple philosophy; when you're playing, don't work. When you do, work like a bastard.

Carver had no physical office. It hovered in a 20-yard radius around him. First was Dan Cabral, his private investigator; if Carver was in a case, Cabral was, too. Carver and Cabral were ham and eggs. Dan was a great sleuth, with the ability to seemingly go nowhere, ask nobody nothing and come away with everything. Cabral stood five nine, weighed between 270 and 300, depending on time of year and type of beer. His neck was wider than his head, his biceps thicker than his neck. Cabral's curly short-cropped red hair finished off the image; a two-legged Red Angus bull.

He survived one hell of a firefight in Bosnia, which degraded into a brawl once the munitions ran out. He fought four men with a five-foot length of speed limit sign. In a burst of adrenaline and Semper Fi improv, Cabral tore it out of the busted sidewalk and started swinging it. Two men died; the others ran at the sight of a two legged bull ripping traffic poles from frozen concrete.

Carver's second was Dave Semple, a lifelong hunting, fishing and drinking partner. Semple also had red hair, but straight and long, for a redneck. He was six three and 250, built like a wide receiver. Dave was an all-around gopher and bodyguard. His loyalty to Howard was unswerving. One time in Wyoming they shot prairie dogs. In moderate winds, Semple consistently potted the diminutive desert doggies out to five hundred yards. He could hold his end of any gunfight... pistols, shotguns, whatever.

Corky Hill stood five six and weighed somewhere around 130, but nobody had the balls to ask her. Twice named high school athlete of the year, she had the hand-eye that most men envied. She also kept Carver out of

51

bars, which is more than the guys could claim. Her appetite ran to women, so Corky's lover had no problem with her running with the grizzled old hetero, who was proud of her. He loved watching her beat some hotshot male who would always pout about losing to 'a girl'. Corky made the accommodations, booked services and basically watched out for the crew's morale. It was hard not to like her.

Kay spent the first month watching the team work. It fascinated her. The posse was an octopus probing every crack and hole, bringing back information to Carver. Its arms could fit under any doorjamb, through any crack. Then if brought the data back to Carver.

Around the fifth week, Carver finally acknowledged her after they caught the serial rapist in Orlando. At their celebratory meal, he leaned back in his chair and called for cigars; "AH, *HELL*... Welcome to the party, Baker." They immediately toasted the newest member of the elite bad-guy catching team. Kay was in heaven.

They would track rape, arson and homicide perps, but they never chased drug kingpins. Early in his career, Carver nailed a major dealer; turned out to be a front for some CIA arms-for-drugs-for-hostages bullshit. Howard got mired in paperwork and apologies. He made no friends and plenty of enemies. From that time on, the rule was carved in stone; *no dope dealers!*

She heard that Howard had a wife and a kid once, but the job was in his blood. His wife left, he still had the kid. Howard seemed too busy to be concerned about his pathetic parenting skills and the horrible relationship with the only person that should matter. He sent him money and occasionally went home to reload for the next safari.

Still, he was sorry, but there was no point in dwelling on failures when success abounded elsewhere. Carver really liked catching crooks. He loved it to the bone. He lived his life by the high-wire artist, Papa Wallenda's famous line; *"Life is on the wire; all else is waiting."* His 'wire' was hunting bad guys. But the waiting was important, too; bodies heal, brains revitalize and cognitive focus reestablishes. So, they waited with the best of 'em; marlin trips, mardi gras, whatever; call it cerebral cross training.

He lit his cigar and thought about Baker; smart as hell, cover-girl looks and a fanatical bad-guy catcher. There was just one problem. He didn't know where she'd fit, but she had too much talent to let her get away. Perhaps he was training his own replacement; he was at the top of his game, with nowhere to go but down.

So, maybe he'd train her to take over, so he could spend his last years doing something else. He didn't know what, but there had to be more to life than stalking criminals, bringing cops up to speed and sleeping in smoky motels.

The more he thought, the better it sounded.

54

NINE...

THE UN-PROFILE

Vincent's paradox haunted him. He was very smart, yet grossly ignorant about his motivation for killing people. The answer was plainly visible to anybody else, yet Vincent couldn't see it. So he sat on the couch, sipping whiskey while the TV played mutely.

So far, he had snuffed two different people while using different identities. The *differences* were the key to not getting caught. The law caught most killers because they ignored the first rule and killed someone who was related to them personally or professionally. Even Keystone cops could catch those assholes.

In the profilers' books he scoured, most serial rapists had signatures, committing each crime the same way. Hell, they couldn't change M.O. if they wanted to. Even a *stupid* cop could see their patterns. But his old man wasn't stupid. He was the best of the best. Obviously, if Vincent wanted to keep killing people, he had to randomize the elements of the crimes; never kill the same way twice. He would have the UN-profile.

He thought back on his killings. At first glance they seemed vastly different; one victim, a crippled old man in a rest home, with no kin. The other victim; OK, not a victim, but a disgusting sexual predator with a long list of youths notched on his bedpost. Hightower really deserved it.

But when he donned a profiler's hat, commonalities instantly emerged; both victims were male, white, old. Both died in their beds and were last seen with an aide of similar age and build. He would have to be much more careful.

Vincent switched to a medium-bodied Napa Pinot from his father's rack. He clicked up the volume the TV; a mind-numbing nature special about rainforest reptiles. A green lizard moved to a lighter spot on a log and changed color. Gradually, blotches of camouflage developed, matching the pattern on the log. A snake slithered down the log, passing within inches without seeing the meal; such a perfect metaphor.

"That's it... 'Ill be a Chameleon."

Actually, he was already becoming one. The cops never crawled on his log. But to be the Chameleon he needed to blend even better. He sipped more wine and wondered where his dad was and what kind of bad guy held his attention. Whoever it was, apparently that guy was more important.

Vincent took pleasure that he'd managed to kill twice, without Howard knowing anything about it. Maybe it was revenge for all those years of disdain and neglect or some deep psychological shit... he perused shrink books when he was 12. The theories were too lame to hold his interest. What was it; Oedipus complex? Some asshole wanted to fuck his own mother, then kill his father? Freud must have been a pervert. No, Vincent didn't want either of those to happen. Still, he glowed at the thought of beating his old man at his best game. Vincent needed a new mark. He decided to kill a homeless guy. He would need a different job first.

TEN...

ARMY SURPLUS

Vincent bought an old four-wheel drive short bed; oversized rock-climber tires set the theme. The truck had a home-brewed lift kit. It was lower on the right, giving a slightly drunken posture. The beast sported an oxidized reddish-orange, from 20 years of summer sun. On the bent front bumper sat a huge winch with a rusty cable wrapped around it. The rear window had a slider made of sun-faded Plexiglas. It sported a bumper sticker; *"Gun control; means hitting what you're aiming at."* Typical of rednecks to dangle prepositions, but who would mention it to a gun toter?

The roll bar with flattened light rack caught the eye. Unlike so many designer bars, it had been used at least once. The bed was layered with acorn dust, mold and loam, spackled into the nooks and crannies. The braided Apache motif seat covers concealed the underlying stains from wet beer farts, taco dust, pecker tracks, deer hair, motor oil and chew stains. Frayed duct tape covered protruding springs. The seat-belt dangled in a state of impotency, but one could still click the buckle with a bit of two-handed foreplay. The heater was busted, the antenna drafted into service as a dipstick. From the mirror dangled old air fresheners, boar's tusk necklace, Golden Eagle pinion feather and Indian talisman; a miniature dream catcher, maybe... It was impossible to tell without untangling, but no way was Vincent touching that shit.

The temperature gauge was the only working instrument. The others died when the truck got air on a mountain two-track. The down-force bent the leaf springs, broke the gauges and knocked the fuses loose. Fucked up the driver too, but that's another story.

The rig fit the redneck image to a tee. He parked near the front door and entered the store. The door swung shut on his heels, making him jump forward. Aromas hit him like a livestock truck; tarpaulins, creosote, cosmoline and a really disgusting cigar. With a more discriminating sniffer he might have discerned the sweet scent of Hoppe's #9, sterno and paraffin. But that would be like a schooner captain tasting a Tsunami as it breaks his vessel in half; a moot point. He found the proprietor sucking on a brown-dick stogie while sorting Israeli camo. He stuck out his hand; "Sir, I'm Jimmy Ray Walker. I'm a lookin' for work."

Vincent created JR with great care; driver license, credit cards, everything. He hailed from Louisiana, but Vincent was lousy with accents, so he had JR move to California when he was six. He could do California OAKIE fairly well, since it wasn't much of a dialect shift; many rednecks emigrated from dust bowl states two generations ago. The Oakie twang softened over the years; everything softens if it stays in California long enough.

The owner surveyed the youth; tall, good shape, looked a man straight in the eyes. Still, a man had to be careful. It's a hard life, selling surplus. He shook hands; "Nice to meet you... Name's Ted Sargent; I own this establishment hook, line and sinker. What kinda work you lookin' for, boy?"
JR shuffled back a half-step and looked at his shoes; "Wellsir, I seen your ad 'n was thinkin' 'bout workin here, if you're still hirin'... are ya?" He raised his eyes to Ted Sargent, who was shorter by six inches but had sixty pounds on the kid. Ted had his poker face on, so JR sold a bit more; "I worked in a truck stop on Idaho state-line; ever hear of the Last Stop Casino & Truck Stop? Wellsir, then I

58

did janitor work in Reno, orderly in a rest home down Pasadena way, but I got purty sick of the southern California faggots so I moved up here. If ya need references, I'll get 'em. That's about it, sir."

Ted hate anybody who carried a resume... Truth is, the kid had him at the Last Stop; Ted won a bundle there once; 11 straight dealer busts paid for his whole elk hunt. The memory put him in a good mood; "Can you run a register, *the way I WANT IT run?*"

"No sir, I don't *KNOW* 'bout cash registers, but I'll do it any way you want. I'm honest and I learn quick. That's about it, sir." Ted hadn't heard "sir" in a long time. None of the three prior applicants impressed him. One came in wearing a bunch of Goth shit. Another had a fag earring and the last was a stupid, selfish fat bitch. She asked Sargent only one question; *'When's payday?'* Jimmy Ray Walker was a godsend. Besides, Ted was sick of sorting camouflage. He hired the kid on the spot. Apparently, the beat-up old pickup wasn't needed for the interview process. Maybe later.

JR wore thick-framed glasses, zero correction, dyed jet-black hair, brows and lashes. The scar on his lower neck protruded just above the tee shirt collar. He wore thick-soled corkers, with a full inch of height on the soles and half-inch inside. He finished the camo, sorted 'em into waist-high plywood bins, labels up. After that, Ted took him on a tour of the huge store, with big semi-open area out back.

Ted's Surplus boasted many diverse items ranging from WWII parachutes to jungle bug sticks. None of his boys ever learned all the inventory. Ted would've been astonished to know JR had it down after the second walk-through. One little shutter snap on the photographic mind... OK, maybe a thousand snaps, but they got filed in the right niches; an interesting diversion for the kid's gluttonous mind. By day three he could find any item on the first pass.

Actually, it wasn't difficult. Ted was meticulous, under the gruff local-yokel façade; *HIS* store was laid out exactly the way he wanted it; logical, efficient, which matched the killer's mental filing method.

In the rear were the bulkiest and stinkiest; monster tarps, dooryard lights on tall beams, half-tracks and jeeps. Everything smelled like Cosmoline; sticky, stinky shit, but one hell of a preservative. He wondered if he coated a cockroach, would it last a thousand years? Toughest things on earth just had to be cockroaches and Cosmoline.

The diversity of items forged customer devotion. A man could look all over town for something, only to learn that Ted had it. If he wanted a shepherd's tent for a trek into the Bitterroots, Aisle Two had 'em; smallest on the left, biggest on the right; could easily shelter 12 hunters and a full cookstove with five-gallon hang-on water heater. True, such a tent MIGHT be available in some cyber catalog, but here a man could see it, sniff it, and if he was serious, haul it out back for a trial set-up.

Aisle Three held related items. Near the tents were woodstoves, double-walled stovepipe, extreme hold down stakes. Jumping over to Four for portage equipment, packboards, packsaddles and fliers for renting strings of horses, mules or llamas. Closer to the front were rafts, again two-mans on the left, 30 on the right. True, they were dusty, but by god, they were there. Next aisle held USCG life jackets, helmets, signal flares, waterproof matches; anything you'd need, once you plunked your ass down in that rapids-running sonofabitch. If it went on or into the river, it was there. Hell,Ted even had drowning kits and body bags.

The next zone closer to the store held smelly plastics; water systems, gas cans, fire extinguishers and extreme weather clothing. JR wondered; the store was in California, which hadn't seen extreme weather since dinosaurs died. But if a man were to outfit for a month in

60

the Arctic, this was the only place to get a Musk Ox coat that would make you sweat at thirty below. And, just to add a little contrast, right next to the extreme cold gear were firefighter suits from the U.S. carrier fleet. Inside the main store were high turnover items; clothing and camping, paintball and archery gear. Under glass were knives and guns. Behind the cashier was a shelf jammed with books on survival, battlefield medicine, martial arts, all of it. He read every one of them in the first month.

Ted soon began to trust the kid. All it took to like JR more was the first payday; "Sir, I have no problem workin' for cash if it saves you any uh, paperwork. Yes, sir. Cash is *fine with me."*

He didn't have to say it twice. With the burdensome endless payroll deductions and the Great Satan of California's entrepreneurs, Workers' Compensation, which sucked 40% of a payroll and paid back nada... He figured the kid had alimony or child support to dodge. But he liked him and didn't want to lose him. JR was a hard worker and smart as hell. If the kid had a shady past, it just made him more likeable. Men with flaws can be trusted.

Ted's cash register cam already proved he hadn't stolen a dime. JR was fast with the drawer, too. He ran it just like Ted told him. Ted's regulars didn't want receipts. With the government bombing third-world countries and paying 5K for toilet seats and bailing out bogus Wall Street scams, his patrons hated seeing their money subsidize that bullshit. So they took a vicarious thrill when Ted went under the table. It was Robin Hood all over again; rob from the king, give to the peasants. Or in this case, Ted.

As for new customers, any of them could be a tax spy or potential hassle. Their transactions went in the register. They weren't hard to spot. They wore nice clothing & shopped without purpose. It might have been overkill on Ted's part, but after his "IRS brush with death" there was no such thing as unjustified paranoia. The ordeal still haunted him; he had to fight the urge to haul a truckload of

C4 to the main office and blow some serious shit out of 'em. So, hell yeah, he'd pay the kid in cash... And trades? The kid loved them. He traded for optics, night vision, infrared trackers and other shit.

By the third month Jimmy Ray had what he needed.
Hell, he even had a mark picked out.

Ted's was at the north end of town, bordered by a vineyard, freeway overpass, dying junkyard and a truck-stop, the only viable enterprise for 300 yards. It was also the only truck stop for 120 miles north or two summits each to the other points of the compass. By the time they made Hidden Crest most truckers needed fuel, oil, coffee or food.

One bum had the cafe Dumpster staked out. He was a real pain in the ass, as far as the owner of the "Fifth Wheel" was concerned, especially now that the cops couldn't hassle him any more. Something about the city's new attitude, civil rights for bums and all that bullshit. The last time Bill Wendell took matters into his own hands, the cops tried to bust *HIM*, for Pete's sake; a Nam veteran, businessman and taxpayer. What did they expect him to do... *Feed the fuckers?* If he would, pretty soon he'd have a whole clan of fuckin' bums livin' under the overpass, just like happened at the south bridge. The county's goin' to hell in a hand basket, for sure.

And so the pain in the ass homeless dude was a perfect mark for the killer; predictable, he frequented isolated areas and nobody would miss him. Best of all, the cops probably wouldn't look too hard for his killer. Hell; they wouldn't look at all, if it looked accidental. JR decided to study the bum's ways.

ELEVEN...

STUDYING TED

Truckstop Ted didn't start out life as a nobody. Originally he wanted to be a professional shortstop, but college revealed that his athletic talents were lacking, so six years at Stanford got him an MBA. Two years at the stock market gained him accolades and riches. Soon he could have any woman and drug he wanted. This met with ill favor from his wife, who sued for divorce and won the house, Beemer, everything. She even got the dog.

Halfway through his divorce, Ted was taking drugs and screwing all the women he could; his life kept spiraling downward. By the time the ink dried on the divorce, Ted had nothing but multiple addictions and a revoked trading license. It took him less time to hit bottom than climb to the top. Soon he was living in a dead van, scrounging to feed his vices. Steadily his brain fried from meth, with his body not far behind. Ted had only one set of clothes shiny from body oil, his formerly sharp brain devoid of purpose other than scoring his next high. The contrast stung at his psyche; Ted's days *used to start* with a workout, sauna and cappuccino. He'd scout the market and call clients with tips. By noon, he'd have them locked into great deals.

Strangely, he felt comfort with his new lifestyle; look out for Number One. Compared to brokering seven-figure deals for greedy dot com assholes, it was a snap. He might arise at eight in summer or nine in winter. He'd take a piss and get out of the grimy old sleeping bag, then hike to the John in the Box to rummage trashcans for a used cup; sham proof that he'd purchased coffee and so was entitled to free refills. Despite his horrid body odor or more likely because of it, the crew let him pump coffee, hoping he'd leave before the regulars came in and complained about the stench. After that, Ted would slither over to Wall Market to take a healthy crap. He'd wash his hands, but the face must be just right; image was everything. By the time he got to his favorite intersection he'd be fully into character; those college drama classes finally paid off.

Ted loved long red lights. Any young moms idling their SUV's with soccer kids in the back, were fair game. All he needed was a long red light, a down-turned mouth and a sign, however cliché. Yuppies ate that up; *"strandid ned gas, dottter's wedding"*. He didn't have a car or a daughter.

He preferred cash, but a sandwich held emotional leverage; it definitely paid to act grateful for the sandwich, one of the bum's best psychic crowbars. He'd rip into it like he was famished, they'd feel compelled to help; *"See, Biff? He's NOT wasting it on alcohol! He really IS hungry! Let's help him out with some cash."* Around eleven he'd toss the once-bitten props to his colleagues' dogs and take his cash to a liquor store. Then Ted would rendezvous with his drug man and carry his booty to the Talbott Bridge. By sunset, the party was on.

It didn't take JR long to get bored with studying the bum's routine. By the third time, JR was ready to kill him.

TWELVE...

KILLING TED

Twice he stalked up close and personal, using the Ghillie suit. It was hot, heavy and butt-ugly, but it worked. The never knew that Jimmy Ray got within ten yards, in broad daylight. What a rush.

His stalking proved that society concealed the real truth about the homeless problem. A soft-thinking school system taught him to think warm fuzzy about them and their signs; *"will work for food", "stranded... need gas"*. The truth was quite different; the were selfish, not helpless. They were ruthless, not innocent. They weren't in trouble, they caused it. Their self-serving lifestyle centered on getting drugs and getting laid. They had no goals, deadlines, no mortgage payments. Theirs was the most carefree lifestyle of all.

Truckstop Ted had wanted to fuck her for a while, but she hung with an asshole that bribed her with chicken nuggets. Luckily she was alone this time. Ted showed her the crack, and she showed hers. Jetta was a former Zoology major, thanks to affluent parents. With the right hygiene she'd clean up fairly cute; but right then, she was screwing a homeless man doggie-style under a bridge, with the tribe trying not to watch. Shortly after Ted came, he walked upstream. He whipped it out to piss and looked up into the skies. The dark of the moon made for a good study of the astral bodies. He felt like a damned king. He had no way of knowing it was almost over.

Jimmy Ray felt hot. He focused on the mark, five yards away. He panned the perimeter with his night vision. He began the final stalk. The gravel bar crunched under the Chameleon's weight. Expecting his lover again, Ted turned around. Imagine his surprise. The Chameleon stuck him above his right clavicle with ten cc's of succynilcholine chloride. Within seconds the greasy bum couldn't move. Jimmy Ray shoved the former stockbroker into the river.

SSC, the pharmaceutical equivalent to Curare, didn't kill. It merely paralyzed his skeletal muscles. He couldn't move or cry for help. That left him free to ponder his fate while he drifted downriver on his back. The tribe didn't notice him float silently past them. Then his air left him and he submerged. There are worse ways to die.

FOURTEEN...

DEATH OF A LEGEND

Howard Carver and posse were hot on their latest perp, having tracked him from Idaho to Iowa, or as Semple joked, *'From steak & potatoes to bacon & eggs.'* The trail was so hot it smoked. Nicholas Bustamonte had a long, distinguished career. While cops knew the arsonist as Zippo, his mob tag was Nicky the Torch. He had a short rap sheet, thanks to many loyal customers eager to see their joints burn down. In fact, that led to his first prison stint; a clever insurance investigator caught him because the client was so happy, he bragged about it to the wrong bartender. The Torch spent eight years in slam, where he completed his Master's in fire forensics and lock-picking under the tutelage of experts. At only five-two and 116 pounds, he was your basic two-legged ferret with a bald spot. His slight build was a godsend, when placing accelerant.

Carver's posse had a hard-on for arsonists. Cabral's only sister died in an arson fire almost five years earlier. It went without saying that that one day they'd catch the bastard that cooked her. Now they were closing in on Nicky the Torch; the whole team panted with hope.

This fire would be Nicky's crowning glory. He didn't really do it for the money. He lived a frugal life and invested heavily in tax-exempt bonds, so he had two reasons to retire. There was that feeling, like a woman feels walking dark streets; a prickly fear, lightly brushing the nape. Surely it couldn't be those charred bodies five years back. How could he know that his delayed fuse would take an extra hour to go off? And *how the hell* did those partying teenagers get into that boarded up building? One of them was a girl, for Chrissakes. He thought he was over it, but a man can't make peace with charred bodies.

Still, he wasn't completely sure if that was screwing with his vestigial conscience. It might be something else making his nape tingle. As a kid in upstate Michigan, Uncle Alfredo was a deer hunter. He schooled young Nickie; *'A trophy deer has a sixth sense. He can sense a hunter on his trail.'* Without knowing it, the Torch had become the stag, feeling Carver's intense lust for the kill. If he'd been more in touch with his feelings it might have saved his ass from a long sentence.

Bustamonte's crowning achievement would be the famous Black Eagle Hotel in Daveyport, Iowa. It was a typical money-laundering job for the mob; put a bunch of dirty money into a multistory fixer-upper, torch it, pull a nice clean insurance check from the ashes; kick some back to the adjuster and everybody's happy.

Never mind that the Black Eagle was an historic landmark. Forget that kings and presidents once slept in the grandest hotel in the Quint Cities. Ignore that the old gal hosted world-famous chiropractors headed for the Fountainhead a few blocks up Brady Street Hill. The Eagle was indelibly linked to Chiropractic. Palmer alumni came from all over the globe to glean new pearls from B.J. Palmer, who often met famous dignitaries from all over the world at the Black Eagle.

69

The fledgling healing profession was long-scorned by organized political medicine. Palmer's annual Lyceum was the main opportunity to recharge. They came to rejuvenate their souls, to learn new technique and to see old friends. They came because there was nowhere else to get what they needed. When they came to Daveyport, the cream of the crop stayed at the Black Eagle.

But she had already seen her finest days. She once sheltered presidents like Roosevelt and Reagan, but now her rooms now held senescent shut-ins and hapless yuppie tourists, none of whom cared a whit for the grand old girl's history. Only the Mezzanine floor remained viable; offices and curio shops did just enough business to keep her on life support.

Still, in spite of her sunspots and wrinkles, the geriatric matriarch clung to her pride; the marble floor, hailed in the twenties as the finest dance floor in Iowa, now had the undeniable stress fractures of old age. Where she once sported spiffy bellhops and a line of shining limos, she boasted trophy-class cockroaches and an occasional puke-smelling taxi trying not to run over bums sleeping in the snow-packed alleys. She had survived other attempts at refurbishing. Once every ten or twelve years someone would scam a new crop of investing suckers. The plan was brutishly simple; take the money, make a sham remodel attempt, skim plenty of cash, then go broke. Still, a girl can have only so many facelifts before her navel becomes a chin dimple. And so it was with the eleven-story matriarch. This time, the operation would be a success, but the patient would die. At the end there would be a big check and a colossal pile of historical rubble. There was only one problem; the Torch didn't want any more charred bodies on his conscience. He needed to vacate the tourists and shut ins. Then as if by magic the plan came while watching the news one rainy night; a small house in Molineau exploded after the woman set off too many bug bombs. When the refrigerator came on, Poof! No more house.

It was no secret; the Black Eagle was chock-full of monster roaches. So in preparation for the facelift the owners scheduled the extermination of half a billion unsavory residents; everyone had to vacate for a long weekend. Nicky saw his chance.

The exterminators taped off every window, opened all the doors, the twin public elevator shafts, dumbwaiter and service shafts. They turned on the poison after double-checking that no residents remained, except for rats, mice, bats and a billion lice, fleas, bedbugs and cockroaches.

He donned his breathing apparatus and entered at midnight, seven hours after the fumigation crew left. The fumigant hung thickly. When he got to the basement the Torch became horrified. His flashlight beam revealed a coffee-colored ocean of undulating, heaving bugs, three feet deep. It was his worst nightmare, an ocean of squirming cockroaches. Rigged for survival like no other species, every roach in the hotel ran warp-speed for the basement at the first whiff of gas. The older bugs knew the drill. It always worked before. It would have been a great plan too, except for the arsonist's plans. A billion spiny legs rubbed against others, creating a horrendous hum. The sight and scent gagged him. He sucked it up and waded into the waist-deep ocean. They climbed inside his pants to his balls. They climbed up his shirt. Smelling fresh air escaping his mask seal, they tried to get into it. But the Torch's will to light the Hawk drove him past his roach phobia. He just clenched his jaw and kept wading through the writhing, reeking sea of dying bugs until he finally located the gas line. Using the pointed end of the fire ax, he started swinging. Soon gas shot from the line so fast that the shrill screech hurt his ears; a thin line of frost quickly rimmed the metal gash. The Torch hurried back through the sea of bugs to set the ignition charge. Meanwhile the roaches smelled the gas and dropped off his body, headed for lower ground. Roach life has one motto; hurdle the dead, trample the wounded… life goes to survivors.

71

Arriving on the third floor, Zippo's lungs convulsed with pain. Sucking air through the decrepit old breathing apparatus made it worse. He set the timer and hauled ass down to ground level. His plan was to drive over the Centennial Bridge to the safety of Molineau's waterfront. He'd see the burning building's double image reflected in the Mississippi. An arsonist could have no finer reward. However, just as he exited the hotel Cabral grabbed him by the throat while Howard Carver clicked the cuffs on the fire-making weasel.

Ordinarily the posse left the arresting part to local law, but with the Torch, everybody wanted Cabral to nab him. The local cops stood by while Kay Baker read him his rights. The posse couldn't be happier, until Howard Carver arched his neck and reached both arms out. A strange light was in Carver's eyes. He clamped onto the Torch's left forearm. He fell, dragging the Torch down with him. They would have to pry his cold, dead fingers from the baby-burning bastard. With one final throb, the profiler's heart stopped, right there on the Black Eagle's sidewalk.

Carver's mind took longer to die; he felt the summer-warmed concrete against his left cheek; it felt good. Kay turned him supine and began mouth-to-mouth. He always wondered what it her kiss would taste like. Now it was the kiss of death and it tasted like shit. It only took a few more seconds before his posse's voices started fading away. He knew it was over. Howard had few regrets, other than his son. He should have spent more quality time. But his job... it was always the job.

In a few more seconds, he would know what lies behind door number one. Was there heaven and hell or was this the whole deal? From far away he felt a deep, rhythmical pressure on his chest; Semple was crying and trying CPR but it was no use denying it; Carver had run down his last bad guy.

Kay Baker takes over

It was obvious that Howard checked out. Kay would mourn later, but for now she had more lives to save; "Dan, please ask our guest *where the fuse is.*" Cabral shook him like a terrier shakes a rat. The torch's jaws rattled; he spewed data so fast it astonished them; "Third floor. Five minutes... *HURRY!*"

He'd serve less time if the Black Eagle remained intact. He would've told more, but Cabral was already hurtling the stairs; didn't even bother with a gas mask. Kay spat commands into her cell phone to have the gas shut off and ten blocks cordoned off. Cabral soon emerged, holding the detonators.

Another ten minutes brought firemen, paramedics and cops directing traffic and evacuating nearby residents. Soon the Eagle shone like a beacon in searchlights of circling media helicopters. It would take a while before the old girl was fire-safe, but at least she didn't blow up. They caught bad guys fairly often, but it's not everyday they saved a historical landmark. The heartland was proud.

But the praise and accolades couldn't do dick for the crew; they were too busy mourning the loss of their boss, best friend and the finest profiler of all time.

FIFTEEN...

VINCENT FEELS IT

He enjoyed watching the greasy homeless bastard float away. His first outdoor murder brought him a higher high. Also he wasn't sure if SSC could be detected in lab work. At any rate, the deed was done; he would hack into the morgue system later to check it out. He went home and searched his gear for incriminating clues, then cleaned and stowed everything. That's when an image of his father flashed; there was no way to know he'd just died in the Heartland. The day after that, the local rag told of a floater.

"Divers recovered a body from the Rushing River,
six miles south of Hidden Crest. Police report is pending,
but it appears to be an adult male itinerant."

He felt betrayed by the lack of information, although it one of the cops' oldest tricks. By exploiting the serial killer's warped psyche his father caught the Candy Man, who killed 32 co-eds. The killer always left a candy cane in the vic's vagina. This info was withheld, preventing copycats and hopefully luring the killer into dialogue. Candy Man suckered for it, placed an ad explaining about the candy canes. His brother recognized a pet phrase and called the cops. Well, Vincent wouldn't fall for it, but he needed to know more.

The next sunrise found him in the Ghillie suit, smack-dab in the middle of a blackberry thicket, spying on the bridge tribe 55 yards away. The Ghillie suit wasn't needed for camo, but to block thorns. Still, once inside the thicket he was glad he wore it. The bushes were cold and damp. He shivered and turned on his hunting ears and adjusted squelch. It took a minute to get it right, due to the background echo from the concrete bridge and pilings.

As the tribe awoke, stretched and farted, it was the usual bullshit; who's going where, which guy had the biggest dick, who's gonna score the best dope. Their conversations were always self-serving. Vincent patiently sifted for morsels on Truckstop Ted. He was rewarded before the last few people left; *"No way... I ain't doin' it, I ain't endin' up like Ted! Knowwhadimsayin?*

The orator stood in the sunshine. His torso rocked back and forth. His head rocked to and fro, a die-hard spinner. The other dude mumbled something JR couldn't catch, because a jackrabbit flushed from the thicket, sounding like a freight train through the earphones. Vincent calmed down to catch the end of it; "He's a badass. *YOU* sell 'em, brah, KNOWWHUDDAHMSAYIN?" He held out a stash of stolen credit cards. That solved a mystery for Vincent; earlier while stalking Truckstop Ted, JR saw these assholes prowling quick-stops...

One dude would distract a young woman after she swiped her plastic at a pump; the other would sneak up and pull her card and disappear; the mark forgot about her card if the pump said *"approved."* She'd pump and drive off while her card found its way into a beat-up old teardrop trailer.

Most people didn't even look at its bone-white paint or faded red stripes. Stealth shelter; too ugly for civilized folks to see. An equally filthy Chevy Vega pulled it. Inside its cracked windows were mounds of trash to discourage the most zealous rookie cop from daring to search it. There were grease-stained bags full of moldy tacos, empty sardine cans and soiled diapers jammed into every nook. Hanging from the mirror were sticky amulets and satanic jewelry. The dashboard was jammed with empty cat food cans. A man could get the crabs just from LOOKING at the mechanical skunk. There'd have to be some serious suspicion before a cop might search that filthy old Vega. So the repellent worked, just like she planned it.

The driver was equally repulsive. Mattie started her life of crime at twelve, when she learned to blackmail her stepfather; she threatened to tell, unless payment came before he did. From there, it was a small step out the door at 13; she fucked and sucked truckers to take her all over the western states. It's amazing how far a man will take a girl that swallows. By 21, Mattie knew how the world works. She could roll a drunk and pick most locks. She could drink with the best of them, but the best didn't want her. The rich get away with everything, the cops ain't always honest nor the crooks always bad. Men are pigs, but pigs ain't always the worst. It's a sick fuckin' world out there; a girl's gotta watch out.

Mattie lost what was left of her looks about the time she lost her teeth; compliments of her fourth husband or live-in or whatever. One night she walked in on him while he was fucking a barfly up the ass. He didn't take the interruption well. With one swing of the Tequila bottle he caved in Mattie's face. Then he started cutting her with the busted bottle. She got her boot knife open and inserted it in his guts. Shocked to see the stiletto buried to the hilt, Mac moaned weakly and rolled off. The knife made a surprisingly wicked gash; dark blood, spleen and pancreas chunks flowed like burgundy clam chowder. Mac prayed for God to save his worthless, woman-beating, trailer-trash ass. He started listing his sins, hoping for atonement, but he ran out of blood before he ran out of sins.

After a plea bargain and 18 months minimum-security, she hit the road. Her time in jail brought her a BS in thievery; how to fence credit cards and phone numbers. When she wasn't brokering plastic she trolled supermarket parking lots. Especially good were cars in handicap spots. She exploited seniors' innate goodwill. Holding out cash, she'd ask them to go back in the store and buy children's aspirin or flu remedy; had a sick granddaughter. Many a senior fell for it. Sometimes in their rush to help, they'd leave their valuables and bags with her. When the mark returned the trailer was long gone, in another lot, targeting fresh do-gooders. Her next best mark was a young person in a sling or cast. Being normally of good cheer, youth usually helps without question; optimism is the handmaiden of crime. Her third choice was the young mother; while teething potions, lice killers and antibiotics weren't as desired as narcotics, they still sold well. Bridge people had toothaches and lice, too.

But her stock and trade was plastic. Mattie got 50%. Her thieves needed her trailer more than she needed them. They'd ride in it and pop out at the next lot. For "handicapped homeless" they sure could move fast. Her thieves would take the stolen cards to convenience stores or smoke shops to buy loot and ferry back to her trailer. They would repeat until the card maxed out.

She left her thieves alone to trade with the homeless troops. She sold her stuff north in Willis or east in Lacqueport. She had to be careful at casinos. The Indians got really pissed when White Man horned in on their business, which was bilking the White Man.....

Suddenly a noise broke JR's flashback; *"Oh, fuck, man… lookaduh berries, dude… I'm gonna get me some, KNOWWHUDDAHMSAYIN?"*

JR froze and hoped his Ghillie suit would work as planned. The doper's jaw muscles worked overtime. He ignored the thorns stabbing his flesh. He just grabbed and chomped and bled. Just as suddenly he stopped and ran back to the bridge. His stench permeated the thicket, gagging JR, but he remained hidden until they left. He mulled it over. Aside from that one tweaker who suspected that Chicken Nuggets killed Truckstop Ted over a credit card sting, nobody really gave a shit about the death.

SIXTEEN...

TROLLING COURTROOMS

Soon Vincent's social conscience started to grow. He recalled helping Clarence cross over. That was good. When he snuffed Reverend Hightower, a bigger pleasure moved him. It lasted longer, too; others besides himself had prospered from the deed. Killing Truckstop Ted was good too, but in a smaller way; the greasy bastard would've lived several more decades under bridges, scratching crabs and screwing crack whores. That was no way for a man to live. Clearly, he'd done him a favor, but compared to his first murders, it was a step down.

JR's talks with his boss usually centered on social issues. In spite of his rough-talking ways, Ted Sargent had a social conscience. JR liked to get his boss ranting about how the world was going to hell... the cops were too soft, liberal judges put crooks right back on the street. Then there were illegal Mexicans committing economic terrorism, taking jobs and mailing cash out of country; the usual boring redneck rhetoric sure, but repetition drove it deep into Jimmy Ray's mind.

Ted wasn't wrong. The kid saw it happening all over. He asked for Tuesdays off, so that, unlike his boss, JR could do something about it. But first, another identity was needed.

Morris Fishbein walked crisply into the Mendonesia County Courthouse. His cheap blue suit, thick glasses and vinyl imitation leather case labeled him a new shark fresh out of law school, the lowest bottom feeder of all. One bailiff eyed the stranger. The retired cop hated defense lawyers... spent his first 20 busting perps, only to watch 'em go free, thanks to assholes like this new shark... no, not even a shark yet, a saltwater guppy.

"Prob'ly from Lacqueport, judging from the tan..."

Lawyers from the lake had more color. The pace was slower and they had plenty of time to jet-ski. Morris dropped his case on the conveyor belt, placing his keys and coins in a plastic tray. Stepping through the metal detector, he claimed his personals and hit the hall. He chose the largest docket; California v. somebody, names changing all the way down. He picked a seat in the back row trying to blend with onlookers, most of whom had a loved one soon to be in the hot seat. He looked around. Hardwood seats, padded only for the jury, a draped window overlooking tar & gravel roofs. The leak-stained, off-white soundboard ceiling was unremarkable, save for a spy cam. Morris' image was probably plastered on a monitor, with some pasty-faced guard watching it. But he had no need to fear. Ever since the World Trade Center disaster spawned tighter security, the camera only managed to film one biker chick throw a hissy fit about her lover's verdict, so they turned it off for routine cases. The bailiff opened the show; "Remain seated come to order; honorable Judge Jason Lenah presiding."

Lenah swiftly entered, sat, adjusted his glasses; "Good morning. People v. Barreras; are principals ready?"

The prosecutor stood and straightened his jacket; "Your Honor. Good morning; this case was pleaded in the hallway, as have the next fourteen, judge."

"Alrighty... skipping down; People v. Lenstad?"

Both lawyers stood in synch; "Yes, Your Honor"

"Geoffrey Lenstad, please stand; you are charged with operating a motor vehicle while under the influence..."

81

The particulars droned, but Fishbein was already bored. Another fucking doper; wasn't worthy of a bullet. And so it went. Most cases were drug and alcohol related. So Ted Sargent was right about drugs clogging our courts. But the penultimate case caught Fishbein's attention. It even forced a change in Lenah's voice; he must be a bad poker player, because a tell that bad would bust him; "The People v. *Lawrence Hopper... **please stand.***"

Hopper's forward-stooping was a nonverbal plea for compassion. His varicose face and bulbous nose shined like Rudolph's nose. The judge glared at the chronic drunkard; "Mr. Hopper, you are charged, as in the past, driving while intoxicated, and *this time...* also **two counts of vehicular manslaughter?**" Although his attorney had coached him to remain silent the alcoholic sang his chronic song; "Judge, if I could get diversion again, I swear I'll learn my lesso..." **"No sir!** You are charged with *MANSLAUGHTER!* Diversion's off the table."

Even his lawyer looked at the floor. Hopper shuffled his feet and tried to look pitiful, but it didn't work this time. The crimes were too big. Cops found Hopper snoring in his car roaring full throttle, propped up by the twisted metal park bench and two young lesbians that had been kissing when the vehicle struck. Their body parts were wedged up into the undercarriage.

Judge Lenah bound him over and set trial date. He banged the gavel, then 50 people left, obviously family and friends of the victims and a few alcoholics supporting Hopper. Morris remained to hear last arraignment, but it wasn't much, just a salmon snagging case, and yet the poacher was the only defendant wearing cuffs and leg irons. Apparently, snagging salmon was worse than cooking meth or killing young women. The good old boy network did love its salmon resource. Morris Fishbein left the courthouse, reflecting hard on what he'd just witnessed. He already wanted to murder that chronic alcoholic, but first he'd need more costumes.

83

SEVENTEEN...

Reggae Ricky

When Hopper's case came up ten days later, Vincent had his disguise ready. This time he was Reggae Ricky; dreadlocks, bright striped pants, baggy yellow and green sweater. Instant tanning lotion did the trick; all exposed flesh looked Jamaican, Mahn. Ricky sat in the back row all alone. Local rednecks didn't like Jamaicans. What is disliked is not studied much; just one of those human nature flaws he learned to exploit.

Believing they had an open and shut case, the prosecution became involuntarily negligent during jury selection; it didn't seem to matter, as far as the DA saw it. Blind monkeys would convict this reprobate before lunch. Then the trial began. Two bartenders and one of his drinking buddies testified; Hopper was falling-down drunk when they split up. Then officers showed photos; two beautiful young lesbian lovers had been peacefully necking on a park bench... and in a minute they were dead meat, parts of their bodies forcibly extruded into the nooks and crannies of the defendant's undercarriage. It took a coroner to place the parts in the proper coffins. The People showed a videotape of Hopper's field Sobriety test and Breathalyzer at the station; sure enough, he was too drunk to stand up, much less blow. By the time the prosecution finished, everyone wanted to kill him, including the judge.

Of course, Defense crossed every witness; in their haste to extricate the girls, nobody read Hopper his rights,

84

according to the dash cams. Not that it mattered; Hopper was borderline comatose. But according to Officer Six Bears, they did read him his rights when he was sober. Defense excused the witness, with one last reasonable doubt arrow being flung; very convenient, how law enforcement always manages to support itself.

Then Defense opened its case in chief. Since the People showed only the parts that bolstered their case, Defense showed the entire videotape, including the part with Hopper piled up in the corner of the holding room, Officer Coopersmith dutifully observing Hopper for all of three minutes. Then Hopper puked all over Coopersmith, the chairs and bone-white vinyl floor. Coopersmith left to clean the disgusting slurry from his uniform. Four minutes passed while Hopper snored, unsupervised. Then Officer Six Bears entered, mopped up the puke and attempted another Breathalyzer.

Defense projected an image of great legal importance, but the jury was dubious; a small form showing Breathalyzer results; 1.9 BAC, which wasn't just beyond legally drunk, it was damned near to the fatal limit. But it was the small print that defense enlarged, the mother of all loopholes. Coopersmith had signed it, saying he had personally watched Hopper continuously for 15 minutes prior to the test. This is to ensure that the drunk hadn't vomited, which would contaminate the test with mouth alcohol. Clearly Coopersmith perjured himself. To make it worse, no videotape evidence showed Coopersmith signing the form; the officer seen signing... was Six Bears.

Several sidebars later, the jury got its instruction. It took two hours for the NOT GUILTY verdict. When the foreman read the verdict, she could barely finish; it was horseshit and everybody knew it... As much as they wanted to kill the bastard, they were legally bound to acquit. Jurors left the courtroom red-faced, heads down. Nine of them had been crying for the young lesbian lovers, so brutally and senselessly murdered.

85

If not for the extra bailiffs, the gallery would've rioted. Not only were the girls' families and friends present, the gay and lesbian community took up three rows. They'd been on the shit end of the stick almost as long as other minorities. The verdict was an anti-gay indictment. The habitual drunk killed two young women, but he wouldn't spend another night in jail.

Reggae Ricky left the room, thinking about the drunkard's reaction; before the the verdict, the worthless drunk looked to be on death's doormat. Afterward, he grinned and threw his arms up in salutation. Obviously the bastard didn't give a shit about the carnage he caused, as long as he was free to drink and drive and maim again.

It was the type of verdict that secures the straight white power structure. It said that one old drunk hetero was worth more than two young gay lovers. It threw raw meat to the dogs of law, turning idealistic cops into badge-heavy, bigoted, perfidious old bastards. The law guards the loophole, which often provides for a civil trial, which mitigates the failings of the criminal justice system. And so the thing seeks its own level, in a perverted way. But any future civil settlement would be meaningless for the grieving parents. They wanted their daughters, not stipends. But to anyone exposed to the legal system, it was just business as usual. One side got screwed, the other won because of a bullshit technicality. Reggae Ricky went to a bistro, ordered food and played it all back at quad speed, especially where the prosecution tried to admit Hopper's six prior DUIs. Defense objection was granted, lest the jury become prejudiced. No mention could be made of his failed attempts at diversion, which were just county-paid hand-holders gorging on county coffers and lecturing fruitlessly to career addicts. The jury never hears sidebars, but Reggae Ricky inadvertently discovered an acoustic oddity; whispers at the bench bounced off it, then ricocheted off the ceiling, caromed off the rear wall. It wasn't exactly Carnegie Hall but the privileged chat managed to hit Ricky's ear.

Halfway through his French Onion soup, he vowed that Hopper was next. He couldn't wait to kill the fucker. On the way home, he cruised the bars Hopper liked, according to testimony. "Happy Hours" first, then "The Weigh Station," which had Hopper's car already in the lot.

Since it was also a restaurant, minors could walk through the bar into the restaurant. He spotted the alkie slouched over the counter; three empty shot glasses said he was celebrating his verdict. Ricky faked like he forgot his wallet and left. He was aching to kill the girl-killing drunk, if only to remove the images of mangled young corpses from his mind. Hopefully it would offset the insane verdict and the sociopath's celebration.

The next night saw Carver with a different identity; Bill Lanier, from Arizona. Blond, tall, twenty-four. Bill bought the poison for Truckstop Ted's murder and a few other weapons in Arizona. He entered Happy Hours. It was a shithole, but its patrons cared not for ambiance or whatever the feng shui yuppies called it. They wanted cold beer, dark booths, cheap drinks and a strong bartender with a weak memory. Forget the snacks. Now and then an extra shot off the tab, and to heck with the decor.

The bar sat near the tracks, near the largest lake in the county. The occasional angler or wakeboarder might drift in for beer and ice, but they sure didn't stay. It was a filthy dump for hard core drinkers who loved their solitude as much as their booze. Bill tried to adjust to the darkness as the barkeep came closer; "Pack of Bud, to go, please."

He squinted; from smoke; "Lessee some I.D, kid."

The Arizona license came out fast. He pointed out the birth date. The barkeep could smell a sting a mile away, but this one was as scentless as a still-wet fawn. He went into the walk-in while Bill spied his mark in a dark corner. He walked over and sat down. "Mind if I buy you a drink?"

Hopper barely moved, but he discerned the buzzwords; "buy, drink".

Pavlov himself would've been proud of the reaction. The bloodshot eyes flitted over the kid; "Sure, buy me *TWO,* if you wanna!" Bill nodded at the bartender; "Put my beer back and bring two of these?"

Mildly curious at the kid's interest in Hopper, he put the Bud back and made the drinks. It didn't pay to ask questions. Bill spoke just loud enough for the barkeep to hear. He wove his web of familiarity, pretending Hopper was his distant uncle's best pal, Lou. Not one to miss free shots, Hopper leaped into character; sure, good old Lou whazzisname. A few drinks later Hopper actually believed the lie. They shot pool and drank. Most of Bill's booze managed to hit the peanut-littered floor or find Hopper's glass. He bought a bottle of off-sale vodka way before last call, before the lights would focus on his disguise. He put his arm around Hopper; "Le's go to *my place 'n* have some of *this stuff!"* "A hella good idea. Damn right…Vamonos!"

The barkeep barely noticed; there was cash to skim, puke to mop and three other drunks to roust soon. Besides, he was glad to see Hopper leave; the prick always got surly at quitting time. The killer helped Hopper into the truck parked a block away, in a darkened outlet lot. Bill looked for cops but they were still stalking kiddy bars, which closed earlier. They'd hunt older drunks in the outlying dives at last call.

Four miles away, a two-track led to the mountains, servicing a few private landowners. Three miles uphill, a locked gate barred traffic. It was a common make-out site, with empty beer cartons, spent condoms and fast food litter to prove it. A short path ran to a seasonal creek. He drove down it. Then he poured Larry a tall one, another and another until Hopper miraculously quit drinking. Bill taped his arms to his sides. Then he pinched Hopper's nose. When the mouth opened to breathe he rammed the bottle deep in his throat; it was swallow or drown. Bill clamped his mouth shut so he couldn't spit it out. After the lesbian killer swallowed it, Bill let him breathe; he sucked air so hard that

88

his nose whistled. His eyes bulged when he got the message; he was being murdered! He fought, but it was a pathetic struggle. Bill let him scramble out of the truck. Hopper pitched face first into the dirt and brambles. Bill was on him fast; "You've killed your last kid, *you prick!*"

It required the same drunken state to see it; for the first time Hopper actually remembered a brunette head flying up into the trees, smells of burnt rubber, sizzling, stinking flesh charring... bodies on gurneys with molten body fat dripping. Apparently he *REALLY* killed those girls. Then everything went black.

Bill palpated the Carotid pulse; nothing. He removed the tape, then drove back to the outlet lot and parked. He hiked to Hopper's beat-up old Chrysler, parked at the closed bar. He donned cotton gloves and drove the filthy shitcan to the kill scene. He wiped down an empty vodka bottle taken from a Dumpster. Actually, Reggae Ricky took it earlier. He pressed Hopper's prints onto the bottle. Then he wiped his footprints away with a Doug Fir branch but it wasn't needed; the hardpan was shit for footprints. He left the driver door open, as if Larry staggered out of his car, then died.

Since he had to walk on the dusty road for the first mile due to the mountain's steep slope, he walked in the thickest dust where the first passing vehicle would obliterate his tracks. Later he found a shortcut straight downhill, cutting two miles off his hike. It was a great night for a walk in the woods while he replayed the kill. He felt wonderful; he wanted to call the victims' families with the good news.

A mountain biker found Hopper's body the next day. The article appeared two days later on page three of the local rag; 'Lawrence J. Hopper, of Hidden Crest, found dead two miles east of Rushing River. An investigation is pending." That was more than any alcoholic deserved, especially one that killed two young women.

Two days later the obituary was a bit softer; "Lawrence James Hopper, 47; died in his sleep due to natural causes. Survived by his loving brother, Judge Justin Hopper, of Coeur d'Alene. Services at Hidden Crest Grange Hall, Friday, 2:00 PM"

Vincent didn't bother to hack the asshole's autopsy. Even if they cut the scumbag open, he knew what it would show; tertiary alcohol poisoning, fatty degeneration, protein catabolism, hepatomegaly and cirrhosis. If they looked, deep into his throat they'd see lacerations , but those would be consistent with a drunken moron falling face down while sucking on his last bottle. Carver hoped the victims' families would have some closure. It wouldn't be as good as killing the bastard themselves, but it had to be better than watching him celebrate his verdict in the courtroom.

Carver felt his embryo growing; killing was getting easier and he was getting better at it. The bad news was that the high didn't last as long. He'd have to take it up a notch; this thought pleased him.

EIGHTEEN...

THE METH HEADS

The weeks rolled by while Vincent's urge kept rebuilding. He would kill another self-absorbed homeless parasite, to scratch his itch. He began stalking the old bitch in the filthy Vega. Following her to the Screaming Bear Casino, he felt his guts tighten with anticipation. He wouldn't kill her tonight, but the foreplay would help allay his craving. He parked facing the lot, under a Bay tree, but suddenly his plan took a turn. Four Caucasian males exited the casino; they moved like a dingo pack, skulking between parked cars, all faces pointing toward their prey.

Cyrus and Bonnie Morris strolled in the warm summer air toward their car. An hour earlier, Bonnie hit a Bingo Letter X, under 18 numbers. With nervous hands she held up her paper six-on, hollering *"BINGO"* with all the gusto an 80 year-old can muster. Cyrus kissed her cheek for luck while they waited for confirmation. It was a good Bingo; the runner counted out 2800 bucks. Of course, the money helps, but cash wasn't really the main attraction; Bingo cultivates hope, which for octogenarians is a fleeting commodity. To hit a Bingo is to align one's self temporarily with the universe; The money's just proof that it happened.

So they walked hand in hand. Cyrus opened the driver's door for her. His night vision was bad. It was a long drive, with hundreds of tight curves and switchbacks before they'd reach their home on the Coast.

91

The thugs grinned when they saw the car turn northeast for the coast road were a lot of bad things could happen on that rugged old pass. The steep switchbacks forced a snail's pace. Following cars always flashed their lights impatiently. There were pullouts every few miles, leftover skid decks from a bygone logging era. Bonnie was eager for the next pullout, since the bright lights in her mirrors hampered her vision.

Following behind the stalkers, Jimmy Ray was trying to connect logistical dots. He hadn't seen weapons, but given the average doper's proclivity for guns, they could be armed. He pulled onto the gravel shoulder to let four vehicles pass. JR didn't want any witnesses behind him. Meanwhile, 12 turns ahead, Bonny pulled onto a turnout. When JR came upon the scene, the cranksters were right on Bonnie's bumper. He saw her frail hand waving cars by, so he hurried past to find a safe spot to turn around. That took three turns.

If the assholes had studied history, they might have taken pleasure in their chosen spot; 140 years earlier, Black Bart robbed stagecoaches stopping to rest horses right there. But they were too stupid to study history. The pullout served their needs, and Black Bart be damned. Bonnie started to pull onto the road again, but the muggers blocked her escape. The first two get out from the left side. The rear dude held a tire iron, the driver a machete, maybe. Tough to see in the dark. Cyrus reached down, tore at the Velcro strap on his left ankle for his insurance policy. Tire Iron reached Bonnie's window and raised his weapon; "TIME FOR MY ALLOWANCE, GRANNY BITC..." The bullet broke glass and punched the asshole's chest. He slouched. The next slug slammed his forehead. Cyrus swung the revolver to Machete Man, running at Cyrus' side of the car. Since the windows muffled the gunshots he didn't know the old coot had a gun.

Adrenaline overrode his spinal arthritis, but it still took Cyrus long two seconds to twist around for the shot. Machete Man broke the passenger side glass a split second before the frangible bullet fragged inside his bladder. He dropped to his knees screaming, but Cyrus' follow up shot centered his Axis vertebra; Machete Man went limp. Bonnie panicked, slammed it in reverse and threw gravel and pine needles on the two dead thugs; the half-assed burial more was than they deserved. The Buick hung its right rear over the cliff, preventing them from escaping. Meanwhile, the last two thugs got out of their ride. One held a Berlinetta 25; the other brandished his favorite persuader, an aluminum bat. Beretta opened with a volley that rattled on the Buick's roof; most people would do anything after that. But they never mugged a geezer like Cyrus before. Just as he'd done in Ribau and Korea, he willed away his panic. He vowed not to waste the last round left in the revolver.

Until then, he'd never thought twice about buying a five-shot wheelgun; the salesman said it was easier to pack. Besides, he'd probably never pull the gun anyhow, so concealment won out over a six shooter. Cyrus never would have suckered for it, back when his platoon lay in frozen shell holes screaming; 'AMMO... *AMMMO!* Now he cursed his peacetime choice in weaponry; he and his soul mate were probably going to die, for the lack of one more bullet. Oh, sure, he had a speed loader in the glove box, but there wasn't time to reach it. So he would center the last round in this asshole's chest, then improvise. If a thousand onrushing gooks couldn't rattle him, these punks sure wouldn't. He yelled at his soul mate; "Bonnie, *GET DOWN!"* Just then Cyrus saw three lights; the center one, just a blink, a muzzle flash. Headlights bracketed Beretta Man; JR's bumper winch slammed him to the gravel. His head rebounded in time for the transfer case to scoop his idiotic brains out; never felt a thing. What a pity.

The last asshole ran for cover behind the Buick. Cyrus swung with him; the frangible caught him in the left

Tibia, just before JR's grill pinned the asshole against a Redwood tree. JR set the brake and checked on the old couple; Bonnie's foot still pegged the gas while Cyrus fumbled with the speed loader; "Are you OK?" Cyrus snapped the cylinder closed on five fresh cartridges; "Yes sir... Didja kill the other two?"

Just then, Beretta Man started screaming, so JR spoke louder; "Killed one, treed that one. Would you come to my truck?" JR hurried because traffic could drive by at any moment. The merciless bully morphed into a deal-making pussy. He didn't deserve a swift death. JR started to get in the truck, to squish the bastard to death, but Cyrus spoke firmly; "Son, let's *DON'T* torture him."

Cyrus' voice was dry. He'd seen enough in Bataan; "*Kill him,* but don't torture him. That ain't right."

JR's senses returned; Borrow your revolver?"

Cyrus handed it over. Meanwhile Beretta Man was sorry, wouldn't do it again, not never, please God... that sort of shit. But on the far side, his left hand scraped away the redwood's bark, trying to get enough clearance to reach the Bowie Knife inside his boot; *"PLEASE DON'T! I'LL DO ANYTHING!"* Then JR knew why his father hated criminals so much; they beat up old folks and raped moms with babies strapped in the car seat next to them. But when the got caught, the cowards sang another tune. JR jammed the muzzle against his skull. Bone conduction announced the cylinder turning, sear engaging, hammer cocking. The crankster shit his pants. Cyrus spoke calmly; "Son, if you shoot him in the head you'll get blood all over your hot hood. It won't wash off." Walker saw his error at once; "Raise your left arm."

'*Please! NO...* OH, GOD! Jimmy Ray placed the muzzle against his lateral thorax, fired and removed the gun in one fluid motion, as smooth as a boot camp flu shot. Just like killing a germ, actually. The bullet slammed the right lung, tore the Aortic knob then collapsed the left lung on the far side. Other than gurgling sucking sounds, the tweaker made no noise. Then they could only hear Bonnie's spinning tire, still charring pine needles. Cyrus walked over to comfort her.

The coast fog is a real bitch; it rolled in as Jimmy Ray backed his truck up. The dead hood ornament slumped to the ground. JR idled over to the Buick to nudge its drive tire back onto the flat spot. He walked to the man behind the wheel, with the panicked wife of a lifetime snuggled tight; "Sir, go home and toss all your empties. Shower and wash away the gunshot residue including your wife's face. Report this gun stolen; may I dispose of it? I promise, it won't show up." "Sure thing; *you saved our lives!*" Cyrus peeled out, but immediately had to slow down on the pavement, since the fog forced a snail's pace. But the peeling out was as much adrenaline as insurance; there were still four rounds left in that gun.

JR put the bodies in the car. He planned to push it over the cliff, but there were too many trees lining the pullout. He saw a dim light glowing in the fog. He turned off his lights. The thick fog concealed him. The state trooper drove right past, unaware of the macabre scene barely 30 yards from center line. JR found two baggies of meth and three bottles of Mattie's cheap bourbon in the car. He poured the booze on the victims and tossed the dope on the ground. He shot the fuel tank. A stream of gasoline obediently began pouring onto the forest duff. Then he fired the last three rounds into the vehicle. With a monumentally loud "whoof" the vehicle and alcohol-saturated corpses briskly caught fire. He drove away. He could see the glow for three turns.

Next stop, Willis town. JR strode into a dingy bar, hollered over the jukebox for a draft and walked to the bathroom. In the grungy mirror he was surprised to see very little spatter. After washing up, he drank his beer and thought about the murders. Killing those assholes was fun, but something was missing. Perhaps the witnesses; there was no telling how the oldsters might react in a few days. He visualized the VFW bumper sticker, which explained the old man's grit; he looked about 85, putting him in WWII, Korea or both. Those men saw some serious shit. He had seen footage of GI's sleeping on the ice with nothing but

95

rubberized raincoats, eating frozen K-rations, losing body parts to frostbite, and still they fought like tigers. That old vet had seen worse than a few worthless cranksters. JR felt in his pocket, examining the wheel gun by feel; two-inch barrel, hard trigger pull, a poor choice for self-defense but the geezer made it work... That took balls. He recalled the Buick's plate frame; *"I heart my grandkids"*. If he needed to kill the old couple he could search coastal VFW halls. But he probably wouldn't have to. He ordered another beer. If they did call the cops, what would they say? A man came to their rescue. Oh by the way, Cyrus killed two, then conspired to kill the last one? No, they'd destroy the evidence and go back to bingo... and they'd be more careful.

While JR ruminated, Trooper Gene Warwick responded to a reported glow in the fog. Black flumes shot up in the white fog while yellow fat-fires roared and sizzled. Warwick hadn't seen people burn before, but he guessed four or five vics. He called CDF; it would only be a matter of time before the whole forest lit up. It took 30 minutes to burn up most of the rubber tires, upholstery and body fat. The flesh itself wasn't a good fuel, so the fire resorted to the liquified fuel puddles at the base of each body, looking like four smoking fondue fires, each exiting its own window. The stinking smoke cooled then billowed back to earth, smelling like burning burgers, so no more cheeseburgers for Warwick. He turned up the AC, pressurizing the cab to keep the smell out. He preserved the scene and waited for crews to show. Two days later it hit front page; four people burned to death on the Coast Road, apparently from a drug-related gunfight. The other big story on the front page was about the ongoing war on Meth in Mendonesia County.

JR vowed to stalk meth dealers next, so he researched methamphetamine, the highly addictive stimulant called speed, chalk, ice, crystal and glass. The odorless bitter powder dissolves rapidly in alcohol or water. Its parent drug amphetamine was first a nasal decongestant. Meth caused increased activity, talkativeness, lowered appetite, much like amphetamines do, but it puts higher levels into the brain, causing cardiac arrhythmia, hypertension and increased core temperature. Meth had limited medicinal use in narcolepsy and ADD, at much lower doses. The pleasurable effects were attributed to dopamine release, which explains the exaggerated torso movements, agitation and egocentric babbling about me, my, mine and I. Long-term abuse caused molecular brain changes, addiction, anxiety, confusion, insomnia, violence and breaks from reality. Such hallucinations can remain for years after quitting, assuming the user quits. Meth addicts had the highest recidivism rate of any type of addiction.

After reading that, Vincent saw no good reason to let meth dealers walk the earth; it was a waste of resource. They tied up the courts, clogged diversion programs, hospitals and addiction clinics. Meth heads are the crabgrass in the Garden of Eden.

The garden needed weeding.

NINETEEN...

DION

Sometimes he'd drive south or east to hear lawyers in neighboring counties at arraignments. It might be Morris, Reggae Ricky or Bill Lanier doing the screening, but no matter; it was a serial killer's buffet. The aisle of potential marks in handcuffs strolled by Vincent. Ah, arraignment; what a great place to eyeball criminals. But lately there weren't any crooks worthy enough to be killed. Just the routine DUI's and wife beaters. Vincent needed more from his next victim.

One night he sat in a bar while the newscasters showed paramedics wheeling a young man. His face was caved in. His lips were blue and swollen like plums. Two paramedics walked alongside holding field IV drips. Two others slid him into the bus. The killer hollered; "Mack, turn it up?" The volume bar scrolled right; *"...apparently from a gang beating. More, at eleven. Back to you, Chuck."*

Something struck a chord in the killer, so he decided to watch it later. Unlike so many teasers, this story actually did get fleshed out at 11. The cutie pie anchorwoman held the big black electronic dick to her collagen-pumped, lacquer-glossed lips; "Gang violence is no longer just a big city matter. Dion Capps of Pedalauna..." His yearbook photo overlaid the lower right corner; "...At sixteen, Dion earned letters in football and wrestling. But he wasn't strong or fast enough to escape the violence that tragically almost ended his life."

She paused quickly to act sad; "Multiple assailants attacked him because he wore... a red jacket. Dion is undergoing neurosurgery. Our prayers go out to Dion and his family. Back to you, Chuck." She smiled her glossy lips. The scene faded out, quickly replaced by a feel-good bite about a rescued cat.

The next day Carver read a better article. Riveted, he just stood in one spot and devoured the data; Dion hadn't screwed someone's girlfriend or picked a fight or hurled insults. He took a different route home after practice; that's all it took to bring him to death's door. The white kid with an athletic lifestyle wasn't aware of gangster rules. The abdominal team removed his spleen while the Neuro team tried to drain the massive hematoma before it killed him. The prognosis was 'extremely guarded.' That's doctor babble for; *"He ain't gonna fuckin' make it."*

JR walked into Ted's. Lately Ted had been dropping hints, to make him a partner. This was unacceptable. The job had served his purpose. He had the gear he needed; time to move on. The sixth customer of the day really flipped his switch. Detective John McMann was Hidden Crest's homicide investigator. Paradoxically, these opposites had become friends; the killer on one side of the counter, master sleuth on the other. JR liked having any cop enter the store, but seeing McMann practically gave him a hard on. He was famous for solving three big crimes in just five years, but he didn't have a clue about JR's inner darkness. McMann came in about once a month, like most of the cops. Ted's support gear sold out fast. But this time, McMann cruised idly. It put Jimmy Ray on full alert.

McMann's life was turning to shit. His wife finally had enough. Frankly, so had he. He was tired of saving lives all day and coming home to a drunken wife. When she wasn't drunk, she was fried on speed. The hypocrisy gnawed at him. So, he stayed out late and went to work early. A common tale for hero cops and their wives.

99

McMann browsed Norwegian ice cleats and Sterno stoves while his mind probed the upcoming divorce logistics. He asked to see the newest "911" knives; flip-outs with serrations for cutting seat belts; heroes can never have enough knives. JR unlocked the display case and let McMann come behind the counter to play. Only cops and firemen had this privilege. Ted said; *"If we can't trust these guys we've got big trouble!"* He eyed the cop; McMann was six three, 190 without the kevlar, Glock and badge. Dark blue eyes, black hair, high and tight. At 45 he cut a figure most women would love to hold. But something was wrong.

The suspense was killing JR. He decided to go for a tell, like poker stars do; "Hey, John; take a look at this; just in from Taiwan." John didn't look; "Yeah, it's nice."

"Hey, did they catch that drive-by yet?" John's eyes cleared. Switched to mode for answering civilians; "We got that perp south of town; stolen car, bags of ice." He was good at hiding personal troubles with his job. In fact, that was why his wife felt betrayed; the control freak never opened up to her. After 15 years of dominant-man silent treatment she had enough.

The subject of Dion turned his eyes smoldering with hatred. They were in poor position to deal with the little fuckers with baggy pants. Back in the day, they could roust 'em and search for weapons and drugs, so the gangs stayed out of Hidden Crest. But the new administration responded to surging Hispanic populations. Cops were reprimanded for 'profiling'. Gangs grew bolder, committing worse acts. He had seen it happen in cities and now, in his hometown. It really pissed him off. He went into his rant; Hidden Crest lost its balls. It was a lesson passed down from Wyatt Earp. Before that, it came from feudal kings and before that, from pharaohs and emperors; riff-raff must be controlled or society collapses.

But yuppies knew better than kings, pharaohs and emperors. Society dealt softly with the bastards, planting the seeds of its own destruction. The newest administration saw graffiti as a form of art. Stabbing and rumbling were just different forms of cross-cultural self-expression. Pretty soon they'd have an art class in tagging. Maybe a class in rape called "Unilateral sexuality, 101." The stand on rape was already softening; they taught women how to survive, instead of demanding stiffer sentencing for rapists. McMann airbrushed the Capps case; the kid's parents and teachers were soft-on-crime, politically-correct fools. They failed to school Dion in reality. Yes, the kid was still in a coma and no, the cops couldn't do shit about it. Then he switched gears. Back in the old days, a man could work hard, come home to a hot meal and a supportive wife. Nowadays, wives were too busy boosting their self-image to cook, much less fuck him right...

He lost Jimmy Ray at that point. The killer didn't want to hear his charismatic nemesis whine like a pussywhipped mailman. Besides, his thoughts were snagged on Dion Capps and all the tubes plugged into him. When the door chimed he never heard McMann's goodbye. The Chameleon decided it right then; his next marks would be the punks that assaulted Dion.

The public wanted to read about fresher tragedies, so Dion's plight quickly faded from the public eye. He used a computer at a coffeehouse, under another alias; Wyatt Urp, but there was no need for this level of paranoia. His search was too common to arouse suspicion. They may as well search for horny hubbies in Victoria's Secrets sites.

Since Capps was in a coma, JR was surprised to see new info on Dion's attack. An eyewitness must have posted to the site. The attack occurred on the tracks near an industrial park. Four gangsters beat him unconscious, then kept beating him. They burned his red jacket. The anonymous tipster called 911 on Dion's phone.

Dion's parents had insurance, but the hospital pillaged the limit cap with the first heroic surgery. Thumbnails started to fill in slowly; the first photo showed a mummy in gauze with black eyes, swollen blue lips and a

101

caved-in face. *IF* he survived at all, they'd fix the face later. Tubes went everywhere. Hell, most of Vincent's victims looked better. The text tried to cheer the readers; *"Dion's left thumb twitched today"*

Then came the paraphrased medi-babble; twitching digits was a good sign, maybe he won't be a complete vegetable... But it was all bullshit. No neuro would say anything so irresponsible. A REAL doctor would steel folks to the grisly reality; *'The kid's in a world of shit; any questions? Gotta go, people to sew.'*

He clicked the latest update; Dion's left eye open. Just one tube, low in his throat. The text alluded to skyrocketing bills, a link to the donations page. JR drove home and gave 2-weeks notice to Ted. It was time to plan revenge for the kid.

TWENTY...

DEATH IN HOP HOLLOW

Fifteen miles south of Hidden Crest, Victor Saldivar from Phoenix got the job instantly; nobody wanted to mop puke for minimum wage. Victor resembled Bill Lanier, except for the dark curly locks and gold earring. Spanish was the easiest language he'd learned; hardly any silent letters, few diphthongs and with its romantic base, he could assimilate as he'd done already with Italian, French and Portuguese. Victor's days took on a simple rhythm. The drive South on the mountain road gave ample time to play a Spanish language tape or listen to Latino musica.

The bar business was boring, compared to Ted's place. There was hardly any inventory. There was nothing to read, so he began reading customers. Basically, there were three kinds at The Hog Cage. The original owner was a biker, but when he died an Italian winemaker bought the Cage; tried to make it work as a pasta and wine joint. It failed in two years. Next were dot com yuppies selling 15-dollar sandwiches and 20-dollar goblets of wine. They went belly up in six months. Actually, they only bought it for a cover to score killer Pot in the Emerald Triangle. Their loss got absorbed in the system, but their Pot contacts lasted a lifetime. Then Juan Carlos Rodriguez-Barreras returned the Cage to its original workmanlike status; pushing cold beer and oily corn chips. The Cage was an icon for Hop Hollow, which used to be just three hop farms, an intersection, a few hundred migrant workers and a post office.

The railroad worked back then, seeing five trains per day running the full length of California. Then they shut down the rails. The hops fields gave way to vineyards and tourist traps. The store took on a façade, compliments of the old hop-drying house. The scavenged lumber was a quaint attractant for thousands of yuppies driving the 101. They craved the old look, as long as state of the art shit was inside.

At 54, Juan Carlos was the poster child for Hispanic businessmen; he'd already folded six restaurants. With a Master's in business and a minor in fine arts, JC could balance a spreadsheet, paint a mural or sing Mariachi with equal mastery. There was Latino cash to pay the bills, but he was clever enough to broaden appeal. He painted the front room with murals of grapes, timber, fishing & hunting. The back room was a raging celebration of Hispanic culture; Aztec and Mayan murals of passion, toreadors and bulls, picadors, blood flying high.

Above those murals was another form of art, centerfolds holding beer bottles. Most were Spanish but a few were white, not to appease the occasional gringo headed to the john but because they were too gorgeous to ignore. They festooned every wall, practically dripping pheromones. Any man walking under them would HAVE to buy another beer purely on the chance that it would get him pussy exactly like those models. Simplistic, crude, yes, but... *Tits sell beer.*

The jukebox in front played country western. The one in back, Tex Mex with one Merle Haggard song. When gringos played pool, 'Oakie' would get 'em through. Everything about the Cage screamed duality; just the way JC wanted it. He was Mexican-American and so was his joint. Still, one picked his night at the Cage carefully. Fridays were Catholic; fish fry, dollar drafts. Whites and Latinos got along on Fridays. Saturdays were solamente Mexican, Coronas, a buck each. Singing two verses of any Latino song got you a shot of tequila, gratis.

Sundays brought plenty of American iron. They stopped out of tradition. For anyone wearing colors, first beer was on the house. Juan Carlos wore a John Deere cap. The bikers saw through the ploy, but they still came. Somehow a ride just wasn't a run without a brew and hickory-smoked ribs, to pay homage to 'Biker Billy' Carter, baddest ass that ever ran a bar. Too bad about his head-on with the log truck, but at least he died quick.

Wednesdays were wide open. On any given Hump Day, the Cage might serve the working man or off-season tourist. Victor learned to spot body language like the theme in a cheap novel. He learned how eye contact varies with culture; stare at a biker and chairs will fly, but returning a Hispanic's stare averts conflict. Stare at a Hmong and he'll shoot you in the back later. Victor learned to spot a punk compensating; the larger the swagger, the bigger his fear. Before long, he thought he knew it all, until early one Wednesday afternoon three white punks entered the Cage; black clothing, spike haircuts, state of the art cell phones. Judging by their loitering, they didn't have jobs or pressing schedules. And yet, they looked bored. He decided to get closer for a better look at the latest bugs in his jar.
"I'm Victor. Whassup?" "Not much; 'sup?" "Oh, hangin'... got this job, you know. You guys need any more sodas? Next one's on me. Later." The trio stuck in his mind long after they drank their free pop and left without thanking him. Victor had never met such lifeless people. Even Horrible Harry had more chi... And *he* was dead.

Those who dismiss life's gift don't deserve it. It only took two more Wednesdays and free soda for the trio to warm up to Victor. Kim was 17. Biff was 19. Emil split the difference. Complacency and affluence stole their passion long ago. They spoke only of death. Their clothing and jewelry also emulated it. But as to *REAL death*, they hadn't a clue. Victor decided to give them one.

The place and date fell into his lap. Kim invited him to a party. His parents were in Aspen for a week-long dentistry seminar. So they decided to indoctrinate him in the ways of death. He could hardly keep a straight face. Considering their Goth fixation, some sort of cult death scenario would work. Biff had access to firearms. Kim liked daggers. Emil loved video games, poisons, potions and shit like that.

On the night of the party, Victor parked half a mile away, then walked to Kim's house. In addition to the trio, there was one more guest. The Chameleon instantly added him to the hit list. Bain was twice their age. He married twice, neither lasting more than a month. He loved to slice heads off chickens and rub the blood over his women. Naturally, he went through a lot of women, so Bain showed because they said girls were coming. Victor took a beer from Kim as he eyed Eric Bain, who returned the look.

Bain didn't know what to make of the kid. Victor wore no Goth shit, only Levi's and black tee shirt. If he wasn't so drunk, Bain might've put a handle on the killer, but all he cared about was the promise of jail-bait pussy, if the Goth punks were telling the truth. With any luck, he'd be rubbing hot bird blood on strange pussy by midnight.

Victor slouched into a recliner. He saw the single teardrop tatt on Bain's cheek; looked too good to be jailhouse work. Maybe the duplicitous geezer had it done in the world, just for the illusion. Anything was possible with chicken fuckers, but one thing was clear; his shifty eyes said Bain wasn't here for Goth. Victor decided to act fast, since they said women were coming. He had a second beer, waiting for them to relax. Then he steered the conversation to weapons; nunchuks, swords and daggers materialized. Kim pulled out 'his' pistol. Technically, his father's, the Markov 22-mag's boxy outline and tactical matte finish gave it a sinister look.

They were drinking, smoking and playing with phallic symbols. The Markov circulated so each man could fondle it. When it got to Victor, he nonchalantly flicked the mag release. Out dropped the fully loaded clip with 20 hollow-points thumbed into it. He rammed it back into the gun. He chambered one as music covered the sound. Nobody was paying attention. Victor stood up and swung the pistol onto Bain, who was reaching for more tequila. Biff watched Victor get fully into character. He thought Vic was going to fit right in with their shock-value, make-believe death-worshiping group.

Victor held on Bain's tattooed cheek, then remembered from Ted's weapons manuals that the rimfire might have trouble penetrating heavy bone. He aimed for the plate-thin Temporal bone instead. The others noticed the ritualized gun-play. Then the Markov roared. The first hollow point scrambled Bain's eggs. He folded so fast, he still held the Tequila bottle. Then he aimed it at the trio.

They sat on the Futon, looking like the 'speak no, speak no, hear no evil' monkeys. Biff covered his mouth, trying to keep his puke in. Emil's hands went to his ears, reacting to the gun blast. Kim was rolling a joint, but his eyes shut in an I-can't-believe-that-just-happened slow-mo blink. Victor shot Biff center-chest, who went stiff with pain as his heart burst. Then he fired two quick ones into Emil. Empty cartridges rattled on the laminated bamboo floor. The CD player went quiet while switching discs, so the rattling seemed extra-loud. Victor swung the sights onto Kim; *"Come here."* Kim yelled; "Please, **DON'T!"**

Victor cocked his head to the left; "Come here or I'll shoot you in the nuts." Fearing his legs wouldn't hold him, Kim crawled while trying to come up with a better lifesaving plea, but Victor was way ahead of him; "You've *practiced* death rituals, right? So, this is a *dress rehearsal.* You stupid bastards got everything handed to ya, but ya got NO PASSION… You don't deserve to live."

107

Victor made Kim stand right where Victor stood when he shot the others. Kim looked at Emil's body, just as Victor put one round into Kim's right Sphenoid Bone. Then he put the gun in the same hand Kim drank with, his right. He raised the youth's dead hand and fired twice, deliberately aiming for the wall, to leave evidence of nervousness, while planting GSR on Kim.

He wiped off his beer bottles, popped out the Markov's magazine, then wiped off his prints and replaced it. He started walking to his car. It was dark, warm and still. The surrounding homes were quiet. A car approached. Raising his forearm to hide his face, he saw only a driver, but no girls. The death-loving punks had told their last lie. Driving away, Victor felt fantastic about his first multiple kill. He could barely wait to see how the cops handled it.

TWENTY ONE...

AVENGING DION

Dion's latest update showed he was conscious, if that meant having both eyes open and cooing just one syllable. He was a fuckin' vegetable only because he wore a red jacket one afternoon. He rested in Fowler's position, with right eye and facial bones still collapsed. The kid still had bigger issues than a pushed-in face. When cued, his head flopped to the left, his right arm flailed in choreo-athetoid spastic-convulsive manner associated with massive upper motor neuron compromise. Fasiculation tremors flashed across the "good" side of his face. His left eye more or less aimed at the camera while his right one cast about. Vincent wondered if Dion could process two different images. Ironically, a chameleon could look for food with one eye and airborne danger with the other, with just a few neurons, while Dion's billions of brain cells couldn't possibly handle it.

The kid no longer had tubes or IV's, so Carver figured Dion wasn't going to get any better. He clicked on the thumbnail for finances. A pie chart popped up, all of it red except for a small blue slice, representing the portion that insurance was obligated to pay. The red part, over 7 million, lay squarely upon his parents. The nonverbal image proved that Dion was tossed out as soon as the media lost interest. Then the hospital filed liens on all Capps properties.

They lost their home in Pedalauna and a rental in Windoor; 21 years of carpet cleaning, re-painting, grinding out one renter after the other, were harvested by the fiduciary combine. Into its gaping maw went equity; shredded deeds flew out its ass. And still the combine rolled on, rapaciously gobbling every asset it found.

The beast's lawyers attached all revenues from Dion's website, interviews, book deals and/or any other potential source of revenue likely to exist in the future. It garnished their wages and levied their savings. If it was a dollar, the combine sucked it up. If it was a coin, it got stuck in its mud-covered tires. A court-appointed keeper opened all Capps mail. Aside from a subsistence pittance, the family was indentured to the medical beast. Gone was their dream, and all because of one brutal event. That's why they call it the American Dream; you'd have to be asleep to believe it.

The young killer was astonished. He grew up thinking hospitals were benevolent institutions where sick people went to get well. But the underbelly was a vastly different side of the beast; a money-hungry, family-killing, asset-ravaging force with too much power. It was anyone's guess which would be the greater tragedy; Dion's vicious beating or the fallout from the impossibly high medical bills. Either way, the undertone was unmistakable; *Don't let this happen to you.*

Carver clicked on the hospital website. Every image was warm and fuzzy; sick kids on chemo, cute little nurses hugging them. Grandma walking & smiling, brand new hip. Now she can dance again; it almost made folks wish they were sick. He clicked on payment icons; first were insurance plans, then ways to pay for deductibles, copays & DME's. A patient could pay with cash, credit card, check, money order or certified check. From the hospital's perspective, it was so easy to pay those mammoth fees. The next option was for Medicare and Medical; they had trained staff to help with paperwork. Then he read the last option, available only to homeless indigents and unskilled river-crossing wetbacks like the gangsters that assaulted Dion; all treatment was free, including obstetrics, abortion and heart surgery. Payment came from a special fund, filled by taxpayers who could never access this fund.

The irony stabbed Carver's heart. The Capps' family paid county, city, state and federal taxes, property taxes, DMV fees, registration and gas taxes. Their every paycheck was gouged with deductions amounting to over 40 percent of gross wages. Yet in spite of all of this, the Capps family got totally screwed. Only the middle class would feel the full crush of the Great White's fiduciary teeth. Carver considered killing a few administrators.

Dion would live out his life as a vegetable. He'd never walk, fuck or play again. The best he could hope for was trying to remember which person in the room might be his mother. He would end up a ward of the state, in a piss-stained cinder-block joint built by the lowest bidder. His parents were in the throes of an ugly divorce, bankruptcy and a black hole of chaos. Meanwhile four gangbangers kept playing their violent little tap-dance, beating and brutalizing others for their own sick amusement, totally uncaring about the carnage they caused.

Vincent had to do something.

TWENTY TWO...

SOUTH

Vincent drove south in his Victor disguise, in Victor's low rider trunk lay his weapons and another disguise, which was more like bait. He had a red jacket, tennis shoes and khaki pants. The trunk held his shotgun, sawed off to the legal 19 inches. Although there is no perfect weapon, a sawed-off comes close. A machine gun would be better, but no cop could ignore the telltale roar of automatic fire. But a couple of blasts with a shotgun were easily labeled backfires in gangland areas. By the time they investigated, the danger would be gone.

Inside were five of the deadliest shotgun loads ever concocted. Popular in the Deep South swamplands where game presents running glimpses, buckshot sold wherever hunters bought beer gas or bait. That's where Charles Cahill bought them. He learned of spreader loads from an old salt that hung out at Ted's store. Market hunters used it to great advantage. A spreader could drop a goose on the wing, running boar or stag. Vincent emptied the buckshot by prying open the crimps. Then he inserted slotted paperboard to make four compartments in each round. Into each he placed a single buckshot, then several bb's, topped with number six shot. He re-crimped the assassin's loads which according to the label still looked legal. His other gun was a 9mm Berlinetta semiauto. Since most gangsters used 'nines' it would blend into his staged scene, gangsters banging each other. As he drove south he thought of the soon to be gangster corpses, laying on autopsy slabs; what would the wounds tell a coroner? That's when it hit him; he fucked up.

It would take just one question to the right gun nut for the secret to out. The resulting search would extend to areas holding old poachers, meaning rural areas such as the one where the Chameleon lived. He stopped at a rest area and tossed his spreader loads into the shit and bloody tampons of a portable toilet. Then he donned gloves and loaded standard buckshot loads. Anywhere in the western USA, anyone could buy them. Even gangsters.

Vincent's error with the spreaders made him wonder if he'd made others in his past murders. Still, they hadn't come after him yet, so that bolstered his confidence. He neared Santa Rosita. Tagged street signs indicated three different gangs. That got him thinking about his marks. There was no way to know if he was killing the right punks. He wanted to be as precise as possible when murdering people.

Checking his watch, he was arriving too early. He needed a place to hang out where nobody would notice him. He pulled into the parking lot of a titty bar. His disguise was little more than dark glasses, ball cap with a "CAT" logo and a Raiders sweatshirt. He quickly hiked toward the dive. His shoes crunched bottle caps, glass, gravel and cigarette butts on the way.

The bartender swiveled his massive head when sunlight burst into the den of iniquity. Victor felt conspicuous, but it was too late to turn back. The door closed and his eyes adjusted to the dark. A few lights under the bar eerily lit the barkeep's mug from below; a 300-pound Vincent Price; "What's your pleasure, buddy?" "A Bud, thanks." "Comin' right up." The barkeep had a dozen brews quick-chilling just for eager beavers like this little asshole. He slid the bottle across the teak; "Eight bucks." Highway robbery, but Carver figured it was the going price. It was his first time in a strip joint. Joe went back to his duties, but studied the kid unobtrusively. It was tough to tell, until alcohol peeled the veneer like psychic paint thinner; worked every time.

113

Joe was a good bartender in a bad bar. He formerly sold swill to the finest stockbrokers San Francisco had to offer. Now he had been reduced to popping beers for perverts in Santa Rosita, tossing girl-groping freaks onto the gravel - busted glass parking lot. He wasn't happy with the situation, but it was better than prison.

Technically, it was a criminal offense which quickly morphed into a civil litigation nightmare. Four disgruntled stockbrokers had a bad day. They took issue with Joe's inadvertent good humor; they got hospitalized and Joe got fired. Anyhow, water under the old Golden Gate. Time to move from Lexus-driving, crooked-bastard stockbrokers to strippers and beered-up hod carriers. Not as much of a demotion as one might think. Joe kept prepping the bar while his only customer sat alone in a booth.

He had a city map opened. The school occupied the 1600 block of Cherry Street. Dion's home on Elm Street sat three miles Southwest; six miles, round trip. Dion must have been in good shape. Victor spotted the probable crime scene midway between school and home, marked with 'RR'. Just then Joe loomed up with another cold Bud in his mitt; "Say, amigo, beer's only 8 bucks when the show starts. I shoulda charged you three; this one's on me." "Oh, thanks." Victor watched him go, wondering if he felt bad or maybe he wanted to get a closer look at the killer. See his map, maybe. No, that wasn't it... Damn, he was getting paranoid. The second beer helped him calm down. He became absorbed in his plan, unaware of the steady influx of patrons. Soon it was almost sundown. He had another half-hour to kill. He sat back to watch the show.
The first three strippers were clones; bleached hair, tits stuffed like plastic grocery bags, ready to tear at the slightest touch. The music was typical stripper four count fuck-beats, no lyrics. Each woman strutted for three minutes, then vanished behind dangling garland and glass beads. Victor had seen finer women. Connie, for example.

114

He got up to leave, but then Candy hit the stage. He got hot immediately; about five feet, 95 fit pounds, all of it on fire. Tina Turner in a white body. No implants; hers were too small to be fake. Candy's hair was fire engine red. Her eyes, a smoldering green, sparkling turquoise or something. They ate right through every bastard in the bar. She moved like smoke. Candy danced, whereas the others merely strutted. Victor wanted to fuck her. Hell, they all did. Hers was the gift of the belly dancer, geisha or top-flight mistress. She could torch a man hotter than any mortal woman ever could.

The joint took on an involuntary tribal rhythm. Even Joe stopped to watch, and he'd seen plenty of strippers. The front-row perverts didn't even try to grope. Hers was another level of performance. To mess with it was inconceivable. So, they paid and watched and lusted. Victor hardened more and more with each movement until his dick felt ready to explode.

Just then she jumped from the stage, alighting on the bar. She leaped again. Her lithe frame and hot, Sandalwood scented skin slid across Victor's tabletop, spilling his beer and rumpling his hair. She ate him up with her eyes, which were more stunning at kissing distance; "You want me, honey?"

Surprised and full of lust, he could only nod. The whole place laughed. Just as quickly, she leaped back on stage. Before she went through the curtain she turned and pointed her turquoise lasers straight at the serial killer. Everyone felt it. Candy vanished behind the curtain. Joe came over; "Man... I don't know what you've got, but she bought this one." Joe turned to go, then wheeled; "That's the first time she ever left the stage *for anybody, dude.*"

Candy quickly dressed into street clothes; light blue tee, levis, running shoes. She normally didn't mess with patrons, but the kid had a smoldering quality. She couldn't wait to fuck his bony ass off. That made it harsh when she opened the door and scanned the parking lot. She saw dust settling; "Damn... the good ones always get away."

It wasn't in his plan to fuck a stripper, but it took all of his willpower to leave. His dick was so hard he couldn't even sit right. Within two blocks, Victor unzipped his pants and gave it three strokes. Semen spurted onto the steering wheel and headliner. Damn that Candy... he romped the gas pedal. It was totally dark when Victor parked near the probable crime scene. It didn't take a Rhodes Scholar to find; gangster tags were on every sign, building and abutment. The stupid bastards were begging him to find them. He double-checked his weapons; safeties taped in fire position. He slung the shotgun on his right shoulder, pistola, right pocket. He scanned the shadows and made a mental note... always bring the night vision. He donned the red clothing, then started walking the tracks like Dion had done so many pain-riddled months ago. The scenario was almost identical, except this time the gringo victim was no unarmed schoolboy. He looked into the dark shadows, to preserve his night iris. After 300 yards the grinding of a hard-soled shoe on gravel sounded behind him, near brambles and weeds and a small creek. They would need to get closer. He walked faster. Soon he heard quiet voices, which quickly turned bolder. By his best guess, they were 30 yards behind. They began blatantly taunting; "Orale, hee's alone... too stupid to know we fuck shit up dat wears our colors. Less fuck heem u..."

His heart pounding, he whirled and saw three barrio buddies. Only instead of 30 yards, it was more like ten. Startled, they stopped. He added a Spanish accent. "OH, You gonna fuck *ME UP?* Like that *other gringo?"* Victor threw his coattail back. In the darkness they couldn't see much. One punk thought Victor had a bat like the one he carried. He lunged ahead. The buckshot sawed through his neck. The head hit the ground first. The others stood there, dicks in their hands; one held a Rambo knife. The other, a metal bat. Victor smirked; "You should bring better weapons, to fuck gringos!" Victor fired from the hip at the dude on the left, knocking him backward while blood and testicle shreds blasted out of the flannel. The other one sprinted for safety. Victor led him two body lengths,

116

remembering to follow through. The gangster took most of the shot string in the upper legs. One pellet severed his lumbar spinal cord. He fell headlong down the railroad embankment clawing for the brambles, as if there were any safety there. Victor ran to the punk arm-crawling for the creek while a fourth gangbanger raised a tiny pistola; "Don't do it, essay or... I fuck you up, bendej..."

The buckshot turned his lungs to cheesecloth, ending his plea. His cheap little ACP barked once; probably a reflex squeeze. The death rattle came instantly from the thorns. As for the world-class crawling coward and beater of young white kids, the last round exploded his skull; gray spatter slowly rained into the creek. Every crawdad for 50 yards waited in cutbanks and burrows; they'd have Mexican for lunch. Victor listened hard, but heard only muffled traffic noise from the distant freeway. A dog barked. Somebody's back door slammed shut. Nobody cared; those barrio boys could knock each other off, as long as they didn't mess with decent white folk. Victor policed his casings, dropped a baggie of coke, then drove off, careful to observe traffic rules. Later, it took every bit of discipline to drive past the "Leather Cup;" damn that Candy.

The chaos of having multiple targets and multiple risks really turned his crank. He could clearly see the first youth's head and neck come unhinged, the bright orange arterial spurts flying up into the clear sky. He wondered how long the brain interpreted images while it fell; for all he knew, maybe that guy heard his buddies get killed before he checked out. One could only hope.

The second gangster looked mean until the buckshot hit and he hurtled backwards. Then Victor surprised himself with that third shot; he led the prick perfectly, recalled the headlong plunge, arms flailing, reaching out for handles that weren't there, as if that could stop his fate. His mouth was open, but spoke not a word.

The fourth goon was unexpected; all Victor saw was the pistola flash, then a big disturbance in the brambles when Victor blasted him. The last image was the most powerful. The buckshot fired at close range entered the youth's brain case as a single mass, blowing a grayish-white cloud of cerebral mist... A crayfish Piñata; tiny bits of scalp, skull and brains creating ripples in the surface of the creek. It rained for 30 seconds. What a fish feed.

He rolled into his garage before dawn, exhausted, but sated. Nothing feels better than a job well done.

TWENTY THREE...

THE NOTE

Maybe it was Dion's compelling tragedy. Or perhaps it was like his famous dad always said; crooks inwardly just want to get caught. Either way, Vincent *HAD TO* write the Capps family. Wearing gloves, using generic office paper, he cut and pasted, forming his first and last Get Well card. Short, sweet, simple;

"The four were for Dion. Sorry for your tragedy."

Knowing better than to lick the envelope, he applied poster glue. The postage stamp got a single drop of tap water. The front address he printed in block text. As to the return address, he merely wrote; "Gen. Delivery Santa Rosita, CA." Naturally he wore a disguise. In the days since 9/11, one could never be too careful. Parking out of range of any spy cameras, he walked to the mailbox. It was only then that his better judgment resurfaced. His dad's team caught plenty of idiots after they sent letters. So in spite of the urge to mail it, he didn't. The Capps family would have to extract closure from the media accounts of the killings. The Chameleon remained camouflaged.

On the drive home, he was amazed at how close he came to giving law enforcement a big clue. The urge was powerful, to share the joy with those so desperately in need of it. The Capps family had been through hell. No; they were *stuck in hell*. Next day it hit the papers.

"Four Hispanic minors were killed in a shootout, allegedly over drugs; names withheld pending notification of kin. An investigation is pending."

The threadbare cliché was called for, to put the public at ease. It meant 'We're doing something; *Not much,* but something.' Most readers didn't give a shit about dead gangbangers. They weren't the lowest rung on the ladder, but close to it. The lowest was for the poor and old. Next rung was for gangs, white trash stabbed at carnivals, crack whores killed by pimps or other stiffs of low repute... Then long arm of the law always got a bit longer for victims who were waspy co-eds, white kids or small-town heroes. The top rung was reserved for whenever a cop is killed; law enforcement red-lines its engines. Of course, the hypocrisy was lost on them. They were sworn to uphold the law equally for all, without prejudice. Then after they got a badge, cops had to take a bigger oath, of fraternity. There is no such thing as equal protection. Police *always* enforce the law with prejudice and bias... There are only two sides; cops v. everybody else. Vincent vowed to *NEVER* kill a cop. Even a chameleon can be found if a snake hunts long and hard enough.

That's why he chose to mimic the gangbanger scene; the 'pending investigation' wouldn't go far.

Detective Ed Mitchell caustically surveyed the scene. He knew gang behavior, signs and tags, but this one didn't smell right. He started with the first-killed dude, coincidentally. He noticed a foreign object in the anterior neck. He raised his magnifying glass; a plastic shot cup, the ballistic equivalent of a badminton shuttlecock. Normally air resistance quickly peels it off the shot column, so this stiff got it at close-range. Ed muttered quietly; *"If I ever take one, I hope it"ll be that quick."*

The second corpse didn't have it so easy. It made his balls hurt to look at the kid's raw-burger groin. His partner squawked from the thicket; "Got a *GUN* here, Ed." "I'm comin'... don't bag it yet". Ed tried to think. *Nobody* takes bats and knives to a drug deal. The sun reflected off of the cheap plating. Tom Adams sniffed the muzzle; "Recently fired. Your typical Saturday Night Special; Universeco, 25 ACP. Hardly a match for a shotgun. Sort of makes you wonder, hah?" Ed snorted; "Hell, I'm too old to wonder." Tom persisted; *"I sure wouldn't use one."*

It was true; designed as a purse gun and barely suitable for that, the .25 gave real handguns a bad name; they were easily concealed and gave women a sense of empowerment, but that was about it for assets. But as for liabilities it had plenty. It had little stopping power. It made a small wound channel. It was prone to jam. Its short sight radius and stamped sights didn't exactly favor accuracy. Still, gangsters loved them; they could shoot a man and make his bones, while minimizing the risk of lethal injection. It was like stabbing someone with a short knife; all of the thrill, half the prison time.

Nonetheless, the tiny pistol was certainly capable of killing. Ed's first partner answered a call just in time to wrestle a graphite driver from the husband, who had been teeing off on his wife. While grappling with the perp, Bill Mahoney heard a pop from the hallway. He stood up and secured the young stepson holding a .25. He started shaking; his vision faded. The puny little bullet macerated

121

his left Femoral Artery. In 90 seconds one good sheriff was dead. All because of one little purse pistol. Ed's flashback faded when his partner spoke; "Hey, what about *this guy*?"

He'd seen decapitations in car crashes, but this man's brains were gone, vaporized. Blood spoor indicated he crawled down the hill before he got blasted. As to the open calvarium, he could only speculate; "Coulda been a contact blast... *or an RPG,* for chrissakes."

Tom tried to lighten it up with a joke; "You know, I got *HALF A MIND* to..." Ed waved him off. Maybe it would be funny later, but not now. The van rolled up to snag the bodies. He had a feeling something was amiss, but Mitchell ignored the hunch and stuck to basics. He wrote what he saw, not felt. Let the legal eagles wrestle with that. No way would he get caught speculating under oath again. Once was enough for that bullshit.

He wrapped up and left the scene, feeling old. When he first started working gangs he thought he could turn some of 'em around; what middle-class bullshit *that* turned out to be. The lazy bastards had no remorse, no social conscience and no goals. The punks always acted glad when the got busted, as if having a criminal record was a good thing.

More than likely, some other gang caught these assholes alone and just wasted them. But one thing was certain; the shooter or shooters were good with shotguns. Mitchell wrote his report. Business as usual for the north coast.

TWENTY FOUR...

VINCENT GETS A LETTER

Victor gave notice after exterminating the gangster vermin. Juan Carlos was sorry to see him go. Victor drove to his mail service, then home to read it. There were several thin envelopes, obviously checks from his father. He opened the thicker one, no transparent window. From the FBI. The first sentence felt like a kick in the nuts;

"Dear Vincent Carver; It is with great regret that we inform you that your father died in the line of duty."

The letter detailed Howard Carver's last act, apprehending some serial arsonist, saving countless lives and a historical landmark in Daveyport fuckin' Iowa. Vincent read with shock and jealousy; even in death, his old man was a hero one more time. The remaining rhetoric was typical; Vincent should be proud, a posthumous medal forthcoming... great loss to the good guys and all that.

Suddenly, he started crying; he wondered where that came from. Hell, he barely knew his old man. On the few times they sat face to face, they never did or said anything meaningful. When Vincent initiated a convo, Howard answered in monosyllables. His dad always acted uncomfortable around him, as if Vincent let a beer fart in church.

He knew his dad didn't really care for him, and he had made his peace with that; or had he? The string of tears indicated otherwise. Clearly, he had loved him in a disjointed, detoured sort of way... It was weird. Vincent thought about his dad's last few moments; did he think of Vincent? Did he have regrets? Hell, did he even feel it coming? But one thing wasn't a surprise; his old man died while grasping a thug. The old bastard sure loved his work, more than his wife, kid or anything. It took him all over the world, made him friends in forty states and two continents. Vincent hadn't been aware of his latent envy, but now it surfaced; he envied Howard's dedication and perfection in catching crooks. Vincent still resented never having a typical father-son relationship, but he finally understood.

Howard wasn't average, he was the Michael Jordan of cops. He was Scott Hamilton, Muhammad Ali, Wayne Gretzki and Tiger Woods. Perfection has a singular quality, which only comes from great sacrifice; his old man sure as hell had it... and paid for it.

That night, Vincent drank himself to sleep. For the first time in his life he placed a single photo of his pop on the nightstand, to guard his slumber.

TWENTY FIVE...

THE PRICE OF POKER

GOES UP

Officers from all over America and a few from Scotland attended Howard's funeral. Or so Vincent heard; he didn't go. He didn't relish the idea of showing his face to 600 profilers. Besides, he rationalized; why should he see his dad then, when he hadn't seen him much before? Last reason? He wanted to remember the man as he lived, not as a stiff in a gel-painted box.

But when he closed his eyes at night, he saw the stark contrast between Howard's monolithic achievements and Vincent's pathetic life. Vincent hadn't achieved shit. Oh sure, he managed to kill some people without getting caught, but they weren't even worth killing. It dawned on him; he needed a legacy, too. It was time to up the ante.

He logged onto the Net, using his newest traceless cyber handle. At first, arsonists came to mind but they were too hard to catch. Then sexual predators hit his monitor. The public awareness websites did it for him. He wanted to kill them all.

Vincent had killed too many people locally, so he set some new parameters for his camoflage. The next mark would have to live at least 90 miles away. He would have to be of minority race, since Vincent had killed mostly whites. Lastly, the perp had to be active, making him easier to target. His first search netted him 12 super-perverts topping a list of thousands. Six lived in Sacramendota, four near Peureka, and two deserving marks resided near Chicontado. He chose Sacramendota; it held more marks.

Vincent didn't want to kill just anybody listed on the site. He had seen enough courtroom antics to know that a man could be wrongfully convicted of damned near anything, especially sex crimes. Paradoxically, Californians were purported to be advanced in their sexuality, yet west coast courtroom sexual bias was Draconian in the extreme. A man didn't have a chance at a fair trial. Earlier, he witnessed such a travesty. The defendant was a 21 year old Hispanic male; good job, no priors. His girlfriend was 16. They had already lived together for a year, with blessings from both sets of parents. However, after an argument the irate girl confided in her friend who worked in the courthouse; her lover got eight years. His only crime? Becoming an adult before his lover did.

Meanwhile, Courtroom TV covered a case where a pretty, white female teacher repeatedly screwed her 6th-grade student; the judge threw the case out of court, claiming the defendant had "emotional issues". Clearly, double standards exist in sex law; *especially* in California.

Before he knew it, Jason Bohannon was headed east for Sacramendota; he hailed from Bakersville. Had dark hair & eyes from colored contacts, and a huge henna tattoo of a sailing ship on his right shoulder. There should be good hunting there, too, since school would start soon. Nothing attracts pedophiles like a noisy schoolyard. Jason paid cash for two nights in a Motel 9, relieved to see the clerk swipe his newest driver license and hand it back; there was always that unsettling moment when a virgin

126

fake license might be detected. He climbed the concrete steps to the 2nd floor. His room at the end of the covered walkway had the usual; two beds, swivel TV cabled down, clean bathroom, two sets of towels. The nightstand held a bible, tourist pamphlets and a local directory. He turned the TV on, to see if it worked. As fate would have it, the scene got his attention; several gurneys rolled out of an upscale wine country home that looked familiar. He bumped the volume and sat on bed. The anchorman's voice floated up;

"...tragic scene in Hop Hollow. Returning after a vacation the Bashfields found their son, Kim Hiram Bashfield, who allegedly shot all three before turning the weapon on himself; More at eleven; Back to you, Lance."

The body bags were bloated. After all, he'd killed them ten days ago. Vincent's guts went cold with panic; the cops would learn that the Goths hung out at the Cage. They'd hear about Victor, certainly. Then he forced himself to be rational; the cops already had their suspect, the asshole with the Markov in his maggot-rotted mitt. He shut off the TV. There was no point in looking back. He locked the door, went down the steps two at a time.

He drove off to find his next mark. He couldn't find the first two perverts; probably fell through the cracks or the predator-alert website hadn't been updated recently. He located the next one quite luckily as he left his apartment; bald, thick glasses and a humorously stereotypical trench coat; August in Sacramendota... and this asshole wore a trench coat. That alone was grounds for killing him. When the mark entered a porn shop, Bohannon broke it off. He'd be easy to find. Jason entered a nice restaurant; or as nice as it ever gets at Denvoy's. Hell, even the waitresses looked better, now that he'd found a mark.

The next morning he parked 80 yards from the flophouse, pulled out his scope and settled in to wait. Shortly after nine Malavai Leroy Johnson stepped into the increasing morning heat. He bent down and re-tied a shoe;

127

surprisingly lithe, for the website-stated 56 years. Johnson began his daily walk. First stop, bagel shop for coffee and a smoke. Jason drove 200 yards past the shop and parked. Soon Johnson reappeared. He walked right past Bohannon's rig. Jason reviewed the file; masturbating in a vehicle, disturbing the peace in a peep show... And 2 stints in the big house. He lured young black girls onto his lap. And then he really loved to tear their panties off and shove his huge dick into their tight little bodies. But more than that, he loved to scare them with a big knife, threatening to kill their families and rape the victim again and kill her, too.

Johnson raped so many girls he couldn't recall them all. But two girls had managed to overcome their fear; the first girl got him 8 to 15, but with overcrowded prisons he got out early. The second conviction netted him 20 years. He served 17 months when a legal snafu forced a new trial. He slid, thanks to a scared-shitless tampered witness. Poor Latisha; the cops promised her he'd never hurt her again if she'd only testify. They promised to put him away forever. So that made it all the more agonizing when Johnson got out, raped her again. She'd never trust white cops again...

Bohannon's thoughts dissipated when Johnson neared the school and sat on a park bench. Pulling a small bag of seed from his coat, he began feeding pigeons in the cool shade of huge Sycamores. Just a harmless old black man feeding the birds; no danger there. But while his head pointed down at the birds, his eyes burned holes through nearby skirts. They were all so pretty; it was hard for him to choose. Soon he narrowed it down to two fifth-graders. The girl on the left was taller and slimmer. Just then Johnson spotted a beat cop; he tossed the seed and blended into the stream of pedestrians. traffic. Bohannon knew where the asshole slept and preyed. One more clue would seal the deal. He walked up to the school office window; "What time does school get out?"

She didn't look up; "2:45, same as every day."
"Thanks"

128

The child raper wouldn't be hard to find at 2:45. Bohannon drove off, ordered a fish sandwich and coffee while he perused the next file. The Mexican was just as bad. But while Johnson raped only black girls, Crystobal Santos was an equal opportunity rapist; any girl between seven and ten. Like his little sister, back in the day.

Santos began raping in east Texas 20 years ago, working his way across Texas, New Mexico, Arizona and finally California. He stayed one step ahead of capture thanks to jurisdiction barriers. There were plenty of cracks in the system. Men like Santos knew every one. He found work as a custodian, janitor or handyman. Churches and small schools badly in need of help with menial positions were glad to hire. Santos had a baby face and a beguiling manner. Most adults never questioned it.

Jason drove to Santos' lair while thinking about the demographic of Santos' victims; 7-10, gregarious, prone to fantasies, keeping secrets and still too young to be shocked by sexual imagery. The hunter and his prey, perfectly suited for each other; it has always been so, from the Serengeti to the modern strip mall.

Just then his daydream shattered; Santos was walking home. Bohannon barely had time to get Santos in the scope before the deviant entered a four-story flophouse. Jason ran over and entered the dilapidated building in time to see the old elevator's twitchy pewter needle stop at three. He found Santos' mailbox; 312, white medical tape, two penciled initials; "cs" Lower case for; *"ignore me, i'm nobody."*

Mailboxes for the fourth floor were empty. He improvised and knocked on the manager's door. The loud TV went down, a heavy grunt, then three locks sequentially clanked. The door cracked open, revealing a frowning, squarish woman of 50. Her scowl dissipated when she saw he wasn't a regular tenant down to bitch about the heat, toilet or whatever.

She wore a dirty tee shirt, faded camo sweatpants and brown bunny slippers full of ashes. In her right hand was a beer. The left held a half-smoked Marlboro. She flicked ash on the floor and her bunnies; "Whaddyawant?"

He flashed his best Sunday School smile. "Good day, m'aam; I'm looking for a room?" He reached for ID, but it was overkill. Maxine sized him up; "Hunnert a week. Two weeks' advance. *Cash*... *Got two hunnert* onya?" Maxine Brown scrutinized the cash more than him. She held it up to the light, looking for the strips. Then she smelled it and thumbed it for palpatory flaws. "412. John's at end hall. Turn faucets off HARD! No women after ten."

The door slammed. Locks rammed home. Just like that he was a tenant of El Escondido. Even better, his flat was directly over his mark's. It was perfect. He turned the worn cast iron skeleton key and opened the warped old Mahogany door. There was a single mattress, dingy sheet, desk and a tiny refrigerator, the kind that holds a burger 'n six pack. He opened it and found a hairy microbiological melting pot. In its former life it was a pizza slice; now gray mold reached upward like hair charged with static. The mold was tired of desiccated pepperoni, so it reached skyward for anything. The first sortie of spores wafted to his nostrils. He shut it and looked around. The walls had no artwork, unless graffiti counted. Decades of smoking embalmed the Sheetrock with nicotine and cannibis residue. There was an oil slick behind the chair and near the headboard. Apparently a huge greasy Afro did the honors. They were the cleanest spots in the joint. He didn't see signs of rats, but cockroaches and lice thrived.

Then he heard Santos moaning below him. Periodically sniffing the panties kept him almost hard. He thought of her, alone in an almond orchard. She got out of his car without panties when a gust of wind hoisted her skirt, new for the first day of school. So innocent and naked. Then he ejaculated and moaned louder.

130

Sissy Sorenson was damn lucky. Santos killed girls after abusing them. But with her genetics for sexual precocity, she already had pubic hair. Ironically, that's what spared her. There was no way he could ever... She was too hairy and scary down there. Good fortune rode with Sissy. She was sort of proud of how she made him get glassy-eyed. It was her first taste of sexual power; she couldn't wait to get breasts, for more power over men.

Jason resisted the urge to go downstairs and stick an ice pick through the deviant's Medulla Oblongata. Instead, he drove to a steak house and ordered a rib eye, rice pilaf and soda. The steak was fantastic.

After dinner he drove to Johnson's territory. Sure enough, he found him fast. It looked like some locals suspected he was a pervert, but they knew better than to call the cops. Usually the caller got cuffed or busted, so the inner city folks solved their own problems or learned to cope without calling Whitey and his tasers, guns and dogs. Which by the way, was fine with the men in blue. They stayed out of White Man's Bermuda Triangle.

The killer wondered if his dad ever profiled anyone from barrios, ghettos, projects, slums, hoods or whatever else they were called. He drove off to a hardware store. After perfecting his disguise he entered and paid cash for lice spray, bug bombs and flypaper. Then he drove to a different store for his tree saw and a hatchet. He only bought the saw for camouflage, because a man buying just an ax might arouse suspicion. Then he drove off to score drugs. By the time he got there, it was dark. Reggae Ricky strolled up to the curbside dealer; "S'up, brah... ya gots roofies, mahn?" The pusher eyed him suspiciously; "Ah... whatyoumean? I doan doo drugs, brah."

"Yah, mahn... gottmeea hot WHITE chick ah wantstafuck, but she don' wanna fuck *ME, Brah. Ah needs some help!*"

The pusher relaxed; no cop's dumb enough to fly solo in the darkening ghetto. He snared the bills, produced a vial of Rohypnol and a little crack, gratis; a pusher couldn't quit prospecting; "Here, Jamaica man...."

Reggae Ricky grinned; "Gotsta find me daht white chick now! PEACE, BRAH!

"Enjoy, brothah."

       On the way to his flat, Reggae Ricky mentally reviewed his data on Rohypnol. It dissolved clear in water or alcohol, odorless, slight salty taste. Pure GHB was shed quickly from the body and invisible in standard blood work. There were specific tests for it, but thanks to anterograde amnesia, most date rape victims didn't report; hence the specific blood tests were rarely called for.' It took effect within 20 minutes and lasted for 2-3 hours; a perfect time frame for his needs. A recreational dose was 1/3 of a teaspoon. Of course it was probably cut with water or alcohol so he'd start with a full teaspoon. If more was called for, it was right there in his pocket.

       He drove to the Escondido and entered his room. Then his plans hit a snag; NO STENCH, meaning Santos was out in the world, instead of 8 feet below the killer. He sprayed lice killer on the mattress and pillow until the shit dripped. He didn't plan on sleeping there, but if he had to roll out a sleeping bag, its former occupants would be dead or incapable of climbing. Triggering the bombs, he locked the door and went outside to find his mark.

       The warmth of the big valley's evening air relaxed him instantly. A few neon signs glowed from closed shops. Around each sign a cloud of moths, midges and lacewings flitted. To the south burned several neon signs in one joint. A beer sounded good, so he walked toward the lights. The front door was open to let fresh air and hopefully a few customers in. The color scheme was tactical red, as if the dump were a submarine on maneuvers. Actually, the red minimized mosquito problems, but the main reason was to try to make the place look better. It almost worked.

Half a dozen patrons didn't look up. The bar lined one side, booths on the other. Behind the bar was a mirror extending the full length of the bar. Jason sat down at the bar away from the others. He put the mirror to good use. It only took a moment to find Santos, alone in semi darkness, making him stick out.

Mac the barkeep approached him; the new kid didn't look like a cop. He was too fit to be a hard core boozer; no strange cars were outside, so the kid *walked in.* No honky tourist would be that stupid, so the boy had to be there for drugs. None of Mac's regulars dealt, so the kid was waiting for a dealer. He'd keep an eye on the drug-scorin', clueless cracker motherfucker.

Halfway through the second draft, the place began to buzz again. Mac turned the tiny b&w TV up. Jason studied the perv in the mirror. Crystobal Santos downed his 4th whiskey. It was a bad day of hunting. His only chance at a girl died quickly; a security officer at the mall spooked him. He waived at Mac for another and thought to himself; *"Pero, there's always manana, Crysto. Claro, there's a river of lil girls. Manana would be..."*

Just then, a stranger busted his thoughts; "Buy you a round, amigo?" The stranger was gringo, but to refuse might attract attention; "Si, muchas gracias." The chameleon played his trump card to allay suspicion; "Oh, sorry, I thought you were my uncle's friend, Bernardo. Ah, what the heck; let's have a drink anyway!" Two drinks later Santos almost trusted him. Jason sensed the moment was right for unspeakable topics; "I shouldn't say it, but what the hell; *we're amigos,* no?" "Si, *estamos amigos!"*

The killer slurred it; "I like to fuck young girls."
"Verdad?"
"Yeah... *REAL young ones"*
"Oh..."

Under the table Santos' hand began rubbing it, so Jason had him; "*Sometimes* I do... *other things too*, eh?" Santos got glassy eyed. Jason kept selling it; "Sometimes I stick things... *in there*." Santos' eyes rolled back, so Jason slipped the roofies into his glass; "AH, you like it too, eh? Maybe we share a bitch sometime, eh?"

Santos wasn't into three-ways, but the booze and chat had him horned up; he'd fuck a goat with his new amigo. He managed one word; "Si."

It was time to bait the trap; "I have a girl in my van *right now!* She's nine. *She's scared, too.* You wanna DO her with me, man? Nobody's gonna know. C'mon, carnal; le'shavsomefun!"

Santos twitched with glee. He tried to say 'ok' but his tongue wouldn't work for some reason, so he nodded. The deviant staggered out of the bar, leaning against his new amigo... good old whazzhizzname.

They wobbled down the sidewalk and into the Escondido. Entering Santos' room with the reeking pervert over his shoulder, he dumped him into the chair. A few wraps of cellophane went over each wrist and ankle first, so the duct tape wouldn't leave any forensics. Then a sock for a gag, taped the same way. He had plenty of time to do it right. Then Jason went up to his room for his tools. When he returned, the mark was still unconscious, so Jason began writing the suicide note; it had to fit the bastard's personality. He recalled details from the incorrigible deviant's rap sheet;

> *"verbally challenged... Soft-spoken...*
> *High opinion of law enforcement."*

Jason revised his plan for a long-winded note; it didn't fit. He scribbled out a few practice versions. The curse of superior intellect is disdain for brevity. Finally he got it stupid enough to pass for the pedophile's work.

> *"Now I cain't hur no more lil girs. Im sorry."*

134

From talking with Doc Jones in the morgue, he knew normal systolic pressure was roughly 4 atmospheres; a severed Radial artery would spray blood all over. At Sacramendota's low elevation, the first few spurts would have pressure equal to a car tire. Subsequent spurts would be weaker, but still shoot several feet, creating a real forensics problem.

Perhaps time flew faster than imagined or maybe the drugs were too diluted. His mark began to stir. His eyes weren't focused, but he was nose-breathing as well as possible. Jason pulled the nightstand closer. He cut his right wrist loose, handed him a pencil and a dingy white envelope from the trashcan. He held up his sample note; "Print this or I'll cut your nuts off!" He pressed the box cutter against his balls for emphasis. Santos went white with fear; he preferred to be the one holding the pointy things. He scrawled the note.
"NOW... Sign it!" Santos scribbled quickly; "c.s." Jason threw him and the chair onto the mattress; "Get ready to die, kiddy fucker."
With the roofies now worn off, Santos moaned and pleaded through the gag. Then it sounded more like praying. Quickly palpating the left Radial artery above the base of the Radius, Jason rolled the palm down so the blood would spurt into the mattress. He used the razor to make just a little surface cut. Give the bastard some time to think about it. Santos' eyes went hollow with terror. His victims would've loved seeing that.

Jason opened Santos' dresser drawers. In spite of his predicament, Santos twisted his head to watch. The middle drawer held panties, some with dried semen, blood and excreta. Jason tried not to feel the pain and terror those girls endured. It steeled his resolve to kill the man; as if he needed more steeling. He opened the bottom drawer, holding Santos' rape kit. There were long, pointy things. His obvious favorite was a well worn attachment for a vacuum cleaner. Santos loved to run it up their asses while getting off on their agonizing screams.

135

The last item was a big silicone dildo, occasionally used for its intended purpose, but mostly for beating them about their bloody mouths. He loved death by dildo. In spite of his predicament, Santos' loins stirred when Jason held it up.

Death by nicked Radial artery suddenly seemed too humane; it took all of his willpower to resist the urge to administer the same punishment that Santos had inflicted on so many young girls. He wanted to shove the dildo down his greasy throat and ram that vacuum cone up his ass until it pierced his dark heart, to hear him scream like a formula one car. But that would put investigators onto his trail. So this kill had to look like a remorseful suicide. He forced willpower over rage, like cold icing on a cake still hot from baking. He leaned close to the bleeding, sweating mark; body odor laced with adrenaline. Apparently Santos knew he was a dead man; "This death's *too good for you.*" I wish I had time to drag it out, you fuckin' baby raper. He sliced the pervert's wrist, but instead of the surgical nick the Chameleon had planned, he cut the wrist down to the bones. Adrenaline can do that.

For a moment denial reigned; Santos hoped it was a sham cut with the dull side of the blade. Something to scare him, before his attacker would let him go. But the hot blood told him the grim truth. The chingado had really cut him. The first spurts made swishy noises against the mattress. Santos struggled, but that just spiked his heart rate, making the spurts hiss louder, like a squirt gun. Jason gazed into the deviant's eyes; "Orale, bitch, you're dying. I'd tell you to pray, but you're going to Hell so pray for your victims instead, you asshole." From the gagged orifice came a muffled word; "hospitaje"

Jason shrugged coldly; "Oh no, the hospital's too busy treating raped little girls. This time, *you die...instead of your victims.*" But Santos was already past the listening stage. He felt cold. His lips were blue. The spurts were over. It amazed the killer to see how fast he bled out, so he

136

turned over the wrist; he'd managed to cut both Radial and Ulnar arteries. Shit, he'd cut everything. Jason thought back on those anatomy texts, the proper acronym... what was it? NAVAL... yeah, that was it; nerves, arteries, veins and lymphatics. The Chameleon cut off Santos' bindings, since the reprobate was too weak to move. Jason wadded them up and put them in his own rape kit, a small backpack with plastic lining. He wrapped Santos' right fingers around the razor for prints, then let it drop to the wood floor. Santos' heart still fluttered and banged, trying frantically to find some blood to pump; what a wonderful muscle, which pumped so long and faithfully from conception to death, but alas, a pump is no good without fluid. Santos' last memories were of wonderful green fields full of little naked girls and not a single pubic hair in sight. If he'd had any blood left for it, he would've died with a hard-on.

Jason placed the note next to the bed. He picked up his murder kit and stepped into the hallway. Placing a credit card against the deadbolt while turning the inner latch, he silently closed the door, then pulled the card; the deadbolt slammed home, making it appear that Santos had locked it from the inside. Finally he placed a small piece of transparent tape high up, spanning the doorjamb and door. He rubbed it firmly to make it invisible. Then he went upstairs to his room. He took a shower and went for breakfast. He felt great.

He pulled into an off-ramp restaurant sharing the huge blacktop parking lot with a truck stop and strip mall. He parked behind the restaurant, near the rank bin of exhausted cooking oil; maggots dripping onto the greasy pavement told him the recycle truck was a week late. He tossed the knife and wadded bloody tape into the maggot mass. Nobody would ever look in that shit. Then he ordered an omelet while planning Mal Johnson's murder.

He got back to Sacramendota just as children stepped off the buses at school. He quickly spotted Johnson perched on his favorite bench. But unlike his

137

former slouch, his head craned forward like a Heron posing to spear his next minnow from the shallow backwaters of a lake. Jason sensed the time was right, so he hurried back to Mal's place and his oxidized lime green Chevy van parked in the alley. He opened the rear doors; inside were lures, fake cast, doggie leashes, pictures of pets and a shabby mattress. Sheets of sound attenuating insulation were glued to the walls. The van had no windows, making it a perfect place to do unspeakable things. He put the magnetically attached transponder which he scored at Ted's store on top of the roof, dead center where Johnson wouldn't likely see it. Jason turned on his receiver; it beeped rapidly. Then we went to the bagel shop.

He ordered, but then his peripheral vision caught the mahogany blur. Mal flew down the street like a black man running from the cops. Jason stayed at the counter, not wanting to look suspicious. It seemed like years, but his order was ready in five seconds. He hustled out to the street. Worried that Johnson might get away, he tried to console himself with what he'd read in the transponder's manual; good for 10 miles, under optimal conditions. Still, he could get on the wrong freeway. By the time he found a clover leaf, the transponder beeps wouldn't mean shit.

But it turned out OK. The beeps showed the rig parked nearby. Bohannon drove past it, hooked a U-turn and parked. Resting his spotting scope on the steering wheel, he focused on the van's windshield. Then the rear doors opened. Malavai Johnson exited and slammed the doors. Bohannon had a perfect seat for the show. Johnson casually approached his mark, limping all the way. On his right forearm was a cast. His left held a leash and a photo. It was a masterful approach; obliquely toward the mark, searching each nook and cranny for his hypothetical dog.

Bonnie Longtree was tall, slender, half Caucasian, half Black. With her stunning looks and outgoing way, she got great grades. Bonnie was a classic optimist. The optimists usually fell for his trap; "Sir, can I help you?"

He slow-played it; "*Maybe*. Yave you seen Emma?"
She saw the photo; "No, I haven't. Cute dog!"

Johnson shrugged sadly; "I think she ran to the park; but with my bad leg, I can't catch her. An' wit mah busted arm *Ah can't shift the gears.*" Bonnie nodded; "Oh, my daddy lets me shift allatime! Let's go find her!"

It amazed Bohannon to see how peacefully the perp took her. Bonnie led the way; she couldn't see that Johnson's limp disappeared. Bohannon waited until he drive out of sight; any pervert that cagey could spot a tail. Soon they took a secondary road toward the vast expanse of orchards northwest of the city. Bohannon figured him for doing his evil under trees, although in the windowless van he could have her wherever. The transponder came to a stop 16 miles later, six rows inside a young olive orchard. The dense foliage shrouded the van from motorists and any chopper's overhead view. But even if a pilot spotted the vehicle, it would look like any other van in the orchard, where workers tended the trees. Bohannon idled three rows deep into the orchard, parking 100 yards behind the van. He was unsure of his next move; a bad sign, for a serial killer.

Things happened fast inside the van. Johnson shed his cast shortly after using it to good effect earlier; she started hollering when she realized her danger. But one solid backhand to her forehead did the trick. Bonnie went quiet for the rest of the drive... Too quiet, actually. He moved her to the mattress, took off her panties. His smooth-talk normally worked, but the vicious blow to her forehead damaged her frontal lobe, while contre-coup damaged her occipital cortex. The former impairs thought; the latter, visual interpretation. As with most pedophiles, Johnson wanted to dominate and scare them. Bonnie wasn't scared enough to arouse Johnson. Not having medical knowledge, he had no way of knowing that he had paradoxically caused his problem. He suddenly needed to piss, so he got out of the van. When he opened the door, Bonnie didn't even look toward the light.

Bohannon's binocs caught the half-naked rapist stepping out to pee. He had a huge tool, way to big to call it a penis. The young girl made no attempt at flight; perhaps she was drugged. The pervert made a big wet spot on the dirt, then crawled into the van again. Jason donned a flannel shirt, ski mask and rubber-dotted gardening gloves. He grabbed his shiny new hatchet. Using a row of olive trees for cover, he sprinted to the van.

His left arm flung the door open. Johnson sat upright with his back to the doors. On his lap, the naked girl writhed a reptilian squirm. Johnson looked around to face the intruder. The hatchet missed center mass, but cleaved off most of his left cheek and jaw. His body fell to the right rear corner. Had the hatchet been sharper, the Trigeminal nerve would have been cleanly severed, but instead it stretched like warm spaghetti, tethering the cleaved cheek and mandible dangling below it. The next swing hacked Johnson's left clavicle and 1st three ribs, creating a sucking sound when the apical lung lost its seal. Tiny pink-orange lung flecks flew. Johnson fell and gasped, trying hard to suck air. The collapsing lung resisted him. The next blow nicked his spinal cord below the Foramen Magnum; he went all-loose. He wasn't dead yet, but it was coming. Jason opened the side door. Bonnie slowly looked his way; a dull expression on her clammy face. Her skirt was soaked in blood. He helped her out and pointed her toward the road; "You're safe now... *GO*." Bonnie walked, trance-like toward the sun and the highway. She never looked back.

Jason wanted the scene to look like an enraged father caught the pervert, so he crawled into the van for some rage blows. According to his dad's notes, a father avenging his daughter's rape would have a pretty fuckin' high rage factor. First he delivered three hard blows to the groin. Half of the humongous penis fell off and the split scrotum offered up clear fluid and one opalescent, hemi-sected testicle; it looked like scrambled brains commingled with pubic hair. The Chameleon didn't enjoy giving rage blows, but had to so he kept on with the hatchet and tried

140

not to think about it. Next he directed his attention to Johnson's cleaved face. A half-dozen light hacks brought the desired affect, a shallow gash-mosaic garnished with tooth parts, tongue shreds and mandible shards. He placed a small crucifix, purchased months ago on the rapist's bloody lap. Then he dropped the hand-ax and closed the door. He got to his car. He drove past Bonnie, still walking like a zombie.

After driving 8 miles he pulled onto a dirt road. At the dead-end of the two-track was a small quarry. Occasionally a bulldozer would load the serpentine into a truck, to fill potholes. The quarry provided other uses, too; good place to drop a stolen car, poached deer remains or empty twelve-packs and spent rubbers from a night of brewing and screwing. Two dead cars were decorated with bullet holes and dents. Tossing his clothes and gloves into the back seat of a soon to be recycled Corolla, he emptied a can of charcoal lighter onto the heap. The fire burned fairly clean, with just a hint of black smoke from the rubber dots on the gloves. Donning fresh clothes, he drove off.

TWENTY SIX...

WHY THEY CALL IT
A RAPE TEAM

The all-white rape crew got there fairly fast, considering that the victim was black. They asked questions, took photos and mined the victim for trace. She distantly felt them examining her with cold tools and warm words. But to Bonnie it was just another rape. In spite of her state of shock, she recalled what her Gramma told her; *'Don't you never trust cops... especially white ones.'* Her fog began to clear. Bonnie started to recognize some words; "...recognize him if you saw him again?"

The white woman wasn't much older than Bonnie. Maybe 23, and pretty. She had fire in her eyes. Bonnie drifted in and out with the psychic tides, while the rape crew continued to gather and label blood, urine, feces, semen and fingernail trace. Her head throbbed. She passed out again.

Bonnie woke up later, in a white bed in a white room. A river of white people flowed past her open door. It was white, too. The fresh sutures in her anus burned, in spite of the painkillers. Kaleidoscopic bits and pieces floated back; the nasty smells, piercing pain, the blow to her forehead, all flitted against her skull, like moths hitting a hot light bulb. Eager to surface, unable to alight, they touched, burned and fell away... into the darkness, anywhere, as long as it was away from the pain. Then that white woman again; "I'm Officer Susan Lightner; You're safe now. May I ask you some questions?" Bonnie nodded; "Good! Now... what happened is NOT YOUR FAULT.

Trust me; he'll never hurt you again! We're going to put him in jail for life, so you never have to see him again!" Bonnie nodded slowly, without making eye contact.

"Can you tell me what he looked like?"

She sucked a big gulp of air and forced her fear away, determined to give a factual description; "He was Black, old, he hit my head with his cast and…"

"No Bonnie, not him. What did the *killer* look like?"

She got confused; *HE SAVED HER.* Then she remembered granmma's words; *"Never trust 'em. Them crackers don't NEVER care 'bout you."*

"I didn't see no killer… He was a *angel* with a ax."

Lightner re-tried; "Ok, was he tall or short?"

"I don't know. He looked big."

Lightner knew this buzzword meant 'up-the-ass-big.' She tried to deflect the imagery; "Was he black or white?"

"I didn't see."

"Did he say anything?"

Somewhere from her dreamland, a vague phrase drifted like a ghost from a neighboring channel on a dying TV; "Said *You're safe'… But* all I saw was a bloody ax."

The eager young cop stifled her disappointment; the witness was a savagely traumatized girl, saved by a faceless vigilante. She read the chart; lacerated rectum, ruptured hymen. Sue thought back to the rapist's mangled corpse; had a cock so huge it would have hurt most adult women. She thought of his dirty, jagged fingernails; the rapist basically dug his fingers into her and pulled her on like a wet sock. She hoped the blood work would be HIV negative. Susan wished she could have been the one swinging that fucking hatchet… What he did to this sweet young girl was unforgivable. Still, she didn't have much. A man of indeterminate race, height and weight killed one Malavai Johnson, a serial rapist with a rap sheet a mile long. But in the back of her mind, Susan hated herself almost as much. She was building a career by lying to vics, just so she could bust perps.

Then they'd get a soft judge or a snake would find a loophole or whatever… Too many perps got off easy, then

143

they'd rape again. Hell, just about everything she told the vics were lies. For openers, that bullshit about 'you're safe now'. What a crock of shit. One of Lightner's first vics heard that promise, only to have the same rapist nail her again, a month later; fucking courts let him walk because some cop abused a search and seizure fine point. Fucking judges.

And that lie about 'you'll never have to see him again?' The accused has a constitutional right to confront his accuser. Bonnie would face him plenty; first in a lineup, then during deposition, later, at trial. And id the perp gets sentenced? Crowded prisons were too happy to let the bastards out early, right back to their neighborhood.

Lightner headed for the precinct for some pencil pushing. On her way, she thought about the disgusting reprobates; no matter how much prison time they got, they never changed. The only things that cured them was a bullet, lethal injection or in this case...

'a angel with a ax.'

After she finished her report she drove to The Club. Normally, they wouldn't talk shop at the cop bar but this case struck a chord with younger females. They didn't have much; a hacked up stiff, no prints and just a few windblown tire tracks in the orchard. The weapon was a shiny new hatchet. There were rage blows. A small crucifix had been placed. Lightner wasn't a profiler, but couldn't help pondering along those lines. He was in his late 20's. The blitz attack meant he had a slight build. He was probably catholic, maybe divorced and had a daughter... And more than likely, he was fucking her.

Susan's third martini lubricated the speculation; she couldn't see a white man killing a black man raping a black vic. But a Latino, now there was something; they loved their revenge up close and personal, preferably with edged weapons like switchblades, machetes or hatchets.

Sue finished the drink, drove home disappointed. Her case wasn't about the rapist or even the victim. She would have to hunt the killer of a pedophile who deserved every hatchet gash, and then some. Johnson's killer deserved a medal, not handcuffs.

With so few clues, Lightner had seen enough dead cases to smell this one rotting on the vine. Turning off the car and closing her townhouse garage door, she headed for the bathroom for a long, hot shower.

TWENTY SEVEN...

PERVERTS FEED THE LOCALS

With fresh clothes and a five-buck truck-stop shower, Jason was free of incriminating clues. He returned to the flophouse. Maxine's door was closed, as usual. Her TV blared a cacophony of white-trash talk-show banter through the thin walls. He took the stairs, pausing to check the tape on Santos' door; still unbroken. He couldn't wait to leave Sacramendota's oppressive heat. Heading back for Hidden Crest, Vincent Carver felt great. The rush of killing two men in such a short span of time brought new heights. He felt so good that he vowed to kill more perverts... There were plenty.

MEANWHILE, SANTOS' BODY...

The first fly found the corpse 30 seconds after the killer left, thanks to liquefaction radicals drifting in the air, drawing blowflies like wine draws fruit flies. She picked the best sites for her eggs. Anything for an advantage over later arriving females. Within the hour, eyelids, lips and even the anus were rimmed with frost-white eggs like salt on the rims of bloody margaritas. Yellow Jackets found the feast after sunup. They eagerly cut off chunks of lips, tongue and eyelids, then flew them to the ground hive in an empty lot near an abandoned drive-in movie theater. Bit by bit, Santos winged his way through the tiny opening, barely big enough for loaded hornets squeezing past exiting workers. The first six ounces of Santos meat energized the queen into full egg production.

Inside Santos, building gas pressure extruded his distal colon and his tongue, exposing more meat for tomorrow's hornets. The 2nd day hatched 90,00 eggs while 200,000 more were laid. The pool of blood became a writhing, heaving maggot mass. The hot summer air accelerated instar cycles. Rats took slightly bigger chunks, but they didn't prefer human flesh; they only took what nature compelled them to take. Then it was back into the wall, down the elevator shaft and out to a Dumpster for tastier food.

The 3rd day Maxine, banging on the door for rent while wondering about the droning noise inside. Maybe Santos passed out and left the TV on a blank channel. Her hearing was shit. She banged rudely; "HEY SANTOS... RENT'S DUE!" 312 was weird but he paid promptly and never made a fuss so she banged again; "SANTOS OPEN UP. *RENT'S DUE, MOTHAFUCKAH!*"

Using her passkey, she swung the door open, just as the corpse let a gassy fart, spewing shit, gas and ass maggots. Simultaneously the stench hit Maxine. She would've fainted, but the ghastly sight riveted the eye too much. A huge cloud of blowflies and hornets swarmed like fire bombers atop a forest fire. Maggots rained onto the dusty hardwood. Mice snatched some, then ran for their holes. Maxine hurried back to her apartment to call the cops. But first she hid her cash; he last time they searched, she lost four grand.

One hour later, detectives showed. They looked relieved to hear the vic lived alone, had no weapons or communicable diseases. With luck, every cop would go home alive. They took photos, interviewed neighbors and bagged evidence. Maxine was glad when it looked like nobody was going to search her place. She locked her door, thinking she was off the hook. Then a cop returned; "Just a few more questions, Ma'am."
"*More?* Sure... how may I help you?"
"Have you had any new renters recently?"

147

She wouldn't tell him about the skinny fucker in 412; it went for 50 a week, but he suckered for double. She'd have to surrender the money for 'evidence'. She donned her 'recalling data from tired old brain cells' look;

"Nope... Why do you *ask,* detective?"

Cops don't answer, they ask; "Have you seen any strange vehicles or people?"

"Nope... Sorry."

"Here's my card if you think of anything."

The detective left the scene without learning much; just as with all ghetto crime scenes, nobody saw, heard or knew anything. The cops would go and file their report. With Santos's trophies, a few cold rape cases would close.

Most importantly, her cash was safe.

TWENTY EIGHT...

AN INVESTIGATION

IS UN-PENDING

Susan Lightner was drawn into the unofficial investigation coincidentally, after overhearing it at the bar. Call it woman's intuition or a veteran cop's hunch, but it piqued her curiosity; she couldn't ignore it. The suicide note was odd. An incurable pedophile suddenly grew a conscience and slit his wrist? *Please.*

She had only seen one bleed-out, but that case had both wrists sliced. Another thing, this dude offed himself in a bed. The other one occurred in a bathtub. She went to Lieutenant Rhodes' desk and sat down. Rhodes' phone was grafted to his good ear. He nodded at the pert young officer while he tried to wrap it up; "Yes, sure thing. We'll look into it Mrs. Whitehouse... uh huh, YES ma'am, I'll put a man on it right now. I'll... you're welcome... uh huh... thanks for your help. You're a good citizen... Goodbye. Yes, **GOODBYE** Mrs. Whitehouse."

Every precinct has a Mrs. Whitehouse. A typical busybody, the first to call with a clue, no matter what or where the crime occurred. Rhodes looked glad to see Lightner; or maybe just happy to hang up on the old bitty. Still, policy dictated that they cultivate relationships, *INCLUDING* lonely old civilian snoops, who on occasion were known to be of value; "What's up, Officer Lightner?" He called most cops by first name, but whenever issues of sexual harassment might arise, it was "Officer"
"That DB, Santos? Anything seem suspicious *to you?"*

"Not really. Perv offed himself with a new razor and an old bottle of sour mash... Why?"

"I've got a hunch... Why did he cut only *one wrist?*" Rhodes saw the look. He knew where she was headed. He started to sneer. They had more important cases. Still, he didn't want to discourage dialogue so he lassoed his sneer before it got out of the barn;

"Oh, *I see...* most slicers do *both wrists...* Well, maybe after he cut his left wrist to the bone he COULDN'T make the other cut... how's that?" Lightner nodded, but she looked dubious, so Rhodes shrugged; "Ok, what else?"

"The suicide note, boss. Pedophiles *NEVER* get remorse. And that other perp? Coroner's TOD's about the same time. And then there's ..."

Rhodes waved the air with a muscled right hand. He used to be a boxer; "*I see...* Eager cop wants to catch serial killer of pedophiles. OK, but before you climb out on that limb, here's some facts. **Fact number one;** Santos was found dead in his room. **Fact number two;** door locked from inside. **Fact number three;** suicide note. **Fact number three;** *ALL PRINTS* belonged to vic. **Fact four;** db's a convicted child raper. So please, Officer Lightner, save your talents for cases that deserve 'em!"

He always miscounted his facts, when he was pissed off. Sue was careful; "But sir, times of death were..." He sighed; "OK, OK, let's see; Santos was killed around the same time as, uh... *Johnson, wa*s it?" "Yeah, Johnson."

OK, let's see; one's killed inside, sliced, door locked, no prints, no... no fiber, nothin'. PERP TWO gets whacked with an ax, outside, broad daylight in front of a witness. Go ahead, impress me; try to link 'em. Hell, even if you could, it won't get you into Quantico..."

She hated his smirk that said "I'm right and you're a chump"; "Sorry to bother you, boss." She walked out. But the hunch still nagged. Fortunately, good cops learn to ignore baseless hunches when no evidence supports them. Like he said; plenty of other cases deserved her, what did he call it... *talents?* Cool!

TWENTY NINE...

A TARGET RICH ENVIRONMENT

After Carver's hunt in Sacramendota, he felt a sense of civic achievement. He wanted to kill more perverts, but that would form a profile, so first he would need a different identity. He logged onto the Net. Soon Jean Paul LeClerc was born; 32, flaming homosexual, loved to party. He was into everything.

Jean Paul began to research the North American Boy Love Association. NABLA formerly met in libraries, swapped kiddy porn and watched man/boy films together. However, librarians complained. The boy-fuckers went back underground. Apparently society wasn't yet ready for 60 year-old men corrupting young boys.

Neither was the Chameleon. This group was more disgusting than the ones he'd just killed. At least with most rank and file pedophiles, the victim stood a chance of recovering, but NABLA weirdos used brainwashing so cult-like that a skilled manipulator could indelibly imprint his message upon a malleable mind, where it became a permanent part of the victim's programming. Jean Paul needed to get closer to his marks. With any luck, it wouldn't take much effort to find NABLA.

The apartment wasn't much, but it was perfect for Jean Paul's needs. It was just a converted attic in Terra Loma, just north of the Golden Gate by 10-50 minutes, depending on traffic. Carole owned the old Victorian. At 82 her hips were too bad to climb stairs, so she used half of the bottom floor. Carole's osteopenia contraindicated surgery. To attempt it on such an advanced disease would be the grossest type of malpractice. One cannot glue metal to sand, and neither could a surgeon mesh steel to those frangible old femurs. So her last years would be bone-on-bone, painful and hopeless.

The rest of the bottom and the full 2nd floor was rented by a semi-retired Army general who only used the place when he flew out for a bit of rock fishing. That left Jean Paul's Spartan attic; small icebox, shower, sink and centralized sleeping/living space. At the center, he could stand up but if he went to a wall, he had to kneel. Floor-level windows afforded a great view, but downward.

Carole barely questioned him beyond the one-page photocopied rent form. She wanted to, but it might spawn a discrimination lawsuit. A landlord, even an octogenarian with bad hips had to be careful in California. She didn't care if the young man was gay or straight, but she wanted a quiet tenant. So far, he seemed perfect for her attic. It was perfect for him, too. He tossed his single duffel on the bed, locked the door and drove off.

His first stop was at the Cocktail in Marklin. One look said it wasn't the place to find pedophiles. Most were gay commuters, young, well-dressed and happy. He didn't have a problem with gay people; whatever consenting adults did was their own business. He turned and left the Cocktail. The other bar advertising for help was in Burlingus. "Chez Dave" was a real dump. The sour stench of beer-soaked Sheetrock assaulted him. He re-christened it 'Chez Dive'.

152

It was a dark, booth & dim streetlight arrangement from the '60's. In the ensuing decades someone should have remodeled it at least once. He bellied up to the bar to inquire about the job.

Kevin liked what he saw; tall, fit and gorgeous, possible lover; time would tell. He shook his ass for the kid; "What will you have, amigo?" Jean Paul smiled; "I was under the impression you're hiring?"

Kevin straightened up; "Yes, we're looking for a bartender-slash-confidant." Kevin loved to 'slash' things; it gave him the illusion of intellect where none existed; "Do you have any references-slash-resumes, honey?" "Yes, but... Well, mostly scorching words from lovers spurned... know what I'm saying?"

"Oh, you have NO IDEA! You start tomorrow at four." He handed the motivated killer a business card; "Call me if you have any problems... and by the way; what you're wearing? It's fabulous for this place."

When he walked outside, fresh bay air catalyzed the bar stench lingering in his nostrils, paradoxically intensifying it. The olfactory phenomenon was short-lived. In its place swirled the vital scents of tidal marsh, grass shrimp and mist, wafting in and out of his nose, cleansing and purging. Before getting into his car, another scent came... barely, but it came; Rain, imagine that. He drove to the south bay. It had been years since he'd been there. He found it odd that an area with so much wealth chose to be so ugly. He ended up in a restaurant in San Joseppe. The Kansas City Strip hit the table, sizzling and oozing droplets of blood from the top. It went down, chunk by wolf-gulping chunk. It tasted too good to chew it much. One more Porter would do the trick. He sipped and thought about how to kill a bunch of NABLA bastards in one swoop.

A bomb could do it, but back when he worked at Ted's, he experimented with explosives. Driving up into the nearby forest to detonate them, he learned that they were too unpredictable to be an ethical killer's weapon.

153

Besides, obtaining explosives left paper trails. Any half-assed investigator could catch the smartest bomber. Transporting a bomb was also risky; in the heightened security since 9/11, placing a bomb was chancy. One could get caught during a routine traffic stop. He finished his beer. He started driving home. It started raining hard. Then it got heavy. It wasn't raining cats and dogs; more like leopards and Rotweilers. He set the wipers at full speed, but they didn't help. He had to slow to 40 to avoid hydroplaning on the freeway already three inches deep.

California has two seasons, dry and wet. There are no blinding snowstorms, blizzards, no changing of colors, unless you'd count winter's dull green transformation to summer's straw-yellow. Some years gradually switch from dry to wet. Others bring it like a slamming door. This was a slammer. When he finally got inside his attic apartment, he was dripping wet, partially hung over and sleepy from the strain of driving through floodwater. His head hit the pillow, the white-noise of the deluge forced the first deep sleep he had in years.

Jean Paul awoke at ten. The rain kept bathing the place in swishy noise. A tiny leak showed at the west window. He saw an old stain in the same spot. He placed a towel to catch the moisture. A bolt of lightning struck a tree somewhere uphill; four seconds later, thunder testified as to the distance; four-fifths of a mile. Then the storm hit high gear. Rainwater gushed from the skies. It rained all day while he got ready for his new job.

He walked into Chez Dave; a virtual photocopy of the day before. He wondered how many coffee-stained photocopies were stacked under this one. He hated the job already. Kevin ushered him behind the bar, putting one hand on his shoulder; Jean Paul stiffened. Kevin quickly retracted the groping hand; "Sorry, Jean Paul; heat of the moment." JP thought fast for a cover story; "No, it's me. I... just broke up with my lover; I need time, that's all." Kevin smiled knowingly; "I can be patient." "Thank you, Kevin. I appreciate it."

It only took one shift to learn the ropes. The regulars always ordered the same drinks and the joint didn't exactly attract new business. But it was a pervert lair. Within a month Jean Paul had picked out six great marks. Five were regulars, when they weren't holed up raping tender young boys. Jean Paul didn't have a game plan for killing them en masse, but at least he had them targeted.

He normally parked in the carpool lot, took a bus to Burlingus, leaving him free to observe people and plan things, while the driver dealt with the rain and traffic. After work Andre, Kevin's ex-lover, would drive him to his parked car, so nobody at Chez Dive knew where the killer lived. Andre was a beautiful man; his mother was Norwegian, his father Cherokee. Andre had bronze skin, curly black hair, blue eyes, long lashes. He was in a solid relationship with a Berkeley realtor. That made him the perfect ride home for a straight man posing.

By the 3rd rain-soaked month Jean Paul knew everything about his marks; where they slept, drank, where they held their meetings. But as for type of death he kept drawing blanks. He blamed the relentless rain for crimping his creativity. The entire Bay Area was soaked to the max. Jean Paul was sick of the rain, the Bay Area and surely, sick of perverts. He thought of canceling the plan, just so he could go north again and dry out. But things worth planning were worth carrying out, if for no other reason than to give his mind ease. Incomplete cycles of action rob one's power. The only remaining glitch was deciding the kill; the fucking rain, it never stopped.

On the last Friday in February he called in sick. He WAS sick, too... Sick of the fog and drizzle that Bay Area lunatics called mist. Thinking a day in the country might help, he drove up to Mount Tamales, well liked by hikers and outdoor types. He got out to take a hike. Almost immediately the killer began feeling better. He was amazed to see how revitalizing the mist was, when encountered on the hill instead of on a freeway at fifty per.

155

The drizzle nourished the micro-niche. All along the trail was evidence of its crucial role in nurturing the coastal biota. Newts were everywhere, burrowing and laying eggs under rotting logs. Frogs reveled, croaking and chirping, extolling the virtues of a bug-rich, dripping wet understory. There were mushrooms, toadstools, molds, slimes and mosses celebrating the rain with boundless enthusiasm. By looking up-slope Jean Paul could see rising mushrooms. As they grew upward, lifting the overburden like tiny thatch roofs, their glistening stalks contrasted sharply against the dun background of topsoil and duff.

But so many months of flatland living robbed his stamina. He turned around after half a mile. When he approached his car, a man walked up with a bucket. He practically whispered; "Hey, wanna buy some 'shrooms?" It had all the charm of a drug deal; "What are *shrooms?"*
Waldo held the bucket for inspection; "I got Chanterelles... *good ones!"* Le Clerc looked in the bucket at brownish-orange shapes; they looked like exhumed bones. He lifted one; damp, firm and surprisingly, not slimy; "Wow, they're heavy... what do you *DO* with them?"
"That's easy, dude; toothbrush away the dirt. Cut off any hard or spoiled spots; they won't hurt you, but they taste like crap. Then rinse *SPARINGLY* in cold distilled water. Don't use tap water; chlorine spoils their flavor. Let 'em dry, slice thin. Sauté in a *DRY pan...* don't use oil or butter 'cuz they have lots of moisture. Then, serve 'em... Dude, they're awesome!"
He saw zeal in Waldo's eyes. He bought the shrooms, making a friend for life of Waldo Trevor Hill; "How you cook 'em, again?" Waldo smiled slyly; "I'll do ya one better. *Follow me!"*

JP followed Waldo's old International. A few miles northeast they took a two-track for seven miles uphill, crested a summit and went down the other side, stopping at a ramshackle cabin in the bottom of a steep canyon. It was almost dark, due to the tall Bays and Redwoods.

Moss and ferns grew everywhere in the steep canyon. Waldo tutored Jean Paul in the preparation of Chanterelles. After all the foreplay, the taste could've been anticlimactic, but the 'shrooms proudly revealed their gustatory secrets. Served alone with a bit of melted butter and hot tea, they were exquisite. Jean Paul learned why folks stalked wild fungi.

He looked around Waldo's cabin; an old-school hippie's lair. He had a pile of shed Blacktail antlers, boars' tusks, eagle feathers and a Pomo dream catcher. A mound of partially lapped wild gemstones and native crystals dominated the bench. The rough-hewn ancient redwood countertops served triple duty, depending upon which bugs hatched, which birds were migrating or which 'shrooms were rising. At the moment, five varieties adorned it, each with a clean white paper towel under it. Two classifying books were weighted open with rusty fletching jigs. Waldo saw his gaze as an invitation to talk more about 'shrooms; "Oh, yeah, see *those?* I'm getting' spore prints, sorta like fingerprints; well, not exactly, but it's a start."

He pulled out a stash pipe, lit a bowl, took a hit and passed it. Jean Paul didn't like Pot, but etiquette dictated at least one puff. Stoners were suspicious of straights. Passing it back, he was relieved to see Waldo put it out. Perhaps he was checking if JP was a cop. And then the dope hit him; powerful shit. Waldo coughed, then kept ranting about mushrooms. Through the building buzz JP caught bits about the tiny shiny, an hallucinogenic from the southwest. Then another bit; "anticoagulant, medicinal applications..." Then JP passed out.

He awoke later, to a dark cabin as if Waldo beamed back into his parallel fungal dimension. A generator started purring. The lights glowed up. He heard footsteps on the gravel. Waldo entered with an armful of firewood; "Hey, dude you were out *for hours;* better go easy on the smoke, bro." Waldo scowled, nodding at the incandescent lights; "I hardly ever use the generator. That's why I bought this place; no power lines, no e-mag

157

radiation. In case of the big blast, we're like totally protected; north-facing slopes, I'd only get a few hundred rads; totally survivable, but anyhow... tonight *we got lights for dinner!"*

Deftly placing kindling over used paper towels, Waldo lit the stove. He strategically placed progressively larger wood in the tiny fire path. Soon he had roaring flames licking forearm-sized Bay logs. He closed the door. The flames died back obediently; the greedy fire would have to make do with the restricted air supply and make heat instead of chaos. Waldo put a pot of water on and started slicing onions; "Yeah, I get I get Chanterelles from Tam and Black Morels near the Kings Range, where there was a hella fire coupla years back. Then I get Matsus, mostly from Mendonesia county."

"HUH? What are Matsus?"

"You never heard of MATSUTAKES? You shittin' me? Great eatin' but the fuckin' Asians buy all the grade Ones I can find..." Waldo added some beef bullion to the pot; "They smell like cinnamon. Ya gotta look for HOPPERS... They dig little holes in 'em. On hopper can ruin a whole load. On a good day, I can make 600 bucks... and with all this rain, it's a *KILLER YEAR for 'shrooms!"* He laughed, lit the pipe and took a short hit. Then he offered it to JP; "No, thanks; learned my lesson!"

Waldo kept rambling while trying to retain smoke in his lungs. Jean Paul never could figure why folks talked while inhaling good Pot. It smacked of Bulimia. At any rate, Waldo kept with tradition; his words emanated weakly; "Yah, depends on rain and this year *really delivered."*

The onion soup was ready. Waldo handed him a wedge of hard Romano and a grater. Waldo had some degrees, dude; botany, microbiology, computer science. An odd mix for an odd man. He married once, had a kid, divorced and got rich in silicone valley, but not in that order. He patented some shit in computers, making him fairly rich, bought this 788 acres of coastal mountain, the center of which held this magical old-growth cabin.

158

Waldo also had a PhD in 'mycology' from the Hard Knocks campus outside his door. His intellect had outgrown the traditional limitations of academia. Hence, his current bathyspheric quest into all things moldy. Waldo was Bubba Gump for 'shrooms. Jean Paul left at midnight, amid pleas to return for more mushroom talk. He promised he'd return; then he drove home and slept it off.

He awoke sluggishly, his consciousness returning in layers, during which the gift came to him; he would kill the NABLA assholes with poison 'shrooms. Somehow it fit; he would kill slime with fungus. And then, of course, he would have to kill Waldo. Killers couldn't allow loose ends, even if they happened to be friendly old hippies.

He searched the Net for mushrooms. One type of Amanita popped up in California's false spring around February, the exact timing varying with each micro-niche's particulars. They liked grassy meadows and had been the bane of sheepherders for 300 years. One tiny Am could kill a ram. One or two finely sliced and sprinkled on say, a pizza, should kill a parlor full of perverts. But it might not be so easy; perverts had weird dietary kinks. He'd have to work on that; maybe an amanita-slash-artichoke pesto.

On his next day off, he drove to Waldo's. Soon they were crawling through the dripping understory. Jean Paul spotted a yellow-white mushroom, hopefully a Death Cap like the ones he'd seen online. He reached for it; "Hey, Waldo; *is this one good to eat?*" "HELL NO! *Don't touch it!* Could be an Amanita, bro!" They went back to the cabin and sautéed up a beautiful black Morel in butter and garlic. Meanwhile, Waldo revisited the Death Cap encounter for his protege; "Ya never go lookin' for *mushrooms to eat*. Ya *STUDY 'EM... GOT IT?* It's a question of mind set." "Whaddyamean?"

Waldo pointed his spatula like a maestro's baton;

"You said, and I QUOTE; *'Hey Waldo, is this one good to eat?'* Believe me, if you swallowed *that one* you would DEFINITELY *EAT IT."* He served up the butter-sauted Morel with hot Colombian coffee. Oddly, the discussion of lethal 'shrooms didn't scare Jean Paul off the wild Morel. Waldo's expertise reassured him. Besides, the Morel was too damn good; "See those diplomas?"

He spied six or eight frames stacked on edge with dust on the tops; "Didn't wanna hang 'em up, but couldn't bring myself to shitcan 'em. One's for slimes 'n molds." He poured more coffee. Waldo liked him enough to start using his initials as a nickname; "Jay Pee, you don't get one o' those without learning *WAY MORE* than you wanna know about Amanitas." With the Morel gone, JP wished he'd found two. The coffee washed away the addictive flavor, helping him bypass his new gustatory fixation; "Anyhow, one thing turned out to be *right on,* man. I call it Waldo's Rule... *'Never eat anything with Death in its name.'*

Waldo slowly sipped coffee for emphasis; "Such as **Death** Caps, **Death** Buttons or **Death** Camas; don't eat that pretty little flower... looks sorta like wild onions, grows right with 'em, up in the high country...they'll fuckin' kill ya. It's bad to eat things with 'Death' in the nomenclature." He reached for the pot pipe; "Now for our friend, Amanita Phalloides, aka the DEATH CAP, it will surely kill a dude; takes about a week."

The Chameleon hunched forward. Waldo had his attention; "The Amatoxins poison your hepatocytes... sorry; liver cells, which fucks up your protein synthesis and RNA transfer. The longer it's in your liver, the worse you get." He passed the pipe. JP took a small hit this time; "With each dead hepatocyte, the liver loses another worker cell. Next time enteric circulation brings the toxins through the liver, more hepatocytes die. Within six hours your liver loses more 'n half its function. There's no antidote. *TREATMENT?* Forget about it." He pulled a bottle of single malt out of nowhere, took a snort and passed it to JP. On top of the building pot high, it tasted great;

160

"The liver fails, then kidneys and the brain starts to swell, aka hepatic encephalopathy and trust me, dude; *All's not swell* that ends swell." But JP was too focused on the message to catch the play on words; "They give ya charcoal, to absorb free circulatin' toxins, but that don't help much. They give acetylcysteine and some other shit... I forget exactly what, but the point being, you stand a great chance of dying, while the best doctors stand by, scratchin' their heads. Most definitely; *DO NOT* eat shit with Death in its name; 'at's WALDO'S RULE"

The hippie capped the point with an anecdote; "This dude from Thailand, where there's a harmless lookalike? He picked some in California and mixed 'em into a stir-fry. He was the only one who survived. Ended up with a liver transplant. But the Death caps killed his whole fuckin' family in nine days."

"NINE *days?*"

"Right fuckin' on; nine miserable days, while you watch your wife and kids die, slow and painful-like. It's like a bad Hitchcock movie, brother." Waldo kept talking, but JP disengaged. He wouldn't poison his marks with shrooms; too much time to call for help, describe the killer and God knows what else. Around ten PM, JP drove down the mountain feeling pretty good. He dodged a bullet and had a side bonus; he wouldn't have to kill Waldo.

The next day he wracked his mind for ways to kill the group en mass. He could use another poison, but multiple perverts dying would surely set loose the dogs of law. As he worked his shift it became clear; he would have to kill them one at a time. Just then, his next mark bellied up to the bar; Ephram Silver; rum and coke, two ice cubes; did they symbolize testicles? Silver used to be a hotshot banker; "One more?"

"Sure thing." He mixed the drink slowly, working up the nerve to initiate an unmentionable topic. Silver already JP handed him the drink and decided to just go for it; "Here, Ephram me BOY... oh boy, I could sure use a boy."

The pervert scrutinized the killer for falsehood; *could it be?* This standoffish barkeep really liked young boys? It would explain why he never appeared with an adult lover. Rum loosened his tongue. Silver whispered; *"Me, too."* He went to his booth and opened a magazine. JP announced last call 20 minutes early. The other patrons drifted out, but Ephram sat there like a boy with a crush on his teacher, holding a shiny red apple. He pointed at his magazine. Sure enough, a hardcore pedophile rag. JP forced a thin smile; "I have that one at home. I have lots; wanna see 'em?" Ephram practically ran out after him. His motto back in his banking days? Strike while the iron's hot.

JP drove to a deserted East Bay industrial complex whose parking lot abutted the breakwater; by day it would be chock full of cars. The last two rows closest to the shore were dark. The salt spray killed off the floodlights years ago. It was a common weekend hang out for old lonely gays, but it was a weeknight; theirs were the only two cars. He watched Ephram park. Silver had his magazines and lotion. Jean Paul baited him; "Let's sit on the breakwater. The salt air will help you. Come on." The fresh air hit him; he wobbled. JP took his arm; "Careful, Ephram... careful." "Yeah, thanks. Never can be too careful." They wobbled-slash-walked up the breakwater. JP passed him a flask. The old man took a huge swig and passed it back, just as Jean Paul caught him flush on the Parietal bone with a breakwater rock. It made a rewarding splat. Ephram listed to the right but didn't fall. JP knew better than to whack him again. He nudged the limp pervert, who fell ten feet to the rip rap. Waves bashing against the rocks did the rest. The scene would show a dead old pervert who got drunk and fell off 'Queer Pier', as the straight cops liked to call it. Walking 150 yards south, he hurled the murder weapon into the saltwater. Tidal action and marine fauna would eat away all clues. Everything in the bay is hungry. He drove away, feeling not much better; it was a chickenshit kill. Rocking a pathetic old drunk left a lot to be desired.

162

Still, he took solace knowing that more boys had been spared. It wasn't as good as cleaving off a rapist's face with a hatchet, but they can't all be home runs.

The next day the corpse drifted south on a rising tide. When it ebbed the corpse ran aground in tidal ooze, after rolling in the briny slurry. When it stopped it looked like much of the other half-buried items in the stinking estuary. It could have been a car tire, dead seal or a bit of Tyvek wrapped around a salt-grass hummock. A thousand cars an hour sped past, all of them intent on going somewhere else.

Six hours later the incoming tide floated the corpse; the cold body was a perfect platform for crabs, insects and resting seabirds. It drifted south where it entered the main current, rolling in the surface chop until it passed some gas, then found neutral buoyancy 20 inches below the surface. Once of surface drag, it picked up speed.

Dave and Guy specialized in big sturgeon, with their biggest measuring nine feet. But when Guy hooked the body, neither man thought it was a sturgeon. Instead of reeling, which would twist his line up, Guy merely reeled slack to keep it out of the prop while Dave backed the boat toward the snag. They saw the hand at 25 yards astern. Guy quit reeling; they didn't want to be blamed for disturbing evidence. Their 911 call netted a game warden. He secured the corpse, then queried the anglers and read their depthfinder way-points. Then he asked to see their driver's & fishing licenses, salmon cards, boat registration, fire extinguisher and proof of insurance.

Soon the sheriff's boat brought another round of questioning, much of which were the same. Before it was over, they lost a day of fishing. Next time they snagged a corpse, they'd cut the line and keep on fishing.

THIRTY...

PLANS CHANGE

The perverts at the bar were too self-centered to notice Silver's absence. Jean Paul already had his next mark picked out. Most women would love to date a man like Lance. He drove a new Porsche. He was rich. Except for his habit of preying on young boys, he was every woman's Mr. Perfect; the prick had carjack written all over his ass. Lance displayed a level of self-protection bordering on paranoia. It would be tough to put one over on him. That explained the snub-nosed .38 in JP's pocket and why he stowed his personal duffel behind the bar. He faked a phone call, then walked to Lance's booth; "I need a ride. Can you help me?" Lance agreed and finished his drink, while JP fetched his duffel. Once in the car, he baited the trap; "Thanks. I can pay for your gas, Lance."

"It's not necessary, really." Lance wouldn't have any skinny-bitch queen gossiping about paying him for mileage. He lit the Porsche. They didn't talk much. Thirty minutes later, JP spoke; "Take this underpass, OK? Funny thing about beer; you don't buy it, you just rent it."

Lance smirked. He thought the kid had more class. He stopped where JP wouldn't be seen from the freeway. The point-blank wadcutter hit him like a freight train, shattering his 9th rib, bursting his liver and ruining both lungs. He shuddered. Then the second slug hit him four inches higher and angling up, obediently tearing through the shrinking right lung, pulmonary artery and vein. It came to rest against the pleural surface of his left fourth rib. Le Clerc reached across Lance and opened the door. He kicked the prick out and slid into the driver's seat.

By the time JP hit the southbound fast lane, his wits controlled the adrenaline rush. He forced himself to stay under 65. An hour later in Oakland, he wiped blood from the seat and shifter, wiped down the steering wheel, door handles and gun. He put it under the seat, grabbed his duffel and walked. With the body 45 miles to the north, the obvious inference would be a fatal carjacking. After a mile he found the right Dumpster. The bloodstained garb went underneath 60 servings of unfinished pasta primavera and rancid butter from the nearby convention hall. He hit the north on-ramp and stuck out his thumb.

ABOUT THE PORSCHE...

Levonne-Shamane Brown watched this honky park a Carrera, then *left it.* When the cracker was out of sight Leroy sprinted to it. The window was down, keys in da switch. HADDA be a sting. He didn't take the bait. He tailed the man two blocks; dude didn't have no backup. Leon ran to the small fortune and hauled ass. Levonne-Shamane warn't stupid. He pulled over 'n searched. He found a snub-nosed hammerless with three live, two spent. And kiddie porn; he felt like driving after the motherfucker an' cappin' his ass wit da dude's own gun. Then he checked da hood 'n trunk. He disabled Onstar, so da Man couldn't lojac his ass. Then he drove to the hide. There were 12 other cars there already; two hummers, one 'vette, six Mercedes, two butched-out 4X4s and a neon lime Dodge Charger RT, a specialty request for a collector. Leroy hooked up with the ringmaster to get credit for the Porsche and to double-check on his hummers. Within the week the roadster and its incriminating DNA would be steaming past Panama, headed for Capetown.

AND LANCE'S BODY...

The trooper saw the Porsche heading north. Officer Art Smith went back to his paperwork. He would've loved a chance to pull it over; he loved everything Porsche. That's what made it so curious when it headed south again, barely ten minutes later; there were only two exits within turnaround time. Why would it turn back *so soon?* Nursing

165

the cruiser out of the darkness, Smith hit his favorite cruise speed of 79. He checked under the first overpass and hit the spotlight. Two turquoise discs shone, then the raccoon covered his eyes. He left the frog-hunter to his foraging. Three miles further north he took the next one; he hit the spotlight. A body lay there, center stage. He swept quickly for suspects; a large dark form materialized high up, near the north end. Smith's adrenaline surged. He broke out the riot gun, jacked a round in the chamber and keyed the PA with as much authority as his trembling lips could muster; "YOU, sleeping bag, *lemme see your hands!*"

Two dirty palms quickly appeared. The transient knew the drill. From Tijuana to Seattle he'd been busted by every kind of lawman. He could already feel the nightstick; *"GET OUT OF THE BAG NOW!"* Burt Thorogood wriggled out and staggered toward the blinding spotlight; *"ON YOUR FACE!"* Burt assumed the position; face down, palms up, carefully. No way would he provide an excuse to get tasered... *or shot; "Yeth, OFFITHUR"* Dispatch said backup was a mile away; if he timed it right he'd look like a hero; knees on the dude's back, cuffs on. Sure enough, backup soon saw. Smith had a suspect in custody, a dead vic on the pavement and the collar of his young career.

Officer Melanie Budros just dropped her partner off. She was on her way home when she got the call. She knew how Smith felt out there, alone in the dark. When she saw the body and burgundy-colored liver blood she radioed for a supervisor and a crime scene unit. Then she turned to the suspect, a typical homeless, worthless drunk, no money or ID, filthy sleeping bag. She got the creeps just from looking at it. With latex gloves she upended the bag; two empty 40-ounce bottles and a penknife, bloodless. Budros went to the stiff and pulled his wallet; platinum cards, 450 cash, current CDL; she read aloud; "Lance W. Cummings, 48. Not a robbery, so what was it?" Art went white with alarm; "Shit... I think I *saw the perp! Nobody buys a Porsche to drive the speed limit!"* He radioed it in. If there were quicker info turnaround... or if black Carreras were rare, they may have caught the perp right then.

166

Supervisor Sergeant Ed Williams arrived. He spoke with the suspect, then the officers; "He don't know shit. Turn him loose." Burton Thorogood sprinted into the darkness. The two-legged urban cockroach evaporated in the surrounding short brush before they could change their minds. He would fetch his bag later.

After a quick sniff of Smith's Glock and backup wheel gun, Ed relaxed. He watched the forensics team dismount, trying to find some clues, but the kill was too squeaky clean to hope for much. He drove to the precinct to write it up. Later that night, he had the make on Lance Cummings; he targeted boys too young to drive. But of the car, nothing surfaced. That wasn't surprising; chop shops loved to dissect foreign beauties, sell the parts and crush the rest. He had an idea about the perp, too; since 38's are easy to control and soft on recoil they were looking for a slightly built or boyish-looking man. Both hits were on the vic's right, so he probably got shot sitting behind the wheel. The first bullet hit liver. Stippling and muzzle blast proved the 2nd was more like an injection than a gunshot. Given the late hour and off-ramp dumpsite, the perp was a pro; nobody else had the balls to dump bodies in plain view. The recovered bullets were Wadcutters, so the shooter had more firearms knowledge than your average carjacker. They caused devastating wound channels and blood loss.

But in the wings, a second profile stood as an understudy; the perp could be an ex-lover. Williams hated second theories like ex-wives, of which he had three. No good thing comes from understudies. If he mentioned it, he'd get his team stuck, wasting time interviewing every pervert and pedophile in the North Bay. He would put an older officer on the case; one who knew which questions *NOT* to ask. That would look good on paper.

THIRTY ONE...

VINCENT GOES HOME

After ditching the Porshe, JP caught a ride, then saw the driver was wired on ice, doing 75 in a 55 zone. The car was a real cop magnet; primer gray paint, expired temporary permit, red-taped tail light and who knows what in the trunk. JP couldn't have it; "Dude; *slow DOWN*... the cops'll get me!" His gas foot lifted at the buzzword; "Fuck me... *cops?*" But soon the tweaker started speeding again. JP ached for his gun. Had to improvise or get busted; "Hey man, that's my street; pull over!" The car screeched to an oil-smoking halt; "Thanks, bro. Catch ya later." Before it got out of sight a cruiser came from nowhere, lit the emergency lights on the magnet. JP's knees knocked from the close call. He walked in a bar and called a cab. As always, he had it drop him four blocks from his lair. He made up his mind; he wouldn't kill any more NABLA assholes. It wasn't as much fun as he thought. And besides, he was leaving clues. He called Kevin from a public phone; "Kevin, sorry to dump this on you, but Mother just had a stroke. Docs say it's bad. I'm rushing to Seattle to see her." Kevin nodded into the phone; "Oh, just go! You'll always have a job-slash-partner here, baby." "Thank you. I appreciate you, Kevin."

JP drove to Waldo's to say goodbye to his only friend. They ate Madrone-grilled Valley Quail with grilled Portabellas and a fine Calpella Zinfandel. The Bellas were store-bought, since the 'shroom season was ending, dude.

By three in the afternoon, JP was heading north.

168

He learned one thing from the NABLA creeps. Society's fixation on low morals and bad parenting was creating pedophiles faster than a thousand Carvers could kill them off. If he wanted to make a bigger dent, he'd have to kill bigger people. It was time to move up the food chain.

Carver's days in court proved that some judges bent over backward to give criminals too many chances. These judges forgot that the law was first created to protect society. Nowadays they cared more for academic minutiae than for the people. His Honor Salvadore Soldana from Lake County came to mind. Carver had seen some weird rulings on Soldana's bench. That slinky prick really deserved to die.

Six hours later Carver rented a ground-level apartment in Lucien on the north shore of Clear Lake, the 2nd largest natural lake in California. While Lake Tahoe had deep pure water, panoramic scenery, gambling and skiing, Clear Lake held no such glamor. True, it had a history of gambling. Sinatra's Rat Pack got it going. The plan was simple; buy low, introduce casinos, sell high. But much like a transplanted organ that doesn't take, the scheme withered. Property values never soared as planned.

Clear Lake was beautiful, but had problems. It was full of Mercury, leached from the surrounding cinnabar-laden mountains. Then there were the annual algae blooms; being a saucepan lake with an average depth of 30 feet, the summer sun heated it to threshold warmth. Algae would bloom, then die off, using up precious oxygen. Massive fish die-offs created stench, which permeated shoreline bergs, impairing tourism and commerce, creating ghost towns. Low rents attract low life. Crack and meth abounded, hence Vincent's good fortune in finding an apartment. Hell, he had his pick of places to rent from eager landlords too broke to ask questions.

Other than commerce generated by tourists, fishing and water skiing (when the lake smelled fine), the city was devoid of commerce. Lucien's three shoreline miles consisted of plenty of closed joints, with just a few chowder houses and pizza parlors still open for business. Lucien had one part time cop. One could always find Officer Dan Lock occupying the 2nd stool at the "Say When". Lock *never* saw anyone snort a line or beat his wife, even it happened on the 3rd stool. He didn't want to ruin a good thing by busting somebody. Besides, Lucien didn't have a jail. He'd have to drive them all the way around the lake to Lacqueport; and if he was driving, he couldn't be drinking.

The citizens liked him more than the badge-heavy prick they had before; that fucker was Barney Fife on steroids. With Lock behind the badge, they could speed, fight or shoot a neighbor's Pit Bull if it got out of hand. It was all the same to Dan. His idea of traffic control was napping in the squad car in the shade near shoreline traffic. Tourists slowed down and Lock slept it off. Perfect.

From his doorway Carver could see the cop sitting across the street, on that stool. At first it unnerved him to have a cop so close by, but actually it was an asset. Carver's place was the least likely to be burglarized. Carver closed the blinds, arranged personal items and fired up his laptop. With a few clicks he discovered that Soldana would have one trial for the week, California v Peebles. A long trial meant a homicide, big drug bust or arson, something like that. Tomorrow would be a good day to stalk judges.

STALKING SOLDANA...

Morris Fishbein strode briskly into court. He sat in the back row among rough-looking biker types with tattoos, bandanas and weathered skin. Their tone? Casual. The skinny prosecutor, whose unofficial nickname was 'Never' Settles, stood up. The moniker originated in defense circles, but it stuck. Lance Settles used it to good effect in campaigns; people were sick of seeing crooks pleading down to slaps on the wrist. He greeted the jury; "Ladies and gentlemen of the jury, Liam Peebles is charged with four counts. Three are MURDER ONE. The other's possession of controlled substance. Please LISTEN to the evidence. I will prove the case beyond a reasonable doubt and you will come to the only possible conclusion; guilty on all counts. Thank you." Jurors loved brevity.

Defense counsel stood up. Fishbein wondered how Peebles could afford him. Custom tailored suit, slicked-back hair, huge diamond cufflinks. His tan came from a booth. Giancarlo Barra, aka Johnny the Suit, addressed the court; "May it please da court... Your Honor, we reserve our opening statement and request we can make it after da state rests. Thanks, judge." Soldana didn't look up; "Granted. Jury is instructed to make no opinions on this. It's perfectly legal. Counselor, begin your case."

The state called their witnesses. Liam Peebles and four un-indicted co-conspirators allegedly broke into a meth house and shot the shit out of Lisa Stafford, 31, her common law live-in, Paul 'Dozer' Dexter, 47 and her daughter Allison McKinney, 15. Dozer's face got shot off with two close-range shotgun blasts. Lisa got it fast and quick; one load of buckshot to the forehead just after she pulled the covers over her head in a failed attempt to *NOT see* their faces. Forensics showed lead shot exiting the rear of her skull, each pellet wrapped in microfibers, looking ever so much like bloody comets; lead ball center, fibrous tail of blood and gray matter.

172

But whereas the parents had only been shot, Allison McKinney got the worst; she was raped and sodomized. Saliva, containing cayenne and pepperoni, matched Peebles. After raping her, Peebles allegedly broke her neck by grabbing her hair and yanking backward. Her Axis vertebra broke in classic hangman's pattern, with partial cord severance. He then allegedly bit off her nipples; the left one, while her heart was still beating. Since they didn't find either nipple, it was presumed Peebles swallowed them. The evidence also showed he ejaculated into her mouth, near time of death.

Before the jury had a chance to vomit, the coroner offered scanty assurance; the girl never felt her nipples getting chewed off, since she was paralyzed from the neck down. However, only one juror took solace in this fact; the others realized that while the poor kid couldn't feel, she sure as hell could see him biting her tits off. Settles tried to leave the gruesome photos up, but the Suit objected successfully. Still, it was a hell of a way for the prosecution to end the first day, with areolar cannibalism burning hotly in the jurors' minds. Fishbein left the court, vowing to return Thursday for the verdict. As far as he could tell, it was a slam-dunk.

He took time off to go fishing; the lake was barely 90 yards from his doorway. He borrowed a neighbor's car-topper. For a change, no afternoon wind whipped the lake into ten-inch whitecaps. He tied up to willow branches near shore. Vincent hadn't fished since long ago, with his dad; one of those rare days when his old man actually took a day off. Ironically, that was also on Clear Lake. Recollections slowly surfaced as he fished, like lyrics from an old song; Vincent let the images come...

He was ten. It was a hot July 4th, over 95 in the shade. For overachievers like Howard Carver, that single day of fishing was supposed to make up for years of neglecting his son. That's how it works with Type A assholes; they spend emotional currency like an accountant; in one column, out the other, so the balance should be even. Howard probably thought he could just drop in, take the kid fishing, then fly off to Mobile to catch a killer. That ought to fill all the voids... Spackle for the psyche so the façade can be repainted enough to last another season. The sun beat down. They finally hooked a huge bass. But just as the bucket-mouth got close to the hull, young Vincent fumbled the net, tapping the fish. With a burst of energy the bass snapped the frayed leader and was gone. Howard's jaw muscles twitched; he didn't say a word, but his face spoke volumes.

Vincent exited the flashback, surprised at its clarity; the bass doubtlessly symbolized some criminal who managed to escape the great Carver's net... Or maybe it was the twitch of a father disappointed in his son, who didn't know the first thing about handling a fishing net... but *how COULD HE*, without Howard around to teach him?

The sun set behind the mountains. The surface got flat and clear. Then his line twitched slightly. He set the hook and played a huge crappie. In three more casts, he had three more. Fuck the mercury; he was going to cook what he caught.

DEFENSE CASE IN CHIEF

When court came to order Johnny the Suit stood up; "Your honor, I would like to make my opening statement, which is my client's right to do... " Soldana nodded. The suit walked closer to the jury, so they could see his gleaming white caps, manicure and tailored suit; he wanted 'em to know he was Mob; "Ladies an' gentlemen, you heard horrible things. You've seen horrible pictures. I'm sorry, for what you had to see... In fact, the pictures were *SO horrible*, I tried to keep 'em out of evidence." The room buzzed a little. He let it soak in, then reiterated; "Dat's right. They were so horrible that anybody could *make the mistake of blaming MY CLIENT.* It's human nature to BLAME ***ANYBODY*** when we see things like that."

He sipped water before continuing; "Cops are human beings too, just like YOU an' me. An' when they see unspeakable things, they also want to blame... ***ANYBODY.*** In this case, they blamed an *INNOCENT MAN,* my client."

The Suit frowned pensively; "AN' BECAUSE of this WRONGFUL BLAME, you're gonna see how my client's CIVIL RIGHTS were *crushed.* You'll see why he confessed to somethin' he didn't do... So I ask you, just like Mr. Peebles did; please keep an open mind, without wrongfully applying blame. Thank you."

Barra could sell saltwater to a drowning man. First of all, there weren't no eyewitnesses; a few neighbors awoke, heard shots and motorcycles race off; coulda been *ANYBODY*, ergo the cops had no cause to search & *seize Liam's stuff.* He showed photos of Liam's bruises, proving they beat him 'til he confessed. There was reasonable doubt about Miranda too, since his client was high on ice; no way could he know his rights. And the DNA? Cops coulda planted it, cuz they HATED his client; looka da bruises if you doubt it. The Suit was sure smooth. When he rested, half da jurors weren't so hot on hanging Peebles;

"Your Honor, dat's about it. Defense rests, judge"

Of course, all of it was true. The cops didn't have much to go on, so they busted the most likely crook. And yeah, they roughed him up a little, but *so what?* A tough guy like Peebles got and gave worse in a bar fight. And the bastard was high on ice, but he'd been arrested plenty of times before, so he knew his fuckin' rights, all right.

But none of it mattered. The jury didn't buy it; no smooth-talking mob lawyer with a ten-grand cocktail ring could erase the images of cannibalized nipples. They came back in 10 minutes; guilty as hell. Then it came time for Judge Soldana to intervene; he set aside the verdict. Just like the rest of the trial, this rare judicial event had nothing to do with a tortured confession or 4th Amendment issues. It was about 326 acres of prime Mendonesia forest with frontage on the Middle Eel River, title transferred to Tracy Thornbird, Soldana's wife's maiden name. The deal was struck in pretrial; Peebles walks, get a free ranch. Peebles was a nobody, but his uncle was top dog in the biggest Northern California meth cartel.

It wasn't exactly the Godfather but they managed to convince Soldana the deal was in his best interest; he could get thumb-tied, head-shot and buried in some quarry. Or he could retire in solitude, never to adjudicate another scumbag. It was a no-brainer. Men like Peebles always got caught another day. Plus, Soldana took bribes before, but compared to this they were small potatoes. So whenever he closed his eyes he saw blacktailed deer, wild turkeys and feral pigs, all within stalking range. He lost a huge block of hunting time, sitting the bench so many years. It was time to catch up.

While the cranksters gave him the ranch, it didn't mean they actually paid for it. A lawyer defended a murderer who couldn't pay the legal fees so he took the ranch. Then cranksters visited his home one night and persuaded the lawyer to sign it over in exchange for his life. Not very legal, but compelling nonetheless.

When he banged the gavel, all His Honor could see were rising trout, strutting toms and browsing deer.

Peebles was free to go. The judgment didn't astonish any bikers. As for the jurors? Flabbergasted. The DA ranted, hissed and threatened to bring motions. But protest has a short shelf life. It took just a few late-night house calls to quell the sanctimonious prosecutor; once he saw his family was vulnerable he didn't make any more waves. The world's chock-full of rats like Peebles.

Morris left court before the ruckus died. Arriving at his apartment, he looked over at the Say When. Sure enough, Officer Lock was a study in habituation. He decided to befriend him. Even a drunken cop ought to be full of opinions on dirty judges. Carver's prior murders were small hills, but a superior court judge was Mount McKinley. Carver cooked up the Crappie fillets, mercury and all, while plotting how to stage the next crime scene. Each type of enemy would have its signature. A mob hit was simple; one shooter, couple taps to the head, small caliber silenced weapon. Nothing would be taken. Most cops wouldn't waste resources trying to pin the tail on the donkey; the Mob's one bad ass to stick.

By contrast, cranksters would send a wrecking crew. They'd use sawed-off shotguns or machine pistols. There'd be massive bloody injuries. If anyone else were there, they'd waste them too; they just didn't give a fuck. The intent was to kill AND post a warning. They'd take liquor, jewelry, drugs, anything.

Victim's survivors might also kill a crooked judge. The killer would buy a gun for the task. There would be random bullet holes, owing to rage and lack of experience. Vendetta slayings were public statements from enraged, hurting people. They wanted more than revenge, they wanted their loved ones back.

He washed up and changed identities; Jimmy Ray Walker walked into the Say When to say hi. It was a typical vintage '70's lakeside bar. The bar took up one wall. The other held obsolete video games and shuffleboard. Fishing items hung on a net tacked to cork-board. A pool table stood on what once was a dance floor, but decades of spilled drinks, floods and puke stains reduced its status. The back wall held yellowed polaroids of past patrons with red noses and blurry eyes.

The place didn't stink as bad as JR expected; open doors at both ends let the afternoon breeze sweep away stale smoke and mold spores. He chose a seat two stools away and scanned Dan Lock, expecting the return gaze of a trained observer, but Lock's red-eyes peered straight into the mahogany. So much for the keen eye of the law.

The first free screwdriver unscrewed the blue wall of silence. Lock told about his formative years. He grew up back when life was good and girls were horny. A guy could fish in the morning, fuck in the afternoon and fight tourists at night, every fuckin' day, all fuckin' summer. There weren't any drugs or gangs or Aids to mess with a man's pursuit of happiness. Then Lock skipped over his two tours in Nam; no need to bore the free-spending stranger with his wartime addiction. Tough monkey to kick, heroin. He also skipped the part about shooting all those gooks for Uncle Sam. Instead, Lock led his listener to the Lake, circa '73. He shook off the dogs of war in time to note the passing of the torch; the lake had changed. Hard drugs spread like cancer. Wherever the Beast alighted, it pillaged. For a while it pillaged Lock too, until rock bottom, when he forced the dragon to spew him back out. After that, it was rehab and odd jobs for seniors in trailer parks. He earned his way with just a beat-up old pickup, rake and a weed whacker.

JR bought another round to keep Dan's lips un-Locked. Yes, Dan had seen hard times. But his labor put him in favor with the voters. He hadda squad car, badge, gun. Not bad for a burned out vet. He made his peace with the Beast flourishing around the lake. It was a horrible dragon, desperately in need of slaying, but Lock was just a tiny knight, too small to kill such a huge beast. Besides, the world didn't want to be saved; it worshiped the beast.

It was that very conflict which forced him to stare at the mahogany every night. You see, at his very core, he always had the heart of a lawman, but never knew it until they swore him in. So he stared at the crime wave, the captain of a tiny ship, watching the Tsunami coming. The only logical choice was to stick his head below decks and swill rum 'til the the wave passes. He didn't like being a drunken whore-cop, but it was better than whackin' weeds for ten bucks an hour; *maybe*. Still, those years at odd jobs gave him the only happy times he'd ever known, back when he made so many folks happy with just the sweat of his brow; ah, the good old days and the 3F's. Lock's rhetoric wore on, until Jimmy Ray said good night. Lock vowed that next time, by god, he would buy.

The next morning found Carver parked near the courthouse. The car came down the street doing 45 in a 25 zone. Nobody else would be so cavalier about speeding. Sure enough, it screeched to a halt, parked in Soldana's space. Carver drove off. At 4:30 PM, he returned, parking where he'd first seen the judge's car appear. Soon Soldana drove past. Carver tailed him for 16 miles. The judge pulled off the road and drove uphill toward the steep volcanic mountain backdrop; the paved driveway went practically straight up. He saw two mailboxes. One had sun-faded hand-painted letters; "Sheppard." The other was a magnanimous brick and mortar tower with anodized aluminum, embossed lettering; "160 Despina Dr." Morris drove off, secure in knowing that was the place.

That night, JR bought more screwdrivers; he queried Lock about Sam Sheppard, no relation to the infamous guy who chased a one-armed man... No, *this* *Sam Sheppard* was a good old boy; left Oklahoma during the dust-bowl. Grapes of Wrath kind of shit. Moved to California, picked nuts 'n row crops, bucked hay from Bakersville to Redding. By god, Old Sam could out-pick any fuckin' Mexican or Oakie ever lived. He bought that house with his wages. It was a helluva view, too; on a clear day, you could see the Pacific Ocean, by god.

179

The next drink hit Lock and he rambled faster; Old Sam would never sell out to developers who prey on oldsters, then flip it for ten times the price. Many a senior learned about lost equity the hard way. But Sam knew what he paid... 30 fuckin' years of stoop labor in the hot sun and cold fog; picked a barge full of fruit and nuts. Maybe two fuckin' barges. With sweat equity like that no fast-talking realty bastard would screw him. Back in his prime, Sam could out-fish, out-fuck 'n outfight anyone on the shoreline. He was the king of the 3 F's, by god. Too bad about his stroke, though; after that he turned bitter and reclusive. It was a hellofa shame.

Then Lock's bloodshot eyes turned a deeper, darker shade; "Nobody sees him much. Once a week he hobbles down for groceries and a shot o' whiskey. Then he limps back up to live alone. Well, almost alone... Soldana lives up there, too."

Jimmy Ray's radar turned on. He bought another round for the crimebuster; "Yeah, Soldana's one mean sumbitch. Big poacher, too. If you hear a rifle shot from that ridge, keep your yap shut! He only takes hindquarters and backstraps, then kicks the carcass into that ravine. You can see the bone pile from the lake, for chrissakes."

JR frowned; "No shit?"

"Yep... But who you gonna call, when it's the judge doin' the poachin'? What an asshole. No wonder his wife left hizzass."

JR could scarcely believe his fortune; Soldana lived alone. The locals were accustomed to gunfire coming from his place. His only neighbor was an old hermit. The icing on the cake had to be Soldana's personality. Arrogant and cocky, he probably didn't use a security system.

JR left the bar when Lock's face hit the mahogany. In the morning he awoke with a headache. The sun was almost up. He packed his spying gear. Driving up a wickedly steep driveway that was one ridge over from Soldana's, he found the perfect spot. He hiked downhill into the bushes. The scope looked down on the judge's house 500 yards away on the opposing ridge.

180

A wispy ribbon of pale gray smoke curled from the chimney, so the judge had embers from the night fire. Then it changed to dark black; Soldana must have tossed plastic into the stove. The prick didn't care about the ozone layer; it would be a pleasure to kill him. Moments later the garage opened; his car rolled down the steep road, snaking in and out of switchbacks, then out of sight, past an old house that had to be Sheppard's.

JR scoped it; no smoke, so the old fart slept in a cold house. Either that or he was dead. He saw a volcanic red line across the sere yellow meadow from the back door up to the gravity-flow spring. Right on cue, Sam hobbled out on his porch, pissed and started hobbling on the path. The killer turned the scope to 36X. In the last moments before sunrise, the cool air gave a crystal clear image without shimmer; Sheppard's left arm curled in classic stroke posture. His left foot dragged, kicking up lava dust. Just then the sun rose above the mountaintops, blazing every nook and cranny. It highlighted the airborne red powder, making it look like Sam's foot was afire.

Over the years, mice, wood rats and frogs had clogged his line. He detached the black hose and shook it, to purge bubbles or any dead thing. Once satisfied he'd have enough water to shave shower and shit, he headed back to his house. Dark blue smoke soon issued from his stovepipe. Twigs of dry Live Oak kindled, he fried up his traditional breakfast - Chock full of everything that was supposed to kill him, that same repast stood him well for seven decades; four bacon strips in his black cast skillet. Later, two eggs. A slice of Wonder bread went onto the hot stove top, for toast. It would sop the bacon grease. Then he added seasoned white oak quarter-rounds, which made great coals but little smoke. JR watched the smoke taper off. Clear heat waves shimmered above the stovepipe while Sam loaded the stove top with his usual dinner; a pot of Navy beans in cold spring water. By the time the fire died down, they'd be in full soak mode. Buttered tortillas and a shot of Scotch would cap his evening repast.

Jimmy Ray's scope swung back to recon Soldana's; no power lines, although they stood half a mile straight-line uphill. He spied the generator house over a small hill, with solar panels all over it; the array was easily worth sixty grand. He wondered which of his subjects offered him that bribe.

He scanned around for neighboring houses but saw only spotted game trails, cut into the steep, red hillsides. Except for rockslides or steep gullies barring their travel, deer took the most level route from one point of interest to the next. He panned one trail weaving in and out of the golden wild oats and Harding Grass; horizontal red dots made a line straight for Soldana's garden. JR didn't see a kennel, so the local deer could snack on the choicest greens without fear of dogs. It looked like he should be able to walk that deer trail and shoot Soldana... a little venison payback. It looked too good to be true, so he scanned the ravine closest to it. A trail of deer bones glinted in the sunshine. JR packed up his scope and left.

Next he searched public records for Soldana's remodel plans. It took an average citizen several months to get a permit, yet his honor's passed in one day. Special clout really yanked Carver's chain. The floor plan showed a huge central living space, bedrooms at opposing ends. Huge kitchen and pantry. The generator house to the southeast served multiple duties as a game-skinning & meat processing shed and last-ditch housing.

The killer thought about that shed; deer, turkey and wild pig trimmings had to get flushed downhill, rotted in the sun until buzzards got around to them. Late morning thermals brought the stench uphill, straight to the gen-house. It didn't take a genius to know that whoever stayed in it was lowest on the judge's ladder. Lastly, JR noticed the plans included a passive IR security system.

The killer drove home and went fishing. Cool waves lapping at the aluminum skiff and gentle summer breezes in his hair put him at ease. He fished and his mind idled. Since Jimmy Ray planned to attack when the judge was home, the alarm might not be an issue. He didn't think Soldana had motion sensors outside the house. He couldn't see him getting nighttime calls from the cops every time some scrawny doe triggered a motion-sensor.

His thinking was interrupted by a slow, steady tug. The fight lasted ten minutes before he netted a monster blue, close to 25 pounds. Big cats were muddy-tasting, so Carver let it go. The huge tail waggled slowly down to the bottom where bluegill eggs waited to be gobbled up.

Re-baiting, he wiped his slimy hands and went back to his reverie. He would go incognito next time, in case there were hidden cameras. Suddenly his line twitched twice and headed for cover. He played a large bull bluegill... Good eating, but he was fishing for ideas, not food. He tossed it back and pondered his weaponry choices.

The shotgun was a no-brainer; point, shoot, dead body. But it was loud. The night woods weren't always empty; poachers and wardens, even lovers might walk the night woods, not to mention dope growers. He played a nice bass and decided to kill the judge with a .22. So he had his approach path and weapon chosen. The last matter was time of death. He would kill him on a Friday or Saturday night, to offer some lag time before anyone noticed him missing. He rowed home, happy.

JR walked to the Say When for beer and popcorn during happy hour. Dan Lock heralded his arrival. "Jimmy Ray! How'zithangin'?" JR grinned; "Long and lean, full of mean, and *YOU?*" "My goose's loose an' full o' juice!" "Glad to hear it; just don't make me choke it!" Before it was over, Lock offered him a job as deputy. Knowing there was no such position didn't dampen the offer. They were drinking buddies. It gave him a thrill, being privy to cop-chat, on what would be his biggest kill. He could hardly wait to shoot the scum-freeing, bribe-taking, venison-

183

wasting bastard. He went home and checked his calendar; June 29, Wednesday. The Fourth would hit on a Monday. He spoke aloud, to himself; *"IF I kill him Friday, court won't miss him 'til Tuesday."* It had a patriotic ring to it; independence from the evil king sitting in his hillside castle, looking down on the peasants. It was perfect.

Friday night found him on the deer trail again. The locals had already driven to the valley, for parties and dates. He started walking the deer trail. Soldana's lights glowed orange from stored solar power. A big buck snorted and sprang up, kicking rocks down the ravine. Muscle memory trained the sights to align with the stag. It took five seconds to calm down. He looked nervously at the house, barely 200 yards distant. He couldn't hear generator noise, so the apparently the judge was running an inverter off his deep-cycles. He stalked within 50 yards of the house, then squatted to load his clip. Just then a yard light went on. JR sprinted for cover behind a tree. The judge walked a landscaped path, flopped back the whirlpool cover and flipped a switch. The generator hummed to life. Malibu lights came up, softly illuminating the walkway. Soldana grunted satisfactorily. He walked back into his house.

It was almost perfect; His honor would be a sitting duck in his whirlpool. The generator and whirlpool hum would cover the final stalk. Soldana came back out. One hand held a bottle and glasses. The other, a huge bath towel. He climbed the steps, dropped the towel and plunked unceremoniously into the Jacuzzi. Taking a small sip, he sighed and leaned his head back. The Malibu lights went off; the control freak had them set for just enough time to enter the whirlpool, so he could watch the stars in total darkness. Jimmy Ray flipped his night vision on.

Sadly, the deer trail didn't keep heading for the chlorinated spa, but veered for the garden. He had to cross 25 yards of crispy twigs and dry leaves. Alternately looking at Soldana and the ground, he inched closer. The night vision made Soldana's dome look like a full moon with

184

black crosshairs splitting it. The little rifle spat twice, making twin plops. Salvadore died so fast, he didn't let the bottle go; his fingers loosely wrapped around it. His head slumped to the left, as if trying to drain water from his ear. JR turned to leave, but a noise made him whirl. The door opened! He crouched and sucked his fear in. The backlight showed a world-class hooker. Except for an open robe, she was naked and incredibly sculpted. He wanted to fuck her on the spot. Instead, he had to kill her; bad timing for both of them.

Tawny strode toward her asshole client. He paid well and *always* had the best Pot, lifted from evidence. This weekend would net her six grand. She knew his kinks; they'd act like strangers in a hotel spa. It sucked, but the pay was too good to pass. Tawny slipped into role; "Oh, sorry, I thought I'd be alone... Oh well, mind if I join you?"
The judge didn't speak, so she thought; *"Oh, so he wants it quiet."* She let the robe fall, entered the spa and waded for the bottle. When the hooch touched her collagen loaded lips, two hollow-points touched her brain case. She never tasted the whiskey. But on the plus side, she wouldn't have to screw the arrogant bastard again.

Jimmy Ray walked down to them. The hooker's tits gave the illusion of life as they floated and jiggled in the whirlpool foam. The judge's left eye eight-balled. JR hit the trail. On the drive home it dawned; he forgot to police his brass, after the prostitute spooked him off his plan. But in a world where a million rounds of .22's were fired each week, the brand imprint wouldn't narrow it down much. There were extractor, firing pin and bolt face marks that matched his rifle, but first they'd have to find the gun to make a comparison. Clear Lake was one big-ass lake. JR was in the boat before sunrise. He dropped the bolt over the side. Then he drifted half a mile and sunk the barrel into the 'wetness protection program.' On July 4 a huge fireworks display showered the monstrous lake while 400 anchored boats and thousands of shoreliners gawked. Two people watched with dead eyes; they were way past enjoying it.

185

SOLDANA AFTERMATH...

Sherry Clarkson was more angry than worried; the asshole was probably in his yacht with some hooker. He should have had the decency to call. The docket was jammed with criminals. Or were they suspects? She never could get the distinction. Sherry had a backup judge en route, but given the holiday traffic on the twisting shoreline two-lane, that would take an hour. She took binocs up to the roof and scanned this side of the lake for his yacht, but no dice. She instructed a bailiff; "Rusty, please GO see what's up?" He nodded; "Sure, Miss Clark!"

"Thanks! Call me *ASAP, HUH?*"

"You got it." Larry Nord reluctantly drove to Soldana's hillside castle, which would surely piss off the judge. He parked on the only level spot, in front of the garage. Something caught his eye out back. They were so bloated, he thought they were party dolls slowly circling in the water. Rusty dialed Sherry; "Miss Clark? I'm sorry, someone killed him... and his female, uh, companion."

"**WHAT?** When? I mean, *that's terrible!*" He nodded into the cell phone; "I've got forensics coming up the hill; I won't be back for a while... sorry."

"It's OK. I'll get Ed to cover for you. Oh my God."

Soon officers swarmed the place like maggots. Every cop, sheriff and CHP drove up to view the hit. It reeked of mob; nothing taken, not even that bottle of top-flight hooch. Just two head-shot stiffs. The only clues? Six tiny brass hulls, readily available at any gun shop. They all suspected Soldana had his hands in so many pockets it would be tough to narrow down, even if they wanted to. So the law milled, took a last look and drove off. An investigation was pending.

186

INVESTIGATION...

Deputy Sheriff Lilly Ballou was tall and lean, with straw-blonde hair 'n sky-blue eyes... the kind that men get lost in. She could open men up with just a glance from those powder blue peepers; they'd tell her shit they wouldn't share with their priest, making her the perfect tool for interviewing people. Peeled paint flecks fell when she rapped on the sun-checked wooden screen door. She spoke loudly through the closed door; "Sheriff's Office, Mr. Sheppard; just need to ask some questions." Shuffling movements from inside, slow and steady, the kind she could trust. The door creaked. He stepped into the light and squinted at the sunshine highlighting her hair and peach-and-cream visage. He wished he was 50 years younger, for just an hour or two; "Morning, ma'am."

Ballou smiled a little. He grinned back. "Mister Sheppard, we..." He interrupted, while trying to straighten up and not look like an old stroke victim; "Call me *SAM,* honey; callin' me mister's like sayin' sir to an old boot."

Horny old bastards, they never changed; "*SAM...* we're investigating a crime at the Judge's; have you seen or heard anything?" He hadn't, but he dragged it out for all it was worth, while trying to store her beauty in his mind's eye; "Oh... what time did you say it happened?" "I *didn't.* Think back, to Friday, Saturday; do you remember any vehicles, sounds, things like that?"

"No Ma'am. Hell, tha's why I moved up here, sixt... *forty years* ago. It's quiet." He was seriously in need of a chat partner, but his eyes were clear and his voice hale, so she took him at his word. He tried to drag out the convo; "Soldana never has company, except his annual poker an' cigar bash; they were a pain in the you know what... Rich, drunk jerks, ever' dad-blamed one of 'em. Add 'em all up and you won't get a single hard day's work."

She smiled and tuned him out, but he kept going; Back in *HIS day,* blah, blah, blah... Ballou drove back down the hill. At the main road, traffic forced her to stop and look both ways. Then she saw the judge's mailbox and spy camera. The cable feed went into the dirt. She hung a

187

U-turn and drove back uphill, found the security system and played the tape. It was an old video loop, where newer footage taped over the older stuff, so all she got was a continuous river of squad cars. She bagged it; maybe forensics could raise something. Lilly went outside for fresh air, to think; the hermit hadn't seen or heard anyone, and he was a sharp old codger. That left one possiblity; the killer came from the woods.

Ballou grew up in Nebraska, hunting pheasants and whitetails. Many of those skills carried over into her work. She studied the deer trail and found a partial print, but the hardpan held no useable detail. The trail rounded the facing ridge 600 yards away. She drove down to the valley floor, took the next ridge road uphill and parked precisely where the killer did. She walked to the deer trail. Sure enough, a partial boot print put a glow in her gut. She turned to leave, then saw a lens cover in the trail. Lilly drove half a mile uphill to a spot wide enough and did a five-point turn to get pointed downhill, then rode the brakes back down to the main road, romped on the gas and headed straight for Ken's.

Ken Barrett sold most of the guns and ammo on the north shore. Lilly purchased her pistol and a fine little Berlinetta backup wheel-gun from Ken. She trusted him, as much as any man could be trusted. She walked into the musty shop and saw Ken grinning. Same shit, different man, but his fatherly ways made her comfortable; "Well Ballou, what can I do?" He liked rhymes. She held out the cover; "You can tell me what you know about this, Pops."
        "Well I'm no dope. It's a cover for a scope."
        No smile from the cop, so he quit rhyme-time and got serious; "Lemme see... hmm, it's for a spotting scope. Could be from half a dozen companies, Lilly."
        She wasn't prone to divulge information to civilians, but it might prime his pump; "I'm investigating Soldana's murder; found this on the opposing ridge. But *you never heard it from ME... Got it?"*

Ken swelled with privilege. "Ah, Soldana, my biggest customer, paid for MY *LIMO.*" She giggled; "You *still have* that piece of junk?" "Sure; can't get rid of it."

One day she'd teased about his old Dodge. The nickname stuck to the truck like cow shit on a hot rock; "Yeah, Soldana was one deer-killing sonofabitch; he'd take a few choice cuts, kick the carcass downhill. When I think of all that wasted meat, it makes me wish *I'D shot him.* Damn judges always think they're gods."

Lilly already knew that the wardens hated him because she used to date one. They called him the Sultan. They tried to put the heat to him once, but Soldana got even. He arranged to hear every fish and game case, then let every defendant go free. So they were forced to let the big fish go, so they could keep frying minnows, but they sure as hell didn't like it. There had to be a few wardens that would love to shoot the Sultan; "Can you narrow it down for me, Ken?"

He sniffed it; "Cheap plastic, could be Tadasko or Busharell but they're so common I don't know how to..." She didn't need to hear another dead end; "Yeah, that's about what I figured. Thanks, Barrett." They flirted for a few minutes, but the evidence part was over. No clues, except for a small bit of red rock dust wedged into the edge where it hit the trail, a metaphor for her case; total dead end, with just a tantalizing trace.

That night Ballou went to the bar; it was a cop's nature to conjure. But try as she might, she couldn't agree with the others about a mob hit. In her mind, the perp was a loner, good in the woods, outdoors or military type. He was mid-thirties and white. He had some disfiguring condition; a limp, stutter, bad acne, something. He had a low-status job, drove a beat-up American truck and lived alone or with an authority figure. Didn't have a steady woman. And he had a lousy relationship with his father. Judges were father figures; shots to the back of the head? Cowardly revenge acts.

She winked at the barkeep for another. As usual, it didn't take two winks. Then Lilly sighed with resignation. The official consensus was a mob hit. Soldana was dirty. Hell, there might even be dirt in the sheriff's office. Mob was into everything else, so *why NOT* the law?

Her report would fall through the cracks. While it was still open, it was as dead as canned mackerel. Still, a mob hit wouldn't normally include the hooker. Killing her would only dilute the message the mob liked to send. Lilly wrestled with it. Hell; she could wrestle all the way to the Olympics, but the case was still canned mackerel to her boss.

THIRTY TWO...
JR
(involuntarily)
GETS IT UP THE ASS

Jimmy Ray swilled lager and swapped jokes with Dan Lock. For a cop, he wasn't very curious. Of course, they paid him not to be. He'd take a drunken kid home, instead of jail. He was "Dial a Ride" with a badge. If some sloppy drunk started manhandling a waitress, he'd put in an appearance. But the Soldana thing? Out of his league 'n jurisdiction. Mob hit. End of story. Any more questions, he could only speculate. For the price of another screwdriver, he did; "Yeah, Soldana pissed off a lot of people. If it was *MY* case I'd start with parolees who were... *unhappy* with a ruling. Then I'd check vics' families."

JR nodded; "You're probably right, Dan, but..."

"Then and *ONLY then* would I fuck with the broken-nosed suits from Vegas... Damn right... *leave the wops alone!*" Lock rambled, while JR's mind ambled; from the sound, the Chameleon's camo worked again; the law still couldn't see the lizard on the log. He finished his beer and went home to plan his next murder.

The next judge on his list was a bad cocksucker. Honorable John Books of Tehaka County was as dirty as a man could get, taking monster bribes for favorable AG rulings regarding environmental impact and water rights issues. The vast majority of people outside of these issues didn't give a shit about them... Especially not the cops. Public apathy is perfect soil for corruption.

The judge ruled and the money flowed, keeping him popular with the largest farmers, the petrochemical and rice lobbies. It didn't win any friends among small organic farmers, sportsmen or anyone else living in the Green world. Books was bad for the ecology, but worse for endangered species. He already killed three salmon runs. JR loved salmon. Books had to go.

He drove to the Big Valley three times to scope out Books. Compared to Soldana's fit body and rigorous hooker-screwing, venison-poaching lifestyle, Books was just a slob with a job; he frequented low class strip joints and drank huge quantities of cheap bourbon. After the obese Books closed the same strip joint the 3rd time JR headed home. The greedy bastard would be easy to find.

JR's drive home brought the killer closer to the law than he ever wanted. He stopped along a desolate piece of Highway 20 to piss. Standing several yards down from the shoulder, he unzipped. Then suddenly a powerful spotlight shocked him so bad that he zipped up his Levi's and turned towards the voice; "You, in the ditch! Raise your hands!" The light blinded him. He stumbled up slope, mind racing; 'Where did he come from? The cop yelled; "Hands on hood! _spread 'em!_" "_Don't fuckin' move!_"
"Yes sir, officer, WHATEVER YOU SAY!" It was a damned desolate stretch of road. There wasn't a house or light for ten miles. Bana shined his flashlight in the vic's rig; no witnesses or weapons, just a telescope. He cuffed JR; "Are you alone, sir?" The unusual question stabbed the killer with fear. The cop didn't ask about booze, drugs, or weapons. Definitely unusual; "Yes, yes sir, I'm alone."
Bana turned him around to face the cop; "Do you have any weapons, needles or drugs on you?" Walker relaxed; "No, I don't use drugs." Bana heard it before. HE patted him down; "May I search your vehicle?" JR shrugged; "Go for it." But Bana didn't bother. He loaded the suspect in the unit and headed for a spot he knew well.

192

Inside JR's mind a time bomb ticked; he had murdered enough people to know he was toast. Instead of wasting time pleading, he searched for anything that might help. But there was nothing. NO use denying it; he was going to get whacked. Sure enough, several miles later the unit turned onto a dirt two-track heading into the hills. Weeds grew in the road, so it didn't get much traffic.

Bana drove three miles, then parked at a locked iron-pipe gate. He exited the unit and pulled JR out. Bana was a changed man. Falsetto voice queried strangely; "Oh, what we got here, some nice TIGHT PUSSY?" The baton rammed his solar plexus; lightning bolts of orange pain shot through his body. He doubled over. The next blow slammed the base of JR's skull. He went unconscious. In the netherworld he felt free, warm and blissful. He wanted to stay forever. He saw old friends, already passed away.

New pain brought him back to earth. He couldn't tell how long he'd been out, but it was long enough for Bana to spread him across the car trunk. JR's face mashed against the hot vinyl trunk mat. His abdomen bent over the edge of the trunk, legs spread wide... now he knew why cops liked the spread 'em position so much. Bana's dick was in his ass, banging like a pile driver. Pain came with every thrust. Bana chanted; "I'm rammin your hot, stinking PUSSSY, bitch. WHATCHA GONNA DO, WHATCHA GONNA DO WHEN I COME *IN* YOU?"

JR's feet flailed in the air with every thrust, then barely touched ground when the cop retracted his pelvis for another brutal push. JR's face kept slamming against road flares and an emergency kit. Only his hands cuffed behind him provided resistance. When Bana rammed, JR tried to scratch the rapist's abdomen. It worked; he felt warm, sticky blood. But instead of repelling the rapist, it just just turned him on; "yeah, bitch, scratch me...*you filthy whore!*"

The final thrust brought all the power the cop could muster. Bana came. The killer never had it in the ass before, but he knew what the hot liquid filling his ass meant. For a full minute Bana spurted and moaned his sick

193

mantra; *"Fuck... OH FUCK ME, momma. Oh momma..."* Then semen finally stopped flowing.

JR lay there, too whipped to do anything but cry. Even if he weren't cuffed, he couldn't have retaliated. His legs were gone. He had a dick in his ass, and if things kept going that way, he'd take a slug through the head and get tossed in a ditch he noticed on the way in. The way he felt, getting shot didn't sound so bad. He felt the dick shrinking as Bana withdrew it. He felt warm liquid dripping down his inner thighs. Thinking it was semen, he tried to take comfort; at least he managed to reject the rapist's cum. Only it wasn't semen, but a slurry of blood and watery shit. Bana turned him around, cracking his nightstick against his JR's left fibula. He cried out and collapsed onto the dirt. The pungent scent of dust and tar weed hit him, while star thistles stung his naked legs and balls. The rapist's voice changed again; "Get on your knees, bitch!"

JR looked up; Bana's dick swelled again, but it was small, compared to how it felt in his ass. That didn't scare him. The voice change sure did. Gone was the falsetto whine. A dark, husky voice with slow cadence proved the man had a third personality. This one wanted head... And maybe murder, too. "I'm gonna fuck your throat, deep and hard! Suck my cock and swallow it, bitch! Make me believe you like it or I'll shoot your cunt off!"

JR knew he would be stone-cold by morning. He ran through his options. He could suck and get shot. He could refuse and get shot. Or he could bite it off and maybe escape while Bana writhed in pain. The last option held promise, except he had no intention of sucking this pig's tool. Bana would have to kill him first.

But the trooper knew it; *they all* hated the sucking part. His baton caught JR's left temple. In a few minutes, JR regained consciousness, then opened his mouth and sucked like a lamb taking a teat. And that idea about biting his dick off? That went south, too; Bana was way ahead of him. He pinned his weapon to JR's temple; "If I feel a tooth I pull this trigger, cunt!"

194

The killer sucked while numbly noting the rhyme; a cop with a glock and a cock; Fortunately Bana came fast in oral mode while fondling his pistol. JR swallowed the tiny strand of goop, the majority of it having already been spent in his ass. Then Bana spoke in a light, nasal twang. He brought JR bottled water and a towel. He began petting him and soothing JR with small talk.

It was preposterous, but there was one glimmer of hope; at least the gun was holstered. JR surfed the ripple of hope like a monster curl at Maverick; he might live if he played the role of wounded victim. That part was easy. Soon Officer Bana shuttled him back to his vehicle. He kissed JR on the forehead, removed the cuffs while Jimmy Ray's photographic memory took the photos; Eric Bana, car 1377. For the two-hour ass-burning ride home he plotted some serious revenge.

The Judge Books could wait.

The next morning he drove into the Mendonesia National Forest. His ass burned worse whenever he hit a washboard, water bar, pothole or pine cone. Walker sympathized with rape victims everywhere.

Earlier he purchased the .243 short mag at Ted's. The stubby rifle had incredible speed. Whereas a normal 6-mm bullet would do 3000 fps, this one could hit 4000, making for low holdover and high retained energy. On the action perched a Soviet scope with star-gathering capability. Technically it was legal, but it was an assassin's scope just the same. At night he could acquire a target out to 800 yards in pitch dark.

The road snaked around switchbacks, offering various ranges from one ridge to the next. Placing targets at likely distances, he placed sandbags and aligned with the target at 405 yards. The earmuffs went on, he fed a 55-grain boat-tail hollow-point into the tube and nestled into the rifle. He rough-aimed, then squeezed the sandbags for final aim. He settled into his finest bench form; butt lightly against shoulder. Right palm on bag. Trigger finger only touching rifle. Left hand to front bag... heartbeat and respiration settle into rhythm. Make final aim; left hand squeezes bag to put crosshairs on bull. *Brush* trigger. The shot registered three inches low. Repeating with three shots each to the farther targets, he drove to check the groups. Under an MOA for all targets. Plenty good enough for shooting rapists.

From hacking the CHP's database, he knew Bana would work swing shift the next two weeks. He wrote many citations on two stretches of road; his favorite spot where he raped Walker, and a similar spot on 162; a rarely traveled forest road that climbed the rugged back way to Caravello. Only a few poachers, drunks and pot growers ever used that washboarded, avalanched, dusty trail.

By the time JR got to I-5 it was sundown. He drove 35 miles, checking every spot that might hide a squad car. He almost missed Bana's unit hiding under a billboard. JR drove 800 yards up into the foothills and found an overview. His scope made out the unit number on the roof, 1377. Somehow that triggered a taste he couldn't shake, that filth-covered cock. He gagged reflexively.

Soon the unit rolled after a lone driver in a second-hand beater. It was tough to focus while panning, until Bana pulled it over. After two minutes the car; apparently the driver didn't suit Bana's twisted taste. Then Bana headed north out of sight. JR turned on his scanner and settled in. Over the next hour, the evening thermals reversed, playing cool breezes back down the sun-baked King Range. There was the usual cop talk, about routine busts. He heard Bana twice, using the big boy voice, not the ass-busting whine or the husky fellatio dominator. Bana called for a dinner break. A half-hour later he informed dispatch he was back in service. Carver sensed Bana would strike when the moon rose; it seemed to turn him on more. 35 minutes later, 77 squawked; running a make on 162, barely three miles north and five west of Jimmy Ray.

JR made the distance in 8 minutes, just in time to see Bana's searchlight blast an isolated male. Walker drove past, but first showed the deferential brake lights, to allay suspicion; everybody taps brakes when surprised by a cop car. Bana was busy frisking, but not too busy to scrutinize the passing vehicle.

Walker went around the corner, then sped up to find Bana's other favorite pullout near mile marker 12.55, about 60 yards from an old dirt road heading south into the desolate foothills. He drove past and pulled off under some oak trees, then pulled the fuses for his lights. The squad car appeared and took the dirt road. When it went out of sight JR gave chase.

Bana idled up the two-track for two miles and stopped at a locked gate. By the time his falsetto rang in the terrified boy's ears, Jimmy Ray had sandbags on his hood and the assassin's scope powered up; he pressed the ranging button; "351 Y" According to his notes, his bullet would print two inches low. He decided to hold high on the torso; in case of a pass-through the victim wouldn't be harmed. True, the hollow-point was designed to frag, but one could never be too careful with innocent lives at stake. JR began taking up what little slack the trigger had.

JR saw one greenish image dragging the other toward the back of the unit. He watched Bana drape him over the trunk. The cop's backside blocked the view, but judging by his twitching gluteal muscles, Bana was really getting into it. JR's guts hurt for the kid. He wanted to shoot Bana right then, but he needed Popoff's hatred. So he would wait until the kid sucked it. Only then would he be an uncompromising ally with a common enemy. Of all the emotions, only outright hatred could be trusted to endure.

Ernie Popoff's dad was a successful rice farmer until a massive stroke ended his life at 46. Ernie had his own style of grieving; he had been out with his girlfriend, whom he'd just dropped off at her home, five minutes before this cop lit him up. Bana liked 'em when they still wore their girlfriends' perfume and pussy scent... and this scent was so strong that he wanted to rape the girlfriend too, so it didn't take long for Bana to spurt in the anal mode. It took less than a minute, but when JR's ass pointed up from the trunk it seemed like an eternity.

The cop pulled the kid from the trunk, then forced him to kneel down. The moon rose over the mountains, boosting his night vision. JR could almost count freckles on Bana' twitching ass. Bana whacked the kid on the head; apparently, Ernie didn't want to suck dick either. JR settled the crosshairs on the base of the rapist's neck. The sight picture settled into a gentle cardiac rhythm, swaying back and forth a few thousandths.

Knowing better than to try to hold it still, he timed the sway. Normally, this was when the thrill was the highest, but this was too personal for thrills. He fought the urge to just blast away. He pressed the trigger; one-twelfth of a second later, Bana's head exploded. The "KA-WHOP" reached JR two seconds later. Call it a nervous flinch or an inadvertent flier, the shot went high, putting 2900 foot-pounds of energy inside the calvarium. The night vision momentarily showed a light-green headless corpse standing there, before the exiting shock wave threw the body paradoxically toward the shooter. He fell supine in front of the confused kid on his knees. Ernie couldn't see Walker but made out a dim reflection; a windshield, maybe. Just then, misted bits of brain spatter began settling; a warm, drizzling fog of brain cells, bone shards and CSF. He was Bana's only victim to touch these bodily fluids.

Through the scope Walker watched the basketball-sized mist-cloud drift down, like cooling campfire smoke on a rainy day. He got in his car and started the long drive home. After five miles he replaced his fuses. Then he listened to the scanner, but it was quiet. Apparently there wasn't much crime going on, other than what Officer Bana committed. He turned off the scanner; he was entering the mountainous canyons, where it wouldn't catch any messages anyway.

He wished he could have done it slow; a bullet to the nuts, baton to the temples; drag it out for a week, long enough to get payback, but the logistics were impossible... abducting and torturing a cop? It couldn't work. So he had to settle for blowing the bastard's head off; he got to see the brain cloud sink to the earth. That was pretty cool. On the drive home, his ass didn't hurt so bad. Walker took some comfort when he thought of the boys he had just spared.

FALLOUT...

Ernest Popoff Jr. emerged from his cocoon of shock after the corpse quit twitching. He was naked from the waist down, bleeding from the ass, with a ring of watery shit and rapidly drying cum around his mouth. When the death sigh issued from Bana's body, nothing registered. But now he replayed it; the fucker's head just... exploded. It sounded like a bomb went off. Now there was a slick layer of cooling, slippery matter and glass-like facial bone splinters everywhere. It didn't make sense.

In spite of the recent tragic loss of his father and his mom's subsequent jump off the wagon, he was a good kid; won a letter for wrestling, kept a B average and managed to stay away from dope in a town that practically drowned in the shit. And for all that,all he had was a mouthful of shit and a heart full of hatred.

As if that weren't bad enough, he was alone on a dirt road that wouldn't see a car for days; but when they found him, they might think he liked cuffs and butt sex. What would his friends think? No way anyone would EVER know about it. Ernie turned his back to the corpse steaming in the moonlight. He felt for the handcuff keys. He assumed he had 10-15 hours before anybody drove that road. Unfortunately for the kid's dignity, it was more like 15 minutes. Just after the Chameleon turned off his scanner, a helicopter en route to Redding got the call. Dispatch had been trying to contact Bana, since his 'cop down' alert was ringing the hell off the switchboard. Officer Annette Laroquette knew Bana; he was probably humping this one particularly bony waitress, but he usually called in first, so Annette radioed the helo to check it out.

Lt. Jeremy Ballister gasped when the spotlight hit the scene. To avoid blowing clues away, he settled the bird amongst weeds and cow pies 140 yards from the scene. The closer they hiked, the more macabre it got. The cop was dead as a post. The squirmer? Naked, bloody and cuffed. His body was spray-painted pinkish-gray. He had his back against the cop and judging from his hurried movements, he was on drugs or just March-Hare crazy.

Ballister and his partner Susie Millicent flashlight-swept the scene, weapons drawn. The aerial scan already showed nobody else there, but survival habits are tough to break. She called it in. What they saw boggled the mind. Bana headless, in a twenty-inch circle of blood. The kid had fingernail scratches on his sides and abdomen. His ass and legs were covered in dust, star thistles and tarweed glue. Ballister un-cuffed and helped him put his pants on. He was rambling, but he wasn't on drugs. They re-cuffed, hands in front, then secured him in Bana's car. The real crime scene photos would come soon enough, but they took photos to cover their asses. They checked for other weapons, but only found Bana's right eye dangling by its optic nerve from the trunk return latch.

They found the right ear and a bit of scalp 15 yards to the west, dangling from barbed wire. Six yards east they found the left ear, attached to a major chunk of tempo-parietal scalp, like a leather-ish Frisbee. Aside from a few teeth reflecting moon-glow, the rest of the brain and face was just gone. They were accustomed to blood and guts, burns and death wails, but they never saw a man's brain turned to mist from a high-velocity rifle bullet. It forced Ballister to puke, but Sue hung tough. She would gag later, thank you very much in the privacy of her apartment. She hadn't risen this far by being frail on-scene. Then distant sirens wailed and lights flashed; one of theirs had been killed and that really pissed 'em off.

Ballister sprinted down the two-track, flashlight sweeping, to get 'em to slow down. He made 200 yards before the first unit blew by, airbrushing all trace from the dusty trail. Disgusted, he returned to the chopper while more units roared by, blasting away any footprints. He wondered why he even bothered.

They had a half-hour of fuel, so he gave her a tour of the mountains. Ballister tried to process it. He hated gays, but this wasn't about gays. It was about Bana using the badge to commit unspeakable crimes on civilians. His voice lacked authority; "Sue, What'll they do *about that*?" She looked sideways at the scrolling mountainside. It was a good question. Hell; it was *THE* question. Her partner didn't want an answer, but reassurance. His straight-arrow paradigm had just been rocked, big-time. How was she supposed un-rock it? The world was fucked up; cops were just as fucked up. The press circled high above with their snooping lenses, whisper-mode rotors and parabolic microphones. They got it all; squad car roof 1377, naked victim, headless corpse, all of it. She would let him sort it for himself; he was a big boy. The great white majority only saw what it wanted. Her first partner beat his suspects, all of which were black. It took just two months of that bullshit before she applied for a transfer, but by the time she left LA, her eyes were wide open on the good cop bad cop crap. When it came to gays, she'd seen cops treat 'em worse; at least they'd bust blacks. Just let a gay man say he'd been raped; they'd snicker. Then if a waspy co-ed made the same claim, swat teams would roll. The double standard was as obvious as it was repulsive.

So they flew along in silence. It would take a great spin doctor to turn this around for the Blue team. Well, they could start by catching the perp, then vilify him. It was a simple matter, too; toss him in a cell with monsters. Deprive him of food, water and sleep, brow-beat him for 18 hours without so much as a restroom break. Then a little media manipulation, a few leaks to rag journalists and the suspect was as good as convicted... But first they had to catch him. Based upon the crime-scene it might not be easy. She finally answered him the best way she knew how; "Partner, what do ya say *I buy, tonight?* Let's head for the barn."

"You got it..." The helo veered for the hangar and more importantly, The Shield, finest cop bar in Nor Cal.

A COP KILLER'S PROFILE

Detective Leonard Finch viewed the rural crime scene with grim curiosity. He'd seen stiffs in just about every scenario, but this? A red-light rapist or as he liked to call it, a "stop and pop". Finch checked the virtually headless stiff for clues. A Frisbee-sized flap of reddish clotty stuff stuck to the shirt front. He took a pencil and attempted to lift it. The pencil broke so he just grabbed it with his gloved hand and reflected it upward and back, to where it would have been if a skull were there to support it.

The flap was Bank's face. Or mask, as the plastic surgeons called it. Tiny cranio-facial shrapnel was blasted into the internal side, indicating extreme ballistic energy. So the suspect had special weapons training. He let the mask flop back down on Bana's chest, then went to the handcuffed teen with brain spatter all over. He looked like a POW victim.

"My name's Leo Finch." He uncuffed the boy; "Have you had a chance to take a piss or anything, since they put you in here?" Finch handed him wet naps; *"No?* Go there in the dark, OK?"

"Yes sir... Thanks"

Meanwhile Finch took a collection; he scrounged two donuts and a can of orange soda. The kid inhaled it hoping it would wash away the taste. He looked better. Finch began; "Mr. Popoff, may I call you Ernie?" "Yes sir."

"Good. Call me Leo. Now son, I know you had a bad time. We're gonna *TRY LIKE HELL* to keep anyone from knowing what went down here, *OK?"* The kid's relief was obvious; *"Thank you."*

Of course, there was no way it could stay quiet, but he needed the kid's confidence, so he sold his lie again; "That's right; NOBODY else needs to know. What you say *stays HERE,* OK? So, tell me what happened, starting when this DIRTY BASTARD pulled you over."

Ernie took the biggest breath of his life; "Well, sir, I uh, just dropped off my girlfriend... we been drinkin' beer an' makin' out on Gold Butte. You know that place?"

"Sure. I used to take my girl there, too."

"When I stopped to piss... uh, he put handcuffs, then took me... *here.*" His story stopped at the dirty part. They always did. Finch helped him through the nasty part, to put him in his debt; "And then he did horrible things and you couldn't fight back. He violated you... *right?*"

It felt better not having to say the ugly shit; "Yeah"

"Did he strike you, Ernie, with your hands cuffed?"

He sobbed quietly, pointing at his baton wounds.

"After he struck you, he RAPED you? You can tell me, son; I won't tell anyone."

Ernie bent forward to hide his face while he purged; "Yeah, *raped*... in my ass, my head was in the trunk... then he tried to make me suck it... but I didn't wanna... then he put a gun to my head; I thought he would kill me so... *I did... IT.*"

"It's OK boy, YOU DID FINE! *YOU'RE <u>ALIVE!</u>* What happened after that?" Ernie straightened up, relieved at the cop's ease in putting the filthy part in the past; "Oh, you mean *next?* I heard KA-WHOP and got covered in guts; then... I think I blacked out."

Finch got closer to the kid; "Ernie, this is *very important*; AFTER the WHOP? You remember a voice, car starting... *anything?*"

He started thinking clearer, after venting his shame; so, *THAT was it!* They didn't give a shit about ERNIE, they wanted whoever saved him. That made TWO cops he couldn't trust; "No I didn't hear a thing."

"Didn't you hear a gunshot?" It wasn't in his character to lie. Besides, Ernie didn't see how this clue could help the cops find his hero; "Yeah, I did." Finch needed this clue; "How long after the bastard's head popped until you heard the bang?"

"'bout a second, maybe two." Finch nodded; "Anything else?" "No sir. That's about it."

Leo called an officer to take the vic to the hospital, but Ernie didn't like being alone with another cop. Once the witness was en route with three cops, Finch assembled his crew; "OK men, this one's gonna get sticky. The press got wind, so let's catch the shooter." Someone in the darkness gave their feedback; *"Absolutely!"* Finch kept it going; "The witness said it took more than a second to hear the report. So our man made a head shot from 300 yards or more, in pitch dark. He's one dangerous son of a bitch. I'm thinking ex-Seal, Special Forces, someone like that. He let the kid live, so maybe our perp's a prior *VICTIM…*"

He waved his arm around, although they couldn't see it; "I spy THREE spots for our shooter; two in that pasture, one on the rise in the road about 400 yards yonder. But since we've had so much traffic, I doubt we'll find anything on that one; Hobbs, Meeker? Check 'em out, pasture first. We might get lucky."

Somebody handed him hot coffee; "He used the terrain and knew how to pick his spot. Maybe the helo will spot a set of headlights going away, up in the forest; maybe he's gone rural and remote. Hell, I would... Daniels, Aguilar? Check out every gun shop in 200 miles. Nobody gets that good without burnin' some serious ammo. Check surplus stores, online shops; see who recently bought night vision."

He sucked half of the coffee down; "Riggs, Burke... Go through Bana's arrests, cell phone logs, for white males 19-35, stopped in the last few weeks. This man don't strike me as the kind that put offs revenge too long."

He killed the coffee; "Ok, *let's get cracking!"*
Finch had caught professional killers twice before, but both times the bastards got off. He wasn't too hopeful this time would be different, but when the brass looked, he wanted them to see he'd been trying.

Soon Leo learned about Bana; had an expunged record as a minor. Despite the judicial seal, Finch's team managed to uncover the story by interviewing childhood friends, siblings and neighbors. Gossip is a twisted vine, but it roots in partial truth. For background work like this, gossip was good enough.

Bana's sister was the source of most of it. The boy liked to light fires. He was mean to animals; torturing cats was a favorite. When it came to the topic of rape, her body went rigid. Apparently, he loved incest as much as he later loved raping boys. He had also been a bed wetter. The expunged records were for a stint in juvenile hall for arson, if one could believe a girl who'd been habitually raped by her little brother. She rubbed her wrists while telling; apparently Bana loved bondage from his youngest days. That is, until the hollow point bullet cured him.

Finch whistled softly, contemplating the hallmark of the sociopath, the classic triad linked with serials; bed wetting, animal cruelty and fire starting. A man like Bana could saw off someone's head at breakfast and pass a lie detector test at noon. To burn an uncle to death, rape a sister or order a cheeseburger were all of equal emotional valence. That was what made spotting them so difficult.

Bana's CHP service record showed he was written up four times on his first stint near Barstow, for undue force. He shot an elderly woman. Apparently gramma was a gun-toting meth head. Either that or Bana planted a gun. No matter; her prior bad acts swayed the inquiry. Bana was cleared, then transferred to Alturas. The brass figured less traffic meant less trouble, so they put him in the loneliest chunk of northern California. Then several unprovable complaints surfaced from young women traveling alone. He was ordered to undergo psychiatric examination; the shrink quickly pronounced him cured. But Finch saw through the smoke; shrinks were hopeless optimists, forming their opinions based upon self-reporting... sociopaths are the best self-reporters of all. Leo recalled the convicted serial killer, Ed Kemper; passed a psychiatric evaluation while having female body parts in the trunk of his car. Later Ed allegedly took the parts out, had sex with them and buried them. So yeah, sociopaths could sing any song a shrink needs to hear.

After Bana's time with the shrink, his record went suspiciously clean, which led Finch to conclude that's when Bana switched to young men, who were less likely to report such a crime; latent homophobia would see to that. Apparently Bana stumbled onto the perfect victims. Then he was suddenly transferred again, with a large raise in pay. Hell, they even gave him a medal for a routine car crash rescue. Plenty of cops performed greater things without getting medals. Maybe Bana found a bigger pervert or uncovered some leverage on a higher-up. But whatever the reason, his paper trail left no more spoor.

The more Finch read, the more he hated Bana; he was the kind of asshole they were supposed to arrest, not hire. Finch wanted to buy his killer a drink, but instead he had to catch him, which wasn't turning out to be so easy. The problem wasn't a lack of leads, but too many. Thousands of night vision units were sold to swat teams, fish cops, border patrol and forest rangers. His guts repulsed at the thought; the perp MIGHT be a cop. He hoped none of his crew bought any night vision units lately.

Leo's other problems were just as daunting. The ballistics dudes had only a few tiny jacket shards having spectral qualities similar to bullets made by High Mountain or Horatio. Those factories cranked out millions of rounds a month. He closed the file and took a slug of bourbon. He might catch this guy. Then again, he might win the Super Lotto, fly a Raptor and get a blowjob from a supermodel, all on the same day.

THIRTY THREE...
THE CHAMELEON
SHEDS A TAIL

JR got home just as the sun rose over Clear Lake. He hurried his gear inside before waking neighbors might see him. He fought the urge to puke; shooting the cop was the biggest rush yet. He took a shot of vodka and tried to think. Panic is the handmaiden of failure. First order of business? Calm down. He tried to think about the clues he had left. His father suddenly haunted him; if Howard were on the case, Vincent would be terrified. The old man had talent for seeing what wasn't there. He could only hope these dudes weren't as good.

The right cop would the see the long range, twilight head-shot as the work of an experienced assassin. Since Carver left a witness alive, a cop would see a vendetta scenario. He might connect the dots. With each additional clue, the right cop might see someone more like Vincent Fuckin' Carver. He decided immediately; Jimmy Ray Walker HAD to die. Just as a lizard leaves its twitching tail behind to distract predators, the Chameleon would leave JR's body... they'd wrangle it, thinking they had something. By the time they grew bored with the twitching tail, the Chameleon would be growing a new one. He polished off the vodka and fell asleep.

MEET FRANCES...

Two weeks after Bana the rapist got killed, Jean Paul Le Clerc strolled into the Blue Lagoon, his 4th gay bar of the evening. He had scoped out so many queers... they began to have the same face. He ordered a Manhattan. The barkeep mixed it and handed it over; "It's on me, luscious; I'm Lance."

JP reflexively twitched; Lance... *Lance*... hadn't he killed a Lance already? The asshole with the Porsche; yeah, that was it; "Lance, thank you. I'm Jean Paul." The drink was perfect. Halfway through the Manhattan, the right boy walked walked through the doors. He looked so much like Jimmy Ray that Jean Paul almost spit his drink. Judging from how the locals reacted, the mark was a stranger; traveler maybe, en route to Portland, Weed or somewhere equally exotic. JP jumped on him before anyone else could; "Say amigo, buy you a drink?" Frances with an 'e' Bottoms smiled a toothy one; "Honey, you can buy me *anything.*" Frances worked fast; too fast, maybe. JP wondered if he was Vice. He scanned Frances quickly; same height, weight. True, Frances was slightly younger, but that wouldn't matter when they found the body.

There was one minor step before he could abduct Frances; make sure he wasn't undercover Vice; they loved to sting gays. JP heard that cops couldn't entrap suspects by exposing their genitals. He wasn't wild about touching another man's tool, but after sucking Bana's shit-covered hard on, merely touching one should be kids' stuff. He reached under the table and petted Frances' crotch. The kid was already getting hard. Frances moaned a guttural moan and whipped it out. He was hung like a donkey, and twice as eager to show it. JP jerked his hand back quickly. He came up with an excuse to keep his cover;

"I'm sorry... it's just... I'm rebounding; I started *that relationship* too fast, also! *When will I ever learn?"*

The cock tease worked like a charm; Frances had a glazed look, a world class hard-on and sitting right next to him was the hottest place to put it; "Why don't we go talk about it, say, in the *men's room?*" But Jean Paul knew it couldn't be the Lav; too many witnesses eyed the new meat; "Too tacky. My place. I have *great weed...*" Frances packed it back in his pants; "I'll just go to the little boy's room; be right back." The stud strutted while patrons ogled. With all eyes on Frances, JP quickly spiked his drink.

Two hours' drive found the lovers in the mountains surrounding Stormyford. Technically, they weren't lovers. One was an unconscious gay hunk; the other, a ruthless killer. He parked Bottoms' roadster on the hilltop where Jimmy Ray Walker's beat-up truck already waited. He left it there earlier and hitched into Sacramendota to troll for the mark. The pocked up two-track serviced only ranchers and teenage lovers needing secrecy, so nobody ought to be on it this time of night. Still, he worked fast.

Frances started coming out of his stupor. His eyes widened. Earlier, he'd imagined having his tight prick inside Le Clerc's gorgeous ass. Instead, Frances was taking it figuratively in the ass. His mouth was full of blood and he was missing some front teeth; it was tough to tongue-count, due to the roofies, the blood and fear.

Le Clerc *had* worked fast, since he didn't know how long it would take to pull teeth and cut off fingertips, so he started while Bottoms was out cold. It took just one tooth before he got the hang of it; clamp the locking pliers, twist, torque; piece of cake. Then he spotted his flaw; nobody lost all their teeth in a car crash. Wedging the jaw open with a thermos cork, Le Clerc lit the bloody mouth with a flashlight; he quickly jotted down Frances' restorations. It would be smarter to change virtual teeth than remove the real ones. Just then, Bottoms began moaning. Le Clerc forced a bottle into the mark's bleeding maw; "Take a big gulp of this, honey. It'll help with the pain. Forgive the play on words, but... *BOTTOMS UP!*"

210

Frances tried to process; denial, rage and desperation wrestled while whiskey burned his bleeding sockets. He sucked it down, blood, clots, whiskey and all; if he really were getting killed, he sure as hell didn't want to feel it coming. He had always been a coward, which strangely comforted him; there wouldn't be any last minute heroics or negotiating. He sucked whiskey like a gorgeous, hard-bodied sailor. He couldn't wait for the juice to deaden his senses. Le Clerc gagged him, then placed a plastic gas can in the cab. Seeing that can changed Bottom's opinion; no amount of whiskey could dull such primal fear.

Satisfied that everything was in place, JP turned on the ignition and wedged the gas pedal down with a tire iron; "Sorry, Frances, but you shouldn't trust strangers in bars... *It's dangerous, honey.*"

The killer shifted into drive and tossed the cigarette in. The truck made 25 yards before vapors found the cigarette, turning the truck into a Malotov cocktail tumbling down the ravine. But he hadn't planned on the fire's rapid spreading, due to the perfect blend of fuel, heat and air at the bottom of the brushy ravine. He barely had time to race Frances' roadster down the mountain as the yellow and orange monster grew in his mirrors.

Inside the cab Bottoms had no more problems. The first few tumbles dislocated his jaw and forced the gag from his mouth; one might have viewed that as a good thing, if not for the flames charring his lungs. He flailed around, banging into melting vinyl, dripping foam and busted safety glass. Fortunately, he died when the rig slammed into the rocky bottom. Hissing, sizzling and popping, the corpse combusted eagerly.

Ironically, Bottoms made a louder protest dead than alive. As for his physical features, they went up in smoke, commingling with other smokes from dry brush, grease-wood, poison oak and conifers, creating a huge flume of burnt Sienna, heathers and browns. Frances would've loved the colors. After all, he was an Autumn, honey.

AFTERMATH...

The bombers were the first line of attack for most California wildfires. Two Grumman S-2A fire-bombers performed flawlessly, dropping royal blue retardant right on the money. The pilots took their clues from the OV-10 circling high above, monitoring weather, air traffic and anything else that might be an issue for the bomber pilots; they had their hands full. They flew into shit that other pilots were trained to avoid. They flew heavily loaded planes at near-stall speed in tar-thick smoke, within scant feet of mountain walls, in ass-kicking superheated updrafts where mid-airs are likely. To top it off, they had to be accurate; missing a drop by two seconds meant another run to cover the miss. With only three passes, the bulk of the Frances fire was out. The pilots headed for the hangar to reload and await the next call to protect California's tinder-dry hillsides.

Hiking from one smoldering ember to the next, ground-based fire crews discovered the carnage. The coroner's team arrived later. Half-walking, half-rappelling, they knew long before hitting bottom that there was a charred body in the truck. The coroner watched with disdain as the bag of brittle remains banged into rocks and root-balls as it slid up the wall. He hated working on burned remains. No matter what he ate afterward, it always smelled like charred people-burgers. Before leaving, he removed the license plate from the truck... or at least, the part that hadn't melted.

RULE-OUTS...

Detective Finch perked up when he heard; some DB found in a fire MIGHT be the man he was hunting. One James R Walker, formerly of Lucien. Daniels and Aguilar found a gun shop owner. The suspect used to buy ammo there. Finch's crew backtracked the lead to Ted's place. According to the owner, hella nice worker, smart 'n *QUIET*. Ted was truly sorry to hear the news of JR's death.

Finch drove to the Temaha County morgue and flashed his badge; an assistant ushered him down the hall, offering Vapor block as they walked. Finch declined. He'd seen plenty of stiffs. Besides, he hated that shit. They split the swinging doors; charred fat stench blasted him. Finch eagerly smeared the goop under his nose. The coroner shook his hand; "You Finch? Call me Arny... Wanna see the stiff?" "Please." "Follow me."

They walked past three normal stiffs to a twisted heap of remains, which looked like rack of lamb that stayed on the grill too long. The long sinews winched the spinal column into a partial, tortuous coil, like a charred Anaconda. The head lay next to the burnt snake, having snapped at the China-glass Atlas while sledding up the canyon wall. Finch felt his legs go loose at the thought of being burned alive. Arny didn't notice; "Sorry; we don't have much. No prints obviously, but I extrapolated from the femur length; height's right. The license plate's a partial match to your man, too. DMV said he was the current owner. That's about it." Finch hated impasses. The remains could be *ANYBODY*. He shook Arny's hand and left. Meanwhile, Leo's cyber-hound gained ground; db's teeth matched Walker's cyber records. That was good enough for Finch. He closed the case. There was no use wasting manpower. Odds were good that the db was Walker. Hell, there was no way to prove otherwise. After chilling for 3 weeks the remains were summarily cremated since Walker had no kin. The irony wasn't lost on him; the state finished the job that fire started.

MEANWHILE, A D.D.S PINES AWAY

Frances' newest lover grew increasingly worried; they'd met in San Diego. Ah, the whirlwind romance of vacations, blissfully full of promise yet too short to discover a routine flaws. When seminar ended he begged the stud to come with him. But first Frances had to sever ties at home, so Biff returned to Port Angeles alone. They emailed and chatted constantly, *at first*. Then Frances' messages started sounding trite. And now, no chat. Biff's sense of rejection gave way to growing dread. He tried to file a missing hunk report, but the local cops didn't give a shit about some fag's lover; the brutes didn't conceal their contempt, either. Then he phoned San Diego PD. They couldn't do much. After all, Frances wasn't his kin, wife or partner. For all they knew, he could be in Vegas right now, blowing gamblers. Bottoms wouldn't be the first one-night stand to jilt a conventioneer.

Biff uncorked an Anderson Valley Chardonnay. After two glasses he could see it from the officers' point of view; after all, he *HAD* jumped into bed rather quickly with Frances. Biff vowed it would be the last time for that. Young men were too fickle. Next time, older lover, definitely. And speaking of next times, it didn't take long. Within a week, Canard was too busy to call cops about anything; he met a luscious young man, a patient, actually. Coincidentally, he just happened to develop his jaw problem from sucking cock too long. Sometimes the world can be so very... *perfect*.

THIRTY FOUR...

THE LIZARD FLIES

At first Jean Paul drove away from the raging fire at mind-numbing speed; the nimble little roadster handled like a wet dream. Then he slowed to 45, normal speed limit for the country two-lane to Williards. He pulled into an all night gas station. It wasn't easy changing clothes inside the Beemer, so he swapped shirts, then exited, changed pants in the darkness, then went inside to wash off any blood.

The cashier's clothes and mood were undeniably Goth, under a polyester logo polo shirt; nose pins, tongue stud, with a tattoo of dragon-claws reaching up from her fleshy cleavage. He couldn't help thinking the Goth bitch might like seeing the bloody clothes he'd just removed. She didn't look when she gave him the key, chained to a small baseball bat. He washed up, then headed north to refuel at a mom & pop where big brother's spy cams weren't likely to spot the stolen roadster.

True, it hadn't been reported stolen, but it paid to be paranoid about small details. He headed north toward Moreford, barely across the border; borders were good for jurisdictional slippage. Parking the sexy roadster in a mall parking lot, he wiped it down, left the keys and started hitching. The first dozen vehicles drove right past. One driver hollered; hitchhiking from the freeway was illegal, didn't he know? Do-gooders always assumed that a man actually wanted advice. Carver breifly fantasized about killing the nitpicker. Too bad he didn't pull over.

215

At 500 yards, its slight deceleration was barely noticeable, but he could spot a ride like a hunter learns to spot which ducks would decoy. The Ford pickup came to rest 20 cautious yards short of the hitchhiker. It paid to stop and eyeball 'em; some stunk like truck-stop whores. Others were beggars, interested only in getting inside to tap their sucker; those bastards never made eye contact. Times sure change. Back when Ray was young a man always picked up hitchers, as normally as waving from your porch. If not for Ray's underlying good nature, tinged with a bit of loneliness, he would've been number 13 driving past the man.

This kid was aware of the scrutiny; he turned completely around for the visual frisking. Ray saw no weapons. He got out and pointed at the rear of his truck; "Put your bag there; watch out for those wings. Where you headed, son?" Distracted by the unexpected cargo, Carver went blank; "Oh, north. I got friends near the border. And you, sir?" Ray noticed the dodge; most people mention a city, not a direction. Still, he had a good haircut and didn't stink; "Going to an RC float fly. Name's Ray." Carver shook his hand; "I'm Ted Morgan. Sir, what's *RC*?"

It felt good to hear 'sir'; "Aw, just call me Ray. RC's a buncha old coots flyin' radio controlled planes off a lake." Ted got the full Monty on toy planes. First of all, you don't call 'em toys; they were were built to tighter standards, had lighter wing loading and higher power-to-weight than 'real' planes. The kid didn't seem to grasp it, so Ray explained; "You know, every full-scale pilot on my buddy box says it's *harder* than flying REAL planes. I don't know why they act so surprised; I mean... *Driving's* a piece of cake, but imagine you're driving a car that's 400 yards away; you'd have trouble. Well, that's two dimensions and you can stop if you get mixed up. RC planes will do 90 in three dimensions and when you make a mistake, you can't stop, *you crash!*"

Ted grew bored. He drifted back to the Bottoms kill; it brought him guilt. Frances burned to death, purely to end one of Carver's identities. Frances' only sin was typical of the young and arrogant; he assumed he was bulletproof, at the top of the food chain. The killer got honest with himself and quickly pinpointed the guilt as if it bobbed to the surface like a floating head; it wasn't about the burning, but his need to end a perfect identity like JR Walker. A perfect chameleon *shouldn't have to* leave twitching tails behind. He tried to assuage his tension by watching the scenery pass by. Traveling Oregon was a study in repetition; climb a summit, descend, repeat.

They neared the lake at dusk. Ray pulled over, two miles from Lake Le Sac; "Say, don't take this wrong, but if you got no place to stay, you're welcome in my camp." It would be good to sleep in the woods, but he didn't want to get known; "Thanks, Mister Mar... I mean, Ray. If it's all the same, could you drop me at that motel?" "Sure... If you run out of things to do, why not come to the lake and watch us old coots fly? Most of my buddies have granddaughters!" The old fart smiled a creepy smile; he still had some gas in the old tank. Ted took out his duffel, carefully avoiding the toy planes.

The room had a bed, TV, rusted galvanized shower stall with roll-painted white latex over the rust. Across the road stood the only greasy spoon for three summits. On the door was a flier for the float fly; apparently it was a big deal for this one-flea town. He ordered their best steak. After that, it was back to the Hokie Hilton for a night's sleep. He awoke early, surprised to see the sunrise. Before he realized it he found himself hiking to Lake Le Sac. The rough pavement woke up his feet; it saw snowplows in winter and log trucks in summer. There were cobblestone pieces of asphalt hodge-podged with coldpatch-embedded pine needles, chipmunk parts and big strips of bark that flew off from Sugar Pines garroted to the rigs with chain binders.

217

The acrid smells of Mountain Misery, pine resin and acorn dust commingled inside his nose. Soon he was spotting animals like a hungry aborigine; sparrows, Stellar Jays, camp robbers and chipmunks were everywhere. By the 2nd mile Ted's body came alive. It had been a long time since he hiked with his good old 'shroom fiend, Waldo. Ted saw a sign; *"Airplanes on the lake"*, but didn't need it. The drone of a toy plane rang through the pines like a mosquito on meth. Half a mile later he made the lake.

They could have seen action in WWII. Old farts sprightly jaunted to and from their vans, temporarily forgetting bad hips and arthritic backs. They carried planes, support gear and portable shade structures. The energy, reminiscent of old time revival shows. Everybody smiled, the sparkle anticipation fresh in their eyes, contagious as sin itself. But what surprised him most was his welcome. Ray promptly showed him off to his buddies like his long lost son. They shook his hand. Nobody treated him that way before.

Some old coot, Leon, was a tail gunner during WWII. He gave the kid donuts and coffee, while offering him a 'ride'. Before he knew it, Ted stood at the shore. Ron and Leon synchronized transmitters while Ray fueled the plane. He read the label; 15% nitromethane, 20% oil, 65% methanol. Ray gave him ground school; "Pull the right stick, the plane climbs... push, it dives." It wasn't quite that simple, but with Ron on the box, there was no need to give him the "reverse input when inverted" lesson; "Move it right, right wing drops, 'n vice-versa." No need to bother him either, with 'reversing commands when plane comes AT YOU; "Pull LEFT stick, engine slows. Push, motor speeds up. Move it left or right, it yaws same way." The killer grunted; "Uh-huh." Ray nodded; "OK, let's fly this turd!" Leon chicken-sticked the prop; she burped to life. Ray put her in the water. She idled past the no-fly buoys. Meanwhile, Ray kept cluing him; "Ron's flying now; when he says 'You got it', start flying!" Ron trimmed the plane; "You got it." It sounded easy when the Telemaster was a static model, but at fifty miles per, it was hardly static; the eight-foot plane rolled on its back. Before it could crash, Ron saved it; "I got it...That's OK, everybody does that; Make smaller moves. *You got it.*" He gave it too much elevator; the bird stalled and spiraled; "I got it. That was *almost* perfect. Smaller moves. OK, you got it."

Determined to get the stupid fucking plane under control, he kept trying. Finally he started having fun. Ron spoke; "We're almost out of fuel… It's time to land. I got it."

Ron greased the water landing and taxied the nine-pounder back; "You did great; I only had to save you nine times!" The kid felt bad; "OH, that's bullshit, but thanks." Ron shook his head; "No, really. See that fat guy flyin' that big Cub? I had to save him 24 times!" The kid sat down at the only picnic bench clear of planes and support gear; "That was way harder than I thought!" The old coots tried to get him to fly again later, but he could only handle so much tension. By the end of the day his head spun. Clearly, RC would be an engaging field, if killing people lost its appeal.

Ray kept a spare sleeping bag in the truck; wasn't gay, just lonely. They stared at the fire while talking planes, pussy and politics. That's what appealed about these fanatics. They were so unlike Carver's dad. He slept like a lamb. The next day was a repeat. He saw crashes; some, from radio failure, deadstick or pilot error, aka dumb thumbs. Each crash was seen as an opportunity to build a new plane. After dinner there was a raffle, then handshakes. It was goodbye, it's been fun, see you next year; but for some of them, there wouldn't be a next year. The old guard wasn't getting any younger. Ray gave him a card; "Look me up, if you're in my neck of the woods."

"Oh, I sure will. Thanks, Mister... ***Ray***"

When he read the card his eyes popped out. *"Ray Marks, Silver Eagle Air Force, Hidden Crest, CA"*

Disney had it right; it's a small world, after all. The killer took off immediately.

219

THIRTY FIVE...

HOMEWARD

Halfway through his Denver Omelet, his ride walked through the doors. He was hauling lodgepole to Bakersville, 850 miles south. Lord knows he was glad to have company for part of the trip. Boredom was a tiresome companion. When the truck fired up, so did Sam; "Them cops got a keen eye for my logbook. Just last week, I forgot to enter my sleep time. It looked like I drove for 18 hours; cost me 1100 bucks! Wellsir, back in the day, Smokey mighta been reasonable, but after 911, it's just an excuse to be Barney Fife with a nightstick, every cussed one."

It wasn't company so much as an audience he wanted. That worked out fine since Carver didn't have a cover story ready. The babbling trucker never let the conversation stall. They saw Mount Shasta. The Kenwart caught tall gears on the downhill southbound. The faster the rig rolled, the faster he talked, as though his tongue were meshed with the drive train. Lake Shasta tempted him. His voice sounded far away;

"Before I got married, lord knows I caught a lot of fish. Drank a lot too. But after I hit rock bottom it's been all good. Got me a new woman, treats me fine, even if she don't like me to fish."

"Really?"

"Now days I drive too much, but back then... there's this one inlet, reaches up the tributary as far as the laws of gravity allow a lake to reach upstream. It narrows down to three feet wide about 900 yards up that canyon. Lord knows, it's peaceful."

221

"Yeah?"

His eyes glazed; "I'd shut the motor off 80 yards out; the boat would drift while I got ready; threaded worm, number six snell, single split shot. I'd ease it over the side. Then, you gotta watch that line; The bait should fall a foot ever four seconds... but if a fish takes it on the drop it falls slower. Or it might stop. Or it might twitch... or straighten out. *Dead giveaways;* **fish on!** Gotta watch that sink rate, lord knows."

"I guess so; I don't fish much."

Sam didn't notice; "Bluegills hit with a single twitch, then two, then swim for cover. Crappies suck it in but don't move. Tough to tell. Black bass are easier to tell, lord knows; one twitch, 'n *wham!* Smallmouth now, there's a fighter. Them smallies just blast your worm like a Jack Dempsey left hook, Lord knows."

"I never caught a smallmouth."

"Best pound for pound fighters; lotta respect. Now, a catfish just drags your line out to deep water like a tractor." Sam's eyes squinted and his vocal cadence slowed; "Then there's trout; never can tell with them moody sunsabitches, pardon my French. One day they'll pound yur worm; next day, barely tickle it. Damned trout... moody sunsabitches, pardon my Fre..."

"I don't like trout either."

"Then there's Squawfish... buncha bait stealin', croakin' slimy little bastards. Even Carp are better 'n those damned Sacramendota Pike."

"I never caught one of *them*, Sam"

This, he heard; "Ya ain't missed nothin'. Of course, details matter... Them fly-fishing purists joke about worm fishin' bein' so easy. It looks simple, but if ya overlook one detail ya get skunked, without ever knowin' why."

"Details; yeah, I know what you..."

"Take your HOOKS, for example; I used ONLY Number Six Hawk Claw Snell short-shank bait holders. A bigger hook sinks too fast, smaller ones go deep in the throat. Kills fish and wastes time."

"Bad to waste fish, huh Sam?"

"For bait, I ONLY used Canadian crawlers purged in corn meal. Some bait farms pack 'em in newspaper; the soy ink makes 'em smell unnatural, kills bites... ya get skunked and never know why..."

Carver nodded; "Yeah?"

"Then I'd use Beerkilly six-pound extra-limp castable for a natural sink rate 'n high surface visibility. If ya don't have a natural sink rate you're losin' bites. A man's gotta watch that line, lord knows. Then splitshot; from ultra tiny to #4, but most of the time I don't use any; them fish love a natural sink rate, lord knows. Anyhow, the terminal tackle matters plenty; worm fishin' is plagued with pitfalls, just like any other kinda fishin'"

By the time Sam came up for air, Mount Shasta was in the mirrors; the grand gem of the valley steadily shrank in size, but not intensity. If anything, it concentrated, much as drying fruit concentrates flavor. The snowy white peak had a French Vanilla corona, thanks to 85 miles of suspended pollen and forest fire smoke. And still the peak dominated the backdrop.

Sam the fishaholic droned on. For a man 'on the wagon' he sounded about one bass away from a relapse. He steered with his knees and poured coffee from a dented old stainless Stanley; it had as many coffee stains as his teeth; "Sam, that's an old thermos..."

"Yep; Mah first wife bought it when I got hired, thank the lord, two million truckers' miles without accident." "Wow!" "Speakin' of accidents, my buddy hooked me through both lips with a Jitterbug, early one morning. We didn't have no pliers. The surface bite was hot, so we just cut the line an' let that plug dangle... boated a *WHOLE* buncha bass. We went home, cut the shanks an' pulled the hooks. I couldn't talk for a week, but it was worth it. A man will do that, if the surface bite's great, lord knows."

After two more hours the Chameleon knew all about mooching cornmeal-purged Canadian crawlers in Lake Shasta, Whiskey Lake and Butte Cliff, lord knows. He climbed down from the Kenwart;

223

"Thanks, Sam; I appreciate it."

"Sure thing, son; you ever get back to Moreford, look me up! You'll see my rig sittin' on Main Street *if I'm home.*" Judging by his glossy eyes, a new boat was forthcoming for the fishaholic; some wagons just ain't worth riding, lord knows.

Ted Morgan snagged a ride west; the driver realed him with casino tips... which games to play, the best buffets. The quiet killer had a way of inviting people to open up. Ted got out near his apartment, then noticed that his blinds were halfway up. He was sure he'd left them down. Instead of entering his place, he went to the Say When for a chance to think. Obviously, someone had searched his room. No, wait, that wasn't Ted Morgan's, it was *Jimmy Ray's* room. And, perhaps he'd left his blinds that way. Oddly, his photo memory couldn't recall that tiny detail.

Panic began to kick his nuts; if they were onto JR, they might be onto Vincent! The second beer went down but didn't help. He ordered a third, then Dan Lock walked in, without recognizing him; his TED disguise was that good. He vowed not to talk, since the Okla-Fornia accent still lingered. The night passed. He began to think he left those blinds as they were. Wishful thinking, maybe, but except for the blinds, nothing else suggested that anyone had any interest in JR's room. After a few more beers he finally believed it. He left the Say When and decided to enter the apartment.

He was just about to cross the street when the hairs on his neck tingled. Trusting his instincts, his eyes probed the shadows. Sure enough, 200 yards away in the half-light of an abandoned seafood joint he spotted glare from a windshield. Then he made out the sedan parked under huge Oleanders. The car faced JR's apartment. It had to be a stakeout. Resisting the urge to bolt and run, he walked a mile east and slipped into a bar. Entering the john, he peeked out its busted window to watch his back-trail. He had one quick draft to make it look good, then skulked along the shoreline willows, returning to the stakeout. He crept within five yards downwind. From the cover of the Oleanders, he heard every word, coffee slurp and burp. Finch's two best men talked of pussy, sports and sitcoms; mundane shit, for a mundane job. Judging from the tone, neither cop thought they should be staking out a dead perp's joint. Their tone hypnotized him. He fell asleep. Then before dawn began to crack, louder voices crashed his slumber; "Well, at least Leo can't say we didn't try; let's kick this pig!"

They peeled out, heading east for Sacramendota. Carver stayed in the bushes, waiting for his legs to stop shaking. It was time to get out of Dodge. But for the moment he needed more sleep; he walked to the shoreline and hit the warm sand.

THIRTY SIX...

LOADED FOR BEAR

Carver woke up and shook the sand off his pants. He needed distance. Arizona was out, because he'd created so many fake identities there. It didn't seem right to kill anyone in Oregon, after all the fun he had. So he picked the Silver State. But first he needed some things from storage in Hidden Crest. He stuck out his thumb. A Subaru quickly pulled over; "Hop in; I've got lotsa room!" Tammy did, too, after they took turns wiping CDs, tapes and books onto the floor. Her warm way put the killer completely at ease. She smelled of coconut, pot and sandalwood. Before they got up to speed, she passed him a pipe; "Wanna hit? It's great stuff."

"Thanks, but I'm trying to quit." The dodge implied a kindred love of dope with a bit of enviable discipline thrown in. She steered with her knees, talked with her hands, nearly shaking pot out of the pipe; "Oh, right on--I did that once. Then, Bush got elected an' I just *HAD to smoke* to get through it." She laughed; twin curls of smoke leaked from her nose. Soon the pot took hold. She slowed to 20 in a zone marked 45; "Tammy, how 'bout I drive an' you smoke?" They switched seats. Soon they were doing 50, perfect speed to avoid police scrutiny. Free of the drudgery, Tammy started talking; she developed her strain of Pot. Not exactly what Darwin envisioned, but what the hell. She sprouted her seeds with deionized water and the finest grow-nutrients. Her strain targeted Parkinson's with some sort of receptor-specific Sativa. If and when medicinal marijuana hit the big-time, Tammy was ready. It

226

forced Carver's thoughts back to Horrible Harry; he sure could have used a toke or two. Tammy pulled over and gave him her number, in case he ever needed a place to hang. She drove off; she reminded him of his mother, a free spirit with a gentle soul unbound by the shackles of traditional mindsets. Her sandalwood lingered.

Carver went to his storage shed for IDs and cash, filling his bag to start a new life in Nevada. He packed his laptop, camping gear and a Pony single action 22. The desert was a bad place to be, without a gun. With the backpack crammed full, sleeping bag and closed cell mattress tied under it, the thing weighed 71 pounds. No matter; he didn't plan on carrying it much. He grabbed a flap of cardboard and drew one word in big letters; *EAST.*

Before the sun set behind the coastal mountains, he caught a ride in a pickup with Bill Starr, bound for Craig. Bill planned to meet his brother in Windemover. The truck bulged with gear and dogs. Bill talked bears, dogs, bait and bear guns, but otherwise he was as mute as a hitching post. Normally, Ed Hazlewood preferred silence, but his recent brush with the cops put him in the need for distraction. The driver started his rant while Hazlewood retraced the same road he'd ridden with Tammy. He wondered if bears ate pot, were they attracted to sandalwood or would they just smell it, go "whoof" and haul ass into the brush. Starr hit full stride when they climbed the mountains to the east of the big lake. They killed a dozen bears up there, back when the knees were good and their clients hale.

In the fading light the mountaintops glowed a purple backdrop, damned near straight up from the narrow canyon. The killer couldn't imagine trying to hike them, much less haul a bear down. So Bill and his brother were the real deal, mountain men whose words were steel. Soon they hit the big valley and Starr's mood changed. His current clients weren't eager to hike. They were a pair of rich flatland bastards. One was an investment broker, the other a developer.

227

The irony wasn't lost on the killer; Theirs was the 'I got mine, so fuck you' attitude, so typical of plunderers everywhere. It didn't bother them that finite forests were falling to strip malls, ski runs and condos. It worried them less that bears needed this space to live.

Starr had a good read on his clients; fuckin' saudis, japs and dot com types, eager to buy up a chunk of Rocky Mountain Wherever. They just needed to prove that their man cave now sat in what was once a wild piece of country; and what better way than display a bear rug or elk rack taken from that very spot?

A man like Starr was smart enough to know he couldn't stop this cancer from creeping across the high country; it already overtook the eastern two-thirds of the nation. Luckily, he wouldn't live long enough to see the country morph into a shore-to-shore strip mall. So he would live out his life among the bears, grouse, fishers and lions. When they finally stuck his ass in a rest home, he would regale candy stripers with tales of extinct high and wild places. His stories would seem preposterous. They'd say; *'No way America was... EVER that wild!'*

So yeah, bring on the fat fuckers who couldn't find a bear if it was in their tree... bring on their platinum credit cards, shiny magnums and stiff new boots; the Starr brothers would do their best to get 'em a bear, even though they didn't deserve it. If their money kept the Starrs in the high country, even better. Their clients were Remora, coasting effortlessly, skimming tidbits while Bill and Rowdy did all the work.

The killer saw pain betraying Bill's rhetoric; it wasn't really about affluent, lazy clients. Starr and his four-legged quarry were simply the latest species about to be extinguished. In a few more decades, there wouldn't be any wild places left for bear, orangutans or arrow-poison frogs. Urban sprawl and mushrooming population would overtake it all. The bears were already dead, and Starr wanted to die with them; Better than seeing the pristine western high country turn into... *Ohio.*

It was the same greed that killed Ishi, extinguished the passenger pigeon and forced countless native Americans to reservations. The cancer was always the same; unconscionable, whorish profiteering masquerading as progress. Two centuries ago, it was the caballero's turn to die. Soon conservationists and hunters would meet the same fate; it was a shrinking world and nobody except hunters gave a rat's ass about the evaporating wilderness. With dwindling numbers of hunters to preserve it all, the future looked pretty fucking grim for all wild things.

Then Starr ended his rant. The rig rolled along in silence; each man absorbed in thought. The killer thought about killing some developers. It couldn't stop the sprawl any more than killing a few perverts stopped perversion, but it might be some symbolic fun. Besides, the pricks had it coming.

They hit Reno. Starr parked in a casino lot. He liked buffets; no time wasted while food was cooked. They wove through aisles full of blue-haired old ladies pumping slot machines. The line moved fast, but it gave the killer a few minutes to prime the pump; "Hey Bill, where are you goin' to hunt?" He reached into his worn Carhart, pulled out a topo map folded to his area of interest. He probably slept with bear maps for blankets; "We'll start there, 'n see what kinda bears we've got."

"Huh?"

"We don't hunt displaced teenagers or sows with cubs. That leaves boars 'n dry sows. Nobody wants a sow on the wall." The line moved while Hazlewood mentally photographed 12 square miles of Routte National Forest; "An area can have lots of sign from teenagers, wet sows or transplants." They reached the cashier; Ed paid for both meals. They found a booth. Ed cracked a snow crab leg; "*What's a transplant?*'

The hunter waved a peeled prawn like an orchestra baton; "Man, you *DON'T* know much about bears, do ya?" Ed stuffed his mouth with sweet snow crab; "not yet." The hunter laughed so hard that he half-spit a prawn, but caught it on his lips; "A wild bear and a transplant's as

229

different as a Boy Scout and a CRACK addict... truth is, crack's the problem." The killer grew tired of begging the bear professor for one byte at a time, but concealed it. Starr started working the scallops; "You got a problem bear at a park, golf course or ski lodge; bear loses its fear of humans. So they dart the bear. They gather data, blood, hair, maybe even pull a tooth to age it." It seemed preposterous, so Hazlewood slurped a few oysters, watching Starr for lies.

Bill forked Haddock chunks while talking. He loved bears; "He wakes up in a fowl mood, with a hangover from the drug, which he ain't physiologically adapted for. He reeks of humans. He's got a tooth yanked out, no gauze or Demerol. To top it off, he's in strange territory. He's gonna get his ass kicked if don't leave; so he hightails straight back to *HIS* territory. It might take him a day or a week but he'll be back unless he gets killed first, an' I don't just mean by people. Other bears figure into the equation."

They went for second helpings, then Starr finished his bear rap; "When I mentioned 'crack' I wasn't joking. They're DRUGGING problem bears with *ANGEL DUST!* Some have been tranked many times. PCP increases aggression and lowers sociability. They turn problem bears into *BAD-ASS*, people-hating crack-bears."

The hunter saw doubt in Ed's eyes; "You don't believe me? Hell, I didn't either, until 11 years ago. My client wanted a Honey Phase bear. There's a ridge high up in California, due east of Corovelo; produces quite a few Honeys. We got the permits for pack-stings, fires, everything. We quarantined the horses, bought provisions, diesel, everything 'n got set for two weeks in the Yolla Bolly Wilderness to try for a honey. They're rare. Anyhow, we finally passed the star thistle quarantine so we trailered 'em up and headed up that hellacious pass."

Starr waved for a coffee refill; "For some reason, we never could get that client to case his rifle. From the time he stepped out of his Land Rover, Bernie hugged that damned Weatherby like a Heissman-winning son. He even held it in the cab while we climbed the pass.

Then we parked at trail-head to start unloading. Meanwhile, my client's walking around, waivin' his Weatherby like a ten-inch dick in a whorehouse. I'm openin' the trailer; I hear him holler. He points straight uphill and fires. This bear comes skiddin' to a halt right at his feet... Bernie got his honey-phase. It was the shortest bear hunt in history! The bear's stone-dead two paces from our client, who pissed his pants. Nothin' like a tusk-poppin', tree-bustin' bear charge for soilin' undies. Anyhow, he had a magnificent pelt, no rubs, scars, nothin'. That bear was huge; took three of us to roll him over... then our bubble burst. His left side had "Ranger Red" all over it."

"Huh?"

"They marked trouble bears with red paint. We tagged it and headed down to the ranger station. Pretty soon, out comes the chief ranger, who radios for a warden. They impound the bear for damage control. Too bad too, 'cuz I knew a guy who could'a taken the paint out of that gorgeous hide." Ed was curious; "They *took it?*"

"Dam right, **TOOK** *IT;* then wrote us a voucher so the client could get a replacement tag. That is damned unusual, so Rowdy an' me started prying. Sure enough, the rangers let the DFG drop that bear off the night before, smack dab in the trail-head parkin' lot. The boar was well known at a park 80 miles away. He'd been tranquilized six times before. He mauled a camper on his last stint, so instead of shootin' him, they relocated... So he slept there all night. Woke up hung over... just waitin' ta take out his mad on somebody.

"Heck of a story"

"But lemme tell you something; never had a client so hell-bent on hauling a loaded rifle around but I sure am glad he did... That bear would have mauled him. The tracks proved he sprinted straight-line downhill, no posturing, no bluff charge. He meant business, brother..."

Ed was flabbergasted; "*Wow!*"

"We found out later that old Bernie couldn't shoot for shit; he couldn't hit water if he fell off a cruise ship... But when it mattered, he managed a lucky head shot on a bear charging straight at him. But that's not the end of the story.

231

Two weeks go by. Bernie calls; *'Hi, Bill, I got that replacement bear tag, but I don't want it... I'm taking up golf."* The guide went teary-eyed from laughter; "A chargin' bear sure can make a man long for his golf game!"

They hit the interstate after dinner. Then, 20 miles east of Sparkston, Starr pulled onto an alkali two-track; "Time to run the dogs." He let his dogs out, hit second gear with the dogs trotting out in front. He made a mile before the first dog squatted. Then like clockwork, each hound followed suit. By the second mile, all dogs voided and were kenneled. Ed had originally planned to stop in Reno, but he liked riding with the hunter. He hadn't met many men with such strong, honest conviction. He decided to ride to Winnemako. If he didn't like that town, there was always the open road. Three hours later, Bill's ring tone cracked the silence; an elk bugling. Starr held it at arm's length to read it. He finally just gave up and turned it on; "Yah? *Cattlemen's? K.*" They wheeled into the lot near a pickup hauling a dented trailer with big tires for ground clearance. Out popped the other half, who grinned and shook the killer's hand; "Howdy; I'm Rowdy. An' whatever my brother's been sayin'... *it's all bullshit."*

Ed grinned; "Ed Hazlewood. Nice to meet you." Bill hugged his brother; "Bullshit, huh? Good to see you, Kid!" They entered the casino bar. Rowdy bought the first round; he ran the computer, trail cams and website. With the second drink he opened up; "Brother Bill's *'OLD SCHOOL'...* I'm New Age'. I'm in my prime!" He ogled a Keno runner for emphasis. "Bill groaned; "Oh, no; here we go again!"

Rowdy resumed; "I use time savers whenever I can; trail cameras, computers, biology reports. I study..." But Bill overran the kid's narrative; "Aw, that fancy shit might help *sometimes*, but 95% of bear huntin's blood, sweat an' blisters!" Old versus new, collided again, right there in the bar; *"Oh yah? I don't see you ignorin' my five percent,* brother!" It was true; he sure as hell exploited little brother's cyber data. That was what made them such a great team.

Ed saw a chance to glean something which might prove useful later; a clue to their website password maybe, which just *had to be bear-related;* "So, Rowdy, what's your *FAVORITE* bear?"

The young hunter was glad someone finally asked his opinion. He sipped his lager pensively; "Good question; which do I love most?" He sipped and straightened up;

"I hunted Polar Bears once up near Umniuk... Man, the White Bear is one incredible animal. He can run 12 miles an hour, across the ice. When that gets too thin, he'll swim at damned near six knots, then get back on the far ice and keep runnin'. He can smell a breathin' hole for miles and catch the seal usin' it. That ain't only smart, it's *tough!"*

His voiced changed timbre, drawing other patrons near; "It was Day Seven of my scheduled 14-day hunt, and it was **SOME KINDA COLD!** Minus 45, wind blowin' 30 miles an hour." The hunter sensed the audience, so he spoke a bit louder; "Wellsir, we saw a big bear about a mile downwind. He sniffed and started trottin' our way. Don't know whether he was plannin' on eatin' us or the dogs, but he was hell-bent for leather comin' straight at us. Lemme tell ya, that will pucker your ass! When he got about half a mile out I made a solid rest on my sled. All I had to do was jack a round in the chamber an' wait for him to get in range. When he got to 500 yards, that bear started galloping; the guide said something in Inuit. Later, I found out what.*"*

He paused to let his audience grasp the scene; "I'll *never* forget that image in my scope; long yellow-white fur shimmerin,' saltwater ice crystals blowin' off his fur like diamonds in the powder blue sky, sparklin' in the arctic sunlight... damn, it was somethin'. I got caught up in the beauty. Then the guide spoke the only English he knew; *'SHOOT NOW'...*

"But it was still too far, with the hellacious stiff wind and the gallopin' bear, so I just kept the crosshairs on his throat and watched him come runnin' an' slingin' blue-white ice diamonds. It sure was pretty."

He put his stein down; "At two hunnert yards, I decided to chamber a round 'n shoot... That's when I got my big lesson in arctic life. My bolt-action was froze up--I couldn't get the bolt to move! Lemme tell you something; that bear suddenly got a whole lot bigger! I looked at the guide, who started rummagin' in his sled for his backup, a beat-up old Savage 99, in .243 caliber!"

Someone smirked at that statement, so Rowdy explained; "Now, the Eskimos kill plenty of sleepin' bears with .243's. One round behind the ear and it's all over. But *THIS bear* wasn't sleepin'! He got on us before the guide got his rifle out. All hell broke loose. The closest string of dogs ran away, sled and all... they were *the only smart ones on the ice pack!"*

The entire bar kept silent. He sipped ale; "The *second* team hit that bear like a pack of bees, riggin', sled and all... So that boar started huggin' dogs. He'd clamp one to his chest an' bite its neck... then he'd reel in the next dog, like a trotline full of squirming sausage links. Then the guide shoots, but he just killed a dog.' I'm still tryin' to get my bolt open. The bear's wrapped up in riggin', dogs and busted sled parts... he's roarin', poppin' teeth and tossin' dead dogs an' huge chunks of ice... Damn, I've never been so scared. The guide puts one through its liver... but the bear just bites his wound and runs straight for the guide, draggin' dogs, poppin' teeth and bleedin' like a stuck pig; That guide was a dead man in about three seconds, but he stood his ground and reloaded. Man, I've never seen more courage! Then the last string of dogs got to him... One dog grabbed an ear, one grabbed his nuts, and the rest just bit fur and hung on. Right about then, my bolt decided to loosen up and I jacked a round in, but he was too close to use my scope, so I sighted down the barrel and blasted him. That 338 blew through him like an arrow. I seen a big cloud of steam outta his chest, so I knew I hit lungs, but that blue-throated bastard just kept comin'. He couldn't roar, but that just made it freakier. I tried to jack another round in, but I was too scared to move."

"I couldn't run; my feet were stuck, like a bad nightmare. He came on like Terminator, then grabbed my legs and started chewin'. It felt like FIRE. Then he caved in and made his death moan."

Again, silence from the crowd; "They really do have blue throats; smelled like rotten fish guts. Anyhow, they pulled me out from under him. I'm not ashamed to say it; sometime during the fracas, I crapped my pants. They lost nine dogs, counting one the guide shot. Then... I passed out." Thinking that was the end, someone tried to applaud but Rowdy wasn't done;

"They put me in the busted-up sled, took me to the village and radioed for a plane; 36 hours and 600 stitches later I woke up. I was surprised to see Jimmy, the head guide. They said he never been in a hospital before; spent his whole life on the ice. He handed me a necklace made from the teeth, claws and sinew. He smiled a toothless grin and said something. The translator didn't want to tell me what it was, but I made him. It was an apology. You see, Jimmy got his rifle reloaded just in time; the bullet went through the bear's throat and *THEN* hit my leg. I'm sure glad he was packing a little 243, 'cuz a big old magnum woulda sawed off my leg!"

The crowd applauded, but one yuppie from California piped up; "Thanks for an entertaining soliloquy, however fanciful it might've been." Rowdy scowled; "You think I'm *LYING*? See for yurself!" He dropped his Levi's to prove it; from hip to knee, ragged scars and suture tracks repulsed some folks. The pants came back up. Yuppie man made his exit, headed to a bar where a man's words weren't likely backed with such steel. Someplace where they spoke of roadsters, mild Merlot and other things that can be merely purchased, instead of lived. When the crowd dwindled to just the barkeep and the Keno runner, Rowdy let them in on the punch line; "Remember I said the guide said something when that bear was way out there? The translator told me later, Jimmy said; *'check gun'*. Apparently, some clients like me ain't used to arctic extremes... Some lubricants freeze your action solid. Damn

235

right, *check gun...*" He smiled for the Keno girl; "So, that covers Polar Bears, which I quit hunting, right then.'

The bartender brought a round; "Thanks, Rowdy, this one's on me." "Thanks, Tim." He turned to the killer; "That leaves Grizzlies, Brownies and Blacks, to answer your question about which is my favorite. Grizzlies are unpredictable. They might not bluff-charge, so they're dangerous... Ever since my run-in with the great white bear, I don't consider danger a necessary ingredient of a successful hunt."

Hazelwood smiled but kept quiet, since Rowdy was still on a roll; "Oh, sure, experts say he'll bluff charge, give you a little swat or two, then leave. Now, if that swat's between bears, it's harmless. But to a HUMAN, it's like a Great White Shark's testing bite; nothing personal, just animal etiquette, played out on soft, helpless people. So, X-NAY on the izzlies-Gray."

That brings us to the monster Browns of Kodiak fame. They are big in size, courage and athletic ability. A client once shot a nine-footer through the top of the heart while it fed on a gut-pile 40 yards away. He whirled, bit the wound and roared so loud the client shit his pants; I myself was sorely tempted. He started spinning, tossin' half-frozen tundra divots and roarin' so loud I never heard Bill's Rigby fire. The bear died in half a minute, but it lasted a lifetime. We'll never forget it."

Rowdy drew breath; "The client wiped his butt with tundra. Bill and I put two insurance rounds into the bear. And just to give you an idea of their power, I picked up one of those waterlogged divots he was tossing 50 yards from ground zero; it wouldn't fit in a five-gallon bucket and weighed 30 pounds with half the water shook out... Man, that's power! That brownie squared nine feet, 700 pounds, with 19 inch paws. One little etiquette slap from *THAT* would cancel your ticket, friend. And, as for athleticism, try to imagine being so fast you can catch a jumping salmon with your teeth or outrun a caribou. And so powerful you could dig up a marmot in half-frozen tundra with your bare hands. Our Brownie does that 'n more, just to make a living. Now, for purely aesthetic considerations, my vote might go to the Brownie; you've got miles of pristine shoreline, clam bakes, halibut, crab, damn, that's tough to beat. But Brownies 'n bad weather are like bacon an' eggs; it can rain, sleet, snow and hail all in the same day; and that's not countin' fog, small craft advisories and tidal problems. I hate week-long stays in a tent eatin' canned vittles, playin' cribbage 'n hopin' for the weather to break."

"So, that leaves the last candidate, and I believe I speak for Bill, too. We vote for the good old Black Bear. But since the night is late and it's my turn to tend the dogs, Monsieur Blackie will have to wait for his homage. And so I bid you bon soir, mes amis." The boy had to be drunk if the lingo went French. Ed got a room away from the noise. He dreamed of Pacific rim forests, hump-backed bears and shoreline mussel feeds. He awoke to the maid's knock. Dressing fast, he ran out and looked for his new friends; gone. So was his duffel. He left it in Starr's truck. Running inside, he asked the clerk; "Hey, when did the Starr brothers check out?" The clerk didn't look up; "Bill and Rowdy? 'bout an hour ago, sir. *Why?*" He thought fast; "They have my bag 'n my insulin! May I use your computer?" "Go for it, but hurry; if Betty sees you, it's my ass."

He quickly found the website, then Rowdy's cell number. The high-tech kid answered; "Kuntrybear, Rowdy." Ed talked fast, in case the high mountain ridges dropped his call; "Rowdy, Ed; you have my pack." "Approachin' Battle Mountain; how 'bout we wait for you?" "That's great; I'll hurry!" "No problemo; we gotta service the trucks, run the dogs and eat. You're breakin' up; If you're late, we'll leave it at the Red Tiger desk, OK?" "Good. On my way!" The killer tipped the clerk and ran to the coffee shop to find a ride east, fast. Two hours later he walked through the doors and found the Starrs, stuffing their faces and talking bears. The killer filled a plate and sat down. He liked the sense of continuity. Rowdy started in, like they'd never stopped; "So, yeah, black bears are our favorite, but there are many kinds; you've got your Citified Dump Bear... He's fat, with little fear of man. He dines on whatever he finds in

237

the dump. We don't like city bears; they won't run, stink like hell. Huntin' em's not sporting work. Still, a bear's a bear, for some clients so we take the fat, stinking city man who can't hike and we set him down on a bear trail barely out of sight of the dump. Soon he's bragging about his "wild bear." They do stink, but those city men pay well."

He sipped coffee; "You've got 'Displaced Bears, teenagers beggin' in ski towns, eatin' dog food, gardens 'n trying to make a living. We don't want clients braggin' about takin' teenage bears; bad for business." Rowdy's eyebrows raised; "That leaves us with the wild free-roaming black." He forked some steak and kept talking; "He camps year-round without a fire. He's stealthy, he just materializes. No snapping twigs give him away. Then when you try to walk those same trails, you sound like a garbage truck at dawn. Big blacks have a civil code; all they want is to not itch, not be hungry and be left alone... Man, we humans should strive for a code like that." "Damn right."

"So, we hunt the wily old black bear, but it's not easy, like the tree-huggers think; they think we drink beer and blast bears from the truck. IF we took a tree-hugger with us, they couldn't handle the work in camp, much less run the dogs!"

They finished the meal and went to the trucks. Ed decided to stay with them for a while. He got into Rowdy's truck. Rowdy re-booted; "Take this hunt for example; we'll spend two days setting tents, digging perimeter trenching. We'll build a kennel, latrine and a corral, in case we need to call a pack-string. We'll cut enough firewood for two weeks of inclement weather. We burn a tank of diesel a day, with Striker on the hood. If Striker hits scent, we check it out; if we see big tracks, we mark it. Hopefully, we'll locate two or three shooters, 'n *TRY* to keep 'em interested until the clients arrive. We make our own lure, and that's not easy. I use rolled oats, cracked corn, alfalfa honey, *TWO* secret ingredients, five gallons molasses. Takes a morning to stir it up. I squeeze out a small glob at each site; takes all afternoon. Meanwhile, Bill's keeping the dogs

238

from killing each other and gettin' camp organized. Then every day we look for sign, re-fresh lures and log bait hits. When I find a good one, I'll hang a trail cam and build two ground blinds and two tree stands, depending on wind and client limitations; some can't climb. Hell, at altitude some clients can *barely walk!*

The time passed. Soon Ed saw a sign for Windemover. Rowdy kept rambling; "Some clients wanna sleep in or don't want to do chores, but we set 'em straight; Everybody pitches in or they go home. It takes initiative 'n effort to hunt the high country. We say so on our website, but what sounds good to a client in a warm kitchen in Tallahassee sounds different at 8,000 feet with freezin' rain runnin' down your butt-crack. Then most clients can't shoot straight or judge bear size. Some can't sit still or shut up. Brother, if you can't, you'll NEVER take an old black bear."

"Sounds hard."

"And then we have the Sultans, want to drink, stay in town and hump women. Our *REAL LIVE sultan* actually wanted us to pimp for him... that didn't last, believe me. Then he threw in another 20 k if we'd just shoot him a bear. It riled us somethin' awful, but we needed the money back then. That was the only bear we ever shot for a client. But I digress... When we finally get our clients on good stands, we maintain camp while they hunt. We'll get word on a walkie-talkie; a hunter made a hit. He's too pumped up to remember much, except how exciting it was. We'll find a weak blood trail, probably a gut shot. That means a long trailing job, always into the nastiest, steepest cover. Bears never make it easy. We'll chainsaw a trail to recover the animal. We skin and hang it, then call for the horses; if the pack-string ain't already busy somewhere else. Otherwise we haul the meat, rug and skull on backpacks; Bill spends a day skinning, caping and salting the rug. He'll drive the meat and trophies to town for processing, while I work the dogs, relocate clients and refresh any hot baits. We keep that up until each client gets a bear or the contract expires. Then we spend two days breaking camp, cleaning everything up so that all we left are footprints. Trust me, amigo; NO bunny-hugger works that hard."

They slowed for Windemover because to the east lay 124 miles of the most extreme landscape in North America. Plenty of pilgrims died while crossing their wagons over that desert. It still posed penalties for anyone foolish enough to cross it unprepared; so hunters, salesmen and tourists opted for a stop at the edge, if only to pay homage. Besides, it was state-line; last chance to gamble before crossing into Mormon-turf. Ed got out and washed the windshields free of alkali and dried bug smears. Bill walked over; "Say, it's none of my business, but I thought you were gettin' off in Reno." He smiled; "Reno'll keep; I liked ridin' with you-didn't want it to end."

But it did. He eyed the lonely stretch of desert fading to the east; if Utah looked that bad, he didn't want any part of it. He said good-bye and grabbed his backpack. The Starr brothers headed for that great mythical nine-foot black bruin, skulking high up near the Continental Divide.

He walked into the store; the sign said they were hiring.

THIRTY SEVEN...

CLEAN SEX &

HONEST POKER

Ed learned fast, how to run the register, selling gas and impulse items to the river of people on I-80. Most eastbound motorists stopped for one last chance to gamble. The westbound, for their first. After they lost they'd head for Toledo, Frisco or wherever. Meanwhile, new tourists warmed their seats in the casinos.

It didn't take long to see the three things to do in the desert; drink, screw and gamble. Ed already knew how to do the first two so he focused on cards. Besides, he didn't have a girl yet. Texas Hold 'em didn't require a great deal of skill. It held mass fascination due to its blend of skillful betting and card-catching luck, like a mixture of slots, stud and blackjack. A slight advantage went to those who read people well. Ted targeted young males; they took big chances and were easy to read. He avoided craggy-faced truckers. Hazlewood soon forged his Poker tenets...

win big, lose small
leave with more chips
than you start with
the rest is bullshit

He met a Keno runner. Bobbie was a closet Mormon, migrating from Salt Lake City as soon as she was free to leave Utah. She had big plans, but her traveling companion, who's name she would never again speak, took her money, virginity and hopes, right there at state-line. Too humiliated to call her parents and too broke to travel further, she got a job running Keno 'for now', which turned into two years. She bought a single-wide nestled against the south-facing bluffs. With her near-virginal innocence and double dimples, she made gonzo tips, had freedom and her pick of men.

The first time she laid eyes on Ed she wanted him; there was danger in his eyes. When her shift ended, she arrived at the rail in time to see the biggest pot of the night. He was in seat 1. Palermo John, 4. 2 & 3 held young Asians. 5-7 were Hispanic workers from another casino. Seat 8 held a tall guy, Spaniard, judging from the thick Castillian accent and fair skin. Nine and ten? white trash; bad teeth, filthy mouths. The casino normally tossed cranksters, but they'd been losing hard at blackjack before poker started. The house wouldn't toss them til they're belly up. The guy in Ten raised. Ed called quietly. The pot was right, at 135.

The flop; 4h 5h Ah

A possible straight flush draw. The Spaniard bet. Ten raised. Her potential lover, seat One, quietly called. Two and Three folded. Palermo John called, but looked miserable. Seat five called without twitching; machismo carved in stone. His amigo re-raised; a typical Macho pissing contest. The Spaniard called. Poor white trash in 9 had wild eyes, folded and reached for beer. Ten called. Her future lover silently tapped felt. Palermo John had seen quiet callers before. He took one last look before mucking his queens, both black. The Mex in 5 called. The pot was right, at 225.

4th St; A, 4,5,6, *all Hearts.*

Seats 8 and 5 were drooling. Ed watched his opponents. The game was 5-10 Limit, or the Latinos would have gone all-in. The Spaniard bet. Crankster raised. Ed called. Five folded. The Spaniard wised up and just called, making the pot 285. Ed went cold inside when he saw the River card made an open ended straight flush draw;

River; A, 4,5,6...7, all Hearts

The 3 or 8 of hearts would crush Hazlewood's nut flush. Luckily, he didn't have to bet first or he might have given it away by checking. The Spaniard looked happy when he bet. White trash twitched; flecks of foam on his lips as he sat forward and raised. Ed saw the Spaniard leaning forward, eyes on the pot; he'd probably re-raise so Ed just called. The Spaniard spoke with thick Castillian dialect, including the obligatory lisp; "I raithe."

Almost simultaneously, seat 10 raised. Ed felt fairly confident of his nut flush, but three re-raises sure shrunk his cards. Lucy, the dealer, interrupted the feeding frenzy. "Betting is capped." White trash got mad; "Hey, *there's NO CAP on Fifth street, bitch!*"

"That's on weekends. This is *Thursday.* Please watch the language, *SIR.*" Her tone said he was an idiot for betting so hard. He sat back and shut up; security was itching to bust his chops. The dealer said; "Turn 'em over."

The Spaniard, last raiser, slow-rolled the deuce of hearts; the way he'd been raising, everyone put him on the straight flush. The crankster showed the Queen of hearts; *"Bigger flush! You lose, pal!"* He tried to rake, but the dealer stopped him; "Sir... we have one more hand to see."

All eyes swiveled to the quiet caller. The crankster scoffed; "He ain't got a hand, he never raised once... *show your cards, man!*" Ed looked him straight in the eyes; "You're right; thought somebody had the straight flush." He slow-rolled the Heart King; "Nut flush... *friend.*" The rail buzzed. Ed raked chips, tipped the dealer and called for trays. The crankster got surly; "So now you gonna HIT 'N RUN, *YOU JERK?*"

Ed couldn't help but jab the prick a little. He pulled one from his archive of TV quotes; "Pappy always said *'You don't have to win all the pots... just the big ones.'*"

When he stood in line at the cashier cage he felt firm breasts pressing into his back. Turning his head slowly, he met Bobbie's gaze. She gave her best imitation of a cowboy-era saloon floozy; "Whacha gonna do with all that cash, handsome?" He smiled; "I'm gonna rent me a room and buy me some purty girls, I reckon. You interested?"

She broke out of character, laughing; "Settle for dinner?" "Yep. They call me Ed." "Nice to meet you, Ed, I'm Bobbie." Lust in the desert has few equals. She had passion, for which no church allowed the servicing; it drove her out of a household with zero tolerance for budding sexuality. Now this Ed had a smoldering hint of the netherworld. It turned her on and turned her loose. He was a good lover. Since she had only had two prior lovers, the comparison field was limited. At any rate, they screwed like death row inmates. Time flew.

SABBATICAL'S OVER...

He got pretty good at Poker. He learned the math fast, but reading people was a nebulous art, part instinctive, part cerebral. With so many tourists joining a game, Ed didn't have time to thoroughly dissect opponents. He hunted just a few basic human nature tells. Eyes that went to the player's stack saw promising cards. Trembling hands meant power cards. Young studs tried too hard to hide tells; they went stone-faced if they had the goods. When a hotshot worked a bluff he would try to sell it. When a player got quiet, it was a trap. Students of the game learned from TV commentators, but as for the subtler nuances, they didn't have a clue. Of course timing for LEAVING a game was critical; if playing tourists, a hit 'n run is OK; the object being brutal pillaging. But if the table held whales he might play again, it was better to lose a few small pots before leaving. They would remember their short winning-spree, instead of the big loss that preceded it.

So he passed the winter learning poker and screwing Bobbie's lights out. But a man could only fuck so much before that too loses its spice. He could feel the growing embryo... And as is so often the case, it took one monster birth-pang to deliver it. Ironically enough, it came during a card game. Wouldn't you know it?

THE FINAL GAME...

It was Friday, prime time for fleecing suckers. Ed arrived early and sat in 5. Ed hoped for young couples, out for dinner and a bit of gaming. It was as easy as trapping the male a few times. The carnie's oldest scam, re-played on a new genre of suckers; step right up, win your girl a stuffed animal. Show her what a man you are. Nothing opens a man's wallet like pheromones.

An Asian man with a label on his wrinkled polo shirt sat down at Two. Ed hated Bus People. They didn't speak English, didn't know the rules and rarely had much cash. A young white couple sat down; shiny necklaces, names engraved. April, Nine, her lover, Eight... Varsity quarterback no doubt. He had the tan, scars and muscles of a fighter. April *had to be* a ski bunny; fake nails, cones and dye blond, but all of the highest quality. Her big tits strained her sweater; she was perfect for Ed's plan. Tits make men stupid. With April at the table, they'd be retards by 8 o'clock. Not that Ed was immune, but he always had sex before playing. With his lust abated, he was immune to her obvious charms, temporarily. Good old Bobbie.

A young stud sat down at Three. The kid had a shot glass full of... whiskey, maybe. With a motion that seemed too natural, he reached for a drink stand. Flannel shirt, gray cowboy hat, chained wallet; *had to be* a ringer.

Two Mexicans staggered to Six & Seven, gesturing for cocktails. Ed turned to greet the dead money; "Hola amigos, me llamo Ed." The taller man, Seven spoke; "I am *Hiraldo.* thees leetle peepsqueek ess mi hermano, *Jose!"*

245

Ed shook their hands, but he was just reaching into their wallets. They were engrossed with April's cleavage. Seats 1,4 & 10 were still empty, but Fernando would deal with seven players seated. He prepared the tray.

A couple sat down. Sticky-back conventioneers' name tags; Dolly took One, Bill Four. They had pasty complexions. Pro bowlers, lawyers and gamblers had such skin. Finally, a man at Ten; 60-65, well groomed, manicure. His pale blue eyes scanned the table, nodding silent greetings to anyone meeting his gaze. Ed and Dolly noticed. Ed nodded back.

There was the usual pre-game tension, like strangers crowded in elevators. Players bought chips while Fernando High-carded for the button. The tradition was as old as Poker. Jose got an ace. Ed folded three hands to watch his opponents play; varsity quarterback tended to sweat with good cards. April rubbed her neck when weak but flaunted her tits when strong. Mex 1 and 2 always raised each other. Bus-man loved to raise pre-flop, then fold on the Turn.

The 4th pre-flop tempted Ed, out of position with red queens. He watched Dolly when Hiraldo raised; a smirk flitted across her face. She called quickly, then capped her cards with two chips. Bill folded quickly. Ed had two eager players; one hell-bent on raising with anything and the other, a woman of unknown skills. Maybe she had him beat; something about how she stared at her partner. Still, he had queens, so he called. Then came a scary flop;

Flop; Ad, Qc, 10c

Dolly's eyes bored holes through the Mex, not the flop. Ed checked. Hiraldo wagered. Dolly called quickly; Ed put her on rockets. He should fold, but his set of queens tempted; he called again. Fernando turned one;

Table; Ad, Qc, 10c Kc

Dolly squinted with disgust at the club-flush draw, then changed her body language. Ed looked longingly, then folded his set of ladies. Hiraldo bet. Dolly morphed into the dragon lady and raised; they re-raised until betting capped. Fernando dealt the River;

table; **Ad, Qc, 10c, Kc, Qs**

Ed inwardly cussed at himself, for missing out on the two-percenter. Dragon lady, who hadn't bothered to look at the River Card, stared through the Mexican, who now looked sick. He checked. She bet, begging for a raise from Macho Man; it took all of his cojones to call the putah. She showed aces and kings. Ed tried not to puke about his four dead queens. The Mexican smiled and turned over 2, 3 of Clubs; his baby flush was good.

Pandemonium; the Mexicans and Bus Man loved it when shit-house luck rewards loose play. Dragon lady took it in stride, which made Ed nervous. He ordered a beer, reset his cap brim lower to study her, then folded three hands. He pretended to watch the TV, runners, anything. But he only studied Dolly. Soon he spotted her looking into the crowd before capping her cards. Her accomplice sat at the slot machine closest to the Poker table, facing it. He wore odd-looking glasses. From his seat he could probably see hole cards for seats 6-8. Ed quit looking at the guy; he wanted to study the thing, not scare it off.

The big blind moved to Ed, with wired red Jacks. Dolly looked at her helper, then put three chips on her cards, nearest the dealer. Bill sagged back in his chair, cocky-like. Jose folded and asked for cocktails. Hiraldo folded, reached for dollars; he wanted to be ready for that sexy Cuban waitress. Quarterback rushed his chips in, forehead beaded with sweat. April raised before he could warn her off. Old blue eyes saw the tell, so he folded. Dolly slow-folded. Bus-man raised, as usual. The young cowboy called quietly; first hand he'd played. Ed and Dan called. Ignoring his 2nd dirty look, April stupidly called the raise.

247

the flop; Ah, 9s, 8s

Dan leaned forward. Beads of sweat trickled down his forehead. He tried to slow-play. If tells were apples, this guy was an orchard. IF Dolly's pre-flop chip signal meant what Ed thought it did, then Dan had pocket rockets. April finally noticed her lover stepping on her feet, so she folded. Bus-man raised. His people were assembling near the doorway, so it would be his last hand. Cowboy silently re-raised, shoving his chips in silky-smooth, like he'd been playing all his life. He was brewing something or hiding a big draw. If so, it was a mature move for such a young player. Then Dan raised; so did the late-for-the-bus, pot-pumping maniac-Manila-motherfucker. Cowboy's face said nothing, but his hands shook a bit when he sipped his bourbon. The Turn Card made more danger on the board;

table; Ah, 9s, 8s, As

The sweating quarterback shucked out chips. Bus-man folded and hauled ass. Dan looked sad when the cowboy only called, instead of raising. Fernando burned a card; Dan blurted, to goad the cowboy; "I'm bettin' dark!" Just then Fernando started to expose the River, and Cowboy got a glimpse; "An' I'ma raisin' in the dark; how's *that feel*, Studly?" Fernando dealt it before Dan answered;

table; Ah, 9s, 8s, As 5s

The betting capped, in spite of the betting snafus. Dan showed his four aces like it was a surprise, but he'd telegraphed them like the Vatican's white smoke. Who could blame him? The cowboy sipped the last of his bourbon then slow-rolled the 6&7 of spades; it's not every day a man Rivers a straight flush.

table; Ah, **9s, 8s,** As, **5s**
Dan; Ad, Ac   *Cowboy; 6s, 7s*

Nobody likes losing with four of a kind. The quarterback started yelling, but everyone else cheered.

The dealer shouted out; *"Dan... you WON the Bad Beat! IT'S at **36 THOUSAND!**"*

"HUH?"

Everyone tried to explain at once, while the Eye in the sky verified that all conditions were met. Half the pot went to Dan. One-fourth went to Cowboy. The remaining 9k split between the other players and Fernando. It took 20 minutes to pay, fill out the forms and restore order. Dan and April promptly left. He finessed her as they walked away; *"See Honey? That's how ya play Hold 'em."* There's nothing like pheromones, a swingin' dick & dumb-ass luck.

Old Blue eyes left too, but for other reasons.

The Bad Beat hubbub attracted new players, which changed the table mood, but Ed finally caught onto their chip signaling system; if the shill saw Eight's cards, Bonnie place chips on the right side of her hole cards. If he saw Six's, she put chips went on the left; chips in center? Seven's cards. When the mark was weak, she'd place a single chip; when strong, more chips. It wasn't a perfect system, but the advantage steadily paid off. As the night wore on, Bill and Dolly's stacks grew. Ed's too, but he had ups and downs; the price off setting up the cheaters.

After the Bad Beat, it took an hour for the table to settle down, but during the chaos, Ed constructed his false tell. He ordered beers, drank a little, then had the waitress replace each nearly full can with a fresh beer, so it looked like he was drinking a lot. He shifted his chair so the shill could glimpse his cards, too. He lifted bad cards just high enough for the cheater to see; 8H 3S. Predictably, Dolly placed one chip on the leading edge of her hole cards. Ed rubbed his forehead and over-bet his rags. The flop didn't help him. He rubbed his forehead again and made a follow-up bet. Dragon Lady folded, but Bill kept raising. Everybody else folded. Turn and River didn't help Ed. On showdown he reluctantly turned over his shitty bluff. Once again her contemptuous smirk flitted across her lips.

Bill won with Kings full. Later he tried the same weak-ass bluff, losing that one, too. Then just a few hands later, he let the cheater see his pocket kings so he could incorporate a false high-confidence tell... He sat upright and leaned forward, in the classic rookie's pose. Dolly placed three chips on her cards, then paid him off to make sure they had the right read on him. At showdown, Ed won a too-small pot. Her smirk flashed again; she knew he was ripe for the picking. But so was she.

Later his chance came. Seats 8-10 held locals. Jose and Hiraldo still occupied 6 & 7, but after ten beers they weren't much for Poker. Still, they kept re-buying and donating, so nobody was going to complain. Cowboy had the button; he had secretly switched to iced tea in that bourbon glass. Bill had small blind, Ed big. He held Big Slick, but didn't let the shill see 'em. So it was time to cue the false tell. He wiped his forehead. Dolly's smirk flitted, knowing he was going for another weak-ass bluff. She placed a single chip in Ed's spot, then signed Bill; closed fist, to pump the pot early and fold later.

Jose called and Hiraldo tried, but in his stupor he turned his hole cards over; red eights. Seat 8 also had a pair of eights. With her outs were dead, she folded. Nine, Ten, Dolly and Cowboy called. Bill's position raise was practically expected. The stage was set. Ed made the most of it. He wiped his brow, then raised. Jose folded. Everybody called. Hell, they were onto his bluff.

Ed; As, Ks   Dolly, **Qd, Qh**   Cowboy; Ad, 3c
Flop; Ac, Kh, **Qc**

Dragon Lady's knuckles went white. Meanwhile, cowboy got quiet, just as he did on the bad beat hand. Big flops didn't scare that boy one bit... he was on another monster draw, probably. Bill opened. Ed raised and wiped his forehead, in case they missed the first two. Players folded around to seat ten, a local short-haul trucker, who called. Dolly already knew Bill would fold, Ed was bluffing and the stupid trucker was on some romantic draw. But she didn't know about the cowboy; with nine grand from the bad beat, he was loose... or the booze was betting for him. Dolly re-raised; time to push her set, before anyone got lucky and filled a big hand.

Cowboy's odds weren't good even if he hit his baby flush. Besides, he was beginning to smell a rat; that conventioneer pair kept making all the right choices; a rare thing at any Poker table. He folded and reached for his fake bourbon. Bill capped the limit. Everybody called. All eyes went to the dealer; except for Dolly; hers flitted between the trucker and Ed. The Turn card ace added excitement;

Ed; As, Ks   Dolly; Qd, Qh   Steve; 6s, 6c
Flop; **Ac, Kh, Qc, Ah**

Ed acted weak and sat back in his chair. Dolly had queens full; with the cowboy out, she had no fear. Bill obediently pumped the pot. Ed quickly re-raised, a common tell with bad bluffers. Steve's sixes shrank; he folded and waved for drinks. It was a hustler's dream hand, with the mark bluffing into her full boat. She re-raised. Bill capped it. Ed called. Another 120 into the pot. Time for the River Card...

Ed; As, Ks   Dolly; Qd, Qh
Flop; Ac, Kh, Qc, Ah, 4c

Fifth Street spiced the hand up for Ed; he could represent a baby flush, one of the worst possible Rivers for a sucker, with a pair on the board. Bill opened. Everyone re-raised. Fernando said; "Betting is capped."

Bill objected; "Hey, ain't the cap just an *OPTION?*"

Ed's guts tightened with sweet revenge when Fernando nodded; "Yes sir, on weekends, deal making's OK if all players agree." Dolly smiled a thin smile; "Fine

251

with me; *how 'bout you, ED?"* He meekly uttered; "Uh, I'm no sissy... didn't come to play like one." He rubbed his forehead again; "Well, I guess... *I'm all in."* He shoved his stack across the track. Fernando counted; " Ed's in for 1255 more. Option for side pot."

Dragon Lady blurted; *"I CALL!"*

Bill folded; "Too rich for *my blood."*

Ed turned the king of spades. Her eyes glazed with greed, since her shill earlier signaled that the beered-up Mexicans folded two kings.... Her Queens full *had to be good.* Ed slow-rolled the ace of spades, and her gut churned. The chump with the big tell wasn't a chump, but a fucking hustler! The asshole harvested their night's profit with one single hand. Worse yet, she felt that hollow feeling a hustler feels *after being hustled.* Fernando announced; "2935 to Mr. Hazlewood, holding ACES FULL..."

The galley applauded. Ed called for trays. It felt great to put the screws to the cheating bastards. He walked to the cashier's while his mind swirled; one thing might feel better. The cashier counted and the impulse swelled. By the time he had his money, the urge commandeered his faculties. It had been a long time between drinks, and he was mighty thirsty.

THIRTY EIGHT...

I SAID; *HONEST POKER!*

Just like the urge to fuck, the urge to kill grows as a function of time since the last event. Ed learned from the staff; the cheaters were staying at the largest casino in Windemover, "Nevada Ben's". He hailed a cab. Soon he was inside the bar near the main entrance. They each had two drinks backing up the one in their hands, so they weren't going anywhere. Ed wheeled and headed for Bobbie's place. He packed and left her a note, saying he'd be gone for a week; trouble with the family in Wichita. He hopped in his truck. The old Ford 150 found its way during a no-limit ring game. Needing a rig and holding second pair and a flush draw, Ed accepted the bet. The River brought his flush and the truck. It leaked oil, like most Fords of that vintage. It was crusted in alkali dust, like most desert rigs were. But it ran... and by god, it blended. He parked on the outskirts of the lot and locked up. He found the cheaters just as he'd left them, well into their third round, trying to wash away the shitty taste.

Maybe it was a holdover from too many childhood westerns, but Ed hated Poker cheats; the worst kind except for hustlers stealing old folks' pensions, maybe. He took the stool on their left and waived at the barkeep; "Drinks are on me; after all, *it is* your money buyin' em." The trio swiveled. A mixture of emotions; curiosity, anger, bewilderment; how could the stranger have the nerve? Bill's lips pursed to speak, but Dolly beat him to it; *"Sir?"* Ed peeled two hundreds off the roll and smiled; "Keep 'em coming, Smitty?"

253

Once the barkeep turned his back, Ed placed the wad in front of Dolly; "Here's your money." She shook her head; nobody, not even cheaters, want their money back *like that*. She pushed it away; "Don't be an asshole."

"Hey... I'm NOT *giving*, I'm investing." He had their attention; "I saw what you do... I want in."

Three poker faces didn't say a word; "I only caught a few of your signals. I liked that trick with the chips, where Dolly..."

"*MONICA*, if you don't mind."

Ed's mock surprise made Bill laugh; "AH, M*onica!* Nice touch, those name tags." Bill liked Ed's style. He nodded and sipped his scotch; "I'm Sam... This here's Tony... aka; "Tri-Tip"; he can look in two directions at once. Besides, he'll gulp down a steak fast! Tony nets us a few fish, so we keep him around." Tony smiled nervously.

While Dragon Lady studied for tells, Sam leaked info. It was a close-knit group; they had fleeced tourists for years. Considering their nominal overhead, tax-exempt status and flexible hours, they did all right. They traveled when they pleased, worked when they wanted. When Ed went to piss, they talked it over. They might consider him, on a trial basis. After all, he was smart enough to spot their scam. The trio was all smiles when he returned. They were staying one more night. In the morning, off to Elk Hole or Winnemako, maybe. They'd decide at brunch, with heads far more sober. Ed watched them go to the elevators. He took a booth overlooking the parking lot, in case they were stiffing him. They had his roll, while he only had a promise. With that and five bucks, he could buy a cup of state-line coffee. They didn't leave. He booked a room for the night.

Sure enough, over brunch the group worked out the probationary details; Ed would work from the crowd, like Tri-Tip. He would set up in Sam's line of view, to signal Sam. Ed's cut would be ten percent. Once he got good with their system,15. They weren't greedy when it came to splitting. It was more about fleecing the stupid lambs. They liked that part.

Time passed swiftly while they clued him on their other tricks. The sun neared the mountains and it was time to leave Windemover. Who would suspect that inside the westbound appliance-white van lurked three Great Whites? Ed's beat-up old truck shimmied and smoked to keep up. After two hours Ed saw what he wanted. The distant summit glowed purple in fading sunlight. At the base of the mountains a thin white horizontal line indicated a desert two-track angling away from the interstate toward played-out mines. In the clear air, it looked like two miles away, but it was really 11. He sped up alongside. They lowered windows and yelled; "What's up?"

"Pit stop... too much coffee!"

Tri Tip nodded; "Good idea!" Tony had to pee. He knew for a fact, miss pea-bladder did, too. He didn't like her snooty way. She wasn't so great at poker or in bed. All she had, really, was a pair of psychic handcuffs on Sam. Tony never could figure that out; Sam was a hell of a card player, capable of winning serious money without cheating. But he was *so pussywhipped* it was disgusting. At any rate, the dirt road up ahead was a chance to stretch and breathe some air that wasn't full of casino smoke and cologne. He kept thinking as he drove; maybe he'd quit and get a real job. Live a normal life. It sounded good. They parked on the dirt road a few hundred yards from the highway, so nobody could see 'em pee. Ed rolled up behind the minivan. The men on the driver's side, Monica on the passenger side, motioning for Ed to go with the other men. She didn't want him peeking at her bush. Not just yet.

He stuffed the revolver in his waist, then went to the driver side while Monica squatted in the sandblasting wind. Her stream blew sideways four feet before hitting parched sand. By then, Sam and Tri-Tip were zipping up, eager to get out of the damnable wind. Ed stuck the muzzle against Tony's temple; "Boys, what do you say let's get inside?" Both men did as told. Tony drove, Sam in the front, hands on dash. Monica sat behind Tony, hands on headrest. Ed sat behind Sam, keeping his gun on them all; "Keep it under 20. I don't want a lot of dust."

255

"Sure thing… go easy with that pistol, Ed." Tri-Tip didn't know guns, but with the barrel pointed at his right ear he didn't need to know much. Ed had them cold. They had no weapons. Hell, they were gamblers, not killers.

Monica worked up nerve to negotiate. "So, Ed or whatever your name is; you gonna rob us? No problem; we can always win more, honey." Ed jammed the muzzle into her throat; "You cheated those people... Pissed me off."

It was the first gun to her neck. In spite of the predicament, she felt raw eroticism. She went speechless. Ed spoke firmly; "Turn here." A less-used two-track angled uphill. After 300 yards it ended at a played-out mine. From its soot-black maw exited a nasty smelling, greenish liquid. Alkali-dusted spider webs spanned the mine's mouth. Ed's voice got grim; "Get out and let me see those hands."

Sam started sweating bullets. Tri Tip Tony was too scared to sweat. They walked toward the mineshaft. Sam panicked and made a dash for the mineshaft. The bullet caught his spine. He dropped like a stone. Paralyzed from the waist down, he arm-crawled in the muck. Tri Tip Tony shit his pants; "Oh, *God!*" But there was no one else to hear it except screech owls and coyotes... And they knew all about death wails. Dragon lady pleaded; "For Chrissakes… *don't!*"

The bullet breached her lungs, interrupting her plea. A tiny trickle leaked from under her armpit. Horror crossed her face. She fell. Her last audio feed was the killer's speech to Tony; "You like to watch, so I decided to kill you last." "NO... you got it wrong! I ain't no cheat. *I was gonna quit,* you know, go **straight!** Wait! I KNOW where the money is!" Ed acted curious; "Tell me an' maybe I won't shoot." "Under the rumble seat… key's in purse… let me…" One tap to the Parietal Bone and Tri-Tip was all done peeking. Ed went to Sam, who by superhuman effort managed 30 yards closer to the mineshaft using just his card-sharping hands. Seeing the grim reaper's shoelaces, he began a wimpy little cry, then took it up a few notches; "Please, for God's sake *DON'T!*" But Ed sneered; "Shut the fuck UP!" Sam prayed for a miracle while Ed ranted; "You're not the first I've killed, but you *ARE* the worst fuckin' cheaters I ever met. It's wrong to cheat folks. Lemme hear you say *'I know it"* Sam pleaded; "Yes, I know it, but..."

Just then Ed sent a karma PAYBACK pill through his Occiput. The cheater died instantly. Ed opened the cylinder; spent cartridges fell into the copper-green tailrace. Soon the hulls would be plated green. He dragged the bodies into the shaft; not that any passersby were likely.

Stealing their wallets and jewelry took precious time, but was necessary for the staging. The stash box held 36K in hundreds. The luggage concealed cognac and colognes. He sliced the bags up, simulating a robbery. Then he hiked uphill half a mile. When he found the air-shaft, he tossed the revolver and jewelry into it. He never heard it splash when it hit bottom, almost1800 feet below.

As he walked down to his truck he felt glad to be free of the building pressure, but he also felt hollow; the kills held surprisingly little thrill. He wondered if his tolerance was increasing, just like any other addiction. There was another thing to consider; his style, much like any artist's, was perfected to the point where no appreciable gains could be had through mere repetition. Perhaps he had reached the point of diminishing returns. His style was so unique no cops ever looked his way. His was actually a LACK of style, without a specific M.O. or signature. That had been the beauty of it, originally. At first it thrilled him to think they'd never look in his direction. Maybe it had something to do with his father, the finest profiler, who never had a clue about his son.

He drove west away from Bobbie. His latest victims cooling in the mineshaft's eerie draft certainly barricaded his return. It wouldn't take a genius cop to ask who were they last seen with." The Hazlewood disguise was good, but not *that good.* Many hours at the Poker tables put an indelible imprint in the minds of a dozen locals, who could easily describe his face, habits, movements *and* his girlfriend. No, he could never see Bobbie again.

Soon Winnemako's glow lit up the western carbon-black sky. The light grew with each passing mile. He stopped at the biggest casino bar for a cold brew while he pondered his next moves; first, get out of Nevada. Second, to not kill any more people; they were just too stupid to be a challenge. In fact, it might be a bigger challenge to resist the urge. That left him with just the bodies in the mineshaft; the latest skeletons in his closet, so to speak. He couldn't recall if the mini-van could be seen from any distance. If so, he'd have little time to work with.

True, Nevada troopers were few and far between, but they had exceptional eyes for unusual things in the desert. For all he knew, they could be on-scene already. He ordered another beer to quench the panic in his gut. But it didn't work, so he just sucked it down. Then he went to his truck and grabbed his duffel. He carried it into the restroom, shaved his head and beard. Then he made a quick henna tatt below the elbow. The Neo Nazi would hold long enough. Quick tan went on exposed areas. Misdirection would save the Chameleon again. He rummaged through the duffel and located the right paperwork for; Charles Bubba Morton, from Biloxi.

Bubba left without a backward glance at Hazlewood's truck. He hoofed it to the interstate junction, two miles north. To the west lay 150 of miles of sagebrush, tumbleweed and ultimately, California. To the north, Idaho, with Arizona or New Mexico as the southern options.

THIRTY NINE...

SOLILOQUY OF DEATH

He chose North, but in the darkness, his chances for hitching a ride were bad. Bubba decided to hike to a good spot and bed down. It wasn't ideal, but it sure beat waiting for state troopers to pick him up. His growing paranoia got his ass walking, and fast. A mile north was an alfalfa field below the highway. Soon crickets chirped him to sleep while the background whine of millions of mosquitoes set the mood. He woke up before the sunrise, thanks to the relentless aerial blood bank; they withdrew six liters... or so it seemed. His face swelled like a prizefighter's. He trudged uphill; couldn't wait to get away from the bloodsuckers that eagerly bred in the irrigation moisture. He burned Hazlewood's paperwork, hiked up to the road and sat on his duffel with his "North" sign. All he needed was a compassionate motorist to complete the transformation. The sun came up. The subtle desert colors spoke for themselves. He eyed the lush pasture below, contrasting with the arid landscape. It didn't look so evil now. A coyote trotted across, its belly full of hay-fed mice and an unwary cottontail. He watched the songdog trot casually, then it caught Carver's sleepover scent; it went into full sprint. Amazed to see such a fast disappearing act, Bubba barely noticed the Volkswagen van approaching. It rolled to a stop, just about the time the coyote rounded a bend in the gully; the 'yote heard the door slam. Engine noises told him the humans were leaving. He went back to hunting, with one ear bent for danger; business as usual in the high-plains food chain.

ROCK BOTTOM...

The gutless van gasped for thin air, while slowly chugging away. Bubba settled into the passenger seat;

"Where you headed, buddy?"

"North. Name's Charlie. Friends call me Bubba."

"Nice to meet you. Name's Joe. I'm headed for Bozeman; 'zat *north enough*?" "Sure. I'm goin' farther, but thanks for stopping for me." Joe noticed his swollen face; mosquitoes, presumably; "Charlie; reach in that glove box."

Bubba saw a few tubes and blister pack of shiny red pills. "See that green tube? Rub some on your face; it will help the swelling." The way he said it made him think Joe was a doctor or nurse; authoritative, nonthreatening. Charlie read the tube; strong cortisone. So Joe was a doctor, RN or a trainer with special clout. He rubbed some on. Relief began immediately; "So... what kind of doctor are you?" Joe hesitated, brewing up an answer that would abort further investigation; "A GOOD doctor, *Charlie!*" They both laughed. Bubba said; "No, I mean, M.D., osteopath, dentist, chiropractor?"

Joe looked sideways. He got the impression 'Charlie,' if that were his real name, wouldn't stop at chitchat if Joe evaded his questions. So he decided to purge; after all, Joe hadn't really opened up to anyone since it all happened. The stranger represented a chance to vent his feelings to someone he was never likely to see again. The more he thought, the clearer it seemed... this was the perfect time to purge the toxic thoughts that ravaged him. Yes, he would tell him, but the time and place needed to be right. He gave him the short story for the moment. *"Medical Doctor;* going to a clinic about 70 miles out of Bozeman. How'd you guess I was a doctor?"

"Just the way you told me to put that on my face; sounded like a sawbones, is all... Sorry; *didn't mean to pry."* Joe liked the way he said that; maybe they both had skeletons. He let it lay right where Charlie dropped it. The miles rolled on while the doc enjoyed his reverie.

Meanwhile, the killer's mind enjoyed no such peace. He worried if the cops had already found the bodies. He was creeping along at a velocity of 48. The fuckin' tumbleweeds rolled faster. He felt cuffs biting into his wrists. Trying to force the premonition from his psyche, he focused on the world slowly rolling by. Northern Nevada gradually changed; sand gave way to rock. It looked volcanic; a continuous undulation of miniature mesas and arroyos. They drove 50 miles before meeting a single car.

After another hour it was time for a break. Joe found a faint dirt road. He shifted into low and crept the bald-tired van slowly off the pavement. Seeing the road was firm, he idled into the desert. "Hey, Charlie, reach in that ice chest... coupla beers."

The trail was bumpy with bunch-grass in bushy hillocks, rattling his ball joints if he tried more than five miles an hour. He kept going. Clearly, the doctor wanted distance from the main road. With the desiccating wind blowing through the cab, the beer tasted splendid. They sipped two more ales before finding a spot out of the wind, nestled in between two small micro-summits. Joe spread out a tarp. It wasn't cold, but somehow a fire seemed right, so Bubba got one going. They unloaded the ice chest and a single folding chair. Soon they were staring at the fire, swapping yarns. With each brew, they got friendlier and their tales more personal.

Joe brought out some snacks. Morton fetched enough firewood for the night. Neither man had pressing business, so camping sounded good. The sun set behind the jagged mountains. It grew darker. The crackling fire served up its magic. Bubba felt bold enough to broach the topic; "So, Doc... you seem like a sharp guy; how come you're headin' off to bum-fuck Montana? What's the deal?"

Bubba noticed a shift in the doc's posture. For a split second, the Chameleon wished he still had his gun. But the change didn't signal aggression; the doc pulled two

261

beers from the chest, handing one over. He sat closer to the fire, took a swig, and settled in to tell his tale; "Well, Charlie, I've hidden it from everybody for a long time. And I'd lie about it now, if we were in a social setting. But we won't ever see each other again, so I'm gonna tell you."

He stared off into the night sky; "You're right; *I AM a sharp guy*. I went to Jamaica for my M.D. Most doctors scoff at diploma mills, but I received a great education. Besides, Jamaica beat the hell out of freezin' my ass off in Iowa!" Bubba stayed silent; he didn't know Iowa. Joe didn't notice; "I had a great wife. She worked, cooked, did my laundry, helped every way. Of course, I was too busy being a brilliant, arrogant prick to notice how great she was."

Doctor Joe drained the bottle; "I did intern work at a clinic in Oklahoma. *That was bad...* Then we moved to California; I treated low-income, Medi-cal, Medicare, medi-everything else... I was Robin Hood, curing the poor and charging the king. I didn't realize it, but I was also risking everything, Just like Robin Hood. But back then I had a monster ego. You need that to get through med school. But once you get your sheepskin; people treat doctors like gods, so I turned into a bigger asshole."

He kicked a log into the fire; "My wife helped me all those years because she loved me, but private practice sure cured her! Patients have two faces; smiling-happy, for me, but snarling and lying for the front desk... So Raylene saw their ugly side. Every one of them was a threat. After all the work she did to create me, she wasn't about to lose me to those conniving bimbos. She tried to tell me, but I was too busy being a good doctor to be a good husband. Then she got pregnant; she grew more insecure. While the fetus grew, so grew her jealousy, Bubba."

The doc shrugged, in abject honesty; "I guess you could say we were ripe for the picking, but I didn't hear the warning shots. Hell it could'a been the S.S. Missouri firing broadside and I would'a missed it!"

Then Joe's voice darkened; "One Saturday morning I was going to play golf. My clinic was closed on weekends, so I unlocked the office to take a crap. I forgot to lock the door. When I came out, two women were in my reception room. The mother was my first Medi-cal patient. She saw my truck and wondered if I'd see her daughter for a quick minute. Now I should have re-scheduled them for Monday, when my staff would be there, but I was stupid... Mom said she had a chest cold. I had Mom take her to the exam room and put a gown on the girl. She was sixteen; had these beautiful, tight young titties. She was proud. She sat there, shoulders back, big grin, pointing her tits like Tomahawk missiles."

He grabbed another beer, so full of self-regret he didn't offer one. Charlie was too immersed in the tale to notice; "Soon I'm almost finished with the exam; mom asks to use the bathroom. I leave the door open, and since I was almost done, finished the exam. Remember, I just took a crap in that restroom; I'm self-conscious about the smell and how it would ruin my doctor Robin Hood façade."

"I can't find more than a latent sinus infection, so I write her a scrip and go check on mom; she's outside, cell phone to her ear, smiling... Now remember, I wanna go golfing, before the REST of my day off gets ruined with more patients trickling through the door. It has happened before. I don't fill out any paperwork. Figure I'll do it Monday. They thank me. I head for the fairways... an hour later, I'm teeing up for the sixth hole, a squad car actually drives across the fairway to bust me! They make me drop my *weapon,* my new 500-dollar *graphite driver!"*

"No bullshit?"

"Bubba, I wish it were. They charged me with battery, rape and giving narcotics to a minor for sex. That's when it dawned on me; no wonder they were all smiles... They won the lottery! Bubba, they had me cold; when a doctor touches someone without first getting written permission, it's battery. Mom claimed she never went inside my clinic. She never went to the can, either; the bitch broke into my cabinet, swiped enough downers to

263

sink the Titanic. Before they went to the hospital, mom gave the kid some. Enter felony number two; drugging a minor for sex. They really set me up for it. They obviously ENJOYED baiting my trap; her boyfriend screwed her brains out the night before, complete with bruises and bite marks on her inner thighs 'n scratches all over her ass... Obviously, they enjoyed that part. I saw the police photos; looked like six convicts raped her. Damn, if I'd done a full exam, I would have seen the marks."

The Chameleon couldn't keep quiet any longer; "But you were *INNOCENT, RIGHT?*"

"Yeah... but *INNOCENCE IS IRRELEVANT*. My lawyer tried to get me to take a plea, but I was hell-bent on my right to be innocent. I was a god... How can you tell God anything? The more I struggled, the more I got stuck in the tar baby, *and* the more facts I left for the civil trial... lawyers LOVE to harvest facts already in evidence. When my lawyer finally convinced me, I was already dead."

"But *you DIDN'T DO IT!*"

"The accusation *is* the conviction. With sex crimes, courts are conviction-oriented. There was no way to defend it; my lawyer knew it. Actually, he wasn't my choice; he was my malpractice company's hired gun. But he DID plea it down. The plaintiffs got their hush money and smiled. When your adversary's smilin', you're losin'! My lawyer said I should kiss his ass. I bet he went to 'Our Lady of Plea Bargains.' He said I could've lost more, and I did..."

"What's that?"

"My soul mate was insecure as only a late term wife can be. She **KNEW** i had to be screwing those firm tits, long lashes and tight little boy-scout-ass... Now I wish I *woulda fucked her;* least I would've had *some pleasure* from it all. Raylene's lawyers took the house, every asset 'n got her a huge settlement; more than my practice grossed. To the jury, I was just another rich prick doctor, cheating on his pregnant wife. Bubba, the awards wouldn't have been so big without her star witness, wigglin' those Tomahawk titties again. When I sat there listening to the judgment, I was glad they couldn't hang me!"

Joe pulled the last two beers from the slush. "Half my patients left when I got busted. The rest left because they thought I was cheating on my wife. Then four other girls filed suit. You see, insurance companies will pay five or ten grand in hush money and everybody's happy... *except* the *doctor.*"

Charlie kicked a smoldering log; a shower of sparks flew into the coal black sky. Joe didn't notice; "My insurance company dropped me like a hot rock. I tried to hire a lawyer, but nobody wants to defend a doctor; the REAL money's in suing us. I did find one guy desperate enough to listen to my story, but he bailed when he checked my credit. It's hard to find a lawyer who works for principle. By then, the California board took my license. So there I was, fighting baseless civil suits, without any experience in the law. I couldn't even get a job flipping burgers, due to bad publicity. It just kept getting worse, like a bad nightmare..."

He staggered to the fire to warm his backside; "My first mistake was treating poor people; they bring 92% of all malpractice suits. They figure doctors are rich and the money's coming from insurance companies, but they never think how it impacts the doc. If you ever jump in shark infested waters, try not to bleed, Bubba."

"I never wanted to be a lawyer but I learned fast! I had no other distractions; did my own investigations. A few small bribes and favors will get you the dirt *on anyone*. I actually beat two plaintiffs by discrediting them before they deposed; they had tried to bilk other doctors. That left me with two cases; it was easy, after I'd seen my lawyer do the first one. It's amazing; money heals. It's The Green Poultice." Then his voice cheered up a notch; "The law is a funny thing. With each new bogus sex case, I gained notoriety. Imagine that; I'm gettin' my guts ripped out, and three different publishing houses start bidding for my book rights!

"Pain can make you do weird things... and brother, *was I in PAIN*. I was on the street, treating junkies and homeless under bridges, just for a spot to sleep without getting stabbed." His demeanor changed again; "Then one day, things changed. Her name was Lori, a hot divorcee; she gave me the eye once in the office, back before it all happened. She took me in, without a question about the crimes they say I committed. We lived high up in the oak forests of Mendonesia. We had no electricity, a gravity-fed spring and no phone. She healed me... She healed my fuckin' brains out. That was one of the best years of my life; no phone calls from shysters or media. We had unbridled passion. Damn, it was great, until I learned the truth... Lori went to town for supplies. I stayed home to clean the cabin. That's when I stumbled upon the documents..."

Joe staggered to the van, returned with hooch and glasses. Campfire smoke made him squint while he poured; "The papers proved it, Bubba... Lori put little miss big titties onto me... She knew I'd never leave my wife, so she orchestrated the whole incident just so she could pick up the pieces. If I live to be a hundred I'll never understand the female psyche. I hated her for taking my wife, unborn son and my practice away! I couldn't think of what to tell her, so I just taped the documents to the fridge door. Then I drove off in her van, right here. Damn, I wanted to kill her."

"Yeah?"

"But I also missed her; the hot sex and good times at her cabin were some of the best in my life... I can still taste that woman... I can still feel her... my god, *what a woman!* I had so many emotions, I couldn't feel them all; there was too much stimulus to sort out. But I knew if I saw her again, I'd kill her. So, I drove, Charlie, I drove! I had my manuscript and a few thousand bucks from her last Pot sale. I drove to the publisher's; took a month to polish, but my book sold like hotcakes. We titled it '*Yes, Doctor.*'

"YOU wrote a book?"

"It's odd, ya know? I authored two medical articles; index medicus, peer reviewed, but my tawdry sex-capades were worth 50 times more! It's a sick world, Bubba."

"Yep; sick as hell."

"Well, my ex-wife's lawyers attached the royalties. That was fine with me; Raylene deserved all of it. I loved her at first sight. Hell, I'll love her 'til I die... right after my scandal, she married a chiropractor in Yubera City; sonofabitch makes three times what I did. He sells vitamins and rubs sore backs. He's not a bad guy. Too bad he was a quack; would've made a good DOCTOR. Anyhow, I'd send her checks when I could, but she never cashed 'em. Her lawyers sure took 'em though."

"We were really something, Raylene and me... A man's lucky to find that kind of love *ONCE* in a lifetime. That's all I learned; *LOVE* is a rare, precious thing. It transcends all. No riches or fame can match it... no higher high when you have it, or lower when you lose it. Love is the whole deal, Bubba... *everything else* is bullshit."

Dr. Joe poured Charlie another, then threw his glass into the fire. He drank straight from the bottle. Something bad was coming, judging from body language; "The chiro and two midwives tried a home birth; something went wrong. My son, James Patrick Muldoon; probably would've died even in a hospital *but...who knows?* The same kind of lawyers that skull-fucked me went after them. They sure charted some rough water. Losing a child is bad enough, but to get tried for it... *Sonofabitch.*" Then he sighed and changed tempo; "So I set out to see who might need a down-on-his-luck unlicensed doctor."

"You actually *FOUND someone* in Montana?"

"Shit, I found plenty! You won't believe who wants to hire a busted doctor."

"Huh?"

"After the trial, I'm a whore in a truck stop with no place to sleep. There's prisons that want me... and cruise ships; in international waters, you can practice all you want! Then there's insurance; I could be a gunfighter, and deny every claim... but they're just whores in cubicles."

He slapped a mosquito; "Well, I won't work in a prison. Cruise ship work's boring, passing out seasick & sunburn potions. And NO WAY would I sleep with the

267

enemy, the insurance pirates. So that left reservations an' nomadic gas towns... all ready to surf your UPIN to death. Anyhow, I picked reservations; they didn't care about my past. They know how fucked up California law is. So here I am, off to Montana and sippin' sour mash with my new blood brother."

Bubba said nothing. Joe took another swig; "You know, Lori used to say something after sex; *'Things always come full circle.'* Now I'll be treating the poor and needy again, just like I started in the first place. Weird, eh?"

The alcohol had them both feeling philosophical. Bubba shot first; "Well, it's too bad you didn't write *THAT* on your goodbye note. It woulda been perfect."

"Yeah, I never think of the right words 'til it's too late. Anyhow, I'm glad I didn't write any smart-ass shit like that. Truth is, I still miss her... When I'm not wantin' to kill her!"

Doctor Joe had opened his psyche to the stranger; now it was time for payback. The booze gave him the guts to go for it; "So, that's my long answer to your short query; **everybody's** hiding something. You're smart, young, in good shape. You could get a job anywhere but you're incognito, hitchin' across Nevada; that henna tattoo is awful, by the way... You got somethin' *YOU* wanna purge? Who's gonna hear it besides the coyotes 'n sagebrush? PURGIN' feels GOOD, Bubba! I highly recommend it."

It might have been the booze, the moment or a space/time warp, but whatever it was, the Chameleon came out of the closet; "Me? I kill people." Joe snorted but the killer insisted; "A *lot* of people. An' you're right, I AM smart as hell... got a photographic memory. I have read 11,612 books. I can quote any one of 'em. Ask me any basic question in medicine, philosophy, art. I know how to stop a suspension bridge from flopping in the wind... Put an inverted airfoil on the bottom; the harder the wind blows, the more stable it gets. I can tell a dominant from a subordinate buck, how to tie a Bimini Twist for Tarpon or roll-cast a dry fly on the Grande Rhonde. I have total recall,

268

Joe... Give me 10 seconds and I'll tell you the page number and day of the week when I read it. My mental file clerk is *perfect,* Doc. I know anatomy... 3405 proper names; Henley's loop, Morgagni's columns in the bowel, the Substantia Gelatinosa of Rolando, Circle of Willis, Aqueductus Sylvius. Something's haywired, so I have to remember shit. I know so much crap, you wouldn't believe: Christianity, Islam, Shinto and Buddhism, Rogers & Hammerstein, poetry, philosophy; Don't even try to test me, doc, it'll blow your fuckin' mind." Joe's head spun from the hooch and the speech.

"You wanna know somethin' Doc? I'd trade it all to know *WHY* people do things. I don't know *WHY people LOVE.* Doc. I don't get it. When I was a kid, I thought acquiring facts would give me pleasure or at least fill the hole in me. So, I kept learning. But after each field of study, I felt worse. It never stopped, my... *emptiness."*

He drank from the bottle, spit-gargling while talking; "Knowledge is pain. By 15, I had three Masters' worth of shit in my skull and I felt worse than ever. So I started thinking of killing somebody. Then I did it. At first... it was *SUCH a rush*; better than sex or dope. Hell, killing was the BEST dope. Then later, I just felt good. Then later, only sated. I killed most of 'em for social causes. I killed one bastard purely for revenge. That left me feeling worse, because I couldn't drag it out long enough to achieve parity; I just blew his fuckin' head off, from 351 yards. Not a bad shot, but it *was* high by about six inches."

"Then later, I left a few small clues for the cops, hoping the added risk might bring the thrill back... but those fuckin' cops are so predictable; foolin' 'em was too easy; if you just randomize the elements of each crime they'll never catch you. So then I took a long vacation. But then I killed three assholes yesterday. I thought I'd feel better if I got 'em off the planet. Truth is, I was bored with the whole thing. People are basically not worth the bullets."

Stunned by the viperous soliloquy, Doc just sat there, paralyzed like a cobra's prey; unable to move or look away. Joe was a dead man, if Charlie's words were true, instead of a rambling drunk fantasy... But he felt icy steel in the words. He voiced his fears; "You gonna kill *ME too*, Charlie?"

Charlie spilled liquor; "Naw, doc; you're already worse than dead. Have some hooch!" He passed the bottle and went introspective, as most drunks do; "Doc, what would you call what I've got?" Joe's only hope for survival lay in abject honesty; "I'd say you had issues with your parents; you didn't measure up. You're obviously a bookworm; I'll bet your old man wanted a jock."

The venomous truth stung Charlie. It was his turn to be paralyzed; "You have the classic signs of addiction; first, curiosity got you into it. Then the intensity hooked you. Later you developed a tolerance; had to increase dosage until you either quit the drug or it kills you." Joe paused for courage, pulled a swig, then kicked smoldering log ends into the fire; "You're as bored with killing as with Henley's Loop. I'll bet you're ready to quit right now. Charlie, y*ou're at "rock bottom."*

Joe passed him the jug. Raw honesty felt good; "Besides, I know what it feels like to kill. Remember when I said my first job out of med school was *'bad'?* It was *worse than bad,* for an idealistic young doctor... I started working in an abortion clinic in Oklahoma. I'm worse than you are... Way worse, Charlie. I killed innocent, healthy babies. It sounds like your marks *deserved to die...* But fetuses? Their only sin is conception. They're as blameless as still-wet fawns. It takes a heartless sonofabitch to put a good spin on that. We staple euphemisms to it, but call it whatever you want, I... *killed* five babies a day, six days a week for thirteen months; that's sixteen hundred babies; *you wanna talk BURNED OUT?* To this day, whenever I see a pregnant woman, ALL I see are hacked up baby parts comin' out of her. You call *YOURSELF* a killer,

270

Bubba? Hell, my profession SPECIALIZES in death. We got abortion, euthanasia, therapeutic misadventures... Hell, we're the death brokers! 'MD' stands for *"More Death"*

He took another swig; "After I killed my first few hundred babies I thought I was over it. I mean, what's the difference if I kill a baby or a bedridden septuagenarian in intractable pain? The former's legal and vigorously protected by federal law; the latter serves no further use to self or society, continues to suffer, even though we could mercifully end his suffering with one injection. We CAN'T kill the geriatric, but the unborn baby's fair game... in fact, *SOCIETY DEMANDS it.* OH Yeah, Bubba, I'm WITH YOU on the death thing!"

He stood up to piss; "I'll tell ya something else; I killed an old patient once, and *I never told anyone.* Foster Beauregard Hibbert was a hell of a good man, back in his prime. Led a good life, great family, raised 'em right. One day he had stroke, the kind nobody comes back from."

He zipped back up; "I ordered a PET scan... the only active part of his brain was the size of a fuckin' marble in the memory center; all he could do was lay there, *REMEMBERING.* It was one of God's sick little jokes; paralyze a man, then force him to lay there, remembering. That's some sick shit, Bubba." I won't bore you with all the other hideous facts, but let me tell you, he was as dead as a man gets with a pulse. Old Foster was fucked and everybody, even FOSTER knew it too. I watched him for a month; nothing improved. One night, I slipped in and I gave him enough Digoxin to kill a plow horse. It stops the heart. Won't show on a standard autopsy. If you ever need to snuff somebody else, I'll show you how to do it *RIGHT.* Anyhow, I said; *"Foster, I'm sending you over. You've got one minute to pray."* Then I pushed the syringe. I saw his right side relax before the Digoxin could possibly take effect; maybe it was the only way he could thank me. Or maybe I'm full of crap. Who the fuck knows for sure?

"Life and Death's a bullshit medical paradigm; one of my best friends pulled a bullet out of some gangster's liver after a gangland shootout. Six months after my friend healed him, he opened up with an Uzi. None of the rival gangsters got hit... just a young mom, her newborn baby and a retired preacher."

"My friend *WAS* a great trauma surgeon. Now he's workin' as a drywall contractor in Vegas. Three innocent people died because he saved a career criminal's life. Ethically speaking, he should have killed the hoodlum during surgery; one slip of the scalpel would've saved three innocents... and a hellofa great surgeon."

"Medicine's 'life for life's sake' is a ruthless, twisted ethic; We save the sinner, the same as the priest. We put a ten year-old girl with a high-cord section on a ventilator, then watch the girl's family torn to shreds while she dies one piece at a time. We drag it out *BECAUSE WE CAN*... not because we *SHOULD.*" Doctor Joe sighed; *"*I'm sorry; I just miss my friend. Damn great surgeon... hellofa racquetball player, too."

Then his eyes blackened with an evil flashback; "And while that girl with severed cord withers into a bag of inert protoplasm, the family goes to hell; a tsunami of medical bills, stress, divorce, alcoholism; a family rarely survives that kinda hell. If I were a *good doctor,* I would've killed her, instead of forcing six years of hopeless life on her, laying there like a bag of rotting carrots while we amputated bed-sore limbs one at a time. She could've died a virgin, instead of a rape victim of a late-night pedophile janitor. Her family could have moved on... because, THAT'S all life is, brother; *MOVING ON!* But instead of *HELPING* her, I hid behind my bullshit ethic, life for life's sake; they said I was a great doc, but I was king of the fuckin' hypocrites."

272

He handed the jug over to Bubba; "You say you killed a few assholes? That's fine with me. Hell, if I had your nerve, I'd whack a few hundred more who *REALLY DESERVE IT!* But there's a bigger issue, Bubba; *ARE you FINISHED KILLING?"*

Bubba tossed more wood on the fire; "You know, doc? I think I might be. I barely remember who I am."

Dr. Joe stared into the uncaring night skies, giving thanks; it sounded like he'd get through the night alive. He propped his wobbly torso up on one elbow and looked at the killer's silhouette; "No offense, Charlie, but *aside from killing*, have you done *anything?* You have a didactic education; you're all hat and no cattle. You're a reader, not a deeder... You think *killing folks* is a challenge? You ought to try *HEALING* 'em. *THAT'S* where the real art lies."

An ember flared up to punctuate Joe's point. The flare contrasted sharply with the soot-black sky; You're right. It might be fun to practice medicine; I'll give it a shot."

Joe wet-burped; "NO, I didn't say medicine, I said *HEALING!* Anyone with two grams of neurons can practice allopathic medicine; a guy has pain, give him painkillers. He's constipated, give laxatives. Housewife's sad, give 'er happy pills. 'Allopathy' means *Reverse the symptom.* If that's not simplistic, what is? People would be astonished at how little their doctor knows, outside the specialty. Hell, even INSIDE, a doctor sucks knowledge from just a few vertical taproots. A cardiologist doesn't know *hearts,* he knows valves and electrical signals. He only sees a heart, not a 56 year-old man with two mortgages, a son gone bad, dog that won't fetch and a wife that won't fuck him. The Doc's too busy fixing the failing *PUMP* to see the breaking *HEART."*

Bubba chewed on that while the Doc rambled on; "We HIDE in our safe-haven, reversing symptoms until the patient gets well, dies or the insurance runs out. Betcha don't know that med students don't learn NUTRITION or

273

EXERCISE... And for the human soul, Charlie, not one classroom hour. I could go on, but trust me; allopathic medicine is a simplistic, drug-based system of disease management. It's *hellaciously good* for crisis care... But as for *HEALING?* Can't heal shit... and everyone in the field knows it. There's another world out there, where people really get cured. That, my ROCK-BOTTOM, born again ex-killin' blood brother... *THAT'S what I'm talkin' about!"*

Bubba got excited; "Damn; it sounds like fun. I could be your assistant; we could keep an eye on each other, now we know each other's secrets. Sonofabitch! *Let's do it!* Let's go to Montana and heal some fuckin' Indians! I'll start readin' tomorrow about Homeopathy, Bach Flowers, Chinese herbology. Then I'll study chiropractic, osteopathy an' aromatherapy. I'll check out Native American medicine in Montana. We can ask the Indians to show us some smoke diagnosis. Doc, *LET'S DO IT!"*

There was only silence; Joe finally passed out. For a doctor, that dude could sure drink.

FORTY...

THE MORNING AFTER

The sun topped the summits. Dr. Joe rose first, hobbled a few yards from camp, pissed and took a high-alcohol low-fiber morning-after shit. With a vow to never again get so completely poisoned, he gingerly paced to the van for aspirin and supplies. In a few minutes he had a fire going and coffee water heating. He tried to think back on the night's conversation; something about killing, maybe.

It would take time before the coals were ready for breakfast, so he got his pistol out; if ever there was a time to refresh his pistol shooting skills, this was it. He slowly walked down the two-track for 200 yards. Then he spotted a small round shape at the base of a cedar tree, barely 15 yards away. The cottontail nibbled a fresh sprig. He filled the rear vee sight with front blade, held under the bunny's chest. The little 380 went off with a mind-splitting roar; to the hung-over doc with no earplugs and atrociously rusty trigger squeeze, it sounded like the Missouri's deck guns.

The puff of sand erupting six inches over the rabbit didn't make it bolt. Instead, it hunkered lower. Joe's trigger control came back. The next bullet found the lumbar spine. She pawed around in circles, trying to run, with just front legs. Joe started to fetch breakfast, pleased with his re-acquired pistol prowess. Then he saw why the bunny hadn't spooked; a hawk swooped down on the cottontail. Powerful wing-beats carried breakfast through the cedar tops, away from the noisy human.

Awed by the hawk's masterful aerobatics, Joe just chalked it up to the food chain. He chuckled, reloaded and continued stalking down the old two-track. The firm sand made for silent travel, and the wind was right. Another 300 yards of stalking served up a second chance; a buck jackrabbit hid in its bunch-grass form, barely ten yards away. The frozen hare slowly lowered its ears until they melted into its back. Joe aimed carefully; the hare's brains splattered all over the form. The big hare twitched twice, death-jumping right to the hunter's feet.

Decades ago, Joe's dad showed him how to unzip a hare using bare hands and an entry wound. In mere seconds, the twitching flesh steamed moisture into the cool breeze. Its heart twitched sporadically when it hit the sand. Unlike human hearts he'd seen in surgery, this one had no fat. Just like the rest of the hare, it was lean and mean. His pocketknife deftly parted the spine at the transitional vertebrae. Discarding the front shoulders, Joe held the delicious back-straps and hinds; a surprisingly bloodless bit of butchering. He took his time hiking back, trying to recall what they talked about last night; dim tidbits returned, stuff about killing people and past mistakes. He could only hope Bubba couldn't recall; after all, that's alcohol's purpose.

Charlie sat with his laptop. He saw the meat; "Damn, I can taste that jack already!" The meat went on cedar skewers at the edge of the coals where smoke wafted to the pristine protein. Joe washed the blood and fluff from his hands and poured coffee; "Whatcha got there, Charlie?" "The future, doc. Remember last night's talk?
Joe's heart skipped a beat; "Uh, not much... *why?*"
"I remember every word, thanks to my photographic memory. You know all my bad stuff and I know YOURS, I can reshape your future; What's your last name?"
"Talbot... Joseph I. Talbot."
"I thought it was Muldoon."
"No, that's my ex-wife's married name; they gave *HIS* surname to my kid! Can you believe that?"
"That's pretty fuckin' *cold,* Doc."

He couldn't erase it, but he could alter the record; the sex crime charges were replaced with a misdemeanor. The new doctor, Joseph O. Talbit, sounded the same, but to federal computers it was apples and space shuttles apart. His UPIN, SSN and new practice license gave him a squeaky clean record. That Caribbean sheepskin went away, too; the new doc graduated from UC in the Bay Area. When the meat sizzled, Talbit's CV sizzled hotter. They ate the hare. It was good, even with a hangover.

Joe ate and grinned; "Charlie, if you want to work with me, you need records, too." "Way ahead of you, Doc. No longer am I Vincent J. Carver; it's been so long since I spoke my own name, it feels weird!" They laughed. "So I now have a P.A. for Van Thomas Carter."

The jackrabbit was good, but the future tasted better. They loaded up the van, killed the fire and drove toward the waiting highway. Montana sounded good.

Damned good.

FORTY ONE...

LONG ARM OF THE LAW

Kay Baker and posse should have been ecstatic to relish their latest catch, but they were too burned out. They had seen too much evil to relish anything right now, not even a serial killer as infamous as this one. He'd been enjoying himself in Colorado, Utah and Wyoming mostly.

It wasn't the abduction or the screwing the hookers disliked, it was the vivisection. Sometimes Charles Binder liked it so much, he'd apply a tourniquet so he could keep savoring their screams. After the victim exanguinated, he'd skewer choice parts and braise them over campfire coals. But if time were a problem, he'd go to the cook stove; the tidbits weren't as tasty that was, but a successful serial killer had to be pragmatic.

He was lucky with his first kills; any clues he left were destroyed by wind, rain and scavengers before the law got to them. Then he got so good that it was almost impossible to nab him. Binder's victims were all dishwater blond, looked young for their age, were pudgy... and all were hookers. They were abducted between ten and midnight on a Saturday night. Each was a willing sex provider until getting dismembered alive and cannibalized post mortem. The dump scenes were always in remote sections of high desert plains or deep forests. They were dumped identically, thus his signature; naked supine torsos, severed legs replaced spread-eagle, knees bent, vulva thrust degradingly upward, supported by rocks.

Enter Kay Baker and posse, compiling data from all murders resembling Cookstove Charlie's. Thanks to Baker's excellent record, every trooper, deputy, ranger and game warden in 11 western states was on full alert; Charlie was as good as caught. All they needed was one good break and maybe a few more partially cannibalized pudgy blonde hookers.

Her profile nailed Charlie down to the eeriest detail; white, 40-50, small stature, truck driver or traveling salesman. He'd have an easygoing charm. He probably talked his way out of prior brushes with the law. He'd killed plenty before the cops got wind of him. He was reared by an a domineering authority figure, an abuser. His victims resembled this person. One more thing; Cookstove Charlie would never stop, until he was killed or caught. He hated women too much to quit.

That's how Deputy Dave Raynaud caught Charles Ranier Binder, 26 miles east of Gillette in the wee small hours. He shined a light on the driver. Charlie flashed his winning smile, which put the deputy on alert. Who smiles when they get pulled over? Binder sweet-talked; sure, he noticed the busted taillight an hour earlier when he stopped for a call of nature. He planned on fixing it in Laramie when the stores opened. Binder put the deputy at ease enough that Dave stopped writing the fix-it ticket. But when he mentioned peeking inside the trailer, he saw the killer's tell; Binder started to sweat, in spite of Wyoming's desiccating wind blowing through the cab. Before long, the deputy had backup en route, the little man in cuffs and one cold, very grateful prostitute freed from the refrigerated trailer. Tiffany expressed her undying gratitude; next time Dave got to Cheyenne, she'd express it again, on the house.

Once the interrogators broke the ice, Charlie spilled his guts. Binder confessed to 125 killings in the 11 western states. To make it worse, he couldn't remember them all.

He'd been killing hookers for over three decades. Charlie kept a suitcase of photos. Each victim got three or four shots; the close-up would be a pose with the living vic's genitalia front and center. Then two, sometimes three shots captured her dismemberment. He loved bleed-outs, and except for the occasional stress-induced myocardial infarct, his victims all died that way. Then he'd cook a chunk of quads or biceps, then usually a bit of tongue for dessert. A little garlic, pepper and butter; damned fine fare for a cannibal.

In spite of their experience catching bad guys, Cookstove Charlie's exploits shocked the Posse. Baker took the longest to get over it, until she forced herself to fast-forward to the jurisdictional problems. That helped.

There would be interstate squabbles over trials, adding years of legal finagling. She shuddered at her next thought; some states didn't have laws preventing criminals from profiting from their crimes. Binder would be an icon, complete with press agent, book deals and god knows how much in movie rights, before his first conviction.

By the time the posse looked through 400-plus pictures they had seen way too much of the beast. They needed a psychic debriefing. It wouldn't erase the images, but she learned her lessons well from Howard Carver; foremost, the one about working hard and then playing hard. Kay saw that they all needed a break. They got in the van; "Forget the airport. Turn left up there, Dan."

Kay paid for the rental RV. The surprised posse gradually got the concept. They loaded the rig full of the finest food, ice and all the alcohol it could hold. Their road trip started with Mount Rushmore. They stood in awe of partially-carved Crazy Horse. The healing magic of the Black Hills began to work on them. They toured the Midwest, trying to forget all the shit they'd seen. They drove the grain belt, through countless miles of corn, soybeans, pigs and hay; a river of green flowing by their windows from dawn to dusk. They stopped at a pheasant club and shot pen-raised birds. Somewhere along the end of the first week, Semple mentioned Vegas, but Sin City didn't seem right for healing psyches. Still, they started west. By the time they got there, they'd be ready.

They toured Flaming Gorge, rented a party boat, fished and tanned like Toledo tourists. Slowly the dark images began to blur into their collective past-crooks database. Baker and crew were finally having fun... That is, until they hit Windemover and caught the news about three bodies in a mineshaft. They weren't exactly looking for work, but a posse is always a posse.

Something didn't add up; if it was a carjack, why leave the mini van? If it was a robbery, why kill the victims? And bodies dragged inside a mineshaft? That didn't fit.

Vacation was definitely over.

AFTERWORD

The ACTUAL number of serial killers *is unknown.*

Police are trained in spotting signatures, but 'chameleons' are never spotted. (forgive the pun) Some serials simply quit, as Vincent did. Some get imprisoned for other charges without disclosing their darker deeds. A few simply go inactive for long periods of time, as BTK did. Some just die or are killed, so nobody learns of their evil ways; it's a dog eat dog world out there.

One thing's sure; the media sure as hell won't tell you the truth. That's the last place you'll get reliable info on people who are killing folks. In a recent (2010) Montana incident that resembled a 'Home Alone' scenario, a nine-year-old girl killed two invaders with a shotgun. The first took a blast to the guts as he climbed the stairs to assault her. The second thug got a load to the chest when he tried to fire upon the 'defenseless' girl. He turned and made it to the sidewalk before he bled out. Police found stolen weapons on the bad guys, taken from a prior burglary the same day; that victim was later found. He'd been killed by the two bad guys.

You'll never hear of this gutsy kid and her remarkably cool-headed survival instincts, because TV's severely slanted to the LEFT, so it rarely portrays gun owners as good people. Neither shall you hear the rest of the truth; these two perps were illegals from Mexico; one committed an earlier homicide in Mexico.

My point is that we must wonder how much the media withholds from us. Hell, there could be serial killers right in your neighborhood and the media wouldn't cover it... until bodies turn up.

Have you ever noticed whenever they catch a serial killer, the neighbors are always surprised?

"He was such a quiet neighbor; never made a fuss."
Jeffrey Dahmer's neighbors

"Pillar of the community..."
John Wayne Gacy's peers.

"Engaging, charming and polite"
terms ladled onto Kemper.

"Such a nice man, and so handsome"
Ted Bundy's landlady.

Need I go on?

Take my advice. Don't hassle your neighbors, especially the quiet, polite ones. And... if you've got the neighbor-from-hell, a middle-twenties, wannabe rock star, shredding his amped-up electric guitar all night long, give thanks to the good Lord above... *It could be worse*.

Sweet dreams.

Love, Lance

TAILING DISCLAIMER...

As mentioned in disclaimers, almost all of it is fiction, although I really did incorporate a scene or two from my life. For example, from 1974-77 I worked in 'DAVEYPORT' Iowa. My first job there was at the Hotel Black Eagle.

And, sure as hell, shortly after its 'facelift' fumigation I had to walk through that ocean of cockroaches (@ page 79) in the sub-basement to retrieve something of great interest to the general manager. Had nightmares for the first 15 years. Even now, I can still smell the odor. I can still feel those roaches climbing inside my pants, on my balls... waist-high cockroaches... ugh.

So when I created Nicky the Torch's last job, somehow I just HAD to weave it into the story.

- ➢ COURT OF LAW; to catch a crafty serial pedophile, three cops must think outside the profile. Filled with sub-plots, quirks, sex, depravity and corruption; pretty good twist ending, too.

- ➢ CHAMELEON; a serial killer has father issues. Dad's a famous profiler. Vincent stays invisible by exploiting profiling data. A few twists, weird sex & bizarre ending.

- ➢ TURNABOUT; a hunter stumbles upon a cartel Pot patch, high up in the coastal mountains. A gunfight ensues, setting Ted on a grisly course of payback. Warning; it's not wise to piss off your average American hunter... Turnabout's such a bitch.

- ➢ Urik-Tah, the Death Rose; Majesty travels at Hawk Speed to check on a mining colony. She finds something that will change the balance of power in the universe. If you like Star Trek, you'll like this. Has the mother of all endings.

- ➢ Mother saves Majesty; Read the Death Rose first, then this prequel. It might warp your mind. Key ingredients; theoretical speeds, black holes, primitive life-form weaponry, insoluble conundrum.

* Owing to various online production glitches, books are either in print now or will be online shortly, at the biggest book site; can't say the name, but it's... *amaz*...ingly big. Search author or title; hell, you'll figure it out.